"It ain't personal," Rhett told the little scorpion, right before he slammed his knife down to chop it in half, along with the wax.

The scorpion curled and uncurled for just a second in agony, and then the giant body surrounding it collapsed into silvery gray dust, leaving Rhett to suddenly fall forward. On his hands and knees in the dirt, he pulled the note off the nasty bit of magic and silently handed it to Dan, who stood closest.

"It's from Trevisan," Dan said.

"Well, no shit, Dan," Rhett said, as he always did.

"It says that if you follow him, he will kill you."

Rhett stood and snorted and walked toward the pile of his clothes.

"Tell me something I don't know," he said.

Praise for
LILA BOWEN

Praise for *Wake of Vultures*

"*Wake of Vultures* will kick your ass up one page and down the other."   —*io9*

"I enjoyed the hell out of it."
—*New York Times* bestselling author Patrick Rothfuss

"*Wake of Vultures* doesn't just fly—it soars. Lila Bowen brings in a wild fantasy quite unlike anything I've ever read, with a voice that's weird and wonderful."
—*New York Times* bestselling author Chuck Wendig

"Gritty and well-realized."
—*Publishers Weekly* (starred review)

"Of all the books I've reviewed this year, *Wake of Vultures'* Nettie Lonesome stands out as the most compelling, well-crafted protagonist I've encountered."
—*RT Book Reviews* (Top Pick)

"I don't care what else you've seen in the bookstore today. Buy this book."
—*New York Times* bestselling author Kevin Hearne

"*Wake of Vultures* is, quite simply, brilliant. A mind-bending mix of history, fantasy and folklore, it's a wild bronco of a read that'll leave you breathless for more."

—*New York Times* bestselling author Rachel Caine

Praise for *Conspiracy of Ravens*

"Frankly, I need more Nettie Lonesome's on my shelf."

—*B&N Sci-Fi & Fantasy Blog*

"The world built in this series is rich and complex. One of my favorite new series."

—*Pop Culture Beast*

"A joy to spend time in Bowen's alt-history world of magic and monsters."

—*SciFiNow*

Praise for *Malice of Crows*

"An appealing hero . . . and his friends are complex, well-drawn characters. The stakes couldn't be higher, and the story couldn't be more absorbing."

—*Kirkus* (starred review)

"Bowen burnishes her particular brand of Western mythic odyssey to a high shine. Outstanding pacing takes us from one exciting, well-crafted scene to another. . . . Extraordinary."

—*RT Book Reviews*

By Lila Bowen

THE SHADOW

Wake of Vultures
Conspiracy of Ravens
Malice of Crows
Treason of Hawks

MALICE OF CROWS

THE SHADOW: BOOK THREE

LILA BOWEN

orbit

www.orbitbooks.net

Copyright © 2017 by D. S. Dawson
Excerpt from *The Tethered Mage* copyright © 2017 by Melissa Caruso
Excerpt from *One of Us* copyright © 2018 by Craig DiLouie

Author photograph by Von Tuck
Cover design by Lisa Marie Pompilio
Cover art by Shutterstock
Cover copyright © 2017 by Hachette Book Group, Inc.
Map illustration by Tim Paul

Orbit
Hachette Book Group
1290 Avenue of the Americas
New York, NY 10104
orbitbooks.net

Originally published in hardcover and ebook by Orbit in October 2017
First Trade Paperback Edition: March 2018

Orbit is an imprint of Hachette Book Group.
The Orbit name and logo are trademarks of Little, Brown Book Group Limited.

The publisher is not responsible for websites (or their content) that are not owned by the publisher.

The Hachette Speakers Bureau provides a wide range of authors for speaking events. To find out more, go to www.hachettespeakersbureau.com or call (866) 376-6591.

Library of Congress has catalogued the hardcover edition as follows:

Names: Bowen, Lila, author.
Title: Malice of crows / Lila Bowen.
Description: New York : Orbit, 2017. | Series: The shadow ; 3
Identifiers: LCCN 2017025901| ISBN 9780316502344 (hardcover) | ISBN
    9780316502368 (ebook)
Subjects: | BISAC: FICTION / Fantasy / Historical. | FICTION / Occult &
    Supernatural. | FICTION / Fantasy / Paranormal. | FICTION / Action &
    Adventure. | FICTION / Coming of Age. | GSAFD: Adventure fiction. |
    Fantasy fiction.
Classification: LCC PS3602.O895625 M35 2017 | DDC 813/.6—dc23
LC record available at https://lccn.loc.gov/2017025901

ISBNs: 978-0-316-50234-4 (hardcover), 978-0-316-50235-1 (trade paperback),
978-0-316-50236-8 (ebook)

Printed in the United States of America

LSC-C

10 9 8 7 6 5 4 3 2 1

To Lindsey, Tim, Ellen, Laura, Lauren, Lisa,
Tim the cartographer, and everyone at Orbit, as well as my
darling Devi. Y'all are the wind beneath this vulture's wings. <3

And thanks to Penny and Sparrow for the inspiration.

© Tim Paul 2017

MAP of
DURANGO
TERRITORY
of THE FEDERAL REPUBLIC of
AMERICA

According to the Newest and most exact Observations of
Timothy dePaul, Geographer

24 Published by Mssres. Howard & dePaul

CHAPTER

1

Rhett Walker woke up feeling like he'd been chained hand and foot to fate. It didn't help that he was in one of the empty train cars of Bernard Trevisan's railroad. It did help that Cora was curled up beside him like a kitten, warm and sweet. But such encumbrances were manacles of their own, weren't they? All his plans had flown away. Meimei was still missing, and Trevisan was on the loose in the little girl's body, hotfooting it back to whatever sort of sordid den such monsters inhabited. And Trevisan had gold. And time.

All Rhett had was a handful of friends twisted up in his destiny, a circumstance none of them had asked for. They had come with him, this time. And they'd all lost something along the way. Would they follow him where he went next? The tug on his belly told him where he was headed, and at least one of his compatriots wasn't going to like it one bit.

Careful and soft, he slipped his bare arm out from under Cora, who muttered something and rolled away, deep asleep still. With so many empty cars, they had taken this one for themselves, and the foreman's bed was just wide enough to hold both of their skinny bodies, whittled away by months working to build this very railroad. He pulled on his clothes in the crisp bite of fall morning and shook his boots for scorpions. Rhett didn't dare pick a fight with the small mirror hanging on the wall. He knew he had a haunted look about him, gaunt and angry and wearing his scars like armor, but he didn't have to meet his own damn eye to know it.

The door opened far more smoothly than the ones that had held him captive every night in the worker cars attached farther along on this same train, and he stepped down onto prairie dirt packed firm by a night of hard rain. The earth had already begun to drink down the wet like a dying babe on the tit, and by noon, all would again be dust. That was life in Durango, and folks without backbone to match that hardness didn't last long.

The once bustling railroad camp was silent as a cemetery, the morning sun just starting to tickle the far, flat horizon to the east. But that wasn't the direction the Shadow was tugging Rhett. He walked around to the engine car and stood where he could see in every direction. Yesterday, he'd told his posse that they would be headed west. But what he hadn't told them was that Trevisan, now in Meimei's body, was headed south.

Such news was bound to be a shock for Cora, but he'd tried to tell her from the start—he wasn't a man who followed a woman's whims. He followed the Shadow, that unwelcome twinge in his belly that told him where the world demanded to be set right, where monsters roamed and evil dwelled and only he could end it. Just now, that angry ache in his belly said that they had to head back to the Las Moras division of the Durango Rangers, and quick.

Rhett didn't like it. Why would the Shadow turn so swiftly away from Trevisan? What could possibly be worse than a necromancer killing people and stealing bodies across the country as he laid railroad tracks toward the sea? There was something heavy and dark about Rhett's destiny just now, some vicious portent that made his hackles rise. The Shadow didn't let go, nor did it usually change its mind before Rhett had destroyed a dangerous target, which suggested the Captain was in trouble.

All the more reason to get headed west as fast as the horses would carry them.

On the other hand, maybe it made plenty of good sense. Maybe it wasn't a problem, but a solution. Now that he and Sam had evidence of Trevisan's evil, maybe the Captain would rally his men, and the Durango Rangers would gallop after the necromancer with the full force of bullets and the law on their side. Cora would surely understand that; she'd proven to be a reasonable woman thus far. But maybe reasonable didn't count for much when it was your family on the line. Far as Cora was concerned, Trevisan was holding her baby sister hostage. Rhett had never had a sibling, but the folks waiting by a cookfire just ahead were the closest things he had to family, and when he saw they already had breakfast set up, he liked them even more.

Well, most of them.

"Took you long enough," Earl said with his usual prickliness.

"Well, after I free an entire camp from servitude, I grant myself the rare treat of a long morning lie-in." Rhett scratched his bedraggled hair. "I never did sign up to be hollered at before noon. And where the hell'd you come from, anyway?"

Earl's nose wrinkled. "Didn't realize how eerie it was in this part of the prairie at night, all by my lonesome. Kept hearing howls. The horse shared my concerns, and here we are."

"I reckon we're stuck with you, then. What's for breakfast?"

"There were no supplies," Dan said, holding up a skewered bit of meat with a shrug, "but most things still die easily enough."

"Unlike Trevisan," Earl added.

At that, Rhett bristled. "I don't believe I'm currently taking criticism from folks who weren't man enough to take on the fight personally. You want to have words with me, you want to gripe about my actions, then you do something besides skulk around with a bottle in your hand."

Earl jumped up, hands in fists and face red. Rhett was already up, and his anger with Earl had become a simmering thing, a wolf pestered by a gnat. Just to mess with him, Rhett reached past the furious Irishman to snag the piece of meat on Dan's stick.

"Thanks mightily, Dan. I do appreciate a feller who can pull his weight."

Dan snorted. "You're too thin, Rhett. We need you whole for what's to come."

"And what's that?"

Dan gave his old coyote grin. "I don't know for sure, but I assume some sort of violent revenge."

"No one thinks you're going to stay here and shack up with your new toy," Winifred added. She'd been silent thus far, sitting demurely by the fire in her dress and leggings, her misaligned ankle crossed over her good one. When Rhett looked to her, he found accusation writ plainly on her face. And was that... jealousy?

Surely not. The girl was standoffish as a cat.

Usually.

"I think you mean my doctor," Rhett snapped back.

"I am no one's toy."

They all looked up to find Cora watching from the open door of the train. Rhett felt a flush creep up his neck and willed it back down.

Cora's face was impassive, a smooth wall. Rhett had seen her look like that at the rude men who came to her and Grandpa Z for doctoring in the train camp, and he reckoned it meant she was feeling insulted. He hadn't known her long, and he hadn't known her well, but she seemed to know her way around patching up a feller's carcass. He could only assume she also knew how to make a feller *into* a carcass. A chill stole over the camp, and no one spoke for a good long while.

"Good rabbit," Rhett observed to Dan when he couldn't handle the silence a moment longer.

But Dan was watching his sister as if she might suddenly do something very dangerous. Recalling Dan's warning about Rhett's own entanglement with the coyote girl, he edged to the left so that he stood between Winifred and Cora, just in case Winifred took it upon herself to scratch Cora's eyes out. His attention flashed to Sam Hennessy, who hadn't spoken yet and was sitting wide-eyed and horrified and gut-punched across the fire, looking like a man caught in the middle of a storm. Rhett's heart shuddered like it'd been mule-kicked.

Sam knew now.

Knew from before that Rhett had been with Winifred. Knew now that Rhett had been with Cora. Only thing Sam didn't know about Rhett's private-type activities was that Sam himself had been a part of them when under a god's spell in the grove at Buckhead.

Knowing what he did know...well, it looked like it had destroyed the boy.

"Goddammit, this is a waste of time!" Rhett shouted, desperate to see Sam's face do something other than look shattered. "Only thing that matters is getting on with life. Don't go stirring the damn pot when the pot is the only thing that keeps us together."

"Camp is a small place," Winifred said, her mouth all tiny and proper as she stood and limped away. "We can't hop out of the damn pot." It was right peculiar, seeing her with two feet again instead of one foot and a stump, but Rhett was surprised to see the girl's old grace had not returned with her foot.

"Not quite right," Cora murmured, coming up behind Rhett as if she could read his mind. She put her hand on his arm. "Nothing heals perfectly."

"That's what's got her riled, most likely," Rhett responded, stepping slightly away from her touch. "She always expects perfection. Wants everybody to be just so. Life ain't like that."

Another snort from Dan, who was starting to sound like a horse with its face in the pepper. "It's not perfection she wants. It's goodness. Rightness."

"Then she can keep waiting." Rhett sat on the log Winifred had abandoned, the bark still warm from her body.

"Let us not wait," Cora said, sitting too close to Rhett on the log. Dan held out the meat, and she nodded her thanks and nibbled it. "Meimei can't be far. When do we break camp and pursue her? You said she'd gone west."

Rhett's discomfort grew. Everyone who was left stared at him. Earl, Dan, Sam, Cora.

They all knew: It was his call.

If this was what the Captain had to deal with every day, no wonder he was a man of so few words. Hard as it was to live a life in which his thoughts didn't count, like his life before the vampire had cornered him at Pap and Mam's, it was a new sensation to be the lynchpin of an entire group of folks, all of whom wanted something different from him.

One thing Rhett couldn't abide, though, was a liar.

So he wasn't going to lie, even if lying would've been a hell of a lot easier.

"That's not quite what I said." He took another piece of meat, chewed and swallowed. It stuck in his craw, and he nearly choked before he got it down. "I said we needed to go west. That's what the Shadow's telling me. But it's also telling me that Trevisan went south."

"You mean Meimei went south."

He shook his head. "I don't know where Meimei went. I just know where the thing I need to kill is."

"But my sister can be saved. She's still in there, somewhere. Perhaps he controls her now, but she's still inside. I know it." He had never heard Cora sound so fierce and so frightened, nor so wrong.

"That's not mine to say," he answered carefully. "What's mine to do is to go west and speak to the Captain of the Las Moras Rangers. So that's my plan."

"I'm with you," Dan said quietly. "There could be trouble."

Sam nodded along earnestly. His red cheeks were the only sign he'd been upset just moments before. "Me, too, Rhett. You know that."

Rhett suspected Winifred would go wherever Dan went, especially if it meant she could needle Rhett some more. That left Earl and Cora, and Rhett couldn't have said what they might choose.

"Might as well," Earl finally offered. "I don't like you much, but you seem to keep your skin. Maybe I'll find a town along the way. Someplace not terribly unkind to Irishmen. Buckhead had a fine feel about it."

"I bet it did," Rhett muttered to himself, remembering Earl and Winifred drunkenly joined under the god's spell.

And with that, he remembered that Winifred was now traveling for two. Pregnant, Cora had said. No wonder she was fussy. No wonder she'd left the campfire. The girl was most likely upchucking her dissatisfaction and her breakfast behind a bush. Rhett suddenly felt like he was rounding up a herd of colts that gleefully defied his control.

"I will go south," Cora said coldly. "If I have to go as a dragon, I will go. Meimei is all I have left."

That got Rhett's dander up. He turned to her slow. "Is she now?" he asked, deadly and soft.

Cora went even colder, as if her scales were just under the surface. "So it would seem."

His rage bubbled up, useless. He'd once punched Winifred, back when he still thought of himself as a girl, and he didn't regret it a bit. Now that he was a man, however, such things felt forbidden. He wouldn't lay a hand on Cora out of anger. But he'd have to convince her that her plan was damned foolish, because knowing what he did about the unforgiving land of Durango and the murderous nature of Trevisan, he could only fear that Cora would die if left to her own devices.

"Cora, darlin', do you want to see Meimei alive again?"

"Obviously."

"Then don't go after her alone. I faced off with Trevisan and barely escaped. He tried to use his magic to pry his way inside me. He held me down and pulled out one of my teeth. You've seen him overcome an entire camp of powerful men, including dragons. Including you. What makes you think you can beat him now just because you care more?"

Cora shot to her feet and screamed, "Because I do care more. Because I'm the only one who cares at all!"

Rhett deflated a little, hoping she could read the sorry in his eye. "Caring don't save lives. Smart planning does. And I'm willing to bet that Trevisan expects us to follow him. That he'll be ready for us."

With his usual calm, Dan broke in. "You have a fantasy in your head, don't you, Cora? That you'll find your sister's small body sleeping on the prairie, alone, and you'll look into her eyes and fix her?" He looked down. "I felt that way, once. I was unable to help my sister when she was lost and broken. Only you were able to do that. And I trusted you to do that."

Cora exhaled a thin line of smoke. "And I failed. Is that what you are saying?"

He shook his head. "No. Quite the opposite. You saved her. You performed a miracle. All miracles are imperfect. You did the impossible. And I'm saying that Rhett can do that for you, too, but you have to trust him. You don't have to like him. But you must understand that his destiny is wiser than any of us. Especially when we're heartsick. Especially when we're scared."

Cora turned slowly in a circle. "Which way is west?"

Without having to think about it, Rhett pointed.

"Which way is Meimei? Which way is south?"

Rhett turned and pointed.

"After you go west, will you go south? Does your destiny tell you?"

His belly churning, Rhett nodded and shrugged at the same time. "I reckon. For now. I mean, it feels that way. Things can change. Destiny's not a biddable thing."

"Neither am I."

Now it was Rhett's turn to snort, his other friends forgotten. "Didn't say you were. Nobody's talking about what you're going to do. We're talking about what I'm going to do. So you can follow me or go kill yourself at Trevisan's feet like a fool. Damn, woman! I thought you were sensible."

"No one is sensible when the thing they love is at stake."

This from Winifred, who'd reappeared, albeit far from Cora's place in the circle.

From one person to the next, Rhett slowly spun, feeling very much like he was sizing up a gunfight. Except when he was in that sort of fight, he felt well nigh invincible, as if he couldn't be touched. Now, for the first time, he felt himself stall and stutter. Now he felt like perhaps he had something to lose, and it sure as hell wasn't as easily fixed as his body.

Sam and Dan were on his side. Cora was flat-out against him. Winifred and Earl…well, on the best of days, he didn't know what passed for their thoughts.

He finally said, "It's just a direction. The ultimate goal is the same."

"It's more than a direction," Cora said, quiet as a viper.

"When the Shadow calls, I have to answer."

"When it's convenient," Winifred hissed.

"This is what I got to do," he finally shouted, all raging with desperation.

"You say that with suspicious frequency, especially when it means you don't have to explain yourself," Earl said, then spit in the dirt for emphasis.

Rhett wouldn't let his head duck down, wouldn't let his shoulders cave in like they had, long ago, when Pap was yelling his worst. There were no lies in what he'd said, no shame in what he was doing. The long and short of it was that folks wanted him to do their business first, and he knew damn well what his own business was. And his business was just more goddamn important.

"Right. So I'll go saddle up, then. If you're with me, you're with me. If you're not…"

It came out all ragged with a little break, almost a sniffle, damn his female vocal chords.

He didn't finish the sentence.

CHAPTER 2

Rhett stomped right back into the train car and slammed the door shut. As if it were in cahoots with everyone else in the camp, the damn thing clanked right back open. He gathered up his saddle and blanket, bridle and bags, and stopped to stare, for just a moment, at the puddle of blankets on the narrow bed. Such comfort could only ever be a fleeting thing. Better the hard ground and smoky fire, tough meat and tougher enemies. At least then he knew where he stood, and it was behind the trigger end of a gun.

It wasn't as if he'd promised Cora anything. Not like he'd lain beside her, whispering pretty dreams of a ranch house and tidy board fences and a snow-white milk cow cropping green grass in the afternoon sun. They'd never spoken of the future. He'd barely known her a few days. And yet he knew, down to his bones, that he was saying good-bye to something of value, something that he might not get the chance to reject a second time. Well, then. As he'd already stated, destiny wasn't a biddable thing, and neither was Rhett Walker. At least now he knew who his true friends were.

He hopped out of the train car with determination and headed for the little knot of horses, where Sam and Dan were already busy with their saddles. Earl, in donkey form and therefore vastly preferable in outlook, waited nearby, ears laid back and tail twitching irritably. Rhett noted that Cora's draft horse, Samson, was gone, and when he looked to the dilapidated open wagon Cora had taken from the train camp originally, he found it abandoned and already lightly dusted with sand, as if it were slowly being consumed by the prairie. Cora was backing the big gelding into place between the traces of Winifred's colorful, cozy purple wagon, once the property of a witch and taken over her dead body. That made sense—Rhett knew the closed-top purple wagon was altogether more comfortable, especially if there was any kind of weather. Winifred was nearby, tossing her saddle onto Kachina's back.

So that's how it was? His women splitting off? Ranging against him?

No. That wasn't right. They weren't his. They only belonged to themselves. And that's why they were about to go and do something stupid. Because it might've been the right thing to do, but it was damn well the wrong time to do it.

He walked toward Cora, trying to make his face look mild, or kind, or something that wasn't his usual rough, brutish, angry expression.

"Cora, I know I can't tell you what to do, but I got a bad feeling about you going off alone, and—"

"I won't be alone. Winifred will go with me. We are quite capable."

"Honey, I know you think that, but—"

"Don't call me honey."

He looked down, struggled to pull his thoughts together in an intelligent and persuasive manner, which had never been his strong point.

"Look. Cora. You go south now without me, chances are

you'll die. Both of you." He looked at Winifred's still-flat belly. "All three of you. You got to trust me on this."

Cora looked back to Winifred and shook her head. "Men. They'll tell you anything to get what they want."

"Yes, except Rhett actually believes what he's saying," Winifred responded. Then, looking daggers at Rhett, she tightened her girth, hard, making Kachina squeal. "You have to do the things you have to do, and the rest of us are left to choose. I choose to help Cora save her sister. She's worried and scared, and that will only get worse with every mile west, every mile that takes you farther away from Meimei. Can you tell us anything about where Trevisan is going besides south?"

His hands made fists at his sides. Asking the Shadow for information was like asking a storm cloud the time of day. But he could feel the answer churning up. "The gulf. He's going to the sea."

Rhett could almost see the wheels turning behind Winifred's dark eyes. "Yes. A ship. It's the fastest way to get... would he go east or west?"

"East," Rhett said without thinking.

"Where the money is. Where the railroads start. He could get a new engine there and just follow his tracks right back to where you found him and start all over again with a new crop of monster slaves. So we have to stop him before he reaches the sea."

"Stop her," Cora added softly, her hand on Samson's soft nose.

Rhett wasn't sure how much *her* was left in Meimei's body, but he wasn't about to add to Cora's sadness—or make her hate him any more.

"Y'all got guns? Ammunition? A spare horse?"

Winifred's smile was wry, and it made Rhett feel a right fool.

"I knew how to travel and fight before you did, Rhett Walker. And we women have our secret weapons." Rhett's eyes strayed to the girl's chest, and she laughed her old, carefree laugh. "I become a sneaky coyote, and she becomes a gigantic dragon, from what I understand. Fool."

She swung up into the saddle and checked her bags with an easy grace, her hair whipping back in the wind. Once she was up there, it was like she became one with her horse, and Rhett couldn't even remember which foot wasn't quite right. He'd once thought women soft, foolish, useless things, but not this woman. Not either of them. Cora finished buckling Samson's harness and climbed up to the wagon seat before Rhett could offer her a hand. She clicked her tongue and urged the big gelding on, the wagon wheels creaking free of the now dry dirt.

Neither girl told Rhett good-bye. Or that they were sorry.

No one said a thing.

Rhett watched them for longer than he should have, feeling a peculiar ache in his bound chest. He didn't love either of the women. Wasn't even sure he liked Winifred that much. Didn't know Cora half as well as he would've liked to. But they had become part of his chosen family, his posse, the few people in the whole goddamn world he'd take a bullet for. He'd give ten of Earl for either of 'em.

Winifred led on Kachina with Cora following behind in the wagon, one of Dan's old chestnut geldings ponied off the back and walking calmly enough. They needed nothing from Rhett, and he didn't necessarily need them, but he didn't like the thought of them out there on their own. The world was unkind to women, especially those without male protection, and doubly so for women who weren't lily white and wearing fine dresses and hoopskirts. Turning into a coyote wouldn't do you any good around a feller who'd just as soon shoot a coyote as an Injun if either creature looked at him wrong. Just the thought of it made Rhett quiver up with anger again. He needed something to do besides burn to follow the women, so he hitched up his gun belt and walked on over to the little herd of horses and the men pretending not to watch him like he was a keg of gunpowder sitting too near a messy fire.

"It'll be good to see the Rangers again," Sam said, his usual cheerful self.

"I wonder what trophies can be had on a sand wyrm. Perhaps Jiddy has worm guts hanging from his belt." Dan chuckled, and Rhett joined him. Hating Jiddy was one of the few things they completely agreed upon.

Earl just switched his tail and took a few impatient steps westward.

"I know, I know," Rhett grumbled as he tossed his blanket on Ragdoll's skinny back.

Dan's hand landed on his shoulder. "Choice is what defines life. I agree that they made the wrong one. We both know your choice is right. Let's move on."

"You ain't worried about your sister and her get?"

"Not until there's a reason to worry. I trust her. You should trust her, too. We must all move forward."

"Feels like we're just running back and forth to the Outpost. Like we're asking the Captain for permission to do the right thing."

"Just because you have a feeling doesn't mean it's real," Dan said.

Rhett didn't know if that was good sense or an insult, so he focused on getting his saddle in place and cinched and sliding the dried-out bridle over Ragdoll's fuzzy forelock. He could use a day at the Outpost, oiling his gear and replenishing his bullets among the men. No fractious women goading him on.

Nobody working him to death or trying to cut on him or... inhabit him. Whatever Trevisan had tried that had landed the alchemist in the body of the six-year-old Chine girl Cora was now chasing, brave fool that she apparently was.

The men were soon in the saddle and checking their kits for the last time before leaving, Sam and Dan just as ready to hit the trail as Rhett was. Cora's wagon was a bright purple smudge against the glowing orange prairie, headed dead south. Rhett look west, and the air tasted better that way. When he looked south again, the air tasted...wrong. Like poison and dust, and...something almost metallic and powdery...something so familiar...

He turned Ragdoll's head south and kicked her hard as all get-out. She sprung awake, furious, and leaped into an angry gallop. Before Dan and Sam could join in, Rhett heard the women screaming.

For a fast horse, it felt like Ragdoll ran forever, time stretching out with her scraggly mane as Rhett lay low and clobbered her ribs with his heels. The purple wagon was stopped up ahead, and the ponied chestnut gelding was pulling back against his rope, digging his heels into the dirt to escape.

"What is it?" Rhett shouted as he drew his pony up near Winifred and held on tight as Ragdoll jigged and struggled to back away.

"The ground," she yelled, jerking her chin since both her hands were struggling to keep Kachina from rearing.

Just ahead, the dirt was collapsing in, sand dribbling down the sides of a new sinkhole. Plants pulled free from the earth and tumbled hellward, and Cora hollered at Samson in her own language, no doubt begging the big feller to back up, to back away from the ever-widening hole. Rhett jumped down off Ragdoll, swatted her rump with his hat to urge her away, and hurried to take Samson's traces in hand, snapping the leather to make the big bastard move. Inch by inch, step by step, his rump nearly against the wagon seat, Samson pushed Cora farther from the danger. Even still, Rhett felt the ground trembling under his boots. The air smelled like evil, like poison, like something Rhett had smelled only once before, in the alchemist's car.

"Get away!" he yelled to Winifred. "It's Trevisan—"

As if the evil bastard had heard his name called and had a trap ready to answer, the air filled with a clicking sound as the hole in the earth bubbled up with a mass of wriggling scorpions. Rhett watched it as he bullied Samson backward, but his brain still didn't quite believe it. Hundreds, thousands, millions of scorpions boiled up and crawled out onto the prairie in a writhing mass of murder. Claws clicked, tails snapped, and the horses made noises Rhett had never heard come out of horses before, a mix of rage, terror, and desperation. His eye flashed down to his boots in caution. For all the times he'd shaken them carefully to avoid a single scorpion, now he was facing an entire cyclone of the damned things, and all he wanted to do was run.

But this was alchemist magic, and he knew running wouldn't goddamn work.

Especially for folks who weren't the Shadow.

The first thing he did was hurry to Winifred and use her dangling lariat to swat Kachina on the rump, sending the surprised horse into a leaping spin and a gallop.

"But—" was all Winifred managed before she was half a mile away, clinging to a fast-as-lightning horse that looked like she'd be all too happy to never turn around again.

Then Rhett was going after Samson and the wagon, pulling the big horse down from his stomping and rearing and carefully walking him around in a circle to avoid breaking the poles holding him to the wagon. Another swat, and Samson was running away, dragging a screaming Cora, a bumping purple wagon, and a terrified chestnut pony with him. Hopefully the big horse would run straight and not cause the wagon to topple over, crushing Cora perhaps beyond what her dragon magic could fix. Rhett's throat whimpered without his consent, and he turned, wholly unburdened by people and horses, to face whatever trap Trevisan must've left for him.

Rhett's fingers itched for his weapons, but it wasn't like a piddly ol' knife or two fine guns could take down a thousand separate, wiggling critters. They aimed for him now, swirling over and around one another like a twister, buzzing and clicking as they came. A low hum started up somewhere, a sound Rhett had only heard one time before, in Trevisan's car. The scorpions glopped together in a big ball, and Rhett went to rip off his clothes to turn into the bird, who could at least eat these little bastards like he had Trevisan's ravens. But his fingers froze on his shirt buttons.

The ball of scorpions was…changing. Shifting. Becoming something else.

Because of course fighting the alchemist's magic, even without the alchemist present, wasn't going to be easy.

"What are you gonna be, you dumb son of a bitch?" Rhett murmured to himself, whipping out his Bowie knife.

The scorpions swarmed and clicked and melded, fusing together into a giant black carapace the size of a shack with pincers as long as a man and six horse-tall legs.

"That's a big scorpion," Dan commented from atop his dancing chestnut.

"Get out of here, Dan. This thing only wants to fight with me."

"Rangers don't let Rangers fight alone," Sam added from his blue roan.

"Goddammit, Sam! Get out of here. This don't concern you," Rhett shouted, worried for the first time. "It'll chop you in half, if it can."

"Then I'll stay out of reach." With a mad grin, Sam maneuvered his horse out of range and started taking potshots at the giant scorpion with his repeater pistols.

"What's your plan, Shadow?" Dan asked.

Rhett looked up at him, briefly, before refocusing on the approaching critter.

"I reckon you can't kill a thing that's not dead, so we just need to stop it and…take it apart. You two keep it occupied."

"What are you going to do?"

"Shut up and watch, Dan."

Rhett ran out of range and finished stripping out of his clothes, dropping everything in a pile. He left the knife on top and stared at it hard while he transformed into the big bird. The lammergeier, the lambhawk, the grandpappy of buzzards. None of those words meant anything to the ugly, red-eyed bird now clutching a Bowie knife's hilt in one clawed foot as it hobbled and flapped up into the sky.

To the bird, the scorpion wasn't an animal, a natural thing. It was a man-thing, cobbled together of trash and poison and sticky strings of magic, but Rhett's will clung to the bird, urging it to fly up behind the scorpion as it snapped at Dan's dancing horse with giant pincers. Although Rhett's first transformation had occurred in midair as he fell from the Cannibal Owl's lair, turning him from man to bird (or girl to bird, then), this was the first time that the transformation had reversed in midair. Rhett popped into his human skin and fell, arms flailing, almost dropping the knife. Naked as the day he was born, he landed right on top of the curve of the scorpion's tail and dug his fingers and nine toes into the little gaps between the plating.

The tail started to whip around, once the critter felt him there. It curled and uncurled its tail before striking the ground, mere feet away from Dan. All the while, a buck-nekkid Rhett clung to the monster like it was a wild bronc he was determined to tame. Even amid the pandemonium, it did not escape Rhett that Dan almost laughed at his predicament, and he swore he'd make him pay, later, for that indignity.

As the tail rose back up and paused, Rhett was able to focus, hold tight with his left hand, and slash off the poisoned barb at the tail's tip with his Bowie knife. It took some sawing, and hot black ichor splashed over his wrist, burning like hellfire. But he didn't stop.

"Aim for its legs!" he shouted before pushing himself off backward into the air, where he pinwheeled for a moment before turning himself inside out and into the ugly, one-eyed bird. He lost track of the knife while he found his wings, damn his clumsy talons, and it clattered to the ground covered in poison tar.

The bird flapped hard for where Ragdoll stood, closer than where any horse with sense would be to such a creature. His mare watched him, canny and disapproving, and didn't so much as stamp a hoof when he landed on the ground and transformed again into a bedraggled man with an arm still slightly smoking and splashed with black.

"If I don't scare you, I reckon you're dumber than you look," he said, but kindly.

The mare just snorted.

He walked up to her barefoot, picking his way around the prickly bits of scrub as quickly as possible, and pulled his lariat off his saddle. For just a moment, he considered swinging up into the saddle in his altogether and running back into the fray, but he wouldn't put the mare at risk. Like Sam, Ragdoll was all too mortal, too easily broken. And Rhett couldn't do without her.

"Stay here," he warned her, and then he was running back to where Dan and Sam were harrying the pissed-off scorpion with their guns.

Out of six legs, two were plum gone, and one was threatening to fall off, dripping black goop into the dirt. An arrow stuck out of one of its great pincers, which couldn't pinch anymore but still made an effective club. Sam shot the critter again, snapping off that dangling leg and making the huge scorpion list to the side.

"I got to reload," he muttered, cantering his gelding out of reach and fumbling with his bullet pouch.

That was perfect timing as far as Rhett was concerned. He bolted forward, whipping the rope around his head like he was aiming for a particularly wild mustang. Clever Dan already knew what was up and had his own rope out as well. They were on opposite sides of the dancing scorpion, and Rhett judged his throw and tossed his loop at a waving pincer, catching it neatly. On the other side, Dan missed, damn his eyes, and Rhett found himself the sole cowpoke in charge of a wagon-sized, angry, magic monster.

He had no gun. No knife. Nothing but a body, already damaged in the fight and not even hidden under clothes. The scorpion turned toward him and waved its pincer in an experimental-type fashion before clicking its mouthparts in delight and skittering right at him on three legs.

"You're too ugly to win this fight," Rhett said, hoping to buy himself a few moments. He backed up, step after step, ignoring all the sharp things and patches of burning black scorpion blood under his feet. The scorpion didn't look like it had understood him, but it also didn't look like it cared.

The unroped pincer struck at Rhett, quick as lightning, and he threw himself on the ground and rolled. Sure, he could probably survive whatever happened, but he didn't want his guts squashed out here in the middle of nowhere. And maybe the alchemist's magic had a poison to it, would make even skin-walker innards stay scrambled. Soon he was trundling away on hands and knees, waiting for Sam to get his guns loaded or Dan to remember how to lasso a goddamn cow, or anything that would get the scorpion to change its focus.

"Any time now would be great!" he hollered over his shoulder.

For a thing half-hobbled, the scorpion wouldn't give up on its goal. Rhett clambered and rolled and crab-walked backward as the giant pincer and leaking tail stabbed, again and again, inches from where he'd just been. Where were his friends, his Rangers? He couldn't even get a good look to see if they were shooting or turning tail. What a way to go, he thought— stabbed to death by a scorpion miles from anywhere, and buck nekkid to boot.

The pincer came down hard, knocking him sideways.

"I hope my goddamn dust blinds all of y'all when this critter gets me!" he yelled.

Something whistled through the air, and the scorpion hit the dirt with a loud *whump* as one of its remaining three legs exploded. As the monster fell, Rhett flopped onto his back, out of range, and tried to get his heart to stop hammering.

"Sorry if I'm late," Winifred said, taking the Henry from her shoulder as she walked up to give Rhett a smug grin. "My horse was misbehaving." Soon she joined Sam in filling the downed scorpion with holes as it struggled to stand again and stabbed at them with a tail that was pretty much a useless stump.

Since the monster couldn't bedevil Rhett anymore, he stood as nonchalantly as a naked feller could and dusted off some of the prickly bits and gravel clinging to his rump. He was hunting around for his dropped knife when he heard a noise unlike anything he'd ever heard before, a scream of rage that sounded something like an eagle, but much bigger and louder. A winged shadow passed over him, and he looked up and shielded his eye.

It was a dragon.

It had to be. Like a sinuous snake covered in scales ranging from gold to orange, with a fiery ruff around its neck and a long mustache and claws the size of Rhett's arm. As he watched, it hovered above the scorpion and snorted, shaking its grand head at the silly people scurrying around on the ground. One by one, they backed away from the scorpion—because they weren't dumb, Rhett's posse, and it was a goddamn dragon. When they were out of range, the dragon's mouth opened to reveal a row of razor teeth, and it belched a plume of flame that left the scorpion screeching and scrabbling in the dirt.

Smoke rose from the critter's black armor, and the giant pincers flailed like an old lady running from a rat, and the dragon turned around and dove again, spraying out even more flame.

Rhett realized in this moment that he was possibly a little more impressed with Cora than he'd thought, but that getting involved with someone who could breathe fire might actually be a death sentence for someone as ornery as he was liable to be. Still, it was a beautiful scene, watching the girl become a dragon and annihilate a monster.

"It ain't dying," Sam offered, sounding perplexed. "Rhett, why won't it die?"

And it wasn't, either. It was still trying, half on fire and with only two legs, to scurry after Rhett in particular. He finally spotted his knife, picked it up, and squinted at the scorpion. When the dragon finished the latest run and kinda looked at him, he waved a hand to indicate that maybe she should stop with the fire for a minute. As the scorpion struggled toward him, he snatched up his trailing lariat and tossed it to Dan. Sam neatly lassoed its other pincer, and they backed up their horses until the critter was strung between them like a taut line of laundry and struggling to stand.

"No tail. No claws. It's not your day, son," Rhett said as he stood in front of it. "I reckon you aren't gonna tell me where your heart is?"

The thing just chittered and struggled like an idjit.

"Guess I'll keep stabbing until I find it, then."

His stomach griped as he plunged his knife into the scorpion's smoking back, and he had to dodge the leaking tail stump as it tried to sting him again and again. Winifred ran up behind it, and the sound of her knife sawing into the tail made Rhett's teeth itch like a dull blade on bone. Soon the tail was half–lopped off like a dead branch and couldn't flick anymore, and Rhett had no choice but to go stab-happy, hunting for whatever controlled the alchemist's creature as his chest burned from the heat rising off its smoking black shell.

"This was a hell of a lot easier with ravens," he muttered, hacking and hacking as more black gunk leaked, burning, onto his hands.

Finally, finally, he must've hit something, as what was left of the scorpion shuddered and stopped moving. Once it was completely on the ground and still, he stabbed some more, because he had the feeling that if it was good and dead, it would... change. Like all the rest of Trevisan's magic, the thing wasn't supposed to just rot out here on the prairie like the bones of an old wagon.

The scorpion's shell was in chunks now, and he pried them away to reveal a wet, crusty tube, black and charred and stringed with more of the ichor.

There.

The thing he was looking for: a ball of wax molded around a bitty black scorpion, the thing still struggling weakly. Stuck in the wax were a sliver of bone, a shard of gold, a bit of scorched paper, and the usual fancy *BT* crest that that Trevisan asshole just couldn't resist stamping on everything he figured he owned.

"It ain't personal," Rhett told the little scorpion, right before he slammed his knife down to chop it in half, along with the wax.

The scorpion curled and uncurled in agony for just a second, and then the giant body surrounding it collapsed into silvery gray dust, leaving Rhett to suddenly fall forward. On his hands and knees in the dirt, he pulled the note off the nasty bit of magic and silently handed it to Dan, who stood closest.

"It's from Trevisan," Dan said.

"Well, no shit, Dan," Rhett said, as he always did.

"It says that if you follow him, he will kill you."

Rhett stood and snorted and walked toward the pile of his clothes.

"Tell me something I don't know," he said.

CHAPTER 3

When Cora walked up, it was the first time Rhett had seen her looking sheepish or shy—or exhausted. He was fully dressed, at least, and had even chuckled to himself as he reflexively shook out his boots for scorpions. His only wounds from the fight were burns from the black gunk that had spurted out of the monster every time he cut on it, and from the looks of the wounds, they would never fully heal. He'd have splattery pink scars on his copper skin forever, most like. Before today, he'd figured he was already as odd as odd got, but he'd apparently been wrong.

He pulled his sleeves down over his scarred forearms as Cora stepped in closer than she should've, considering how they'd left that this morning. Her chin was down, her eyes burning and her forehead rumpled. A sheen of sweat glittered on her skin, and she was trembling, just a little.

"Go on, Rhett Walker. Say it."

Rhett cocked his hat up to give her a teasing grin. "Say what?"

"That I should've listened to you."

A waterfall of feelings tumbled through his mind, but in the end, what came out was, "I don't say things I don't mean, if I can help it."

Cora looked up at him, curious. The others listened in from a comfortable distance, like the nosy fools just couldn't help themselves.

"But you said we shouldn't go south alone, and when we did, it nearly killed us all."

Rhett looked away and rubbed the back of his head. He wasn't used to people acting all . . . well, like he was an authority and they were looking to get punished for their mistakes. It was a new feeling, and a strange one.

He didn't like it.

"Hellfire, Cora. It didn't nearly kill anybody. I got a few burns, but it's not like I can get any uglier. It was just a scorpion. Or, I guess, a bunch of bitty little scorpions that decided to be a big ol' mama scorpion. It's gone. We're fine. There's nothing to fret about." Then he patted her on the shoulder, like he figured the Captain or Monty would do to make a feller who was shamefaced feel like there were no hard feelings.

But Cora still couldn't quite look him in the eye. "Where I come from, a woman who opposed authority and put everyone at risk would be punished severely."

He snorted. "Well, that's pretty dumb. Women got just as much right to make dumb mistakes as fellers do. Look, I told you: Dangerous things gather to me, and I'm called to them. You just tripped a trap before I could, that's all. That note was for me. It's me he wants dead." He held her shoulder longer this time, gave it a comforting squeeze. "But maybe you'll consider coming with us now. If Trevisan's the bastard I reckon he is, the trail he's left from here to the sea's gonna be chock-full of traps like this. Everywhere he's stepped, he's left death in his footprint."

"In Meimei's footprint."

That got him to look her in the eyes. He had to make sure

that what he said this time sunk in, and sunk in good. "That right there? It's gonna be the death of you. You got to think of it as Trevisan now, or one day you're gonna look at your sister's little face and go soft when you got to go hard. I believe she's still in there. Okay? I believe. I *want* to believe. But I got to get him out first so we can find her. What she is now will kill you as soon as look at you. Today should've made that pretty clear. So you come with me to Las Moras, and we'll regroup and start the hunt again, but sideways. Where he won't have laid any traps. Where he won't be expecting us. That sound like a plan?"

Cora sighed the sort of long-suffering sigh women do when they know they're going to be hostage to a fool's whims for a while. "I don't like it, but it's better than facing another monster like that one. I thought my dragon's fire would be enough, but it is not. And now I am exhausted, too exhausted to fight another trap. I can barely stand." She gave the saddest chuckle and clicked her fingernails together. "I always thought that if only Meimei were free, Grandfather and I could lay the entire camp to waste, could destroy Trevisan with one deep breath. But it would appear he and his magic are something beyond what we are."

"What he does—it ain't natural," Rhett agreed. "But we can fight it. Together." He toed the heap of glittering gray ash that had been the scorpion. "We make a pretty good team, truth be told."

"Well, you had help," Winifred said, walking up and putting a hand on her hip.

"*We*'s a pretty big word," Rhett growled. "You were included in it, which you'd recognize if you weren't so damned ready to take offense all the time."

He used up his annoyance with her by grinding the ball of wax into the earth with the heel of his boot. The gold chip glimmered, and suddenly Earl was there, plucking it from the trash and pocketing it. Something about that gave Rhett the willies, so he covered up the bone chip with some dirt, effectively burying the bit of whoever had powered the scorpion with stolen magic. Hell, for all he knew, it could've been a sliver of his stolen toe bone. Feeling a sudden rush of sympathy, he dug the bone chip back out, studied the bitty thing about the size of his fingernail, and tucked it into the leather bag around his neck. Now it could stay with him, wherever it'd come from. For all the damage he did, it felt right nice, sometimes, to carry remnants of folks with him, to know they wouldn't be alone or forgotten. Wherever his toe bone ended up, he hoped it wasn't in the service of hurting anybody.

His head jerked up.

"Wait. Coyote Dan, does that book the Captain gave us say anything about tying magic to particular folks? Like, could Trevisan be using my own bone bits to draw his monsters to me? I know we only seen this one, but I'd be a damn fool if I didn't think there'd be more waiting along this trail."

Dan shrugged. "The book doesn't have much information on making alchemy work, it just identifies alchemists as another monster to be wary of. Your theory is possible. That could be your bone. But also remember that you weren't the one who triggered the trap."

Rhett chewed his ragged lip. "So anybody who comes across one of Trevisan's traps might get et up by a monster? All the way from here to the gulf?"

Dan's look was a hard thing, a warning not to stray too far from the path. "There's no way to tell. Maybe it's just monsters that can set them off. Maybe it's just people with your stink on 'em. We can deal with that after we've got the Captain's blessing and more weapons, as the Shadow wills it."

A trill of worry something close to fear went down Rhett's neck. Whichever direction he went, he wasn't headed toward anything good.

Rhett looked at his posse, one by one. Sweet Sam, sour Earl, steady if annoying Dan, defiant Winifred, and poor, out-of-her-depth Cora, caught halfway between guilt and terror. His main goal now was to keep them near him, where he could help protect them.

Clearly, breaking up the group spelled disaster.

Clearly, keeping them nearby wasn't just him being selfish.

"Then let's saddle up," he said. "The plan's the same. We go west. For now."

But what would they find there? The queasy churning of his gut suggested it was going to be even worse than usual, which was saying a hell of a lot.

The posse was back on the trail. Nothing unusual happened for quite some time. The horses found their calm and still had plenty of stamina. The first day on the road was always Rhett's favorite, when the sun was out and the food was plentiful and nobody'd gotten sick or shot yet. They'd been lucky with the scorpion—Rhett was the only one who'd taken damage, and even that was just his skin. He was out front on Ragdoll, working like a mostly human compass to guide the group in the right direction. Sam rode by his side with Dan in back, keeping an eye on the trail behind. A drained and weakened Cora wobbled on the box seat of the purple wagon, relying on Samson to follow the other horses. They'd left her original wagon from the train camp behind to mark their old path, so Earl trotted along in donkey form instead of driving, which seemed to work best for all involved.

Winifred hung back near Cora's wagon, and Rhett was glad to see them smile shyly at each other instead of raising their hackles. With so few women roughing it in the wide spaces of Durango, they had quite a lot in common, once Winifred got over herself and her ridiculous jealousy. Cora was still exhausted, so he was glad to know someone else was watching over her. In any case, with all the ponied horses tied up off the wagon and Rhett free of most of what had dogged him, he felt right fine.

They broke for lunch after Sam shot a fine, fluffy bird. Winifred and Cora worked up some taters and greens, both claiming that if Rhett didn't eat better, he was liable to lose his teeth and get bow legs. Considering how the train camp had left him so wiry he could count every rib, even with his binder on, he was glad enough to take an extra helping, if that made the women fuss less.

Everything went just fine until they stopped just a bit before sunset. As soon as they spotted the little creek, the fellers nodded to one another and split off to do the chores. Even Earl had learned well enough how to find things that would burn, and he'd nearly mastered the art of fetching enough tinder that the fire didn't go out by morning. Sam was off hunting, Dan cleared the camp and started up the fire from Earl's pile of sticks, and Rhett took care of the horses. Cora's wagon was just a bit behind, and he watched it trundle across the ground, imagining that the girl's rump would be sore as hell after such treatment. He immediately blushed for having thought something so personal, but he wasn't the sort of man who would ever choose a seat over a saddle.

As Samson strained toward the little creek, Rhett took hold of the gelding's bridle and walked by his side to a pretty field of green. Cora didn't say anything, and Rhett didn't say anything.

Samson made happy, snuffling noises. When Cora disappeared through the canvas curtain into the back of the wagon, it was like a weight had lifted from Rhett's chest. He talked to Samson as he unhitched him and hobbled him in the field, then went over the ponies one by one, checking for ticks and burrs and thorns and stones hiding in hooves. Next to being alone with Sam, this was probably his favorite thing to do. Horses were simple. They made sense. They had clear, honest personalities that rarely changed, and they knew almost immediately how they felt about a body. Humans and monsters, as far as Rhett figured, were just about the opposite of that.

Once all the horses were hobbled and gulping from the stream, Rhett stretched out until his back popped and headed for the fire. Everyone was there already, drinking from their canteens and watching a fat rattlesnake sizzle over the fire.

Rhett looked at Sam in surprise. "Are we that bad off that we're eating snake?"

Sam gave him a pained smile. "It's not that I missed a shot, Rhett. It's awful strange, how few animals there are around here. I ain't seen anything edible in hours, not since that bird at lunch."

Rhett inclined his head to concede the point. It was true, now that he considered it. They hadn't seen any game, much less the signs of anything big enough to fill them up or leave a trail. No deer, no scat, nothing bigger than a bluebird bursting from the bushes in surprise. And yet it was a lush place, as far as Durango went, with plenty of grass and little scrubby forests poking up around the creeks.

"It's right peculiar," Rhett agreed.

He stood and slowly spun in place. The Shadow didn't feel anything out of order, no pull to put some horrible, game-murdering monster to dust. No, what the Shadow mostly wanted right now was to sit the hell down and eat some snake without getting attacked by anything or having further uncomfortable conversations. After a long day in the saddle following a fight to the death with a giant scorpion, no one seemed liable to argue the matter.

The snake didn't go far among six people, and that was after they'd dug out the remains of lunch. Rhett felt like his middle was a gaping hole that could never quite be filled. Back at Mam and Pap's place, at least he hadn't known he was mostly starving to death. But he'd gotten accustomed to living on proper vittles with the Double TK ranch hands and then the Rangers, and now one sixth of a snake and a cold potato wouldn't cut it. He guzzled water just to feel full.

He settled on down for the night, leaning against his saddle with Sam on one side and Dan on the other. Winifred and Cora were on the other side of the fire, and everyone was keeping mostly silent. It was like that, after a fight—folks tended to sink into their feelings, replaying the fight or worrying about the future or just enjoying a quiet moment after the flood of energy. It wasn't much to slide his saddle back and tip his hat over his eyes, enjoying the soft flicker of firelight and the silence of a calm autumn night, not too hot and not too cool, broken only by the gentle wufflings of the horses nearby and Earl's donkey snores. He heard the women murmuring, and then their footsteps retreating, probably toward the wagon.

Good. They didn't have expectations of him, neither one. One more weight off his mind.

"Hey, Rhett?"

Rhett rolled on over when he heard his favorite sound and curled on his side to grin at Sam Hennessy. The feller hadn't shaved in a while, and his burly golden beard made Rhett's heart do somersaults.

"Yeah, Sam?"

"Aren't you going to the wagon with Cora?"

Sam's eyes were giving Rhett that puppy dog look, like he was hopeful but also afraid of being kicked. Rhett had to choose his words carefully, not only because the truth was a tricky thing, but also because he never wanted to cause Sam any pain.

"I don't reckon she wants me there," he said, voice low, hoping Dan wasn't listening in.

"Seems right comfortable. You two did, I mean. And the wagon."

Even a few weeks ago, Rhett would've turned away from Sam's plaintive look, from the torture of untangling his feelings. But Rhett had learned a lot about himself, and one thing he'd learned was that hard things were often worth doing and didn't keep well if ignored.

"It was comfortable, I guess. But the girls are the ones who need the wagon's comfort. Not me. I...I'm accustomed to rough living. And I reckon it did Cora a fright today, facing off with that monster. She's never faced anything like that, and it plum tuckered her out."

"But she knew Mister Trevisan personally?"

"Well, it's different, ain't it? One man looking you in the eye, making you be obedient, but knowing that as long as you do what he says, you'll survive. And then you're free, and devils are rising up from the ground to claim you. I don't think she's ever been in a fight for her life before, and she told me herself she thought her fire would kill it, lickety-split. Must be quite a blow to a person, realizing that you're not as dangerous as you thought you were."

Sam nodded as if tucking that wisdom away. "You-all sure seem to have a lot in common."

Rhett's lips twisted. "Oh, because we ain't white and we've been enslaved? Yeah, I guess her and me and half of the Federal goddamn Republic got that in common." Sam flinched like he'd been slapped, and Rhett softened. "Sorry, Sam. Sore subject, I reckon."

"I meant more like…how you're both…I mean…" Sam turned red as an apple and looked like he was liable to choke. "You seem to like the same thing, I guess. Hellfire, Rhett. I don't know what I'm saying."

But suddenly Rhett did know what Sam was saying, and he felt a blush creep up his own cheeks. "Oh. Oh. Well. Sam. I reckon…I mean, I figure…well, some folks won't eat snake, and some folks won't eat squirrel. Some folks'll eat both, and other folks prefer citified salt pork. But I reckon it depends more on how the meal is prepared, far as I'm concerned."

Sam's face went through a series of changes then, confusion and surprise and understanding. "Oh, well, I reckon that makes plenty of sense," he finally said, and then he gave Rhett a sweet and private smile.

"And what I prefer is to sleep right here. By the fire," Rhett said.

"Well, I prefer that, too, Rhett."

And then they stared at each other so long that it got right peculiar, and Rhett ducked his head and said good night and lay on his back, trembling, until sleep claimed him.

In the morning, they found no game and had to subsist on jerky they'd stored while waiting for Rhett to finish his business at the railroad camp. Poor Cora had never had jerky before and suffered a horrible stomachache after just a few hours on the trail. Winifred gathered what wild plants she could, but vegetables never filled a body up without some good, bloody meat to cling to.

Racking his mind for reasons such edible creatures wouldn't be around, Rhett let Puddin' fall back behind the wagon to walk beside Dan's latest forgettable chestnut, a mare with a wide blaze and one blue eye.

"Dan, you got any idea why we can't find supper?"

Dan stared between his mare's ears with his usual annoying calm. "Sometimes, there is no reason. Creatures move here and there."

"But I ain't even seen a vulture. It's unnatural."

"Wrong. Adversity is natural. Going hungry is natural. Ask me after ten days, and then I'll look for something sinister."

"Well shit, Dan. It only takes one meal without food to make me curious."

The stare Dan gave him reminded Rhett how little he knew about his vexful friend's past. "I've gone hungry much longer and for far more significant reasons." Then the shade seemed to pass by like a cloud, and Dan's smile was friendly again. "Ride ahead if you like, or become the bird and range farther. Perhaps such a large party and the wagon make them run. Perhaps they smell a dragon and flee."

"Fair enough. Watch my horse, will you?"

Dan nodded, so Rhett pulled Puddin' to a stop, dismounted, shucked his clothes, and tucked them into the saddlebag, all while keeping the pony between him and Dan, who had also obligingly halted his mount. Sam was ranging far ahead, on the lookout for game, and Rhett didn't give a shit if either of the women saw him in his altogether. Soon the bird was flapping into the sky, sighing the sigh of the truly free and light of heart. He passed over a tiny bright dot, Sam on his palomino, and kept flying. The grasses spread out beneath him like an endless blanket, rippling in the wind. The sun was high and warm for fall, the sky blue and clear. After the rainy, miserable days in the train camp, Rhett would never take a sunny day for granted again. He turned off his people brain and let the bird take over, tasting the air for something good and dead.

He managed to find an old deer, mostly rotten but meaty enough for his needs. After he'd plucked the carcass clean, he rubbed his face on some grass and took back to the sky, wheeling in ever wider circles. Below him, no creatures moved. Not a deer, not a bird, not even a fanged rabbit, which were generally plentiful. And yet nothing else seemed off to him, nothing at all.

Except...

The bird wobbled in the air. Too close to human thoughts to stay aloft, he twitched his feathers and headed back toward his posse. He saw Sam first, then the others, all sitting around a campfire that didn't smell delicious at all, thanks to a lack of cooking meat. Earl, still in donkey form, cropped a tiny patch of sparse grass, far off, his back to the group. Landing in his usual ungainly fashion behind the knot of horses, the bird transformed back into Rhett Walker, dressed, and considered his words carefully as he took his place at the fire.

"No game?" Dan asked.

Rhett shook his head and took the piece of jerky Sam held out. "Nothing. Nothing as far as I got. Only found one carcass, and it was ancient." He put a fist over his burp, which reminded him exactly how old it had been. "Didn't see anything unusual. The Shadow didn't feel anything. And yet..."

"And yet?" Winifred asked.

Rhett stared at her hard. "And yet I got this feeling." Nobody interrupted him for once, so he chewed his jerky and considered. "Like the world's holding its breath. Like something's coming, but all the critters had plenty of time to clear the way. Like they know something we don't."

Dan cocked his head. "I've felt the earth move. I've seen tornadoes. I've stood under the sky raining frogs. The animals sometimes sense such things before the humans do."

Rhett looked up at the clear sky. "Don't seem like tornado weather. And I didn't see a single frog-colored cloud."

"The earth moves often, where I'm from," Cora said, looking up as well. "There is never any warning. In the city, we shrug and rebuild and move on. The animals don't appear to notice." She seemed, to Rhett, more quiet and demure than she'd been before, as if she were holding part of herself back. It made his heart ache, to see her dimmed, but it wasn't so much his business anymore, was it? Far as he understood relationships, she was done with him. There was some color in her cheeks, at least, so Rhett figured she was recovering from the fight.

"Anybody have any particular feelings about frogs?" he asked, just to take the spotlight away from someone who obviously felt uncomfortable in it just then.

Sam chuckled, but no one said anything. It felt as if they, much like the larger world, were all waiting for something, but damn if Rhett knew what it was.

"Then I reckon we go to sleep in shifts so there's always someone awake, should something happen. I'll take first shift."

"I'll take second," Sam said, and Rhett rewarded him with a smile.

Nothing happened on Rhett's watch, except that Sam gave him a sleepy grin and clutched his shoulder tight as they traded places. Nothing happened on Sam's watch, either.

In fact, nothing happened all night.

The next day, though?

That brought a hell of a surprise.

CHAPTER

4

Breakfast was a dim affair. They sat around the fire they didn't need, the orange flames doing very little to brighten a dull gray morning. Nobody said much. The clouds seemed heavy as lead, oppressive and suffocating. Rhett was anxious to be on the road and out from under the looming dread. Even the horses were spooky. Ragdoll nipped at Rhett's hand when he went to tighten her girth, and since he understood exactly why she felt twitchy, he didn't blame her much.

His belly grumbled something awful as they doggedly forged a path through heavy scrub. Rhett was out front on Ragdoll, the Shadow pulling him west like it had him on a string. Sam trotted by his side on his blue roan, the whites of the gelding's eyes showing as he blew against his bit and frothed.

"Sure do wish you'd choose a peaceable horse," Rhett muttered to his friend as Sam again had to tighten reins on the dancing critter.

"It would appear I rarely choose what's easy, Rhett," Sam said, giving him a look that said a lot of things that Rhett couldn't quite decipher but that gave him goose bumps nevertheless.

The prairie was headed uphill, with a range of mountains far off. Rhett knew that up close, the rock formations were probably orange and rounded and that they were a good sign in regards to getting close to their goal of the craggy range surrounding the Ranger outpost, but from here, they looked black and sharp as rotten teeth. Thunder roiled, and the pressure in the air made Rhett wince. A dull ache started up behind his eye. The ground trembled under Ragdoll's hooves, and she sidestepped and planted her legs more firmly, snorting as if to tell the world all was not well.

"Earthquake?" Sam asked.

Rhett looked back to where Dan rode, closer to Winifred's place by Cora's wagon.

"This is not an earthquake," Cora called, struggling to hold Samson's reins as the usually calm gelding danced backward. "It's something else."

The thunder was louder, and it wasn't stopping, and the ground was shaking so hard that the horses looked like they were standing on a hot cast-iron pan. A great funk rose up, a cloud of orange-brown dust that smelled like...

"Oh, shit," Rhett yelled. "Run!"

Because something was coming, and whatever it was, it was big.

Earl was already galloping back the way they'd come as fast as his little donkey trotters would carry him. The horses were more than glad to spin and gallop in his wake, but Cora was having trouble with Samson. He was big, and the wagon didn't allow him much room to maneuver, but he wanted to follow the other horses and kept getting tangled up.

"Goddammit," Rhett muttered, cantering over and skidding off Ragdoll to take Samson's bridle in hand and laboriously turn the terrified critter in the other direction.

"Rhett, look."

Dan's voice was calm, but the kind of calm that spoke volumes. Rhett did look, and what he saw chilled him to the bone. He slapped Samson's rump to urge the beast away and just stood there, frozen, staring at the mass of woolly brown careening down the far hill.

"Buffalo," he murmured. "Never thought I'd see 'em."

"You're going to see them very close up if you don't get moving," Dan barked, his voice barely carrying over the oncoming roar.

But Ragdoll had had enough, and she knew her limits. The mare squealed and galloped away, leaving Rhett to stand there alone. Pounding hoofbeats approached, and Rhett spun around to find Samuel Hennessy holding out his hand.

"I reckon you don't mind riding double on a prancey horse?"

Sam's grin said everything, and Rhett put his foot in Sam's stirrup and took the hand up, landing on the roan's rump. Sam kicked the horse, and Rhett wrapped his arms around his best friend's waist and dug his face into Sam's shoulder, holding on for dear life. Even after weeks on the trail, living wild, Sam still smelled better than anything Rhett had ever encountered, and he figured he'd maybe thank a buffalo one day for this spare moment, should he and Sam live long enough to see it.

Oh, goddammit.

Sam.

"Head for the wagon," Rhett hollered in Sam's ear.

"Why?"

"Because we can't outrun the buffalo, and you're human."

"So?"

"So they'll trample you to death, fool! Now git!"

It was easy enough for the leggy gelding to overtake big ol' Samson and the wagon, even with two rangy cowpokes on his back. Cora was yelling at Samson in her own language, shaking the traces, but Samson was a smart horse and wouldn't go any faster. He knew, even if Cora didn't, that going too fast on uneven ground with a top-heavy wagon would kill them both. Rhett looked over his shoulder and saw miles and miles of buffalo, dirty brown fleece and sparking black eyes. East, west, south: there was no way to avoid them, to outrun them, to skitter past them.

Rhett jumped down from Sam's horse and grabbed Cora's arm, but gentle enough. "Turn into a dragon and get into the air. Now."

"But what about you?" she asked, already untying the strings that held her shirt together.

"I got to protect Sam. Wait, when you're a dragon, can you—"

She shucked her pants and stood there in her altogether, pretty and defiant. "No. I'm sorry. I can't carry anyone when I fly. Too heavy. I've tried."

He nodded. "Go on, then. If I don't make it through, whoever's left will help you. The Rangers will help you. You'll get Meimei back."

Pain crossed over her face, followed by a sweetness that hurt Rhett's heart. "I'll see you again, Rhett Walker. The wheel isn't done turning."

She stepped away, bent her neck, and rippled into the magnificent, scaled beast. Shaking out her mane, she waggle-galloped and leaped into the sky, where she circled once and hovered, wide wings beating, watching the scene below keenly. Rhett looked around but couldn't find Dan or Winifred or Earl. It was just him and Sam now, and the buffalo were close enough that he could hear their collective snorting and smell their wet, hot breath. Sam stood by the wagon, holding his panicking horse's reins, waiting for Rhett's word.

"Let him loose and get in the wagon, Sam!"

Sam slid the roan's bridle over his ears and smacked the gelding's rump before dutifully climbing into the wagon. Rhett cut Samson out of his traces and urged the horse away, then ran around to where the second string horses and mules were ponied. They were all tangled up and yanking, so he slipped their halters off their ears one by one and sent them all running in Samson's wake. Even loyal old Blue the mule galloped off without a second thought. When they were well out of the way, he went to the little door in the back of the wagon, the one he'd entered himself a time or two for a night of pleasantries with Winifred. Opening it, he followed Sam into the muted light of the canvas-roofed caravan car.

When he'd taken it from Prospera's camp after freeing all her magical beasts, it had still smelled like the old witch, sharp and green with herbs and age and black dirt. Now it smelled like Winifred, like flowers drying in the sun and that little ball of rose soap the dwarves had given the girl what now seemed like a lifetime ago. Rhett reached around Sam to close the door and fix it with a piece of leather they'd rigged up for privacy, him and Winifred. Better not to see the millions of buffalo bearing down on them. Dead was dead, but a feller didn't need to watch it happen outright.

"Plenty homey in here," Sam said, and Rhett smiled at the way his friend had of focusing on something nice and light even as the world was falling down.

"I like a place I can stand up in without scraping my head, but I reckon it'll do. Compared to the alternative." Rhett tried to give Sam a comforting, confident smile, but he was et up with worry.

If those buffalo didn't have the sense to go around the wagon, Sam would get crushed to pulp, and maybe Rhett, too, although Rhett would probably still be alive to feel it. For some reason, Sam didn't seem at all troubled by the prospect. He sat down on the bed, then scooted over to make room for Rhett. Considering there was nothing back here but the bed and Prospera's old trunk, it was pretty much the only place to sit, so Rhett shyly joined him, being careful not to sit too close or lean in or do anything that would remind Sam of Rhett's peculiar feelings. Even after last night's strange conversation, Rhett would've rather been stung by a hundred scorpions than knowingly make Sam uncomfortable. But whatever he did now, Sam didn't move away. In fact, he moved just a little closer, his knee bumping into Rhett's.

"I reckon—" Sam started, but the buffalo arrived like all the thunder the gods had ever made.

The wagon juddered and tipped as massive, powerful bodies skimmed around it. Rhett panicked and threw his arms around Sam, tackling him to the bed, which was still covered by Rhett's own buffalo coat, soft and deep. It smelled of Cora, but all Rhett cared about was Sam.

"Uh, Rhett?" Sam's lips were near Rhett's ear, and his hot breath made Rhett shudder.

Rhett drew a shaky breath and spoke into the fuzzy fleece.

"Sam, it's not what it looks like...I'm not...Look. If they break up this wagon, I might be the only thing that'll keep you safe. Better they hurt me than you. So just forgive me and try not to think about it. Ignore me. Pretend I'm armor, if you have to."

For a long moment, the only sound was the buffalo herd outside, just a few inches away, separated by wood and canvas and sheer luck. The stutter of hooves, the rumble of breath, the occasional bellow, the shakes and tremors as the wood creaked against muscles and horn. Rhett saw it go a thousand ways, but one image in particular haunted him. The beasts bashed in the wagon and caught Rhett and Sam on their horns, on their hooves, carrying their bodies away on a wave of brown like gory trophies. A little sob ripped unbidden out of his throat when he thought about how far they'd come only to lose now, and not even to a clever, powerful monster or villain, but to a dumb herd of buffalo just doing what comes natural. All the other animals knew what was coming and had the good sense to get the hell out before the pilgrimage of hooves and horns came over the horizon. But not the dumb humans, who just sat there, innocently marching toward their own goddamn doom.

Maybe such thoughts were the reason it took Rhett several long moments to realize that Sam was clutching him back, fiercely, his arms snaked tight around Rhett's back and his hips pressed forward more urgently than how a boy about to die should've managed. Sam's breath was ragged in his ear, their hats tumbled off, the sound of thunder merging with their heartbeats, pressed chest to chest.

Rhett's head untucked from Sam's shoulder, and he ventured a look-see. Sam pulled back, too, and they stared at each other with wide, baby-doe eyes. The black of Sam's eyes was endless, the blue sparkling with...sweet hell, was it tenderness? And something else, something Rhett had only seen when they'd drunk the god's wine at Buckhead and began to pay their delicious toll?

"I could never ignore you, Rhett," Sam whispered.

"You okay, Sam?" Rhett asked, cautious and terrified of being hurt again.

Sam swallowed hard. "I...I reckon I am. The buffalo don't seem to want us dead."

Rhett nodded. "Loud as hell but not downright murderous."

"I never dreamed there were so many of 'em. You think it'll ever stop?"

Rhett felt about like he had before leaping off that cliff at the Cannibal Owl's lair and learning he could fly. He'd jumped then, and that had turned out pretty good, so he jumped now.

"I wouldn't mind if it didn't, Sam," he murmured, a bare whisper against the backdrop of the stampede.

Sam inhaled, and Rhett knew that whatever he said next was as sure as a bullet and just as likely to shatter something as fragile as what they had.

"It's just us in here, ain't it?" Sam whispered. "Like our own little world. Everything outside is thunder and noise, but in here, it's just you and me."

Rhett let himself relax a little, his head pillowed on Sam's shoulder. "Nobody can see, nobody can hear. Not like we can go anywhere. Makes me feel downright cozy."

As the buffalo didn't seem intent on bashing the wagon in just then, he rolled over onto his back, his elbows out and his hands behind his head. It was a position that said "I'm harmless and I'm not trying anything," but it was also a position that said, "But you go on ahead, if that's your inclination."

Sam sat up on his elbow and grinned. "It's like being in the middle of a thunderstorm, ain't it? So much energy in the air. So much…"

"Passion?" Rhett supplied, feeling like a dog rolled belly up. He was trembling now, and not just because of the wagon shaking around him. Energy, yes. Electricity. His heart felt like the buffalo herd, a cacophonous, endless tumult of desperation and fury and power, and he didn't even have the words to explain to Sam how it felt, how when he looked up at Sam in the low light, he wanted to believe in a god so he'd have somebody to thank.

"That's one word for it," Sam agreed.

He licked his lips, and Rhett could've died.

"It's funny," Sam began.

When he didn't elaborate, Rhett said, "What is?"

Sam swallowed again and thought about it for a moment, and then the wagon rocked hard to the tune of a buffalo's grunt, and Sam fell over, right on top of Rhett. He quickly pressed away, set himself up on his elbows, and Rhett was looking right up into his favorite face in the world, Sam's body half-splayed over his, Sam's knee pressing down between his, Sam's fine blue eyes blinking closed with golden lashes, Sam's face dipping down to his, and finally, finally, bless all the damn gods, Sam's warm, soft lips brushing Rhett's own with an electric jolt more powerful than a million buffalo. Rhett froze, accepting the kiss, praying for more and terrified to scare Sam off by liking it too much.

Sam backed off just a little, his beard scraping Rhett's chin, his eyes looking hurt.

"Well, ain't you going to kiss me back?" he whispered.

Rhett gulped in a breath, reached for Sam's face, and showed him exactly how much he wanted to do exactly that, and it was everything he'd ever dreamed of in his entire life, and it was over far too goddamn soon.

Sam pulled away, and Rhett drew in a ragged breath, seeing stars.

"What's wrong?" he asked.

Sitting back, Sam ran a hand through his hair, still mussed from Rhett's fingers. "I don't rightly. It got quiet. The wagon's not shaking."

When he listened, Rhett heard the same thing. A few clopping hooves here and there, but no more beasts shouldered the wagon, and the ground wasn't quaking as hard. He hopped up quick and headed for the door.

"Sam, we got people to feed. Let's find us a straggler and take it down."

Sam blushed red as he adjusted himself and put on his hat. "Your mind moves fast, other Hennessy."

Rhett gave him a serious look, a smoldery look. "Well, I can change my mind back the other way just about anytime you like," he said. "But I reckon we'd both prefer it on a full belly."

"There's hungry and then there's hungry, other Hennessy."

Sam laughed, a light and friendly sound that assured Rhett that things wouldn't be awkward between them, not now. Rhett untied the door and scouted about before hopping down to the churned-up dirt. Little tumbleweeds of brown fuzz rolled everywhere, along with fresh, wet cow patties and overturned stones and hoofprints. The grass was all tore up, and the wagon's wood was dented and cracked, brown gouges in the purple paint.

"There!" Sam shouted, and Rhett followed him toward a limping buffalo cow holding up a damaged leg. It wasn't any work at all to shoot the poor thing in the head—more of a kindness, really.

"I reckon they get running like that, all bunched together, and they're bound to hurt one another," Rhett said.

"She's not hurting anymore, at least, you soft-hearted fool. You go find our people." Sam looked up, and his eyes were back to being Ranger-sharp, not at all dreamy, but still tender in their way. "My palomino might come if you whistle like this." He demonstrated, and Rhett could only look at his kiss-swollen lips. But he nodded.

"I'll do my best for you, Sam."

"I always know you will, Rhett."

They traded goofy smiles, and Rhett lit out in the direction the horses had run before the stampede hit. After walking long enough to get up a sweat, he cussed to himself, shucked his clothes on a boulder, and took to the sky, where he could see farther and with much less effort. He found the horses first,

Ragdoll and Samson and Puddin' and Kachina and the two Blues all huddled together with the second-stringers that hadn't earned names yet. Sam's palomino wasn't around, so Rhett rubbed noses and checked hooves and let out a few whistles before taking back to the sky, knowing the worried herd would stay right there until someone came to fetch them.

In the air, he followed his nose to a disappointing scene: Sam's palomino, trampled and torn open by unapologetic hooves. Even as a carrion bird, Rhett kept enough of his soft heart about him that he didn't eat a single bite. Back in the air, he flew in ever wider circles until he found a creature that made him feel ten kinds of strange.

Dragon, his mind flashed.

Friend.

Kind of.

He landed and turned back into a human, and the dragon did the same, and they stood there, all alone in the wide, trampled prairie, buck nekkid and shy.

"You seen the coyotes?" Rhett asked. "And Earl?"

Cora nodded. "Yes. All are safe and headed back to where the wagon stood. I was looking for you."

"You found me. Only critter we lost was Sam's leggy horse, as far as I know. We'll have some leathers to fix, but we did bag a hurt buffalo, so we'll eat tonight, at least."

Cora dipped her head, careful not to look down. It was strange, Rhett figured, to know and like someone's bare body just fine yet find moments in life where it was the last damn thing you wanted to look at.

"I will fly back, then," she said.

She turned away, and Rhett said, "You're a right beautiful dragon, you know. Pretty girl, too. But I always wanted to see a dragon, and I reckon I ain't disappointed."

Cora turned around and gave him a shy smile, tucking her hair behind her ear. "Thank you, Red-Eye Ned. There is a season for everything, is there not? And how quickly they can change. Buds bloom; leaves fall. A natural progression, I think."

And then she rippled over with scales and launched into the air. Rhett watched her, considering. He'd liked her sensible nature from the start, and as far as he was concerned, she'd just cut him completely loose in the most polite way possible. If he couldn't still taste Sam on his lips, maybe that would've bothered him. But it didn't.

He felt one of his favorite things, just then: sweet freedom.

He turned into a bird and hurried back to his clothes, then the waiting horses.

When Rhett rode up to the camp on Ragdoll's back and fully dressed, followed by a small but happy herd, he was cheered to smell fresh buffalo meat already cooking over a nice-sized fire. Dan and Winifred carved on the carcass, and Cora walked around gathering buffalo fluff. Rhett thought it was a right silly thing to do until he realized that buffalo fluff was a damn sight softer and more absorbent than the rags he used for his hated monthlies, so he snatched up a few rolling balls of fuzz, too, stuffing them into his saddlebags when nobody was looking.

Seeing as how everyone else was working contentedly, except Earl, who was blessedly silent due to being asleep, Rhett set to fixing Samson's sliced traces and tying up the horses to the wagon. The grass had been entirely ruined, kicked up and trampled by the buffaloes' huge hooves, so they'd have to wait until they'd got to live ground again to graze and drink. Too much grain would be dangerous. That meant they couldn't camp here long, which Rhett figured everybody knew but he had to mention anyway.

"How long do y'all expect to stay here?" he asked as he moseyed up to the fire. "No water, all the grass gone, and the horses near scared to death. We can make a few miles by sundown, head southwesterly and maybe get beyond the herd's damage."

"That's right, Rhett," Sam said, giving him a sunny smile. "Give the meat an hour or so to cook up and let us get something in our bellies, and we can store the rest and get moving."

"That suit you-all, Dan?" Rhett asked.

Dan glared at him from the buffalo carcass, just a stone's throw from the campfire. Dan knew his way around a butchering and was stripped down to his breechclout, his skin coated in slick, dark blood as he sliced and dug and sorted.

"You try my patience, Shadow," he said, each word dropping slow and deadly as he lifted a dark purple mass of muck out of the critter's gut. Dan was usually a sunny enough feller, which made it all the worse when he was angry. He sliced off a bit of whatever he was cutting on and handed it to Winifred, who ate it. Rhett shuddered at the thought of slimy, raw guts.

"It's the liver," Winifred said, rolling her eyes. "Good for the baby."

Rhett looked from her to her brother. "Is that why you're mad at me, Dan? Because I yet again failed to protect your sister?"

"My sister and her child, yes."

Guilt settled like a fist in Rhett's gut, but he wasn't about to give Dan that satisfaction.

"Well, hellfire, Coyote Dan. It ain't mine, if that's what you're thinking."

Dan dropped the liver and stood, seeming to rise from the

ground like some spectre, some bloody god enlivened by rage. He didn't bother to rub the gore from his skin, just walked to where Rhett stood, leaving rusty red footprints in the shape of his long, bare feet. He stopped, his nose inches from Rhett's, the scent of him heavy with death.

"I thought you were a hero, Rhett Walker."

"*I am* a hero."

"But you bring only death. No life."

Rhett swallowed but wouldn't let himself back down. "Maybe there's different kinds of heroes. Maybe death's all I got to offer."

Dan shook his head like he was disappointed. "Maybe each man chooses what sort of hero he'll be, and you choose the actions that release you from responsibility. Killing puts problems to rest. I hoped that as you grew, as you learned, you would begin to choose life."

Rage simmered up Rhett's spine, and his teeth ground together. "I did choose life, Dan. I chose to protect the only one of us that the buffalo could kill. Your sister and her god's get are well-nigh indestructible, far as I know. But if we lose Sam—"

"If *you* lose Sam, you mean."

Rhett's hands made tight fists at his sides. The entire prairie went silent. Even the horses watched them, curious, ears pricked. Every eye at the campfire was on them. Now would not be a good time to punch Dan in the teeth, much as Rhett wanted to do so. Because that would mean Dan was right, wouldn't it? That Rhett always chose violence. And that it was a bad thing to do.

"Are you saying you don't care if Sam lives or dies, Dan?"

Dan snorted, his chin going up an inch.

"I'm saying you choose him for selfish reasons. Yourself first, then him, then the womenfolk, maybe, if there's time. Me, you didn't even think about. And we all know it. Don't think I don't notice that you always save the white man and let the brown folk fend for themselves. That's not what the Shadow was fabled to be. You were our hero. You were supposed to stand up to white men, not fawn all over them like a puppy."

"It ain't because he's white," Rhett said, each word careful and sharp. "It's because he's Sam."

"Someone with your power should protect the weakest. And Sam isn't weak."

Earl, still in donkey form, brayed his agreement.

"Fair enough, Dan. I didn't think of you when the herd of buffalo arrived because you're the cleverest, wiliest, hardest-to-kill asshole I ever met, myself excluded. And I didn't think of the critter with four goddamn hooves because he's as stubborn as a damn buffalo. I helped Cora. I slapped Kachina to get Winifred far off. And, yes, damn my eye, I went and protected the most helpless among us, because whatever's in your sister is just as immortal as she is and probably the size of a goddamn gnat. I'm not saying Sam's weak, but his body isn't made of...hell, whatever ours are. Magic and stubbornness, I reckon. I'm not sorry for my actions, and I don't need your approval. I'm sorry you grew up thinking the Shadow was a savior built just for you, but I'm doing the best I can. You know well enough how I feel about white folks in general, and you also know that Sam is goddamn different. So's the Captain. I follow my gut, no matter what. And considering not a one of us took a single injury, I suspect that whatever I'm doing, I'm doing right."

Dan stepped back, his body ramrod straight, and shook his head sadly. "I hope I'm not there the day you find out you're wrong, Rhett. And I hope my sister never takes harm on your watch."

Turning his back, he returned to butchering the buffalo. Winifred spoke to him in their language, and she sounded like maybe she was chewing him out, but a lot of their language sounded like that to Rhett. Feeling like every eye was still stuck to him, he exhaled and moseyed over to the fire, all nonchalant-like.

"Any of this buffalo ready to eat?" he asked.

Sam selected a skewer and handed it to him, leaning close. "Don't let Dan hurt your feelings, Rhett. You know how he gets. Real protective of his sister. Can't much blame a feller for that."

"I guess you can't," Rhett agreed, nibbling the hot meat.

"This is a feeling I, too, understand," Cora said gently.

Rhett's eye flashed to her. She didn't look angry or annoyed. More like a rabbit always waiting to feel a hawk's shadow. Alert and twitchy and softer than she ought to be. The bones shone through her face, purple bags under her eyes like she hadn't eaten or slept in weeks. Whether it was changing to the dragon or being worried about her sister and grieving her grandfather, Rhett wouldn't have ventured to guess.

"You ain't mad?" he asked her, genuinely curious.

"Oh, I am very mad." She nibbled her own meat and chewed thoughtfully before continuing. "I am mad that Trevisan took my sister. I am mad that he held me hostage so long. I am mad that my grandfather is gone. I am mad that my sister is trapped, that she's being used. And I am mad that we can't go save her right now. But I see the greater plan around you, Red-Eye. You are like a bit of iron, drawn always north. Your north changes, and it does not always make sense. But when the scorpions came, I learned that to go against you would end in my death, or at least my grand discomfort. So I go with you, even though it stretches me thin and breaks my heart and fills my every moment with terror and dread."

"That's right poetical," Rhett mumbled, feeling like she had just used a whole bunch of words he'd never even heard of before. "You understand...I don't like it. The way it all works. I like to just ride after something and kill it, dust my hands off and walk away."

Cora laughed her light laugh. "Oh, I know. We all know."

"But what you-all got to understand is that even if my way is death, like Dan says, that still serves you. Serves the world, I reckon. I didn't ask for it. The burden or the pulling."

Cora cocked her head at him. "In your own way, you're a prisoner, aren't you?"

Rhett stood and dropped his empty skewer in the fire. "Rightly so."

He looked to Sam then, whether for sympathy or a friendly grin, he didn't know. Sam stood and held his shoulder. "You got to do what you got to do, Rhett. Nobody can blame you for that."

Eyes burning, Rhett nodded tightly and clapped Sam on the shoulder, then walked off to a couple of boulders out beyond the horses where he pretended to relieve himself but really just hunkered down, head in hands, to cry.

Dan was mad. Winifred was hurt. Cora was angry. At least Sam understood.

It wasn't easy, having a destiny.

And the road before them never seemed to get any shorter.

CHAPTER

5

By the time they reached potable water and untrampled grass, the horses were in real danger of falling over. Rhett's canteens were more sand than water, and he was holding off on the tough buffalo meat, knowing it would sit in his belly like a stone. Ragdoll sensed the greenery up ahead before Rhett did and picked up the pace, her dull yellow ears pricked up in the shape of a heart and the whole herd of ponies bugling excitedly from where they were hitched to Cora's wagon. Sam's blue roan jigged along, and Rhett wondered when Sam would find another unreasonably leggy pony to take on, now that the palomino and black were both gone. Rhett felt more than a little lucky that he still had both Ragdoll and Puddin', and even old Blue the one-eyed mule, who was enthusiastically braying his excitement about drinking, and pawing at the creek like he always did, muddying up the water like a fool.

It was funny, how too long between creeks could kill them perhaps more easily than one of Trevisan's traps. Durango was a hard place, and soft things wouldn't last there for long. Rhett glanced back at Cora as Ragdoll tried to break into a canter. The girl was smiling like she knew a secret no one else did. He didn't love her, and he knew that now. If the circumstances had been different—if there had been no Sam Hennessy—maybe that would've changed. But he could appreciate her positive, sensible attitude, especially considering Dan and Winifred had ridden together, behind the wagon, silent and accusatory—at least around the eyes. Cora was worried, but she let it wear on herself instead of taking it out on others, which was a right gift.

A few moments later, the mounts were all lined up at the fast-running creek as if companionably sharing a trough. Rhett hopped off Ragdoll and headed for the wagon, where he carefully released Samson and the other ponies from their leathers to join the saddled horses. He held up a hand to help Cora down from the wagon, and she took it and gathered her canteens and went upstream to fill them like a smart person did on the trail.

Surrounded again, finally, by the shrinking brush and increasingly more orange ground of his blessed Durango, Rhett realized he'd felt off ever since the incident with the buffalo. He'd heard tell of such seemingly endless herds overrunning the prairies, coming down from Montana del Norte when it got cold and icy. But he'd never seen it before, and he hadn't understood just how many of the beasts there were, nor the damage that could be done by thousands upon thousands of trampling hooves.

"Dan, I know you're still mad at me, but do you know if the buffalo ruined that place we were in? Will the plants grow back? And where'd the buffalo go?"

Dan looked up from the fire he was lighting and gave Rhett a tired glance, almost like what somebody would give a troublesome child who just couldn't stay out from underfoot.

"It is nature, Rhett. The herds move, and the local animals hide, and when the buffalo have moved on, the animals return. The churned ground brings up grubs and roots and bugs. They move seeds and pollen, destroy old stumps. It's good for the earth, to be stirred up now and again. As for where the buffalo go, I suspect, much like you, they take their destruction in the direction of their destiny and don't exactly know why."

"But aren't there buffalo tribes, shifters like you?"

The fire caught, and Dan smiled briefly at it before turning back to Rhett. "There are, but they are not so many. They have never been so many. Every day, there are fewer. The world is changing, Rhett. Can you feel it?"

Rhett looked around, hands on his hips. He saw a world he knew and understood. Hard ground, jagged mountains, fast water, boulders that could hide a man from bullets or likewise hide the rattler that ended him.

"Looks about the same to me as it ever did," Rhett said, feeling like Dan was maybe setting him up for a preachin'. "I'm a damn sight better off than I was a year ago, I know that much."

"Did you learn nothing from the railroad? The white men are coming, and they don't need magic to destroy our world and our people. Their treaties mean nothing. They step over every line they draw in the sand and cut the world into portions with their fences. Soon there will be no place for the buffalo to roam. No place for the people, either."

"And what the Sam Hill do you want me to do about it, Dan? I'm trying to go kill about the whitest white feller I've ever seen, right now."

Dan looked up steadily from where he crouched by the fire, easy in his skin. "We were taught the Shadow would be our redemption. That you would save our people."

Rhett bristled at that.

"You saying I can't do it?"

"I'm saying no one can. We couldn't stop the buffalo. We

couldn't turn them or kill them or fight them. All we could do was live through them. And that's what the white men will do to Durango. Overrun it, stupidly and carelessly." He looked at Earl and then Sam in a pitying sort of way, and Sam shrugged in apology. "Current company excluded, Sam. But they are coming, and they will destroy my way of life and yours."

"What's your point?"

Dan stood up then and dropped his britches and shucked his shirt, which was no longer shocking or strange at all. "I have been angry for a long time, Rhett. But now I grow sad. We're bickering over nothing. You are not enough. We are not enough. The Shadow is not enough. We are ants fighting more ants. And we are losing." Still shaking his head, he turned into a coyote and ran away.

"Well, that's a chickenshit way to insult somebody," Rhett muttered.

"He wasn't insulting you as much as he was insulting the world," Winifred countered. "He's just frustrated. There is no safety for him, for us. Where can I go and know that my child and I will never face persecution? The land we grew up on is now someone else's ranch. We know you can't own land, that land owns itself, but someone else has decided differently."

"This is not a problem only in the Federal Republic," Cora said. "My homeland is overrun with petty dictators and wars that kill people for land. My grandfather and parents came here for a better chance. They gambled everything." She looked down and sighed. "Now you know why I am not a betting woman."

"Well, hellfire. If a fire-breathing dragon can't feel safe, I reckon we're all doomed," Rhett said.

That earned one of Cora's smiles. "There is always a bigger dragon," she said.

They drifted away from the fire after that. The silence grew uncomfortable, for things both said and unsaid. Cora and Winifred went to gather greens and tubers, anything to soften the taste of hard meat. Sam took his gun, muttering about prairie chicken and eggs not belonging to anybody, yet. Earl pulled a dingy bottle of Buckhead wine from somewhere in the wagon and collapsed in an angry heap by the fire. Rhett was getting ready to shed his clothes and fly away when Earl chucked the empty bottle at him. Luckily, his aim was bad, and it just tumbled over in the dust at Rhett's feet.

"You got a problem with me, too, donkey-boy?"

A snort of derision. "Only since you first opened your mouth. Don't suppose that'll be changing anytime soon."

"And what would you have me do? Campaign for the rights of donkeys?"

Earl's head shook, his shaggy red hair now grown out into ringlets. "I'm fine with your way of doing things, lad. Kill this, kill that. Seems a handy way to deal with what ails you. But the coyote's wrong. It's not white men that are the problem—it's rich men. You don't see me going about drawing lines in the sand and planting flags. I just want what everyone wants: a little plot of land to live for, and a family to tend there. I'm as far from having it as you. Best I reckon the world holds for me now is to find a wee job in a city so full of immigrants that it won't notice me in particular."

"Then why are you angry at me?"

Earl lay back in the dirt and flapped a hand. "I'm angry. You're just here. Easy to be angry at you, lad. You only kill things as deserve it, but you know the likes o' me only deserve pity. And I hate you for knowing that, too."

Before Rhett could untangle his tongue to respond, the feller was snoring the snores of the drunk, a sound Rhett knew well from his life before the Rangers and the monsters and the destiny. Once upon a time, he had been nothing but a scared little girl named Nettie Lonesome, living among people who drank themselves near to death nightly, who hated her and used her, and she'd ever been unsure that she'd find a place in the world to call her own.

That girl was gone, but Rhett was damned sure Winifred's child—be it a boy or a girl, closer to brown or to white—would never feel so helpless. He'd make sure of that, even if it was the only part of his destiny that didn't involve killing what needed to die. He owed her that much.

It was close to midnight when Rhett was done flying. He landed on clumsy talons and stumbled forward on human feet, glutted on a young buffalo he'd found half-trampled and that hadn't required him to make polite conversation around the campfire. The horses were accustomed to him now, showing up at strange hours, naked and smelling of death. Pulling his clothes from his saddlebag, he slipped his feet into his boots and slunk through the darkness to the creek, where he accepted the shock of chill water and scrubbed himself clean with sand. The air was cool but kind, and he spent a few shivering minutes pondering the future before he was dry enough to wind on his clean binder and step into his clothes.

His saddle was already by the fire, a bit closer to Sam than usual, which warmed his frozen heart. He stopped to look around, hands on his skinny hips. The women were absent; in the wagon, most like, and maybe even curled together like kittens in the narrow bed. And may they find much joy in it.

Hell, he had, in both their embraces. He had no yearning for that now, for losing himself in a woman's softness by dark of night and facing her bright, hungry eyes come morning. He knew their skin but not their minds and hearts—most especially not Winifred's. Too damn complicated by a mile. A few hours' pleasure encumbered by...hellfire. Emotions. Expectations. It was only natural that here, alone in the nothingness, bodies would seek any comfort they could find. Cora had told him she only liked women, and Winifred, Dan had said, liked whatever she wanted, whenever she wanted, especially when it got under somebody's skin.

What they did from here on out was none of Rhett's goddamn business. He knew what he wanted, and that was all that mattered.

There, by the fire, was what truly called him, body and mind. Samuel Hennessy. He'd yearned to be near that boy since he'd met him years ago at the Double TK Ranch, not that Sam remembered the dark, lanky neighbor girl named Nettie with her long pigtails, thank goodness. Nettie had watched Sam from the top rail of a white picket fence, never dreaming she'd ever actually speak to the sunny young cowhand. And then...hell, last year had happened. Nettie was Rhett, and Sam Hennessy was, somehow, Rhett's best friend.

And Sam had broken Rhett's heart back at the creek near Burlesville, sure, the first time he'd seen what Rhett kept so carefully hidden under his clothes. But Sam was slowly mending that heart again, wasn't he? The kiss in the wagon...that had been real. More real than anything. And now Rhett's saddle and blanket were laid out by Sam's sleeping form, Sam's kind face turned toward the bedroll like he was waiting for the feller who'd occupy it.

Across the fire, Dan lay on his back like a corpse, breathing steady with his face as set and stern as judgment itself. Even when he was in a mostly good mood, Dan looked angry while he was sleeping. Well, and to hell with Coyote Dan. He couldn't lay the sins of the world on Rhett's shoulders. Rhett was one man, and even the Shadow had limitations. His fingers crept down to the two leather bags now around his neck. The first one contained what was left of Prospera's magic dust, which had the ability to show the world Rhett's monster eye instead of keeping the Shadow's identity secret. He didn't need it anymore, but he somehow hadn't wanted to tuck it back in the chest with the witch's other trinkets. The second bag had been with Rhett since before he could remember, probably since he was somebody's papoose that got stolen away. It contained four vampire teeth, Rhett's first quarter, the bone chip that had powered Trevisan's monster scorpion, and a variety of other remembrances from his life, then and now. He gave that one a squeeze and tucked them both back under his collar before arranging his saddle and blanket and lying down with a sigh.

"Tried waiting up for you," Sam murmured, his voice honey-sweet and sleepy.

"Sorry, Sam. Sometimes I just got to fly, I guess."

"Don't fret. I know that about you. I'd fly, too, if I could. Did you see Cora while you was out there? She flew off, too."

Sam was awake now, his head pillowed on his arm. Was that worry Rhett saw in his eyes?

Rhett shook his head and gave Sam his fondest grin. "Nope. Only thing I found was half a buffalo. Cora doesn't want nothing to do with me, Sam. Not anymore."

"Why not?"

Turning on his side and pillowing his own head, he scooted a little closer to Sam, close enough to whisper. "I reckon I was just something new and shiny in a drab place. A new kind of pie to try. Cold comfort in a dark world and all. She…she was, too. For me, I'm saying. Nothing wrong with her, mind, just not the flavor for me. She lost any interest as soon as I chose my destiny over hers. Cora wants her sister more than she ever wanted me."

"Then she's a damn fool."

A shiver went up Rhett's spine at the earnest look in Sam's eyes, at how Sam's big, warm hand reached out and landed on Rhett's own where it lay on the cooling sand between them.

"Sam," Rhett's whisper got even lower, his head leaned in. "Sam, none of it meant anything. Neither of 'em. I…I always known what I wanted."

Sam's voice went just as low and gravelly. "I know that, Rhett. Fellers don't hold such things against one another. I reckon I tasted some pie in my time, too. Things change. Tastes change. It just takes some time to figure things out, I guess."

"Sam, I—"

"Kiss him already!" Earl yelled in annoyance, but this time, Rhett didn't curse him and blush. This time, Rhett followed the donkey boy's direction. He leaned over, slow and gentle, and kissed Sam Hennessy on the goddamn mouth.

And that was all, but that was everything.

They fell asleep side by side, staring into each other's eyes and smiling like fools.

The next morning was quiet and pleasant and normal, or as normal as things could be in such abnormal circumstances. There was enough water and food, at least, plus some grain mush the girls had put together with some honey. Rhett discovered it tasted like horse feed and went to saddle up, figuring that the more ground they could cover, the better life would get. Dawdling only made his posse grouchy, and as he'd become the de facto leader, that meant they were grouchy with him in particular, and Coyote Dan wasn't the only one.

As a gesture of goodwill, Rhett got Kachina brushed and saddled. Forcing himself not to frown, he picked out her hooves and walked her and Samson over to where Winifred and Cora talked by the wagon, their smiles warm and genuine. Until he got near, at least. Then they both closed up like angry turtles.

"I got your horses ready," Rhett said, trying to sound casual.

"Is this because I limp now? Do you think we're helpless?" Winifred shot back.

"Of course not. I seen you both in action. I just...well, I ain't by nature particularly thoughtful, as your brother has been kind enough to point out, so I thought I'd give it a try."

Winifred just glared, but Cora softened and smiled. "Thank you, Rhett," she said, taking Samson's bridle and backing him between the traces. "The sooner we're on the road, the better."

"This doesn't fix things," Winifred said finally, snatching the mare's reins from Rhett.

"Well, what would, then?"

Winifred mounted up, ignoring the hand Rhett held out to her, like he even knew how to help an angry woman into a saddle.

"Talk to your Captain and take me with you to find Cora's sister. That's to start."

Rhett's jaw flat-out dropped. "Take you, a breeding woman, on an adventure to kill an alchemist that's cut toes off goddamn dragons? Your brother would stab me himself if I tried that."

Dan walked up just then with his usual fantastic timing.

"Much as I'd like to stab you a few times, supporting my sister means letting her make her own decisions. The last time I tried to take care of her by leaving her behind in a proper town with a proper job, she escaped and hunted me down and tore me a new one. It's her body. It's her baby. It's her life. If she wants to join the hunt, it's her decision."

"Well, I reckon I won't stop her, then. Why's she so goddamn mad at me?"

Dan's smile was wry and vexful. "Women talk, Rhett. She knows what you've been up to."

"And that's my own goddamn decision!"

"I told you this would happen."

Winifred snorted and looked down her nose at them. "The two of you are so kind and gentlemanly, talking about me like I'm not here."

Dan shrugged. "Breeding women can be...sensitive."

"I'll sensitive your damn hide," Winifred hissed.

With a long sigh, Rhett shook his head. "I will never in my life figure out what it is you two want me to be." He turned to walk back to the horses, who he at least understood and who didn't talk back.

"Sensible, Rhett," Dan shouted. "We just want you to be sensible."

"And smart," Winifred added. "Loyal, too."

"Goddamn coyotes," Rhett muttered, tightening his cinch and swinging into the saddle. They wanted a hell of a lot more than that, but damned if he knew what it was.

"Don't let 'em get to you," Sam said. "He's right. Breeding women are always frachetty, and I reckon Dan feels like he's got to protect her."

"What do you think, Sam? Am I doing things wrong?"

Sam shook his shaggy blond hair. "Nobody's ever done it

before, so I reckon there's no wrong way. No leader can make all his followers happy. Look at the Rangers. Captain's a fair man, but Jiddy and the Scarsdales question everything he says and grumble afterward. A good leader needs folks to speak up and keep him walking the straight and narrow, or else he just becomes a tyrant."

As they trotted up ahead to where Earl waited, switching his tail impatiently, Rhett considered.

"That's pretty fancy talk, Sam," he admitted. "I hadn't thought of it that way."

"I had some schooling," Sam said, chest puffed up. "But I mostly learned it from this older feller on a ranch where I worked one summer. His name was Monty, and he had a lot of fine thoughts. Helped me grow up, Monty did. Wonder what ever happened to that old coot?"

Rhett's breath stopped in his chest, but he tried to hide the terror on his face. He knew what had happened to Monty. He'd held Monty as the kind old feller had died, ripped up by chupacabras and a stray bullet—from Rhett's gun. But Sam didn't know about that part of his life, didn't know Rhett used to be Nettie Lonesome, couldn't ever know it was Rhett's fault that Monty was dead. By the time Nettie had taken her place at the Double TK Ranch under the name Nat, Sam had already been a Ranger. Monty had helped her along just as he'd helped Sam along. And Monty's death was the thing that had sent Nettie and Ragdoll on the run—to the Rangers, and to becoming Rhett and the Shadow.

"He sounds like a right fine feller," Rhett said, his voice husky.

"He was. I learned a lot that summer. Nobody knew more about gentling colts." He looked at Rhett, eyes sparkling. "'Cept you, I reckon."

They rode on in silence, and soon the clop of hooves and the creak of the wagon followed. Rhett was their compass, always in front, always following the Shadow's tug. Their path hadn't wavered, but there was an...urgency to the pull. Whatever needed to be done, Rhett reckoned, was now on a timetable. Although every step toward his goal lessened the tightness in his gut, every step also carried increased dread. What had happened to the Rangers that had such a powerful call? What fight could be more important and more terrible than the fight against Trevisan?

Rhett tried to swallow down the ball of worry, replace it with optimism, or something like it.

"Good weather, plenty of water," he shouted. "Let's get some miles while the getting's good!" Turning to Sam with a grin, he took off his hat, whooped, and slapped Ragdoll's rump. She felt it, too, that electric thrill in the air, and the appaloosa mare eagerly sprung into her gallop, low and flat to the prairie, ears tight to her skull. Sam caught up a few moments later on his blue roan, whooping and hollering, his grin a mad and vibrant thing. Dan and Winifred joined them, likewise urging their mounts in the race, their troubles momentarily forgotten. This joy and peace—it was what kept Rhett going even when things seemed especially hopeless. No darkness could take it from him, the feeling of flying, of freedom, of blue sky and a swift horse. It didn't matter what he was running from or toward, there were moments of mercy that reminded him that being alive was a gift, and that folks experiencing joy didn't stop to bellyache about it.

A wobble up ahead made Rhett rein Ragdoll down to a trot and throw out a hand in warning, and his friends fell back behind him. They knew, by now, that look. The one that said there might be trouble up ahead. Following his belly, he saw a black smear on the prairie, far off. From here, it might've been anything: Rangers, chupacabras, a winged buffalo, maybe even Bill the Sasquatch. Rhett didn't sense malevolence—more just curiosity.

"Let me trot up first," he said, shooing them back. Then his eye met Dan's. "Keep 'em safe."

"But Rhett," Sam started.

Rhett gave him a grin. "Don't worry. There's enough room out here for more sand. Just stay back so I won't worry for you."

Sam gave him a nod, and Rhett trotted on out toward the monstery black blot.

As he drew closer, he felt something familiar about whatever waited up ahead. Two figures stood from where they'd been hunched over something on the ground. Rhett squinted, hunting for the sun's gleam on a six-shooter or the flicker of an arrow being nocked, but the two figures just stood there, leaning in like they were whispering. Like they were worried, too.

A little closer, and he recognized them and breathed out a sigh of relief. Taking his hand off his gun, he cantered the rest of the way.

"Beans and Notch! Well, this is a fine howdy-do."

"Red-Eye Ned," Beans said, using Rhett's alias and nickname from the train camp and giving a respectful nod that Notch copied. "What're you doing out here?"

"Getting my people to safety back west," Rhett said, not sure how far he could trust these two fellers who had been part of his work detail at Trevisan's hellhole. Spending time with a large group in a small train car meant that Rhett knew the scent of their unwashed bodies, knew if they were costive, knew what they murmured in their sleep, yet he had no idea to whom their allegiance lay when they were out from under Trevisan's thumb and Digby Freeman's management of their crew. "Where are you-all headed?"

Beans waved an arm over a young buffalo torn jaggedly open. "We were headed west, looking for our people. We lost our mule among the buffalo, but at least we got enough food now. Pretty tough to butcher without proper knives, but Notch's claws came in handy."

Rhett saw now that the buffalo's belly had been scored open by four sharp slices. He looked at Notch with a new respect and interest. The man had never struck him as a predator, twitchy and proud and skulky as he was, but he had enough power to slice open a carcass and a strong enough sort of mind to focus it in animal form—and not to eat Beans. He wanted to ask what Notch was but knew by now that such things were beyond personal and couldn't just be asked outright like he was inquiring about the weather.

"You want some buffalo, Ned?" Notch asked.

The rest of Rhett's posse rode up just then, reining their horses in at a respectful distance. Quick as a blink, Beans had a heavy stone in hand, seemingly out of nowhere, and Notch had a railroad spike held like a knife.

"Easy, fellers," Rhett said, hands in the air. "These are my friends. They ain't gonna hurt you."

"But he's a Ranger," Notch said, pointing to the shiny upside-down star on Sam's shirt. "Oh, shit my britches, so's he." His shaking finger swung to Dan.

Rhett took a deep breath. "Well, as it so happens, so am I." He moved his vest aside to show his own star, the one the Captain had given him special when naming him Scout. "But we ain't here on official business. And if you're accustomed to the ways of the Lamartine Outpost, you'll find Captain Walker and the men of the Las Moras Outpost farther west to be more than fair. We want no trouble, and we mean you no harm." Neither feller had put down his impromptu weapon, though, so Rhett added, "And if you mean us trouble, for whatever god-forsaken reason, know that we've got enough firepower to turn you into dust." He sunk his thumbs into his gun belt to high-light this fact, in case his old carmates had any doubts.

Notch and Beans looked at each other, and the air seemed to squeak out of them both.

"Well, shit, Ned," Beans said. "We don't want trouble. We just want to get home alive."

"That's all we want, too." Rhett looked in turn at Sam, Dan, and Winifred, then made a decision they very well might hate. "If you need safe passage, you can ride with us, at least to Las Moras. We got a wagon and a few spare horses. Even an ornery, bony old mule, if you're missing yours too much. Long as you'll mind your manners, pull your share, and..." Here he looked at Beans in particular. "Sleep downwind."

It was telling, how Beans and Notch both looked to Sam as if hunting for his agreement. He gaped at them, somewhat bewildered. "He's the boss," Sam said, pointing at Rhett. "Don't look to me."

Rhett nearly swallowed his tongue, hearing a white man say that.

"We got to talk a minute," Beans said, and he and Notch hurried a bit away, around a skinny little tree that didn't do a damn thing to hide them as they whispered and gesticulated. From back here, they looked even scrawnier and more run-down that Rhett recalled. How quickly he'd bounced back from his own hell on wheels, once he was surrounded by his friends.

"Taking in more strays," Winifred mused. "Rhett, you're getting soft."

Rhett blushed and fiddled with his saddle strings. "Well, Dan wanted me to do more than kill, and I reckon taking in

Trevisan's lost folks is the right thing to do." Rhett shifted in the saddle, uneasy. "Y'all don't mind, do you? They're peaceable enough fellers, and they deserve a chance."

Dan nudged his horse closer. "It's good of you to offer them passage, and I won't argue. But it would be best if they found a stop before Las Moras. The Captain took to you, and he tolerates me, but he's not as kind as we'd both hope to Injuns without our particular skills. He's not as bad as Haskell, but he's still a white man with a job to do. The Durango Rangers as a whole are more prone to shoot Injun shifters than invite them in for tea, you know. That's their job. We're lucky our Captain uses his conscience more than his Henry, but he won't owe any respect to brown fellers he can't use."

That made Rhett grit his teeth; he hated hearing anything bad said against the Captain, even if he knew in his heart it was probably true. Tolerance only went so deep, in most men.

"Any other thoughts?" Rhett asked, his eye on Notch and Beans.

"If they try to touch me, I'll knife them," Winifred said coldly. Rhett raised a surprised eyebrow at her, and she sniffed and added, "Men without tribes forget their manners sometimes, especially after they've been prisoners."

"Well, obviously that'd be your right," Rhett allowed. "It's only fair. Hell, I'd be second in line with a knife to finish 'em off if they dared. Sam?"

"We're starting to run low on ponies, I guess, but they could maybe double up. Or ride in the wagon, if Cora don't mind."

"Then let me speak for Earl, since he hasn't bothered to ride out." Rhett played at Earl's thick Irish brogue. "*Oh, and so you'll be taking on more mouths to feed, lad, and that's two more jobs gone in whatever city we find. Perhaps you could start a collection of injured puppies and hungry vipers.* That sound about like him?"

Sam chuckled, and even Dan smiled. About that time, Beans and Notch returned, looking as hangdog as Rhett remembered them, like they'd forgotten how to hold up their heads and like their arms had forgotten what it was like not being weighed down by a dull pickax.

"We'd be glad to travel with you awhile, but we'll earn our keep," Beans said, chin up and scrawny bird-chest out. "Like you said."

Rhett held his hand out and slipped his boot from his stirrup. "Well, come on, then. We got miles to ride yet, a fire to build, and supper to cook, and none of it will wait." Beans took his hand and landed in the saddle behind him. The man was so slight, Ragdoll didn't even dance or snort. Rhett was glad to see Dan putting a hand down to Notch, who was agile enough to hop up on the chestnut gelding, even though Dan preferred to ride without a saddle. Turning to find the wagon and Earl not too far off, Rhett kicked his mare on and followed the wobble in his stomach until they were back on track, having gone a little off course to pick up the fellers.

"Good to see you, Ned," Beans said.

"Call me Rhett."

"Rhett, then. And why ain't your eye red anymore?"

Rhett sighed. It was a long story, but he didn't like to have lies on his tally count, so he told it, and loud enough for Notch to hear, too. His friends listened quietly as they rode across the wide prairie in a loose bunch, and he realized that in their haste to return to the train camp and then get on the road to Las Moras, he'd neglected to tell them the full story of his time in Trevisan's camp, living and working and suffering alongside these men as they carved land and laid tracks for a monster. They didn't ask any questions, thank goodness, and Notch and Beans didn't seem to mind too much that he'd lied to them about his name and station, considering those lies had been in service to their freedom.

"So you don't know if you're even Comanche?" Beans asked.

Rhett shook his head. "Not for certain, but a feller can hope. This is my original pouch, the one I've had as long as I can remember." He pulled the pouch out from under his shirt and held it over his back to Beans, who considered it briefly before handing it back.

"Reckon it's not your fault if you don't know," he said. Then, to Dan, he murmured a string of syllables, but Dan just shook his head.

"Different tribe," Dan said. Then he said something in his language.

Both Beans and Notch shook their heads this time.

"At least we all got English," Notch noted. "Who's the lady?"

Rhett realized that he'd forgotten introductions and felt like a right ass. "Well, that's Winifred, and you're riding with her brother, Dan. This up here is Sam Hennessy, and my full name is Rhett Walker. You'll see Earl and Cora soon. Me and these two fellers are Durango Rangers of the Las Moras Outpost, and we're headed back there to report to our Captain."

"I never heard of Rangers taking on folks with Injun blood," Beans said.

"The world is changing," Dan said again and more forcefully.

"Reckon it's up to us to make sure it's always for the better," Rhett added.

They rode on toward the setting sun, quiet and maybe hopeful.

CHAPTER 6

They rode as far and as long as they could, stopping near the usual sort of scraggly little creek and setting up camp at dusk. Notch and Beans were not bold men, and watching them skulk around the campfire like beaten dogs, Rhett doubted they had ever been so. Their clothes were the color of soot, and they clearly hadn't stopped to wash since Rhett had watched them depart the camp, perched double on the swayback of an old mule.

As the wagon rode up and they saw Cora, both fellers took on a look of terror and held their hats against their chests like shields. Rhett wasn't sure if that was because they knew she could saw parts of them off at will and magically seal the stumps over or because they'd heard all the camp's stories about the eventual revenge of dragons held hostage. Still, it was a relief that they wouldn't be chasing after the women. Beans even asked Winifred, softly, if he could fetch her anything and seemed relatively in awe of the girl, despite her grouchiness.

"Got any dice?" Notch asked, settling down by the fire Earl was building out of twigs, and the Irishman jabbed him in the side with a stout stick.

"No dice. Work or get out," he grunted. "Not that anyone asked me if we needed more mouths to feed."

"Well, with all the hunting you do, we naturally have more than enough meat already," Rhett drawled.

In response, Earl growled, and Rhett moved over to Sam and Dan. "You fellers want to go scare up some grub?" he asked.

Dan looked at him like he was a damn fool. "All three of us go off and leave my breeding sister alone with strangers? They're your friends, Rhett. You stay behind with the women. Sam and I will go." He jerked his chin at Sam and began walking away, and Sam gave Rhett a sheepish shrug, took up his rifle, and followed. Without a word, Winifred unwound her sling and hurried to catch up with them.

"Don't take it personal," Rhett said, frowning at Notch and Beans as they squatted uneasily by the growing pile of kindling and pretended they hadn't heard the discussion. "Dan's a prickly feller when his sister's involved, and I've pushed him past reason recently. You-all got any useful skills? Besides hunting?"

"I can tan skin and dry meat," Beans said.

"I can shine shoes, tie a tie, and fold gloves," Notch added.

"Well, one set of skills is a bit more useful than the other around here. Cora, ain't we got that buffalo's hide somewhere?"

Cora looked up from where she sorted leaves and sliced roots she'd brought up dripping wet from the creek after foraging all day. Frowning, she pushed her hair out of her eyes. "Rolled up in the back of the wagon." She didn't bother to get up and fetch it, though, so Rhett brought it out, along with the tools Winifred kept around for whatever magic she did to turn bloody skin into buttery soft leather. Beans went to work, and Notch edged away, looking disgusted.

"Notch, you know anything about horses?"

"I grew up in a town, Rhett. They scare me, if I'm honest.

One stomped my brother's foot once, and his toenails popped off like corn on the cob."

"Then he was dumb as a possum. C'mon. I'll introduce you."

As Rhett soon learned, Notch was dumb as a possum, too. Being handsome must've been enough to get him through life, as he couldn't make heads nor tails of the horses, literally. Rhett eventually set him to refilling the canteens hanging off the saddles as the ponies drank from the stream and Rhett went to hobbling them.

It was getting toward that part of the day when it was almost barely night and everything felt dreamy. Rhett still wasn't fully reaccustomed to life in the saddle, and his bowels hadn't straightened out since the train, and all he wanted to do was eat something that wasn't squirming or rock hard and curl up as close to Sam as felt safe with two new bodies around the campfire. The hunting party had good luck, what with all the local critters returning to their stomping grounds after the buffalo had passed, and Cora managed to cook up a stew of greasy bird and rabbit in the witch's old cauldron. Rhett's belly was soon hard and round, his lips slicked with fat and his smile sleepy.

He placed his bedroll as close to Sam's as seemed polite and settled down. Notch and Beans, as it turned out, had grown too used to the confinement of the train and dragged a saddle blanket under the wagon to sleep without the stars overhead. But Rhett stretched out on his back and stared up at the glittering mass of dots so like the holes torn in his old shirt at Mam and Pap's. Things felt finer, tonight, for some reason. Dan had returned with his old smile, some of his iciness toward Rhett melted. Winifred had disappeared with Cora into the wagon, but even she had thawed a little with a bellyful of good food.

Far as Rhett could figure, something must've happened, out there on the prairie, without him.

"Hey, Sam," he murmured, once it seemed like everyone else was settled down and Dan had finally fallen asleep.

"Yeah, Rhett?"

"What did you-all talk about while you were out hunting?"

Sam rolled over looking thoughtful. "Lots of things, but I reckon most of it's not mine to tell. I think we'll be okay, though."

Rhett noticed he didn't mention whether that *we* meant the entire posse or Sam and himself and whatever this was, their nightly saddle-talk session and that kiss in the wagon and the way their fingers brushed, softly, just once as Sam passed Rhett a tin cup of stew. They hadn't mentioned it, either one, but there was a tentative sweetness around Sam's face whenever their eyes locked.

"You have never understood me so well, have you Rhett?"

Rhett exhaled, annoyed that Dan was still awake and had overhead them and interrupted them during a time that Rhett considered special and private, even if it happened under the moon for all to see.

"I reckon not, Coyote Dan," he answered. "You'd think after this long on the trail together, I'd know when you were faking sleep to listen to me gossip." His eye flitted to where Beans and Notch snored and farted under the wagon. "You reckon this'll turn into a party now? We all gonna have a little pillow talk?"

Dan's soft, easy chuckle took Rhett back to the days before he'd bedded the man's sister and things between them got particularly strained. "No, they're asleep. I was waiting to speak to you, actually. This is important. Sam helped me understand something today. The thing is, Rhett, you are a lustful man, a hungry man. Like a boy first feeling his thews, you long to taste everything, and you seem to like everything you taste. You are driven and possessed, sometimes unwisely, by your body's urges. But me? I hunger for nothing. I don't even wish to taste."

Rhett sat up on his elbows to stare at Dan. "You saying what I think you're saying? Because that ain't natural."

Dan barked a laugh. "It's as natural as you are. As natural as Sam is. As natural as Winifred or Cora or Jiddy. Only townfolk would see two wild boy dogs humping in the forest and call it unnatural. Is it so hard to grasp, that I might be your opposite? That I might grow frustrated when you can't control yourself and focus?"

Rhett's sleepy brain considered. It was true enough that he'd never seen Dan's eyes trail after a woman, a man, a cowpoke, a whore. He'd taken it for a preacher-like fussiness, but Dan was laying it out for him, right here.

"So you think what I am is wrong?" Rhett asked.

"No, fool," Dan said, like he was chiding a child. "I think you're acting like a tomcat, and instead you should focus on your goal and spend your energy on purer tasks. I was angry, once, that you changed your mind so quickly from this to that. Now I see that... well, you never actually changed your mind at all."

Rhett swallowed and looked anywhere but at Sam. "No, I reckon I didn't."

Because he'd felt the same damn way about Sam since that summer at the Double TK, and he'd even felt the same way since that day in the river when Sam had learned the truth of him, and Rhett had learned the truth of Sam.

All those...things he'd tasted, as Dan had said? Well, he wasn't settling into a meal, wasn't even looking for a full belly, as far as that went. He was just trying things thus far unknown. Just taking comfort where comfort came in a cold, hard world. But when it came to his heart, he knew what he craved, and it was more than a willing partner in the dark.

"So we're all good, then, Coyote Dan?"

For a moment, the only noise was the crackle of the fire. And then he heard Dan settle back down and sigh.

"We're good, Rhett Walker. Just stop it with the goddamn Coyote. My name is Dan."

"Goodnight, Dan."

"Goodnight, you ridiculous son of a bitch."

Rhett settled on his side and stared into Sam's eyes, seeing something there like a promise, like permission.

"Good night, Sam."

Quick as a blink, he reached out his knuckles and stroked ever so gently along Sam's bearded jaw. Sam's eyes closed briefly like a cat in the sun.

"Good night, Rhett."

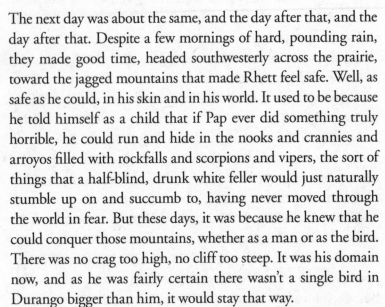

The next day was about the same, and the day after that, and the day after that. Despite a few mornings of hard, pounding rain, they made good time, headed southwesterly across the prairie, toward the jagged mountains that made Rhett feel safe. Well, as safe as he could, in his skin and in his world. It used to be because he told himself as a child that if Pap ever did something truly horrible, he could run and hide in the nooks and crannies and arroyos filled with rockfalls and scorpions and vipers, the sort of things that a half-blind, drunk white feller would just naturally stumble up on and succumb to, having never moved through the world in fear. But these days, it was because he knew that he could conquer those mountains, whether as a man or as the bird. There was no crag too high, no cliff too steep. It was his domain now, and as he was fairly certain there wasn't a single bird in Durango bigger than him, it would stay that way.

The closer they were to the mountains, the closer they were

to Las Moras and the Captain and getting rid of Earl and Notch and Beans and getting the hell back to killing Trevisan. And the closer he was to getting rid of the ball of dread that suggested something horrible might have happened back at the Ranger outpost. Just because Rhett wasn't with Cora didn't lessen his resolve to wrestle Meimei away from the monster and throttle whatever was left of the old alchemist. At least, for once, the Shadow's destiny was mostly aligned with what Rhett would've chosen on his own—although Rhett would've gone after Trevisan first, given the choice.

A few days on, his courses returned, spotty and brown but annoying enough. He hadn't missed the painful reminder of his body's stubborn femininity while he'd been starving near to death in the train camp; hell, it was one of the only good things about the experience. When he veered Ragdoll away from the others and toward some rocks, yanking out his rags and cussing like hell, Cora called him over and gave him some god-damn piece of stick to chew, swearing it would ease the pain, which it probably did, a little.

They were past lunch and headed into the longest, hottest, dullest part of the afternoon. It was October, and it was cooler than it had been, but when the sky was empty of clouds and the sun wanted to burn down some punishment, Rhett felt it in every bone of his body. Hot and dry, his belly crunching in pain, he was called back to the days he'd wandered in the desert, dying of guilt and a mesquite thorn both, back before he'd met and been saved by the then-mysterious nekkid feller he now called Dan.

What had happened then—Dan had called it a vision quest. Said it made Rhett a man. Said it named him the Shadow. Because that was what he'd seen, thrown harsh and dark against the orange canyon walls. Rhett could almost see it now, wavering on the hot, baked earth: a shadow too big to be any bird he'd ever seen, soaring overhead, wings wide enough to blot out the harsh sun.

A brief moment of coolness passed, and he squinted. And then he knew.

He *was* seeing it. A shadow.

When he looked up, he was pretty sure he was having one of those famous oasis dreams rumor had it madmen got in the desert, when they'd had too much sun and not enough water or sense. Sure enough, it was a bird, and like no bird he'd ever seen. Was it another vision? Was that what he looked like when he flew overhead as the lammergeier, the lambhawk? Even from this far away, he could see that it was clearly like a vulture, with a pinkish-orange belly and throat and broader wingspan than the local carrion birds and harpies both. It soared over him and his posse in a leisurely, intelligent fashion, then circled a little lower.

That's when Rhett realized he wasn't hallucinating. Dreams don't get suspicious and come in for a closer look.

Quick as a lick, Rhett was off Ragdoll and stuffing his clothes in his saddlebags, rags and all, not even caring that the others could see his body.

"What're you doing, Rhett?" Sam asked.

Rhett pointed up. "That about what I look like when I'm a bird?"

Sam followed his finger. "Aw, that's just a vul—Wait. Yeah. Yeah, that's exactly what you look like."

By then, Rhett had shucked off his boots and was taking a running leap.

"Be careful!" Sam shouted in his wake.

Not that Rhett had any plans to do so.

In midair, the gawky girl's body he hated so much turned inside out, felt like, and became the bird. He'd finally got it down so he didn't have to land and lollop around before taking flight, just started pumping his wide wings toward the hard blue sky. The feathers around his face lifted, a strange mixture of excitement and something that tasted halfway between rage and fear.

What was this…this…*thing*? In his space, in his sky? He was the only one of his kind, and this interloper was unwelcome. His belly wobbled as his will solidified. He would take the bird down.

A human thought poked through. *What if it was a friend?*

Maybe, dare he say it?

Family?

The bird shook off that nonsense.

Interloper, the bird said.

Attack, the bird said.

A scream, and now he knew that it saw him, and that it felt the same way about him. The other bird streaked toward him in a dive, pulling up at the last minute, talons outstretched. Rhett spun around and slung up his own claws, and they locked into a raging ball of feathers that spiraled down toward the ground as they screeched. At the last minute, the other bird pulled away and pumped back upward, and Rhett found his air, mere feet above the ground, and laughed as he gave chase.

It was smaller than him, this bird, by just a little. Even if it had been the aggressor, it was no longer in power. Rhett would've fallen to the ground, taking the little bastard with him. Still would, if things shook out that way.

Although Rhett had driven off other vultures and attacked hawks in flight and eaten his fair share of ravens and crows, he'd never faced a feathered foe anywhere close to his size. Far as he was concerned, he still hadn't faced one with his drive. The smaller lammergeier was flapping hard now, not riding the thermals or anything so relaxing. It was flying for its life, giving short cries that sounded less like screams of rage and more like a lost child.

Cheek-acheek! the other bird cried.

I'll get you, cheeky critter, Rhett thought.

He was chasing it at top speed, away from his posse, but he could find them easily enough. He had to know the truth of this bird, of the human body he knew it hid. He could've attacked it at this point; he was bigger and faster. But even as the bird, Rhett wanted answers more than he wanted blood, so he slowed and let it fly, following it up over the jagged rocks and north a bit, felt like. When it finally angled down toward the ground, Rhett scanned the area for signs of a tribe but found only a strange little shelter of poles and skin with meat drying on racks outside and a buffalo robe spread out in the sun. A rough-looking coydog rose from sleeping and took up barking furiously, leaping toward the sky.

Cheek-acheek! the bird called again, frantic, and an older woman stepped out of the dwelling, knife in hand and shielding her eyes against the sun. The bird tumbled to the ground, lolloped behind the woman, and disappeared into the dwelling. The woman slashed threateningly at the air with her knife and shouted at Rhett in a language of sharp sounds, proud and confident.

Rhett circled low. Not low enough for her to throw the knife, but low enough to see her face, warm brown and fierce. Her hair was ink black with just a few sparks of silver, cut short and parted down the middle. Her dress was a simple leather tunic to her knees with soft leggings and moccasins. The man might've seen more, but that was all that the bird saw.

Not food, the bird thought.

His aggressor had fled, his scent gone. He was human again, hiding in the tent. The bird knew well enough that there was nothing here for a creature like him, no juicy bones full of marrow. He circled higher, as thoughtful as a bird could be, and flapped toward his posse on strong wings. A few times, he dared to think human thoughts, wobbled, and let the bird take over again. Some time later, he landed near Ragdoll, who was being ponied off Sam's horse, and stumbled to his dusty human feet.

"What happened?" Sam asked, reining in to give Rhett access to his kit. "You okay?"

Rhett was careful to keep the mare between him and Sam as he bound his chest, tied on his rags, and dressed. Now was not the time to be thinking about bodies, and he was shy, anyway, still worried about scaring Sam off, if Sam had too much cause to remember what sort of parts he actually had and hid.

"Followed him to his camp. Just him and an older lady and a coydog, looked like. He hid from me, though. I reckon he's younger, maybe, so he doesn't have as much control. After that first tangle, he hightailed."

"So who was he?" Dan had ridden up now, with Winifred not far behind.

Rhett shook his head and hopped on his horse. "I don't rightly, but I aim to find out. There's a pass up ahead. We're going north."

Dan cocked his head in that irritating way he had that meant maybe Rhett was wrong and was about to rush into something stupid and get everybody killed. "Is that what the Shadow tells you to do?"

"Fuck the Shadow, Dan. This is personal."

He gave Dan a significant look, turned his horse's head, and aimed for the pass. They could follow or not. That wasn't his business. Finding out about that other lammergeier—that was his business.

They followed, though.

They always did.

CHAPTER 7

It was only a couple of miles before they came close enough to the small camp that Rhett could feel his stomach wobble. Dan and Winifred felt it, too, judging by how they both perked up and subtly checked their weapons. Maybe Earl and Notch and Beans did—Rhett didn't ask and didn't much care. Sam rode by his side, and as the tent came into view, he had his hand on his pistol.

Rhett turned to face his posse. "I'm going in. Cora, Notch, Beans, you-all stay behind. Dan, if you'd consider having your bow ready, I'd be obliged. Winifred, I'd never dream of telling you what to do with yourself, but please stay safe enough that Dan won't holler at me. Sam—"

"I'm coming with you, fool," Sam said with affection.

Looking down, Rhett flushed with shame. "I was actually hoping you might hold back and cover me, should I need gunfire. The woman I saw looked pure Injun, shouted in a language I didn't understand. You might make her nervous."

"You trying to keep me safe again?"

"Let's say that, sure."

Sam nodded and made a show of settling into his saddle.

"So you're going in alone?" Winifred asked.

"It makes sense. Nobody else needs to get hurt on my fool errand."

She snorted. "Fool indeed. I'll go with you. A woman will make her feel safer."

Rhett gave her a real smile. "I'd appreciate that, if your brother don't mind."

"What I do is none of his goddamn business."

In response, Rhett just tipped his hat to her and Dan, who was tight-lipped and stringing his bow. Rhett and Winifred dismounted and walked toward the camp side by side. It was right peculiar, how small and fragile Rhett felt on his own two feet. Something about a horse gave a man size and weight and speed, as if they became one while he was in the saddle. In the air, he felt the freedom and recklessness of a creature without laws or gods to hold his soul hostage. But here, putting one foot in front of the other in the endless sand, he felt like a tiny, easily squashed creature moving slowly through eternity.

A click behind him told him Sam had his back, gun at the ready. There was no sound to tell him that Dan had an arrow ready, but he could feel the tension of the bow, anyway. Although Cora hadn't argued with him when he'd asked her to stay back—hell, told her; he had to work on that—he knew that she wouldn't hesitate to turn into a dragon and raze the tent to the ground, if she thought it would help. Even Earl would probably give someone a donkey kick, if it wasn't too much trouble. They were a right solid bunch, for all that they bickered constantly when times were good and allowed them time for bickering. He only remembered such things when life and death were on the line, another thing he needed to work on.

The tent sat lonely on the prairie, nothing but the fussing coydog betraying any life nearby. The ugly critter was the dusty brown of the ground, hair going every which-a-way and teeth bared like a goddamn Lobo. It stood rigid in front of the door flap, hackles raised and growling.

"Nice dog," Rhett murmured. "Anyone to home?"

The leather tent flap opened, and a feller emerged and stood to plant his moccasined feet firmly in front of the door. Seeing him, Rhett was speechless.

It was like looking in a mirror.

A slightly warped mirror that showed him exactly who he wanted to be, and maybe two years younger than he currently was. Around fifteen and lanky as a strip of hardwood, his skin the same color as Rhett's and his bared teeth white under eyes so brown they were nearly black. His hair, like Rhett's had once been, was in two long braids that wouldn't quite sit, greased with a white stripe painted down his part. He had a knife in each hand, and he looked like he knew how to use them.

"Well, howdy there, feller," Rhett said, hands up in the universal *how 'bout you don't stick me?* gesture.

The boy—man?—said something in the same guttural language the woman had spoken.

"You got any English?"

The boy just barked harder at that, pointing the knife repeatedly at Rhett's chest.

Winifred tried a few different words, and finally one struck home. She said it repeatedly, and the boy said it once, questioningly, before snorting.

"Rhett, they're Comanche. Do you remember…anything? Any words?" She said it gently, her eyes all full-up with feeling.

"Beans might," he muttered. Holding up a finger to the feller to indicate he shouldn't get stabby just yet, Rhett turned around, cupped his hands around his mouth, and hollered, "Beans, you speak Comanche?"

It was a long, painful moment as the three of them stood

there waiting for Beans to trundle across the prairie. The coy-dog didn't let up growling, although the boy did run a fond, proud hand over the flat of the dog's head and murmur something sweet to it. The woman didn't show, and every time Rhett acted like he wanted to look in the flap, the boy nearly prodded him with the tip of his knife. Winifred showed an unusual kind of patience, and Rhett for the first time wondered what her life had been like up until they'd met, how many places she'd felt like she didn't quite fit in but had to play nice anyway.

When Beans arrived, Rhett wished he'd made the feller bathe, as he looked like last year's long johns. As soon as he saw the boy, though, his entire demeanor changed. His chin went up, his spine went straight, his lips set in a firm line, and he gave a curt nod and muttered the longest string of sounds Rhett had ever heard him put together. The boy's face lit up, although he struggled to maintain his proud composure. They gabbled excitedly for a bit, and Rhett and Winifred stared at each other and the tent and the increasingly confused dog and tried to figure out what the hell was being said.

"His name is Revenge for the Stolen," Beans said. "He's traveling with his mother. He asks if you're the same creature who attacked him, and if so, he wishes to kill you now."

Rhett considered the younger feller. "Please tell him my name is Rhett Walker, I'm the creature he *tried* to attack that nearly whooped his ass, and I'd rather talk than fight, as I've never met anybody like me before and I think we might be kin." In punctuation, he pointed to his arm, then the boy's arm, and the boy gasped and threatened a slash at Rhett's arm with his knife. "And please let him know that there's a rifle and a bow pointed at him right now, and also that my other friend's a dragon, so he can settle the hell down."

Beans added that on in an apologetic type fashion, and the boy settled into an angry silence.

A woman's voice came from the tent, soft and tentative and ending in a question. The boy barked at her, and her voice rose firmly to answer.

"She asks why you think you might be family, and who your people are," Beans said.

"I was found out here somewhere by white folk with no love for me," Rhett said, voice husky. "I don't know who my people are, but I got memories of a paint horse's rump and being carried away by the Cannibal Owl. Other than that, I know what I look like now and what I can turn into, and both of those things are rare enough."

"Pia Mupitsi?" The woman's voice broke as she pushed out of the tent flap.

The younger boy spun and tried to hustle her back inside, but she disentangled from him and stood, stepping forward, eyes wet, to touch Rhett's face with her hand. It was dry and lined; she'd had a hard life, as everyone did here.

"I killed it," Rhett said, his voice breaking, too. "It can't steal no more babies."

Beans translated, and the woman broke into bright tears, her smile wobbling as she spoke.

"You are a brave warrior, and you have the look. But my child was a daughter," Beans said.

Rhett's eye slashed sideways, his jaw hard. "I was maybe born a girl, but that's not how I live. Not who I am. Don't make me show you."

Beans had some trouble translating that, and the woman's eyes narrowed as she looked Rhett up and down, searching perhaps for signs of the child she'd once known. Reaching into a pouch identical to the one Rhett wore around his neck, she pulled out a tiny beaded moccasin and held it out on her palm. Rhett marveled at it, remembering a similar one he'd found in the Cannibal Owl's lair. He tentatively touched the cracked old leather, amazed that anything but his thumb had ever fit in something so small. She smiled and tucked it back in its pouch.

Rhett pulled out his own pouch, and she exclaimed and ran a thumb over it. Her smile told him everything he needed to know.

When his mother spoke, it was low and slow and with the feeling one reserves for babies.

"We called you Fierce Rabbit," Beans translated. "Forehead always furrowed, so serious. You'd only been out of the cradle-board for two years when you were taken. Told your papa you could kill a buffalo, if he'd just give you a bow. Did not like the women's work. I was heavy with this one when the Cannibal Owl came." She gestured to the boy. "But I never got over it. I grew angry. Your papa was like a cat—I always knew he would wander away. His name was Stars Against Midnight, for the white of his smile against the dark of his face. He came from the Seminole, and before that, over the ocean. He became the great bird, like you, like your brother. Lambkiller, he called it."

She smiled like she wanted to hug him but didn't know how. He looked down at himself briefly and wished he'd taken off his goddamn Rangers badge. No wonder the boy didn't trust him. He'd been right to leave Sam out of it.

She said something else, and Beans asked for her, "Is this your woman?"

The woman looked at Winifred hopefully, and Rhett chuckled. "She's her own damn woman, and that ain't my child, if you're asking. I'm not that magic. She's my friend, Winifred."

"You are a Ranger?" the woman asked next.

Rhett held out his badge, proud and a little sheepish. "I'm a Scout for the Durango Rangers, Las Moras Company. But I only kill what needs to die. No...innocents. No tribes."

At that, the boy nearly exploded, his knife in his fist. "He says Rangers are evil and deserve to die. That Rangers..." Beans listened carefully and turned to Rhett looking somber. "Rangers killed what was left of their band. Only they two escaped, and only because he shielded her. He was shot three times."

"Haskell?" Rhett asked, fury building.

The woman nodded once. "Haskell," she repeated, making it a guttural curse.

"You tell her Eugene Haskell is a devil and I'll kill him myself. You tell her, Beans! Him, too."

Beans did, and they both relaxed. Rhett added, "Tell her my Captain ain't like that. That there are good Rangers in the world, and that I'm one of 'em, and that we don't go killing folks for fun."

Winifred murmured, "You know that's not true, don't you? Your Captain is only a man, and he has soaked the prairie in blood. Less now that he's older. The Rangers were created to wipe out the Comanche, to destroy anyone who opposed the white man's interests."

"Don't you go speaking ill of the Captain around me," Rhett said, deadly.

"Ask them. Ask Dan. Ask yourself. I will always speak the truth when it must be heard."

A dark silence settled over them, despite the white-hot sun.

Rhett shook his head and turned back to the woman. "I reckon those dues can be tallied later against another man's soul than mine. Are you saying...this feller's my brother?"

After Beans translated, the woman smiled. "I think so. You are very alike. Angry, fierce, strong. There are no other lamb-killers in Durango, unless Stars is still warming beds." She stepped forward and put her hands on his shoulders. He was a little taller than her, a little lankier, but the lines of her face were so familiar that it made his chest ache. "What happened to your eye?"

He ran a thumb over the kerchief hiding the ugly hole. "Pia Mupitsi. But I took both of his before I killed him and I'm still here, so I figure I win. When did you-all lose your band?"

She smudged a hand through the air. "Years ago. We do fine together. Our old horse died recently, though, and traveling is harder now. We need to move south before the weather turns."

"We'll give you a horse," Rhett said without thinking. "Whatever you need."

She—the woman—his mother—smiled fondly. "We will take it. Life without horses is not really life."

"I feel the same way."

Rhett had forgotten now that Beans was translating between them. He was lost in her eyes, in the curve of her smile. Memories were tumbling back, half-formed things. Misty feelings, mostly. He knew, deep in his heart of hearts, that this really was his mother. He wanted to hug her tight, to be held by her, but he'd become aloof as a wild cat and didn't know how such sentiments were approached among her people. Not to mention the fact that his newfound brother was glaring at him with the hate of a thousand suns.

"Why's this feller so mad?" he asked, flipping a thumb at the angry boy.

His mother—their mother—turned to the boy, muttered what sounded like a good scolding, and said, "He has grown up with only one goal: to become a man and kill the Cannibal

Owl for stealing his sister. Now you are here, and you are not what he expected. And you have stolen his destiny."

Rhett struggled to hold in a chuckle. "Brother, if it's a destiny you want, you can have mine. I'd be glad to have a nice lie-in for a while out of the elements." Then, more seriously, "Is that something he wants me to apologize for? Will that set him right? Because I ain't sorry I killed Pia Mupitsi and got that baby-eating monster the hell out of our world, but I am sorry that I accidentally stole something he held dear. I got a destiny myself." He looked to Winifred, and she nodded her encouragement. "You ever heard of the Shadow?"

Beans translated, and Rhett's mother shook her head.

"It means Rhett has a calling," Winifred said. "That he is here to fight for us."

The woman's eyes searched Rhett's face, and she said something that sounded worried. "Then you won't stay with us? You will move on?" Beans said.

Rhett hung his head. "Yeah, that's what it means. I can't stay in one place. Things call to me, things that need killing, and I got to go. I'm on my way to kill something bad right now."

Beans translated, and the woman and the boy argued, which Beans didn't translate. Finally, the woman spoke emphatically to Beans, moving her arms with conviction.

"She says she understands, but you should take your brother with you. Two great birds together, as it should be. You can train him. He's smart and strong."

Tears pricked at Rhett's eyes. "I ain't taking a child into this battle. I already got enough people to worry about. And I can't train anybody. I'm barely trained myself. But you tell him to learn English and come find me when he's a man."

After Beans translated, the boy barked at Rhett, nearly pressing his chest against Rhett's like he wanted to start a fight.

Rhett wanted to shove him away, hard, but he knew pretty well that hotheadedness was one trait they shared, and he didn't need to stoke this feller's fire and start a real fight. "Look here now, Revenge. You want to be a good man, you take care of your mama. You can't just leave her out here on the prairie alone."

"That's what you're doing," the boy said back, with Beans's help.

"I'm giving you a horse. I'm giving you the truth. You-all stay safe, and when you're ready, you come to the Las Moras Outpost of the Durango Rangers and ask for Rhett Walker. Then I'll do what I can, and you can come fight monsters with me. But from what I can tell, our mama ain't a monster, and that means you got to protect her with your life. Like you been doing."

Because sure enough, Rhett didn't feel that familiar wobble when he stood near his mama, just that old familiar terror he felt around Sam, like just about anything could kill that fragile mortal body. And even if the boy was a pushy little snot just now, he wouldn't risk his brother in his hunt for Trevisan. No, the best way to care for the family he'd just found was to push them as far away from the Shadow as possible, as much as it hurt to do so.

That's what a hero did, he reckoned: what had to be done, even when it hurt, even when it was hard.

Rhett's mother listened to this speech, then reached up and touched Rhett's face with calloused fingers. She'd looked soft up until then, motherly and a little sad. But now she went over sharp and fierce, and Rhett saw maybe where he'd got some of his backbone from. "You do what you must, and we will do as you ask. You honor me with the gift of a horse. You are a good son. My only regret is that you were taken from me, but I am proud to see you now. I tell you this: You will see us again, and your brother will fight by your side one day."

"Well, hell. At least let's make camp together tonight. We got plenty of meat." He glanced back at the rest of his posse, waiting and worrying, the sun flashing off Sam's silver gun. He could almost feel Cora's judgment and worry, her need to press on toward finding her sister, but he reckoned that if she could have just one more day with her sister or her grandfather, she'd take it, and she couldn't keep him from his own such reunion. Feeling kinship with folks was a strange new feeling for Rhett, and he wanted to roll around in it like a dog in stink while he had the chance.

"With your permission, I'm gonna bring my friends over, and we'll get a fire going and tell some stories," he said. "That suit everybody?"

"It won't suit Cora," Winifred added with her usual smirk.

"Then she can fly the hell away," Rhett shot back. "This is for me. I don't reckon I've ever asked for anything for myself, so don't you try to stop me."

Winifred dipped her head. "You're right. I'd give anything for another day with my mother. And it'll be good for you to see what it's like."

"What what is like?"

She grinned. "Dealing with an annoying brother."

Everyone settled in quick, and they ate well that night. Only Earl and Cora kept themselves separate, out of stubbornness and frustration, respectively, Rhett knew. It didn't trouble him. The Shadow wasn't bugging him to move on, and so he reckoned that if his own goddamn destiny could give him a night's break, so could the friends he'd dedicated his life to saving and helping. He felt just about as relaxed as he'd ever been, sitting there next to his mother with Beans nearby to translate. Beans was even coming out of his shell a bit, having conversations of his own with her and the boy both. Notch got along well with Dan and Winifred, being some sort of distant cousin, as tribes went, and Sam was just his usual sunny self and seemed pleased to see Rhett so happy.

Rhett's mother told stories of him as a baby, about the time he found a fledgling hawk on the ground and brought it to his mama to save it and ended up in a fight with the hawk's mother instead. She confirmed his memories of his father, known for his good stories and laughter and ferocity in a fight, as well as his predilection for roaming. She had loved them, Rhett knew, his father and himself, and he could read the lines of worry across her face, understand that her life had been one of loss and that she'd continually stood up against her tears and kept on moving.

His brother was quiet at first but then began asking questions, mostly about Rhett's travels and fights and what the Rangers were like when they weren't trying to kill your whole family in a night raid. Rhett told him of his time with the Rangers, of the siren of Reveille and the fight with the Lobos and what it was like to gentle a unicorn. His brother's eyes went from suspicion to something a little like awe, which made Rhett feel right proud.

For once, Rhett didn't mind that Sam's bedroll was around the other side of the fire. Sam's sleepy smile and wave across the flames were enough to tell Rhett that Sam was happy for him and glad to give him this time with his family. He would've stayed up all night talking with his mama, if Beans hadn't started yawning his fool head off. The three of them were the last ones awake, and Rhett finally had a jaw-cracker of a yawn himself.

"Go to bed, Fierce Rabbit," his mother said through Beans with a fond smile. "You have fought enough for one day."

"Yes, ma'am," he said, settling down against his saddle as she likewise curled into her furs. It was getting cooler now, and he pulled his buffalo coat up to his chin.

She started singing then, a sweet and liquid lullaby, and Rhett's heart filled up with a rush of warmth and remembrance, with the strange new feeling of being loved. He was willing to bet this song was the same one Winifred had sung to him in the Cannibal Owl's lair, the one that taught little children how to seek their second skin and turn. It was the rarest and strangest of gifts, and he went to sleep feeling complete and content.

It was hard to say good-bye, but destiny was calling. Rhett kept finding excuses to stay around a little longer, fetching water and tying up buffalo meat and trying to give pretty much everything that wasn't nailed down to his mama while his brother watched, half impressed and half annoyed.

"His name is Puddin'," Rhett said to Beans. "They got a word for that?"

Beans shook his head as he watched the sleek black-and-white paint horse sniff Revenge and stamp a foot. "I guess they got something like Mush."

"Well, he won't answer to that," Rhett said. "His name ain't Mush." He stepped over to Revenge, who held the gelding's reins, pointed at the horse, and said, "Puddin'. Puddin'. Say it."

With Beans's help, Revenge was calling the horse Puttun, but Rhett figured it was close enough. He was gonna miss the hell out of the stout little paint, who'd carried him all over Durango when Ragdoll was having her day of rest.

"Check his hooves regular. Make sure he gets some feed. He likes to have his withers scratched."

After Beans translated, Revenge barked something back and patted Puddin's neck.

"He says he could ride a horse before he was two, and he don't need your help."

Rhett glared at the boy. "Have your people got any rules about brothers getting in a tussle?" he asked.

Beans shook his head. "Not if it's in good fun."

Rhett snatched the reins from Revenge.

"Hold the horse," Rhett said to Beans, and then he jumped on his brother and punched him in the ribs. Revenge shouted something angry, and they were soon rolling around in the dust, kicking and punching and scratching and shouting as the coydog barked and growled excitedly like it was the best thing he'd ever seen. The boy was smaller, but he might've been made from stone, he was so lithe and tough. Rhett didn't want to hurt him, really; just wanted to get out some of their aggression and let the little turkey know he couldn't sass an elder. He got in a couple of good punches and took one in his bad eye before his mother's sharp voice broke in, and they both pulled away looking a little sheepish.

Revenge shouted something that sounded very much like "He started it."

"I'll finish it, too," Rhett muttered.

"She says to stop acting like children before you upset the horse," Beans added.

When Rhett stood up and dusted himself off, he found his mother holding Puddin's reins, looking vexed.

"Sorry, Ma," he said, and Revenge said something similar.

Winifred just chuckled. "Now you're getting the hang of it," she said.

Dan just snorted. "If you were a man, Sister, we'd fight like that more often. I suspect your fists are less sharp than your tongue." When Winifred punched his arm, he winced and chuckled, too.

Rhett was surprised to find that in the short time they'd been talking horses and brawling, his mother had deconstructed the tent and bunched the wood and skin up into a travois. Now, as they watched, she led Puddin' over to it, introduced him to the travois, and hooked leather straps around the horse like a harness. Rhett was gratified to see how competent his mama was with horses, and how well Puddin' took to the strange new burden, and how bruised up his brother was from their tumble. Of course, as he was the same thing Rhett was, the boy would be all healed up within hours with no sign of the dark splotches now painting his arms, chest, and face.

Soon they stood, two people, a horse, and a now-friendly coydog on one side, Rhett and his posse on the other side. It was a strange enough grouping, but Rhett reckoned it was a good one. Injuns, whites, Irish, Chine, all smiling. Such a scene could never happen in a town like Gloomy Bluebird, and in a place like Lamartine, where Haskell's Rascals might catch wind of it, it could've started a riot. But here, it was just a bunch of folks Rhett liked, mostly respected, and would continue to fight for, even when he'd rather spend another night around the campfire, grinning and sharing buffalo stew.

It was his turn to talk, so he went with the truth.

"I'm worried about you-all," he said, feeling like there wasn't a damn useful thing to do with his hands.

"We're strong," his mother said through Beans. "We got this far. We will survive."

Then Beans spoke for himself. "Me and Notch could stay

with 'em. They need people, and we need people. I can teach Revenge some English. Right, Notch?"

Notch nodded. "Rather stay out here than meet the Rangers, if I'm being honest."

Rhett looked them up and down and contemplated the pros and cons. "They got to agree to it. And we'll give y'all a gun and some bullets. You can keep one of the ponies. But if either of you-all touch my mama, I'll skin you alive and roll you around in an anthill." He looked to his mother. "If that suits you."

His mother and Beans had a hurried and somewhat awkward discussion that ended up with shrugs. "She says she don't mind, and she sleeps with a knife, anyway," Beans said with his usual unflappableness.

So that was one less thing to worry about. And further proof that when Rhett let the Shadow lead, problems tended to solve themselves one way or another. They'd taken in Beans and Notch, and Beans had served his purpose. The feller had earned his horse.

Rhett sighed and looked at the dwindling pony herd. "So I guess that's that."

"Be strong, my son," Rhett's mother said. She threw a stern look at his brother, urging him to say something.

"I will find you," his brother said in halting, practiced English, and Beans gave him a grin, which the boy returned.

"I hope you will," Rhett answered, holding out his hand, which his brother took for a punishing, bone-grinding sort of shake that ended in smiles.

"I guess it's west, then," Rhett said, dashing at his eye and wishing the good-byes were already over.

He gave Puddin' one last pat and turned away. At the last minute, not really able to stop himself, he threw himself into his mother's arms for a rough, tight hug that ended with a few hiccupping sobs into her shoulder. She rubbed his back and crooned to him, private quiet things that Beans didn't need to translate. Rhett knew well enough what she meant. She'd lost him, and she'd found him again at last, and now they were losing each other all over again.

"I love you, Ma," he whispered, and he reckoned she said the same thing back in her way.

And then he was swinging up on Ragdoll's back and rolling with her walk. He knew damn well that if he turned around to look back, he'd start crying all over again.

"Good-bye, Ned," Beans called, and his mother echoed it.

"Good-bye, you-all," Rhett called back, a hand up in the air.

The posse formed up around Rhett, Sam and Dan and Winifred up front and Cora behind with the wagon, silent and lost in her own thoughts. Earl trotted in their wake, more sour than ever.

"She told me she's changing her name," Winifred said, once they were over the next ridge.

"I never asked her name," Rhett said, suddenly feeling like a complete ass.

"It used to be I Will Find Her, but now she's going to be I Found Him."

Rhett kicked his horse and galloped up ahead to cry in private, alone on his horse.

CHAPTER 8

Rhett glared at seven crows sitting on a skeletal tree, staring right at him with dead stone eyes. His stomach didn't wobble, but had Trevisan's birds ever made him feel anything? He couldn't remember, but he didn't like the way these smug bastards were staring, like they wished for nothing more than to peck out his remaining eye and swallow it. Had crows always been around, or was he just noticing them now? He pulled out his gun and shot it from his bedroll by the cold fire—not aiming to kill, just to annoy. The birds rose in a screeching clamor and winged up to a higher branch, resettling to fuss with their feathers. His friends sat up, grumbling.

"It's not wise to kill crows," Winifred warned, already awake and returning from the wagon.

"But it's just fine to vex them, I reckon," he shot back.

He'd felt prickly and standoffish ever since they'd parted ways with his mother and brother and Beans and Notch. It wasn't that he was sad, exactly. It had, after all, been his quest that had forced their parting. It was more that in as big and dangerous a place as Durango, there was no way to know for certain if he'd ever be able to find them again. Not like he could write up a letter and hand it off to a Pony Express rider and expect a letter back in a week, written out on creamy white paper. He could search his entire goddamn life and never see them again unless the Shadow decided that that was what was needed.

Rhett sat up and stumbled off to deal with his private needs, and when he came back, Sam offered him a chunk of cold meat, and Winifred rolled a potato from the ashes with a stick, nudging it toward him with a sympathetic smile. Well, hell. If anybody knew what it was like to figure you'd never see your mother again, it was her and Dan. He turned to Sam.

"Sam, you think you'll ever go back to Tanasi?"

Sam shrugged as he ate and looked off toward the rising sun in the east. "No, I don't reckon I will. Tanasi was getting awful crowded, and the war was making everybody choose sides, and following my brother to Durango seemed like a good idea. It was lonely, for a while, but I guess there are always gonna be fellers to josh around with." He grinned at Rhett. "It all worked out, far as I can see."

Rhett's heart fluttered, and he felt a blush creeping up, so he rammed some cold meat and hot tater in his mouth to keep himself from saying something awkward. Dan appeared carrying a fat prairie bird by the feet, and Earl wandered up in nothing but his shirt, scratching himself.

"What about you, Earl? You think you'll ever go back home?"

The look Earl gave him showed a level of suspicion Rhett thought they had long ago bypassed. "Of course I can't go home, ye great idjit. Not only do I have no money nor prospects of making money, but what am I supposed to tell me mam? That I ran away and let wee Shaunie die? Oh, and she'd welcome me home with open arms, then." He snatched the piece of buffalo Sam held out and added, for emphasis, "Idjit."

"You still mad at me, then, donkey-boy?"

Earl stood, threw the bit of buffalo in the fire, and stomped away.

"What the Sam Hill?" Rhett asked the group.

"He's mad at himself," Dan said as he began stripping feathers from the bird, which Winifred gathered in an old sack. "But it's easier to focus the anger on you. You're stronger. You can take it."

"Well, I don't appreciate that."

"He clearly doesn't care what you appreciate, Rhett."

Rhett snorted and watched as Earl stripped, stuck his rust-colored shirt into his old bag, and turned into a donkey.

"So not only do I have to be the Shadow and get yanked all over the damn place, but now I got to…what? Be the scapegoat? Accept everybody else's anger? Guilt? Whatever?"

Dan didn't even look up from his work. "The weak rely on the strong. That's the way it's always been, and that's the way it will always be."

"Gets like that with the Rangers sometimes," Sam added. "Beg us for help, then get angry when we don't help the way they wanted."

"Just like the dwarves," Rhett muttered. "Just like Regina."

"You've never had power before." Winifred gave him her cutting grin. "It's easier to have no responsibility and receive no complaints. I was a governess to a town man in Nueva Orleans, and people rang our bell, day and night, with the most foolish requests and grievances."

Rhett looked at each of them in turn and wished he'd left Earl behind with Notch and Beans. A feller with a chip on his shoulder made himself a burden, that much was for certain. But he couldn't forget the good turn Earl had done him when they'd first met, long before Earl had reason to speak against him. Without the Irishman's help, Rhett might not've understood how to move between his skins, between man and bird, nor to accept for certain that he was a man and not the scared little girl he'd been born.

"Then I reckon he's my burden to carry," he grumbled. "But I don't know how long I can go being fussed at without punching a feller."

Winifred laughed at that. "Well, we wouldn't complain if you punched him. He's not the best trail companion. When he's a donkey, he shits all over the place." As she stood to take a potato to Cora, Rhett could see her travel dress starting to bulge around her belly. How far along was she now? Three months, maybe? Rhett knew plenty about birthing horses and cows and next to goddamn nothing about humans or demigods, so he didn't have any idea when the critter inside Winifred would see the sun. And he wasn't about to ask, neither. Seemed downright personal, asking such things. Perhaps he'd ask Dan in a private moment, when the feller wasn't feeling too preachy.

Cora next caught his eye, and he considered her. The girl had as much reason to hate him as Earl, but she either didn't lay the blame at his feet, or she kept her cards closer to her chest. She didn't seem to want to confide in him just now, he knew that much. And he wasn't going to press her. The best thing he could do to help her was to move on, following the Shadow's call back to Las Moras and then on to dealing with Trevisan.

"You doing all right, Cora?" he asked.

She looked up, smiled tightly, and said, "Yes, thank you, Ned."

And that was all. Whatever else she felt or thought, she didn't say it, but she looked like a frayed rope, like her mind and heart were somewhere else, and it wasn't someplace good.

Rhett frowned and looked at Winifred. "How 'bout you?"

"I didn't like vomiting constantly, but it seems like that's stopped, so I'm much better. I think we're all ready to get on the road and move forward. Not that we minded yesterday's stop. It's just...well, hard to relax, isn't it?"

Rhett stood and sniffed the air. She was right, dang it. There was nothing in particular that he could put his finger on, nothing that made the morning peculiar, as it had been before the buffalo herd had arrived. But he'd woken up antsy and still felt that way, even with a good breakfast in his belly. High up in the dead tree, the crows laughed. There were more now, twice as many as before, glossy and black. When Rhett pulled out his gun and shot at them again, the cloud of birds exploded into the air, leaving a sinuous black shape behind.

"What the hell is that?" he asked as the thing unwound from around the tree's trunk.

Even from far away, great yellow eyes bored into Rhett as claws unfurled and the thing stretched out along a branch.

"We called 'em painters back in Tanasi, but they were brown," Sam said, his gun cocking.

"It's not a shifter," Winifred said.

"Must be some kind of monster cat," Dan confirmed.

"Well, no shit, Dan," Rhett snapped before aiming right between the critter's eyes and pulling the trigger.

The giant cat shook its head in annoyance, as if the bullet did no damage. It recovered quickly and slunk down the tree headfirst, long tail curling around the trunk behind it. Rhett figured it had to be the size of a horse, but with shorter legs and much bigger teeth.

"Winifred and Cora, I respectfully ask that you get the hell out of here, and Sam, please keep your distance while keeping your gun about you," he said, and before waiting for an answer, he pulled his other gun and unloaded everything he had, hoping to hit the cat's heart before its feet touched the ground. But again, it was like striking a cloud, like shooting at midnight. Nothing had any effect.

"Ideas, Dan?"

"I got nothing, but I'll try."

Dan's arrow should've hit the cat-thing right between the eyes, but it just slipped out the other side to clatter uselessly against some rocks. Dan's next arrow, aimed perfectly at the thing's chest, did likewise. As the beast stalked the fifty yards between its tree and the camp, Sam whipped out his Henry and pulled the trigger seventeen times. Seventeen bullets passed through the critter and pinged off the tree and ground behind it.

"Sam, you go, too. Get out of here. Protect the women, if you can."

"I'm a Ranger, Rhett. I'll stay and fight beside you."

As the thing crept closer and closer, haunches up and claws crumbling rocks, Rhett watched Sam standing there like a goddamn golden beacon and shouted, "You got to take care of yourself, Sam! You're the only one of us who can get broken, and I can't fight when I'm this worried for you."

"I'm not the only one who can get broken, Rhett." Sam's voice was ragged with feeling, but his feet were stepping backward, one after the other, as if he just couldn't deny Rhett at all.

"Then do it for me. Please."

Sam's eyes met Rhett's, and he nodded and spun and hotfooted it away, back behind Rhett and Dan, toward the wagon where Cora had already gone. Winifred, damn her, hadn't budged.

"Goddammit, Win—"

The cat wiggled its tail and sprang right for Rhett, and time seemed to slow as it flew through the air, paws outstretched, black claws curled and murderous. Rhett grabbed his Bowie knife and slashed right up with it as the beast hit him, knocking him onto his back and slamming the air from his lungs. Perhaps it couldn't be shot, but the creature's weight was real, as was its rancid death breath. Its claws sunk into Rhett's shoulders, its mouth open and teeth angling for his throat. He caught its face in his hands, digging his fingers into the soft fur and slashing for its eyes with his thumbs. It growled and spat and tucked its head against him.

"A little help?" Rhett sputtered.

"No weapons can touch it," Dan shouted from very near. "It's like smoke."

"It's nothing goddamn like smoke at all. It weighs more than a cow. I can feel its fur!"

His knife, though, felt like it was playing with the breeze. It wasn't lodged in muscle or bone or skin. Maybe Dan was onto something. Maybe...

"Try to grab it," he shouted, and the cat growled as Dan and Winifred tried to wrestle it off him. The huge thing resisted, grappling and writhing.

"Yank out its whiskers," Rhett shouted. He didn't have an arm to spare, since his hands were the only thing holding the cat back from ripping out his throat with its impossible teeth.

With his eye closed and his hands fighting for purchase, he couldn't see what was happening, but he sure as hell heard the cat scream and felt it shake its head, loosening its claws to bat at something, probably whichever of Rhett's friends had managed to mangle it. Rhett peeked out his eye just in time to see the pissed-off cat's mouth open in a hiss, and he figured he'd go ahead and do something dumb as hell that just might work.

He stuck his arm down the cat's mouth and punched it in the back of the throat, although its wetness burned like acid.

Well, to be more clear, he reached as far down as he could,

felt his knuckles scrape innards, grabbed a handful of whatever he could, and yanked.

Teeth bit into his shoulder, and claws sank into his ribs, but he scrabbled his fingers in deep, pushing his arm as far into the critter as it would go, feeling his skin tear against fangs as it went. The cat was spitting and fighting, and he shouted "Hold it down!" to his friends and reached in farther. If this didn't work, or if he didn't do it quick enough, he was liable to lose the whole damn arm, and from what he knew, it wasn't going to grow back. That just made him ram his fingers down all the harder.

His fingertips scraped something hard—something that didn't feel like it belonged in any sort of cat's guts. It felt like... a ball of wax, maybe. Rhett knew what to do with that, so he wrapped it up in burning fingers and dug his bitten nails into whatever it was and crushed it. He felt the exact moment it happened, the wax crumbling and the cat exploding to silvery black dust around him. He exhaled, his lungs finally free to expand without the weight of the cat, and let his head fall back to the ground. Dan and Winifred nearly fell on him without the cat there, but they managed to get untangled and roll away.

Rhett held up his torn, bleeding, burned arm and uncurled his wet, bloody fingers to show exactly what he goddamn expected: a black ball of wax tangled with a whisker, a tiny flake of gold, and a bitty chip of bone.

"We got to hurry," he said, once he caught his breath. "This shit is getting old."

And then he passed out.

Rhett didn't fall into dark dreams—his sleep was deep and quiet, like being lost. When he woke up, Cora was tending to his wounds. Thankfully, they were in the privacy of her wagon, which meant no one else would be forced to look at his chest unwound and covered in salve. Seemed like she'd been at it for a while, seeing as how there were ugly, waxed black stitches holding flaps of his brown skin together. When she noticed he was awake, she sat back on her heels and tried to smile. The pain of her looking at him like that, with pity, was almost worse than what the ghost cat's claws and teeth had done to his body.

"If you were human, these cuts would go putrid and kill you," Cora said, almost like she was scolding him.

"If I was human, none of us would be here in the first place," he muttered, flushing and looking down as she rubbed her ointment into the ticklish skin over his ribs, where her hands had once roved in a far more entertaining manner.

Neither of them said anything about how much uglier he was now, pieced together like an old pair of long johns.

"It is fascinating to see what finds you," she observed. "The way your destiny unfolds like a flower, every petal in its place, the bees called by some strange perfume."

"Are you calling me a flower?"

"Perhaps. You have much in common with the lotus. Born of mud, floating toward greatness. But of course, it is a flower of purity..."

As she went for more salve, her fingers brushed over his nipple, and he gasped and huddled away. "Don't."

Her chuckle was soft and not cruel. "You are very conflicted. I am also conflicted. You frustrate me. Sometimes you anger me. Sometimes I feel my heart soften toward you. But still I follow you. Still, when you tell me to run, I do. I am not accustomed to such encumbrances. Winifred feels much the same. We are free women in a world that wishes to bind us, and it is odd to find ourselves already bound to something we did not choose. We can't seem to quit you, either of us."

She turned away and handed him his binder, and he gladly wound it tight around his chest. The skin itched as it knitted back together, leaving yet more scars. "I didn't choose it, either. At least you two got each other now."

"In some ways," she said mysteriously. But most of the things Cora said sounded mysterious.

"I'm happy for you, then. You're both . . . real good folks. You deserve comfort." It was as close as he could come to giving his blessing for whatever stood between them, and Cora smiled and dipped her head.

"I do not need your permission, Rhett. Bees go from flower to flower. It is their nature. We are both, perhaps, bees, in that way."

"You still mad we're not after Meimei?"

She was behind him, and when her hand landed on his gored shoulder, she had her dragon claws out. Bigger than the ghost cat's had been, they pricked into his skin. It was a warning, and he went still to show her he understood.

"I can be patient. I do not like being patient. But Winifred assures me that when you do not do the Shadow's bidding, life becomes uncomfortable for everyone. I'm uncomfortable enough as it is. We will see Las Moras soon, she says, and I believe her. You will do your business there, and then you will lead us to Trevisan, and together, we will end him. One way or another, he will not wear my sister's body. Yes?"

"Yes."

She dug in her talons a little more, just to show him she could, before releasing him. He gasped—he hadn't even realized he was holding his breath—and the pain rushed back in. The warmth of her human hand replaced the claws, rubbing the slightly numbing salve into the fresh punctures.

"One day, you will be made of nothing but scars," Cora observed.

"Already am," Rhett answered, glad they were finally on the same page.

For days, they pushed hard, dawn to dusk. They ate in the saddle, killed more meat on the road, and set the meat to dry in strings off the wagon, brown ribbons twisting in the wind. If Rhett felt a minor wobble here or there, they didn't turn off their course. They even saw a column of smoke rising up from a small town at one point, but when Rhett turned that way, he felt nothing.

"We keep on to Las Moras," he repeated, shaking his head. "Whatever troubles that town is being done by the hands of man, and he can clean up his own goddamn mess."

Dan's second-to-last chestnut stumbled over a rattler, which they killed and ate over that night's fire. The horse barely escaped a nasty bite, and it was a near miss that made everyone cranky. Earl muttered under his breath about the use of giving away ponies when they had none left to spare, and Rhett told him that when he could capture, tame, and ride a mustang himself, he could complain about it, and Earl shut right up and went back to being a donkey.

By the time they stopped each night, everyone was beyond exhausted. They fell to their duties, fell to their dinner, and fell to bed without much to say. Rhett, strangely enough, was happy this way. It reminded him of life on a ranch or of his time hunting the Cannibal Owl with the Rangers. It was a hard life but a simple one, and each person knew their place. There was no time to shirk, no time to fret, no time to look at the patchwork of ugliness that was his arm and feel like he'd lost something, like he had one more thing to keep hidden. No time to quarrel. Just calm and steady pacing toward a goal.

His only concern, besides Earl's hatefulness and Cora's miserable jitters, was old Blue, his one-eyed mule. The critter was hardy and just about made of gristle, but the punishing pace was taking its toll. Blue had to be thirty if he was a day, and his nose had started to go white before Rhett had left Pap's farm. Each morning when Blue welcomed Rhett with a bugle and pulled his skinny bones up to standing, Rhett was grateful. One morning, he knew the old critter would stay down, and he knew that Blue would get left behind—although no matter how hungry they were at the time, Rhett outright refused to eat him or let anyone else do so. He'd have shot 'em first.

Rhett's world was not one in which life stopped to accommodate a loyal old mule.

One night, Rhett was up late rolling a piece of gold between his fingers as he stared into the fire, too consternated to sleep. The girls were gone to their wagon, and Earl and Sam had already succumbed. Rhett was thinking about how the gold reminded him of Sam's hair, grown long on the trip and curling at the ends in a way that made Rhett's chest feel funny.

"What is that?" Dan asked.

"The gold I pulled from the cat."

Dan was around the fire in seconds, snatching the gold from Rhett's dirt-stained fingers. "You kept it? Are you truly that stupid?"

Rhett hopped up to his feet, as he hated to be on a lower level than a feller who already thought him there. "Far as I know, collecting gold is smart." He reached to take it back, but Dan winged it off into the darkness.

"What the hell, Dan? You think money grows on trees? Because if so, I got bad news for you about the desert."

"Rhett. Think about it. Trevisan is sending creatures after you. How do you think they're finding you?" He stepped closer in a menacing sort of way. "Wait. Now I remember. You keep the gold from the scorpion, too?"

Rhett's eye shifted away, and he hunched his shoulders. "Earl did."

They both looked to Earl, who was clearly pretending their argument hadn't woken him. His red eyelashes quivered around squinched eyes. Dan stood over him, looming.

"Give it."

When that didn't work, Dan nudged Earl with his boot and stuck his palm out, and Earl glared sullenly for as long as he was able, up until Dan's hand crept to his knife. Earl winced and withdrew the tiny chunk of gold from his pocket, putting it into Dan's hand. Dan tossed it out into the night.

"You got anything else from Trevisan?"

Poking around in his pouch, Rhett pulled out the two tiny bone fragments he'd kept, and Dan chucked them out, too, in different directions.

"Anything else in there? One of Trevisan's eyelashes, maybe?"

Rhett grumbled unpleasant things about Dan under his breath. Coming up with nothing, he stuffed the pouch back down his shirt and said, "No, I don't got anything else from Trevisan, save all these scars. You want to pat me down to make sure? He's got my own toe-bone, don't forget, and I can't do nothing about that."

Dan rolled his eyes. "I just want to be sure you're not carrying a beacon that allows our enemy to find us. The scorpions made sense; that was a trap. But if he can send creatures after us, if he can find you wherever you go, then we're never safe. We'll have to start sleeping in turns, and when we get to Las Moras, we'll bring Trevisan's wrath to the Rangers' doorstep."

"Well, if anybody's up for fighting him, it's them."

Dan gave Rhett the don't-be-dumb look. "Oh, because more guns would've ended that ghost cat?"

At the memory, the healing white scars up and down Rhett's shoulders and ribs seemed to itch and beat in time with his heart. "What do you want from me? You-all can leave anytime you please, if my company is proving unpleasant. I didn't ask for this."

"You keep saying that."

"Because it's true, Dan! You said yourself that I can't escape it."

"Did you ever consider that we didn't ask for our roles, either, but that still we will play them? You forget that I was drawn to you by strange means. And then my sister showed up after years away in Nueva Orleans, found us out in the middle of thousands of miles of prairie. And then Earl found you when both of you were lost. Your own mother and brother appeared as if from nowhere. We are all just as captive to your destiny as you are. And we can complain about it just as often, if we like."

They were nearly toe to toe, then, whisper-shouting by the fire. Sam rolled over, and Rhett looked at him with a ping of guilt.

"Sorry to wake you, Sam."

"You-all should sleep," Sam muttered. "We got miles to go yet."

"That's right, Sam," Rhett said gently. "That's right."

He nodded at Dan and resettled into his bedroll, into the warmth under his buffalo-skin coat. He and Sam slept mighty close these nights, close enough to touch, if a moment allowed it. Sam's hand landed on Rhett's fingers, soft as a dove's call. When Rhett looked up, Sam blinked at him like a baby owl and squeezed his fingers.

"We can't quit you, Rhett. Lord, I know I can't." And then he was asleep again.

It took a long time for Rhett to calm his heart down enough to join him.

Maybe Dan had been right about the bits of bone and gold, much as Rhett hated to admit it. There were no more attacks, although they slept in shifts and the crows gathered in increasingly large, dreary parties to watch them pass. At first, Rhett took small pleasure in scaring them off with his guns, but then he realized they were getting low on bullets and took to throwing rocks and shouting obscenities. Even this close to the Rangers, it wouldn't do to be out of bullets when only bullets would work, especially the silver ones.

It rained, hard and cold, and that night they all bundled up together in the tiny wagon, breathing in one another's breath and funk and farts. Every movement meant touching someone else, and they were all skitty as cats and just as grouchy, although Rhett secretly felt like he caught on fire every time Sam's body twitched against his. He woke up with his head on Sam's shoulder and feigned sleep a little longer just to enjoy the sensation.

When they ventured out in the morning, everything had turned brown and wet, a dreary land of mud. Winter had arrived. Earl had slept under the wagon in donkey form and spent the next day miserable and looking like he was caked in cow shit. The wagon wheels constantly caught and spun in the mud, and by the end of the day, Rhett was pretty sure he had a wagon-shaped bruise on his shoulder from shoving it free. The weather got dry again for a spell after that, thank goodness.

A few days later, Rhett began to recognize the terrain. They crossed a river that looked familiar and tasted sweet. The bulky rock formations and mountains seemed like arms held out to embrace him. The wobble in his belly felt like a hunger that was about to be slaked, and he urged Ragdoll on. She could sense it, too, could maybe even smell the Captain's good grain on the air, and soon they were cantering up a well-trod road toward a familiar cabin with smoke merrily tooting out the chimney and a whole passel of horses bugling their welcome.

A line of figures emerged to stand along the porch, weapons held casually but on the ready. There were fewer Rangers than Rhett expected, but it had been months since he'd been here, and there could already be another posse out on a job. One figure was more than familiar, causing a monster ripple in Rhett's belly, along with a lurch of abject dislike.

Jiddy stepped down off the porch, grinning with tobacco-stained teeth. His bear-like beard was longer than ever, and he moseyed up to where Rhett's horse stood.

"You almost missed it," Jiddy said.

"Missed what?" Rhett asked, voice low and growling.

Jiddy spit on Rhett's boot. "The Captain's dying breath."

CHAPTER
9

Rhett was off Ragdoll and up those stairs before Jiddy could say anything else. Hands reached out to stop him, and more than one gun cocked, but Rhett threw out his bony elbows and skittered in the door and down the long hall to what he knew was the Captain's private room. Once inside, he slammed and bolted the door against Jiddy and anybody else who'd think to come between him and the closest thing he currently had to a father. He'd never actually been in the Captain's room before—nobody had, according to Sam—but he wasn't about to ask permission if things were as dire as Jiddy said. With his back against the door that rattled with fists, Rhett let out a cry of dismay at what he found within. For all the dread and fear that had dogged his steps, for every foe he'd imagined facing down, he'd never reckoned that he might be racing death itself to the Captain's door.

The Captain's bed was a simple affair, just a straw tick mattress on a low wood platform, and the Captain was a sickly shape barely taking up room in it. His skin was nearly gray, his closed eyes sunk back in his balding skull and his lips dry and chapped. A town-looking feller frowned at Rhett's interruption as he pinched the Captain's spindly wrist.

"What's wrong, doc?" Rhett asked.

"Same thing I tell you boys every time you ask. The wound's gone putrid. I've tried vinegar and salt and mud and poultices and every goddamn receipt I know, but the creature that bit him didn't much want him alive." The doctor gently placed the Captain's wrist on the mattress, and the old man flinched like even that small movement hurt.

Rhett stepped closer, his hand hovering near the Captain's forehead. He'd never have touched the man otherwise, but he had to make some connection. Hell, maybe the Shadow would have some instinct on how to help, since the Shadow had driven him here. His palm touched sweaty skin so hot Rhett was surprised the man's head wasn't letting off visible steam.

"Hellfire. What got him?"

"The Rangers say it was a sand wyrm. I never heard of one, but I've never seen anything like this, either. It's not like a snake's venom, nor even a spider or scorpion. It's like gangrene, like the wound is eating into him with acid. I can't stop it. Stitches won't hold it. He's just...falling apart at the seams." The doc slipped off his pince-nez and shined them on his shirt. The feller looked like he didn't get or want much sleep and like he was personally annoyed that the case refused to be solved reasonably.

"So you can't fix it?"

"I reckon nobody can."

"How long's he got?"

The doc gently pulled back the light blue sheet over the Captain's half-naked body to show a huge circular ring of red on his torso, not quite a bite. The outside looked like a burn, and then there was a curling layer of wet yellow, and then...meat. The doctor gently pressed on the red burn, and the Captain whimpered like a child, his eyes springing open.

"Goddammit, let a man die in peace, you sadist," he barked.

"Not long," the doctor murmured.

120

The feller apologized and went to wash his instruments in the ewer, and the Captain's eyes focused on Rhett. The old man swallowed hard and licked his scabbed lips and reached toward Rhett with one clawed hand. Rhett held his hand out, feeling downright foolish but never wanting to deny the Captain anything. But the Captain reached past his hand to the Scout badge he wore on his shirt.

"Give me that."

"Sir?"

"Your goddamn badge. Give it here."

Rage and grief surged through Rhett, but so too did a glimmer of hope. The Captain had always done well by him. Surely the man's dying act wouldn't be to strip Rhett of his Ranger Star. So Rhett undid the pin and put the heavy badge in the Captain's palm, much as he hated doing so. The Captain held it up to eyes going rheumy and coughed, and Rhett slipped an arm behind his bony back to support him.

"The son-of-a-bitching doctor's right. I ain't got long, son," the Captain began, all while Jiddy banged on the door and hollered. "Either those boys'll get in here, or I'll die, and I got things that need to be said, things you need to hear."

"You ain't gonna die, Captain. And I'll kill any man who speaks against you."

"You're doing it now, fool. I most surely am going to die, and soon. So shut your smart mouth." The Captain fumbled around with something on a little table by his bed and pulled Rhett closer by his shirt. When Rhett straightened up again, he was completely shocked to see that he was wearing a Durango Rangers Captain badge. He stared at it like it might bite him and fumbled for words.

"Captain, no. I can't. We can get you better."

The Captain's laugh turned into a wracking cough. "Doc just

showed you what's killing me. Eating me, outside in. Nothing can stop it. Damn sand wyrms. We sure could've used you out there, Rhett. These boys rush in at the wrong time and pussyfoot when they should attack." He sat up a little straighter and pinned Rhett with the old familiar glare. "How'd your job go?"

It was Rhett's turn to give a dark laugh that almost became a sob. "Well, Haskell's working with Trevisan, and if I hadn't noticed his ring before we mentioned our job, I reckon the Rascals would've shot us on sight and made a few dollars in scalps. So I went into the train camp alone, spent a few weeks digging ditches and running rails, broke a few bones, got in a fight—"

"I don't have much time, son. Did you kill him or not?"

Rhett hung his head. "Thought I did. He was an alchemist. Jumped bodies. We didn't know he was still alive till he'd killed a good man and took off in an innocent child's body. So now we got to track him down, try to save that little girl. My destiny, it led me here first. Reckon I need your help. The book you gave us, it's got nothing about how to kill alchemists."

The Captain shook his head. "I don't know everything, nor even a little slice of it. We got books you can use. Sounds like you're dealing with a lich. Worse comes to worst, head down toward San Anton. Just west of the city, there's a mission there, mostly abandoned, but a nun keeps track of all the books and nonsense. She's helped me a few times, these last years. There's more out there in heaven and earth than I ever goddamn reckoned, Rhett Walker."

"I believe it, Captain."

"But why'd you come back? How come you aren't chasing your alchemist?"

"I wanted to chase him. Hell, I still need to. But my destiny…it brought me here. Dragged me here, pretty much. Guess it knew…"

"That I need you here, son. I can't leave this outpost to Jiddy. He's the strongest of who's left. He's a good scout, but he ain't a good man, and he'll end up more Haskell than me without somebody to keep him in check. Now I did some things when I was a younger man, led my Rangers into the wrong fights. Many's a grave in Durango ground or a pile of sand and ashes above it that keeps me up at night, wondering if I done right. But you understand it, Rhett. You know what needs to die, and you know how to reason with what ought to get to live. We can't just kill, son. That makes us…" He coughed up a splatter of blood. "That makes us the monsters."

"But Captain. They'll never believe me, never accept me as…"

The Captain sat up, blankets slipping off his skeletal frame. "You'd better believe they'll accept it. They'll do as I tell 'em to, by God. Open that door right now, and let them come in and hear it straight from me."

Rhett caught the Captain as he almost slumped over and guided him back onto his pillows. "This can't be good for you, Captain."

"You don't tell me my business, and I won't tell you yours. Now open that door."

Rhett arranged the man's blankets, straightened the new star on his own dusty shirt, threw back his shoulders, and unbolted the door. Jiddy burst through it, his hands turned into giant brown bear paws tipped in long black claws.

"This here sick room is off-limits, you little upstart shit!" Jiddy growled, getting closer to the bear than Rhett ever wanted to see. The other Rangers were behind him, six or seven men that Rhett knew but didn't much like. Troublemakers, he'd have pegged them. Dan and Sam followed, too, both wearing their badges and resting fingers lightly on their guns. Seeing them there, faces closed down and hard, bolstered Rhett and helped him keep his head high.

"I can still maintain control of my own goddamn outpost, Jiddy, you ass," the Captain said, his voice just as strong as ever, even if Rhett could see his hands trembling under the sheet.

"Sorry, Captain. As your number two man, I want to make sure your rules are followed," Jiddy said with a shit-eating grin that shouldn't have fooled anyone and certainly didn't escape the Captain.

"I'm glad to hear that, as I need you to continue that care for my rules when I'm passed on." Everybody interrupted him then to explain how he was going to be just fine, and he slashed at the air with a skeletal hand. "Oh, now don't pretend I'm going to pull through. You all know I'm for it and soon. So get everybody in here, quick and snappy, and listen up."

Rhett didn't budge from his place by the Captain's side, and Jiddy managed to squeeze around to the other side of the bed and pretend like he belonged there. Runners went out and fetched the other Rangers from their work and bunks. Milo and Virgil Scarsdale, the Captain's oldest and grouchiest Rangers, pressed up near Jiddy, giving Rhett a double stare of doom. In just a few months, the group had already changed, with some folks missing and some new faces popping up, fresh and un-scarred and still grinning. Rhett felt like he'd been gone a hundred years, and damn if the Captain didn't look like he'd lived through that much pain and sorrow since their last meeting.

"We all here? Good. Then I'm going to say my piece, and we got plenty of witnesses. I'm dying, boys, and I still got enough strength to pull the trigger if anybody wants to argue. Doc's doing the best he can, but we all know there's no magic that can stop a sand wyrm bite from taking its toll, so hold your tears and let's move on. It's my responsibility and my right to select my successor, and that man is Rhett Walker."

The room went so quiet you could hear the soft hiss of sand wyrm spit gnawing a hole in the Captain's side. No one said a word.

"Now I know you boys are all loyal, both to me and to your Ranger duties, and that means I know you'll all do your best to support your new Captain. If you haven't had the privilege of working with Rhett Walker before, you'll quickly learn that he's smart, well-trained, courageous, and will do anything to save a fellow Ranger. He's got a good head on his shoulders and will continue to lead you down the road of justice and protection to which we've all sworn our lives. Virgil and Milo, I want you to counsel him. Jiddy, you scout for him. Dan and Sam, you be his deputies. If you work together, I feel certain that you will continue the good work I've begun here. I know you'll keep Durango safe. For everybody."

When the room's silence grew chilly, Rhett removed his hat. "I don't reckon anybody can be half the man you are, Captain, but I'll do my very best."

The sound of Jiddy's spit hitting the floor caused more than a few guns to be silently drawn from their holsters.

The Captain shifted, his lip curling. "If you don't like it, Jiddy, you and your friends can head right on over to Haskell's outpost. He'll put up with insubordination, a lack of bathing habits, and unnecessary violence, but I didn't, and Rhett won't. Will you, Captain Walker?"

It took Rhett a moment to realize that the Captain, his Captain, had just asked him a question and called him . . . Captain.

He stood a little straighter, raised his chin a little higher, tucked his thumbs in his vest to let his badge catch the light.

"No, I don't reckon I will."

The Captain went into another cough just then, and Rhett turned to support him and hand him a bandanna. When the fit was over and Rhett stood back up, bloody fabric in hand, half the fellers in the room were gone, most notably including Jiddy and the Scarsdales. The Captain noticed, too.

"They're going to give you trouble, son. Most new Captains cut their teeth on hunting a monster, or maybe a big pack of Lobos. Looks like your first challenge will be winning over the weakest of your own men."

Rhett looked down at him. "Weakest? They never seemed weak to me."

"Their hearts are. Those men went to war too young and came back twisted. Right and wrong is only shades of gray. Their hearts are dark. They need a firm hand, a leader who won't back down but who can still listen to good advice. You reckon that's still you?"

Their eyes locked, and Rhett bit his goddamn lip to keep it from wobbling with feeling.

"I reckon that's always been me, Captain."

The Captain shook his head sadly. "You can't call me that anymore. I'm just Old Man Walker now. So go on and call your boys to supper and see if you can't bring 'em around. Might take joshing, might take hollerin', might take a few well-timed threats, but a barrel of liquor would help."

"I do believe they call that a wake, old man."

The Captain sighed, and it was like all the air and life went out of him as he sunk back down into the bed with a crackle of straw. "Well, don't wake me. I'm tired, and I'd like to rest. Man can't attend his own wake, anyway. It's undignified."

His papery eyelids fluttered down, his breathing shallow as he fell into a light sleep.

"Go on out, fellers," Rhett said, his voice low. "He needs rest."

Most everybody else cleared out, hats in hand. Dan and Sam stayed, shuffling up close to Rhett, their boots the loudest sound in the room.

"I'm sorry I can't do anything else," the doctor said, standing there looking awkward and small in a room recently cleared of fighting men, his white hands wrapped around the handle of his black bag. Rhett had completely forgotten he was there at all. "I'll leave laudanum for the pain. Just a drop on the tongue, as he needs it. You can't really overdo it, at this point. He's near the end. I'm so sorry."

Remembering his new role, Rhett held up a hand. "Wait. What do we owe you, doc?"

He had no money, but surely someone among the Rangers knew how such things worked.

The doc shook his head. "Nothing. We got a deal, me and the Rangers. Captain leaves me to mine, and I help out when someone's injured." Rhett could feel it now, a wobble in his belly as he shook the doctor's clammy hand.

"If I can ask, which I reckon I need to, as the next Captain: What are you?"

The doc shrugged. "Wendigo's the name they give it around here, although I'd rather you just called me Doc. I have the unfortunate need to feed on human flesh, but I'm averse to killing, so I do what I can with the patients I lose. I keep mostly to myself, in a small village a few miles northwest."

"You don't worry about him, he won't worry 'bout you," the Captain whispered.

"Fair enough, then," Rhett said, making a note to find out more about wendigos when the time was available. "Go on, then, Doc, with our thanks. Captain, you got any more such arrangements I need to know about?"

The Captain's hand flapped at a worn book sitting on the table, and Rhett took it, opening it up to see a whole bunch of letters and numbers that of course made no sense to him. Writing still made him angry and uncomfortable, so he handed it to Sam.

"Would you give it a look-through, let me know what's important, please, Sam?"

Sam smiled and took the book, flipping through it. "You know I'll help in any way I can, Rhett. Jiddy's liable to cause a ruckus, seems like."

Dan grunted. "If by 'ruckus,' you mean 'mutiny,' I agree. But I'll help, too." He gave a wistful grin. "Of all the people you've punched in the teeth, Jiddy deserves it the most. He's been unkind to me since the day I showed up. To you, too, I reckon. Nothing worse than a shifter who hates shifters."

Rhett smiled as he pictured it. "As long as he didn't turn into a bear and kill me, I reckon punching Jiddy would be mighty…"

"Cathartic?" Dan offered.

"Pleasant, more like."

"That, too."

"Y'all go on," Rhett said. "Make sure Conchita's got dinner ready with plenty of extra helpings, and rustle up a cask of booze, if you can find one. Make sure none of the fellers are skulking around, talking bad. Make sure Cora and Winifred are safe and Earl isn't getting into fights."

"What will you be doing, Captain?" Sam smiled like the morning and flicked Rhett's new badge, making him blush.

"I'm gonna sit here with the real Captain for a few minutes and try to make my hands stop shaking and make sure I don't upchuck in a spittoon."

They each patted him on a shoulder and left him there. Rhett's legs gave out a few moments later, and he landed on the corner of the Captain's bed, careful not to touch the man's feet and cause him pain. The world seemed to spin and land square on his head, heavier than a house. He was really Captain now? Him? The half-breed critter from nowhere? The newest Ranger? The Shadow with a destiny that had to be followed, regardless of what orders came down from...well, wherever the Captain got his orders? Hellfire, Rhett had a lot to learn. And now he was supposed to mosey over to some Rangers' meeting in a big city and sit at a table with Eugene Haskell and a bunch of other smug white fellers and try to remind them he was an equal when such a statement would just make them draw their guns?

"This is dumb as hell," he muttered, head in his hands.

"No it ain't, son."

He looked up. The Captain hadn't moved, hadn't opened his eyes. His breathing was shallow and quick, sometimes stopping for a good long while. A clicky whistle in the back of his throat made Rhett downright uncomfortable, but he would stare at those rough lips until they spoke again.

The Captain's desiccated tongue slipped out, licked, and he cleared his throat. "You're the only one strong and stubborn enough," he rasped.

Desperate for something to do, Rhett tipped his canteen onto his handkerchief and used it to gently pat water on the Captain's lips.

When the Captain spoke next, he sounded like he always had before, strong and certain.

"The Lord sent me an incomplete set of utensils, Rhett. He does it to everybody, just to see what we can make. The Scarsdales are too egotistical. Jiddy is ignorant and vulgar. Sam's too sweet. Dan's too spiritual and he hates white men too much. All the other men are inferior in their own ways, too. It comes down to you. I seen what's special in you, son. I seen you run into fights you can't win. I seen you sacrifice yourself for your friends without a thought. And you never hold it against nobody. You don't judge a man by what he looks like, but by how he treats his inferiors. You're a good man, the kind of man I tried to be, once I knew enough about the world to want to leave it better than I found it. I ain't saying it's gonna be easy, but it's the only road I see."

"But what if I fail, Captain?"

There were tears in Rhett's eyes now, for himself and for this good man moving on. With Monty, he'd barely had a moment to speak, to apologize, to beg. But here, it was just him and the Captain, his hand curling around the man's old bony fist and feeling those fingers cling tightly like Rhett was the only thing tethering him to this world.

"You can't fail, son. That's why I picked you. You won't settle for failure." He let out a sad, windy chuckle. "I figured you'd punch failure in the mouth, if it came to that."

"Yes, sir, I reckon I would."

Rhett moved to sit alongside the old man, his back against the wall. They sat there in the gloaming, in the silence, holding hands. They sat there when Conchita rang the bell and the building shuddered with boot stomps and filled with the rough talk of rougher men. They sat there as the whippoorwills began to call and the horses nickered their good nights across the yard. The old man's grip never lessened, and Rhett didn't think of letting go, either. No matter that his stomach grumbled, and no matter that his lips were parched. No matter that he was slowly falling asleep, his head sliding down the wall to rest near the Captain's wrinkled pate. The man was much diminished from what he'd been, but people were made to bounce back, to get stronger.

Sometime in the long, dark night, Rhett fell asleep in the Captain's bed.

When he woke up in the morning, the Captain was dead, his gnarled fingers gone cold in Rhett's hand.

CHAPTER
10

Rhett had to get himself back together. The new Captain of the Durango Rangers Las Moras Outpost couldn't be seen like this, with sobs jerking his body as he cried like a goddamn baby. He shook his bloodless fingers loose from the Captain's stiff fist and closed the old man's sightless eyes and went to stare at himself in a small, cracked mirror hanging over a ewer beside a man's shaving supplies. Rhett's face was gaunt, but it always had been. His eye was red from crying with a dark purple circle underneath from constantly troubled sleep, and his hair was starting to get spiky as it grew out. He found his hat on the floor and resettled it, mashing it down. He flicked water from the ewer onto his face, but it didn't do a damn thing. His mouth kept trembling, so he focused on firming it up. He straightened his shirt and vest, settled his gun belt at the right angle, and adjusted his kerchief over his gone eye.

The feller glaring back from the mirror didn't look one goddamn jot like a Captain, no matter what the badge said.

Although it hurt to do so, he looked at the Captain, his Captain, so small and shriveled in the bed. What about the man had given him such a respectable and imposing visage? Rhett couldn't grow facial hair, so that was out. He wasn't much for smoking, so that wouldn't work, either. But the Captain had worn a nice vest and a necktie, so Rhett murmured his apologies and dug a tie out of the heap of cloth draped over a chest. It slightly choked him, but he puffed out his chest and felt a little better. He could never be as great as the Captain had been, so he would have to be the best damn Captain he, Rhett Walker, could be.

Picking up the Captain's well-known Henry repeating rifle and slinging it over his shoulder as the Captain often had, Rhett took a deep breath and put his palm against the door to the hallway. The noises of the company at breakfast had been building all along, while Rhett privately grieved and prepared himself. But when he pushed the door open and walked down the hall, every boot step echoing, all the men of the Las Moras company stopped their eating and jawing to stare. Rhett wouldn't allow himself to quake or cave in or apologize or do anything that showed cowardice or an unCaptainish lack of confidence.

Chin up, mouth grimly set, the Captain's Henry in hand, he said, "I regret to inform you-all that our great Captain has passed in the night. He went quiet-like. Peaceful. I reckon he was asleep. I know I was. And I assure you that I will do my level best to lead this outpost of the Durango Rangers in his name and spirit, according to his wishes."

Rhett reckoned it was the best speech he'd ever made or would make in his life, and he felt pretty good about it up until Jiddy stood, chair slamming back on the wood floor behind him with a clatter.

"That man killed the Captain!" he shouted.

Rhett was surprised as hell to see that Jiddy was pointing at him.

"Me? Hell no! You can ask the doc, Jiddy. The Captain…

he was a great man, but he was human. He couldn't make it through. The wounds were too much. You can't think I would...that I...Hell. C'mon, Jiddy. Even you ain't that dumb."

Jiddy pulled his revolver and aimed it at Rhett's heart. "You calling me a liar?"

"No, fool. I'm calling you dumb."

Jiddy pulled the trigger, and Rhett felt the hot punch of a bullet in his arm, grateful that the other man was as bad a shot as Rhett had always suspected him of being.

Every man stood. Every hand held a weapon. The air in the room went still and thick enough to bite. Rhett found Sam, Dan, Winifred, and Earl bunched together at one end of the table, just as armed and angry as the rest of the Rangers, most of whom were white and human. Rhett did not reckon himself a smart man, but he also figured intelligence wasn't what would get an outnumbered crew out of a situation like this one.

"You were there last night when the Captain declared Rhett his successor," Dan said in a level, matter-of-fact voice. "Jiddy has just shot the acting Captain. Let's see a show of hands if you think Jiddy was right to do so."

Jiddy glared around the room, and hands went up one by one. Both of the Scarsdales, Jiddy himself, and at least half of the remaining fellers. It was a pretty even split.

"Well, then," Dan said, and quick as a blink, he reached into the holster of the man beside him, whipped out the feller's pistol, and shot Jiddy in the chest.

Rhett flung up the Captain's Henry and popped off two shots at Virgil and Milo Scarsdale before he was dragged to the ground as a hail of bullets whispered overhead. It was Winifred who had pinned him, and she clambered off him and whispered, "Go for feet and knees. Most of them are human." She had a knife in hand, and she slammed it down into the boot of the nearest man, who screamed and fell over blubbering like a baby.

Gunshots peppered the air and pinged off the wood walls. Cries of rage and pain gulped and squawked, and Rhett's vision went razor sharp as he looked for the familiar spurs of Sam's boots. Sam was just as human as the Captain had been, and any one of these bullets could land him in the same place: dead.

Winifred was stabbing feet and legs and tossing guns aside as their owners fell, and Rhett used the relative cover to crawl under the table to Sam's boots. He could tell by Sam's stance and the sounds above that the feller was in the heat of the gun-fight, not paying any attention to just how easily he could get hurt. He tugged on Sam's pant leg and got a pistol in the face.

"Get down here, fool," he hissed, batting it away.

"Fight's up here," Sam growled, looking so determined and dangerous Rhett could've swooned.

"Fight's wherever you take it," Rhett said, and he shot Virgil Scarsdale in the knee from under the table and landed the old son of a bitch on his ass.

Another bullet caught Rhett somewhere in the back, but in a meaty place that didn't stop him from shooting Milo Scarsdale in the thigh. Up above, Sam cried out in pain and crumpled over, falling right where Rhett had wanted him but bearing a red splotch on his shoulder that Rhett didn't like a bit.

"Winifred! Cover him!" he called.

When the girl let up on foot-stabbing to crawl over, Rhett dropped the Henry, took a pistol in each hand, and popped up where Sam had just been, shooting every goddamn traitor who'd raised his hand for Jiddy.

His aim was pretty good, and for all that he took three or

four bullets, he killed or hobbled three or four fellers in a row up until something exploded against his face. He dropped both of his guns and staggered back. When the red blur cleared off and he stopped seeing stars, he found Jiddy's hand wrapped in his neck cloth, the man's fist reared back for another punch. There was something shiny over Jiddy's knuckles. Rhett's hands went up, but too late. Well, shit. Silver knuckles. No wonder it hurt so goddamn much when Jiddy popped him in the nose.

He wanted to punch Jiddy back, but he was at a disadvantage and gushing blood like a well pump, so Rhett threw himself backward, yanking Jiddy with him. As the man fell, his beard seemed to spread over his face, the silver knuckles dropping as his thick fingers sprouted claws and bristly black fur. Rhett was on his back now, Jiddy's weight getting heavier and heavier as the ass-hole turned into a bear. Rhett scrabbled at his belt for his Bowie knife and punched it right up into Jiddy's gut.

The bear just laughed.

Through teeth half turned into fangs, Jiddy growled, "You ain't my Captain."

Rhett scrabbled the knife up, sawing through whatever Jiddy had for guts. "You self-hating son of a bitch. You hate me because I'm a monster, too, or because you know I'm the better man?"

"You're a mongrel..." The words came out jumbled as Jiddy's nose stretched out into a snout.

"You ain't all white, you bear-changing son of a bitch, so you might as well stop pretending." Rhett's knife stopped, scraping up against bone, and Jiddy's mouth snapped open in a bear's scream.

Rhett's arms were trembling now, holding up the bulk of a bear getting near to the size of a horse, the butt of the knife's hilt starting to press into his own belly. Rhett let go with his other hand and scrabbled for a gun but couldn't find anything under the table except sticky blood. His fingers tugged on Sam's boot, and Sam ducked back under the table.

"Gun," Rhett muttered.

"What the hellfire? Is that—"

"GUN, Sam."

Sam put the gun to the side of Jiddy's bear head as the black snout snarled and bristled.

"Do it," Rhett urged.

The gun went off, and Jiddy's head splattered all over Rhett, half its face gone. The mouth was still screeching, though, and the other eye was mad as hell.

"Give it here."

Sam put the pistol in Rhett's hand, wrapped his fingers around it, and Rhett pushed it against the side of Jiddy's chest and shot him straight through. The bear didn't turn to sand, though, just fell over sideways, pawing at the quickly healing hole. It should've been easy enough to hit the critter's heart, but it was Jiddy, so maybe the damn thing was smaller than usual.

Rhett sat up, drawing a full breath, and shot Jiddy in the face again. What was left was half bear, half human, and mostly ground meat. But Rhett wasn't done. He would keep shooting until he found Jiddy's goddamn heart—for disrespecting him and the Captain both. He crawled over to where he'd left the Captain's Henry, dragged it back, put it up against Jiddy's chest, and pulled the trigger.

Finally!

The man-bear exploded in gray sand that filled the room like smoke. A few of the fellers coughed, and the gunshots stopped for a moment as they got their bearings. Rhett coughed, covered his mouth and nose with his neck cloth, and stood up holding the Henry and breathing hard through his mouth as his nose tried to knit up from being split open with silver.

"Anybody who wants to live can drop his goddamn gun," he said.

Milo Scarsdale, just about riddled with holes but running on anger, shot Rhett right in the belly, twice, before his gun clicked, empty. The shots went straight through, and for a moment, Rhett felt the air whistle straight through him. Then it just hurt, the way Rhett's guts wriggled around and re-formed, but Rhett didn't let that show. He didn't even bother to put the Henry to his shoulder as he shot Milo in the gut. The old man fell to the ground beside his brother, Virgil, blubbering and pissing himself in a satisfying sort of way.

Rhett looked around again. There wasn't a man there without wounds, and even Winifred had a new gash along her hairline, still dripping blood.

"Anybody else want to take a goddamn shot? Because I can do this all day, and I reckon most of you fellers can't."

One feller shot him in the leg, and then another shot and missed, and then some complete fool led a charge in from the porch, and Rhett roared, "Let's get out of here!"

He fell to his knees, rammed his pistols home, snatched up the Henry and his knife from the pile of sand, and bolted down the hall to the Captain's old room. He could hear his friends behind him, but he didn't bother to look back to see how many there were. Despite all the death he'd wrought, there were still more of Jiddy's boys than his own, and he didn't like the odds. The ones who hadn't raised their hands—well, they'd been shooting at him, too, the cowards. It's not like he was going to win over men who wanted him dead, anyway. Better to get the hell out than keep fighting a bunch of assholes he could never lead.

Bullets pinged off the floor and walls, and the glass window at the end of the hall shattered. Rhett felt a bullet punch into the back of his leg, cussed at it, and kept on clambering. Once inside the Captain's room, he dove sideways. Winifred, then Dan, then Sam scuttled in after him, and he put his foot against the door and prepared to kick it shut once Earl had joined them. But Earl didn't arrive. Rhett had seen him at breakfast, his hat down over his hungover eyes and his plate full of extra bacon. But he'd lost sight of the Irishman in the battle, and now he was notably absent.

"Did donkey-boy go out the back door?" Rhett asked.

"Don't think so. But I didn't see sand, neither." Sam was up against the wall now, teeth clenched as he held a kerchief to his shoulder wound.

"Cora is in the wagon, at least," Winifred said.

Rhett peeked out the Captain's window to confirm but didn't dare make his head visible to anyone outside. Jiddy might've lived through having half his face blown off, if he hadn't taken a bullet in the heart, but Rhett wasn't interested in trying such a strategy for himself, considering he was already full of holes and could feel each separate bullet singing its wretched discontent in his flesh. He couldn't see the wagon, but the horrible thought occurred to him that some of Jiddy's men, some of his own Ranger brethren, might mean the girl harm.

"Anybody hurt bad?"

Dan snorted. "Just a few bullet wounds and stabbings."

"As long as you're not complaining."

"Oh, I'm complaining. About those traitorous cowards too proud to call a brown man Captain." Dan looked down, poked a finger through a bloody bullet hole in his shirt. "Days like this, I wish I shifted into something dangerous."

Rhett dusted gray sand out of his hat brim. "Yeah, well, that didn't do Jiddy much good, did it? Look, you-all stay here. I'm going out there for Earl."

Winifred gave him the look she almost always gave him—at least during daytime. The one that said he was a born fool hell-bent on dying young. "You're going to walk into a room full of men who want nothing more than to see you dead, all to save a man with a death wish who doesn't even like you?"

Rhett stood, feeling a little wobbly. The knitting holes in his belly felt heavy, and the fresh new scars pulled and burned across his legs and back and arm. Everything he had hurt, including his heart.

"I most certainly am, and if it's any comfort, I'd do the same for you. You-all are my posse, and whether or not those shit-heads out there acknowledge it, I'm the Captain. I'm gonna kill what needs to die and save what must be saved."

He stomped over and picked up the Captain's metal piss pan off the floor. It might've once been used to pan for gold, and then it had been part of a dying man's sick room, but now it was dry as a bone, about the size for making a pie, and he hefted it and looked around the room a bit more. There was a bible on the bedside table, a smallish and beat-up thing that he only recognized thanks to the gold cross on front and the red ribbon sticking out of it like a snake's tongue. He placed the bible in the piss pan, opened up his shirt, and slipped the whole thing under his binder.

"What the hell is that?" Sam asked, looking up from his wound as Rhett rebuttoned his shirt and arranged his vest over the slight lump.

"The only thing between me and a pile of sand, I reckon," Rhett said.

He checked his guns and found fewer bullets than he pre-ferred, but the Henry was still half-full, probably.

"You want me to go see to the horses?" Dan asked. "Outside looks clear."

"Those fools are probably planning on barging in here," Rhett said. "Without a leader, it's what a damn goat would do. Just keep butting heads. Go on and sort our ponies, if you can. We might not have enough time to saddle up, though. Maybe throw the saddles in the wagon, if there's a chance."

Dan nodded once, wrenched the window open, and slithered out.

"What do you want us to do?" Winifred asked.

Rhett gave her a hard look that brooked no refusal. "Keep Sam safe, and your own self as well. Once Dan has your ponies ready, get out and ride west, the way we came. We'll find our trail to Trevisan once we're all out of harm's way."

"But you're the Captain," Sam said, wincing as Winifred helped him stand.

"And as far as I'm concerned, I've got the better posse. Wait until I'm in the hall and they're focused on me before you run, you hear?" Winifred and Sam nodded, and Rhett touched each of his weapons again. Gun, gun, knife. The Henry was in his right hand and ready to fire. Far as he reckoned, there were maybe ten fellers still in the dining room who could fight. And they'd be fighting to kill.

Rhett hadn't lived with the Rangers long enough to learn their ways, to absorb whatever tactics the Captain taught. His fights with them—well, they'd all gone cattywampus, and Rhett had used his wits and hot-headed bravado to singlehandedly save their ungrateful asses. What would they expect him to do, now that the tides had turned? Stand, fight, or run?

He walked to Sam, stood close enough to hear the man's labored breathing.

"What are they expecting?" he whispered.

In the peculiar silence, Sam gave a small chuckle. "They're expecting to kick your ass. Probably hanging back, seeing as how there's nobody smart or brave left to lead the charge. You seem like the kind of man to take advantage of that."

Rhett's grin was a slow, dangerous thing. "I am that kind of man, yes. Wish me luck, Sam."

Before he could think twice about it, before Sam could answer, he kissed Sam, brief and hard and glancing. He didn't hang around to see what Sam thought about it, neither, just went for the door, threw it open so hard it banged against the wall, and screamed a ululating war cry as he flung himself into the hallway, guns up and aiming to kill.

CHAPTER
11

Rhett expected a pile of bullets, and that's exactly what he got. It took the boys a minute to catch up, though, so he leaped onto the long table and shot the Henry at each man in turn as he stalked along its length. He took two bullets that he felt, but they no longer bothered him, so long as they went into meat. Everything hurt but he felt nothing. Nothing but rage. His aim wasn't ideal, but the men he shot fell over no matter where he shot them. Humans were like that, he'd noticed.

When he ran out of bullets, he dropped the Henry on the table and went for his pistols. Three fellers made a break for the door, and although Rhett winged one of them in the back, they didn't stop running.

Rhett was the only man still standing, high up on the long table. The Rangers who were left squirmed on the wood boards, their breakfast forgotten and splattered all over the walls, along with more blood than any reasonable person wanted to see at a meal. The table shook with every step as Rhett walked to where he remembered Virgil and Milo falling side by side. When he looked down, he saw Virgil slumped against the wall, a kerchief around his busted knee. Beside him, Milo had clearly fled the mortal plane; a good gut shot would do that to a man who wasn't made of sterner stuff.

"You shoulda chose better sides," Rhett observed, looking down.

"Go to hell."

Virgil fumbled for his pistol, and Rhett didn't budge. When the old man's hammer clicked harmlessly on an empty chamber, Rhett snorted.

"Thought you were loyal to the Captain, Scarsdale."

"You ain't the Captain, cur."

"The old Captain said different. You were there."

Virgil spit, his tobacco a brown spot of slime mixing with his brother's blood.

"There ain't no proof of that."

Rhett couldn't stop chuckling. "You forget. Only the man who walks away gets to tell the story." And he shot Virgil in the chest, easy as pie.

Rhett didn't like what happened next. It reminded him all too much of those burned-out villages that left folks like his mama and brother alone and on the run. But he also understood enough about the world to know that if he left any of the turncoat Rangers alive, they'd rain down hell on his head for the rest of his days. They'd join up with Haskell or head back to the main office, wherever it was, and the whole damn territory would be hunting the Shadow and his ragtag band of supposedly turncoat murderers.

The Captain had understood Rhett and his destiny. These fellers just saw an uppity Injun claiming what they figured was theirs.

He reloaded his guns from a dead man's bullet pouch and walked around the table, stopping at each feller still drawing breath.

"Would you call me Captain?" he asked the first one.

The man spit on Rhett's boot and took a bullet for his trouble.

The second man he asked called him a cocksucker, and he took a bullet, too.

Three of the fellers were too far gone to answer. One just whispered, "Kill me." That feller had a hole in his head and wasn't gonna last long anyway, so Rhett obliged him. Of all the men left, of the ones who could speak, not a one admitted he would call Rhett Captain.

Not a one survived.

When Rhett got around to the final corner, he saw a flash of the familiar faded red he was looking for, so he jumped down to move a big dead feller aside and found Earl cowering, covered in somebody else's blood and shaking. Earl looked up at Rhett, his eyes white around with terror.

"I never killed anybody before," he said.

"There's a first time for everything," Rhett said. "They'd have done the same to you. Hell, looks like they tried pretty hard."

Earl touched the red splotch on his arm. "Never been shot before, face on and point blank, neither. I could see his eyes, Rhett. They were full of hate. So I . . . I killed him."

Rhett exhaled and shrugged. "You get used to it."

"That's just it, lad. Don't think I will. It's a sin to kill. Sure, I had many a sin to my name, but nothing like this. I saw his eyes go empty, heard his last words. Not even a priest within a hundred miles, I bet. No one to hear his confession."

"Reckon he didn't feel like confessing. Considering the name he called me and the bullet he put in my own hide, he didn't strike me as a religious man."

"He couldn't confess, even if he wanted to. Even if he needed to. He died too fast. But I'll be heard, by God. So listen well. Bless me, Father, for I have sinned. Oh, I have sinned many and much, and my last confession was so long ago I can't even remember it. Some firebox of a church in New Amsterdam. I've lusted, and I've drank, and I've gambled, and I pretty much met the golden calf I was warned about, and I smiled at him. And I've taken the Lord's name in vain."

"Well, goddamn, boy, who hasn't?" Rhett was feeling impatient and knew that the longer they waited around, the braver the fellers outside would get.

"Every moment of my life is like being trapped in a box, lad. I can't get out. It's dark in here and dreary, and my brother's always telling me I failed him, and the drink's not enough to take it away. I wake in the night crying, feeling my every loss, my every defeat. Anger's been the only thing keeping me going, and I thought it was you I was angry at, but it was me. It was always me."

"That's bullshit, and you know it. You just got to get up and keep walking until things get better."

Earl grabbed Rhett's pant leg and yanked, his eyes going wide and desperate. "I'm not done, and you'll listen, lad! I swear you will! Somebody has to hear it, and since the worst of my sins happened after I met you, you'll damn well take in every word. I remember what happened in Buckhead, and I would do it again. So tell that to God, when you see him, will you?"

"I'm doing my best not to have that happen to either of us, donkey-boy, so get up and let's get the hell out of here."

Earl shook his head, fat tears squeezing out of his green eyes. "I can't."

"Well, I'll help you, then." Rhett held out his hand.

Earl clenched his teeth and closed his eyes and shook his

head harder. "No, lad. That's just it. It's not that I can't get up. It's that I don't want to. That I don't deserve to."

"Deserving's got nothing to do with it. You just got to—"

"I'm sorry, Rhett. I'm done. This will be my last sin, and a mortal one it is. God will understand."

Before Rhett could ask him what he was sorry for this time, Earl put a pistol to his chest and pulled the trigger. In the silence, the gun was nearly deafening, and the air filled with silvery-gold sand. The pistol fell with a thump, and Earl's clothes fluttered softly down.

Rhett scrabbled at his eye with his fist, fighting the dust and the tears all at once. It hit him like a silver bullet to the gut and left him gasping. He couldn't grasp it. Couldn't understand what he'd just seen.

"Goddammit, donkey-boy," Rhett gasped, surprised at the rage and sadness that welled up in his chest. "I didn't like you, and you didn't like me, but you would've called me Captain. We could've found a good place for you. I can't believe you would do it, I can't..."

Falling to his knees, he plunged his fingers into the pile of sand and squeezed the slippery grains in bloody hands that couldn't quite grasp enough.

"Goddammit, Earl! Why'd you do it? Why'd you...Didn't you know...Didn't you know people cared about your dumb ass? Goddammit. You never said...I didn't know...I mean, you were sad, and we knew it, but...hellfire!"

Rhett carefully opened the pouch around his neck and poured in some of the golden sand, wishing for something more concrete to carry with him. Earl's bag was beside his clothes, and Rhett picked it up and poked through it, but all he found were an empty wine bottle, a ball of old cheese, and the jar that held Earl's brother's ashes. Not knowing what else to do,

Rhett opened it up, scooped in Earl's ashes, and tucked it back in the bag, along with all the pistols and knives it could hold. If he was leaving here without the full backing of the goddamn Rangers, he was going to take every weapon he could. Even for monsters, life came with a one-way ticket, and he wasn't ready to get on that dusty coach.

After reloading his pistols with more spare bullets from the dead Rangers, Rhett stood and surveyed the scene. At least Conchita had managed to get away. He hoped.

"I'm coming out," he called, standing just inside the open door.

Far as he could figure, there were at least three Rangers still walking, maybe more if anybody had slept in, finished eating early, or taken to hiding in the outhouse. He hadn't heard any gunshots besides Earl's and his own in quite some time, which meant his posse hopefully had the ponies ready to go and had alerted Cora to, well, whatever the hell had just happened.

There was no answer to his shout, but just in case, he grabbed a hat off the nearest Ranger, slung it up on Conchita's switch broom, and waggled it in the doorway. Nobody shot at it, which he took as a good sign. Readjusting the piss pan under his binder and glad so far nobody had been able to test its ability to stop bullets, he stepped out into the dull shine of a mostly gloomy day. Every hair on his body was up and quivering, every inch of him sang with pain, and the air was filled with a deep disquiet. Some of the excitement had sloughed off, and he ached in every bone, felt the tug of every inch of healing flesh. A deep, painful thrum in the meat of his buttock suggested that at least one silver bullet had found him, and somebody would probably have to dig it out, and soon.

Still no one shot at him. Heart in his throat and et up with worry, he looked to Cora's wagon, which was turned the way he'd requested with Samson already up in his traces, calmly waiting. There was no sign of Cora, though. Then, out by the pony corral, Rhett saw the last goddamn thing he wanted to see: Dan and Winifred with their hands up, and a roughed-up Ranger with a rifle against Sam Hennessy's spine. Two more Rangers—or ex-Rangers, by Rhett's count, and young, scared ones at that—had their guns turned on Dan and Winifred. Except for these last two, they were all staring at him.

"You drop your guns and hand over that Captain's star, or your friends die," the leader said.

Rhett racked his brain but couldn't put a name to the man's snarling, ugly face.

"Are you even a Ranger?" he asked, handing over neither the star nor the guns.

The man poked Sam's back with the rifle, and Sam cried out, wrenching Rhett's heart.

"Hell yes, I'm a Ranger. Rode with the Captain for ten years. Who the hell are you?"

"I'm the man he wanted to be Captain. I rode with him for a couple of months. I killed the siren at Reveille and the Cannibal Owl, up north in the mountains. Also took down some Lobos that had captured the Captain and most of the Rangers. But I don't remember seeing you around."

"Drop your guns and shut up," the man growled.

"Don't believe I will. Now where were you when I was saving the Captain's ass these last few months?"

"I was on patrol, you little shit, and even though he didn't do a thing to deserve it, I will blow Sam Hennessy's spine out of his belly if you don't drop those guns."

Rhett's eye flickered to Dan and Winifred. Winifred looked furious, but Dan just winked. Which was just like the coyote, to go making fun when shit was serious. Dan's eyes flicked down to the gun pointed at...his belly. So these new Rangers didn't know that Dan and Winifred were coyotes, which meant they most likely didn't know Rhett was a skinwalker, too.

The head man cocked his rifle. "Last chance to drop the guns. I don't wanna hurt Sam, but I will."

Rhett put the Henry down gently and was just reaching for his pistols when a cold shadow swooped overhead. Considering how big it was, he didn't have to look up to know that there was only one critter in the area that could throw so much shade.

"Holy shit! A dragon!" he hollered.

When the Ranger looked up for just a second, Rhett whipped out his pistols and shot the feller. His aim was off, but he got him in the thigh, and the man fell to the ground hugging his leg, his rifle forgotten. The other fellers popped off their shots, but Dan and Winifred were already moving in for the kill. Sam staggered and fell to the ground, and Rhett hurried to his side to make sure he hadn't actually taken a bullet.

"You little—" the Ranger started from the ground, but Rhett shot him in the chest without a second thought and kneeled by Sam.

"Did they get you, Sam? You gonna be okay?"

He helped Sam sit up and kinda cradled the man in a way that felt both enormously awkward and fantastically intimate. Sam looked up at him, face streaked with grit and blood, and smiled that sunny smile that made everything better.

"Just the bullet in the shoulder and a twisted ankle, I reckon."

They just stared at each other for a long moment while Dan and Winifred killed the other two Rangers with their own pistols. Cora landed nearby and huffed smoke like a question mark.

"Did we get them all?" Rhett asked. "Looks like Cora's hungry."

Dan and Winifred looked at one another, and Dan nodded, shucked his clothes, and became a coyote. The coyote sniffed the ground and took off for the chain of outbuildings at a gallop. Rhett inspected Sam's bullet wound with the tenderness he would show a newborn baby and determined that the bullet had gone in one side and out the other, leaving a nice, clean hole. He was so accustomed to his own bullet wounds closing up that it felt right peculiar to gently pluck Sam's shirt away from the bleeding wound and stuff his own kerchief over the hole that was making no attempt to heal itself.

Winifred kneeled, too, but a respectful distance away from Sam. "Rhett, did you take any damage?"

He shrugged and wiggled, hunting for pain. "Just twenty bullets or so, some in and some out. Reckon there's a silver bullet in my buttock. Damn thing's rattling around but won't quite heal up. Another ugly scar."

"Your scars aren't ugly, Rhett," Sam said softly. His hand landed on Rhett's.

"I'll leave you to it," Winifred said, standing with a knowing smirk and walking back over to the half-saddled ponies.

"I don't know, Sam," Rhett said, feeling a flush creep up. "Nobody much prizes mangled eyes, far as I can tell."

"Then they're not looking hard enough. We all got scars. You just wear yours closer to the surface than most. I'm gonna have a fine one from this damn bullet. Cora can fix me up, right?"

Rhett nodded. "Yep. She's handy with that sort of thing. I broke my leg plum in half once, and she sorted it back, good as new."

"Did you like being with her?" Sam asked, real low.

"I...I got other things on my mind right now. You, for example."

Rhett was getting pretty good at looking into Sam's eyes, his heart racing and his skin tingling. For his part, Sam did not seem to mind.

Dan walked up, pants on and slipping his bloodied shirt over his arms. "All I found was Conchita, and she's got no quarrel. Everyone else is dead. All the Rangers. And I found this."

Looking pained and sorrowful, he held up Earl's rust-red shirt, once the only beacon that drew Rhett back to humanity. It looked sad and empty now, silvered with sand. The stains of wine and grease dotted it, and that simple reminder of Earl's last moments was like a screw turning painfully in Rhett's heart.

"One of the Rangers must've got him," Dan said.

Rhett hated how much relief he felt, hearing someone else say it. It wasn't a pretty lie, but it was prettier than the goddamn truth. Rhett owed it to Earl to never let the others know what had really happened.

"He didn't deserve that," Sam said.

"Hell no, he didn't."

"Help me up, will you, Rhett? We got work to do. Folks can't see...what's left of this place. They wouldn't understand."

Rhett stood and helped Sam to his feet. The three men shared the kind of look that Rhett figured a feller took to the grave, the kind of look that said they were going to do something down and dirty and necessary, and there was no going back once it was done.

"We got to burn it, then," Rhett said.

Dan and Sam nodded their agreement, but like Rhett was the slow one just catching up.

"But first, we take everything we need. We load up that wagon, maybe take another. Bullets, guns, food, magic shit. Clothes that ain't covered in Ranger blood and shot full of holes. And we bury the Captain."

"No!"

Rhett and Dan turned in surprise to stare at Sam, who looked stricken at first but firmed it up into confidence.

"Rangers don't get buried, they get burned. We burn him with the rest. It's what he would've wanted."

"You're right," Dan said. "He would."

"Then let's get to looting and start setting fires," Rhett said, feeling the tug on his belly from the east, already pulling him back on the trail. "We still got a lich to kill."

It was right pretty, the sight of a fire that big. When they'd burned Reveille on top of the siren's husband, Rhett had felt a profound sense of waste and loss, like maybe that half-built little town could've found finer folks to run it. But considering what had passed that morning at breakfast, Rhett knew that the best of the Rangers had left the earthly plane with the Captain, and the dregs that were left would've brought no good to the world. They were like a pack of dogs turned wild by the loss of their master, and no one else could've taken them in hand. Rhett knew they would've spread only violence across the land. He knew that putting down those beasts meant other, more peaceful folk could go on living.

Their hate—for monsters, for Injuns, for anything other— was like rabies, a thing that spread man to man and did more destruction than any one feller could ever do alone. It was, like all hatred, sprung from fear. The world needed fewer men like that with power and guns. For his part, Rhett was glad to take on the burden of fighting them. But he still wondered, not for the first time, if maybe he wasn't the most dangerous thing around, and whether that was actually a good thing or not.

They stood far away from the fire, although the wagons and

horses were farther off still. Sam, Dan, Winifred, Cora, and Rhett, who held a glass jar under one arm. At Rhett's urging, Conchita had taken what she wanted from the larder and set off in a packed-up wagon with a loaded gun, fast as two stout geldings could pull her. They'd looted, and Rhett reckoned he'd never feel anything but slimy, rootling through a feller's pockets and saddlebags. He'd found all sorts of Ranger correspondence in the Captain's bureau, but he'd left it all to burn. If the Captain's men, hearing it from his own mouth, couldn't accept Rhett as the new Captain, why the hell would the head fellers back east take him on? And that was before they learned what had befallen the outpost. No, better to let it burn. Better to let anyone in charge think all the Rangers had gone down in flames. If pressed, Rhett's little posse was still officially out scouting, Captain's orders.

The Captain's badge went right into Rhett's pouch. He couldn't wear it. He couldn't tell anybody the truth of what the old man had entrusted him to do. But he could keep it with him always to help remember another fine man who had died fighting the good fight. From now on, Rhett would be a Ranger Scout, even if he knew in his heart he was the goddamn Captain. He'd found his own badge still on the Captain's side table and would continue to wear it with pride.

"It's right pretty," Sam said, sounding all hangdog. "For a pyre."

Rhett squeezed Sam's shoulder. "A pyre should be pretty. It's got the best fuel."

"The Captain was a good man." This from Dan, whose face was hard, set in lines like it'd been carved from wood.

"Jiddy wasn't," Rhett admitted. "Never was too fond of them Scarsdale boys, neither."

"I reckon the fellers would've followed you if not for those three. They were trouble before you ever showed up. I don't like to speak ill of the dead, but Virgil caught me..." Sam trailed off and fidgeted about. "Well, doing something he didn't like, once...and he about thrashed me bloody."

Seeing the red of Sam's face, Rhett had a pretty good idea what Virgil had caught him doing, and he wondered briefly if the other guilty party was currently on fire, too, or if it had been someone already long gone. Rangers seemed to die at a fast clip, and Rhett at least reckoned these fellers knew what they were in for when they signed up for the job. Monsters were everywhere in Durango, whether they wore human skin or showed their true colors on the outside.

"Then good riddance," Rhett said. "I can't abide rudeness. And there's nothing ruder than a feller who don't like somebody for all the wrong reasons." He looked down at the jar in his hands and sighed. "Speaking of rude fellers, anybody know how the Irish do their funerals? I scraped up as much of donkey-boy as I could and put most of him in with his brother's remains, and it feels like somebody ought to say something or sing something or, I don't know, get drunk and yell at me."

"I know the Irish like to sing," Sam said. "But I don't know any of their songs."

Much to Rhett's surprise, Winifred's voice rang loud in the valley, rising over the crackle of the fire. Rhett had heard the song before, something about amazing grace. They'd sung it in the church in Gloomy Bluebird, from time to time. It didn't sound particularly Irish to him, but it did sound sad and talked a good bit about being lost and a wretch, which he figured Earl could relate to, wherever he was now. Winifred had a fine voice, sweet and tremulous, and Rhett took off his hat and held it over his heart. Sam and Dan did the same. Cora crept up beside Rhett, took the jar from him, and said something before throwing the sand into the wind, as she had with her grandfather. When Winifred's song came to a close, Rhett cleared his throat.

"Earl, you were a vexful feller. From the first time I saw you, I knew you were gonna be trouble, and you did not disappoint. But you taught me a lesson I sorely needed, and for that I'll be eternally grateful. You had a fine sense of humor, and a love of good fun. I won't say you were a pleasant companion, but you were stubborn and loyal, and that goes a far piece. Wherever you are, I hope you found your brother Shaunie, and I hope between the two of you, you found a bottle of something to celebrate with. I hope you find what you were looking for, whatever it is. I hope you find peace."

"Amen," Sam murmured.

But Rhett still felt antsy. "What about the Captain? Shouldn't we say something for him, too?"

Dan stepped forward, to Rhett's surprise. He was in his Ranger get-up, patched-up navy shirt and butternut pants, his hands folded in front of him. "The Captain took me in when I was in a dark place. My heart was filled with revenge, but he saw light in the darkness. He called me useful, said it would be a sin to squander such aptitude. He pulled me back from the edge of a cliff, and today I'm glad I never found what waited at the bottom of that chasm. He stood up for me, fought for me, defended me. When Jiddy tried to beat me, the Captain struck him in the face with his quirt. That's when I gave him my allegiance, because if a white man will strike a mostly white man for the sake of a brown man, that means something. I am sorry he is gone. For myself, and for the world. His Rangers were something more because he was something more. Without him, they became squabbling children, but squabbling children with many bullets. What happened this morning was justice.

155

Many lives will be spared because those men did not ride forth, empty of judgment and kindness. Any man who looks at me and sees an animal instead of a man deserves to die like an animal. May the Captain rest in peace, and may the rest of his Rangers haunt this valley, forever denied what they seek." He spit on the ground, turned, and walked toward the horses.

"Well, shit, Dan. Tell us how you really feel," Rhett muttered, but he watched Dan check the saddles and stare grimly into the fire and realized that for all that Dan had tried to teach him, the man had revealed very little about himself. Now that they understood each other better, Rhett owed it to Dan to treat him less like an annoyance and more like a goddamn equal. He realized, to his own consternation, that he'd fallen into the same trap and had seen Dan as less than a person somehow. The flames felt hot on his cheeks, and he followed Dan to the horses with the others in his wake.

"So where'd he find you, Dan?" he asked.

Dan looked up and gave his old, cocky grin. "Sneaking up to kill him. I'd found the remains of a band of skinwalkers, or so I thought. Followed the horses here and planned to take down the Captain after dark. But Jiddy found me, and when I confronted the Captain, he tried to convince me that it had been a band of Lobos, which had recently preyed upon another tribe. Gave me directions to where he'd left the survivors, and I went there myself and saw that he'd given the Lobo horses to the band, plus their coin. I realized that maybe the Rangers, his Rangers at least, weren't what I'd been told."

The horses milled uneasily in their paddock, pricking their ears and snorting at the unwelcome invasion of the fire's smoke. There had to be a hundred of 'em just now, divided into three pens for the Rangers' regular mounts, secondary mounts, and miscellaneous broncs, mules, and unrideable beasts. Dan had two halters in hand and slipped into the main pen, whickering to his chestnut and selecting another chestnut, considering he'd given one of his horses away. Ragdoll met Rhett at the fence, butting his shoulder with her long nose for a proper rub. He looked over the herd, hunting for the sort of horse that would suit him, now that Puddin' was gone.

His gaze landed on the Captain's mount, a gelded unicorn named Big Bastard, called BB. BB was a sturdy, friendly, courageous critter, at least seventeen hands and built like a brick shithouse. Rhett hated to think of him roaming free on the prairie, which is what would happen to any horses they didn't take. Wild unicorns wouldn't accept him, since his horn and balls were gone, and wild horses probably wouldn't cotton to him, either. Rhett knew what it was like to have a foot in both worlds and a friendly smile in neither.

"Dan, you reckon anyone will complain if I take on BB here?" he asked.

Dan shook his head. "He ain't a chestnut, so you'll see no complaint from me."

"The Captain would've wanted you to have him," Sam said. "He'd want BB to be with you. He's a Captain's mount, sure enough."

Rhett jogged out to the barn and brought an armful of halters, dumping them on the ground. As he waded into the first-string pen, Ragdoll was hot on his heels, nudging him with her nose as if to suggest he didn't need another pony. When he reached BB, the great beast blinked down at him with long, white eyelashes and gentle, intelligent dark eyes. He was one of the finest mounts Rhett had ever seen, and his dappled white coat and elegant lion's tail never seemed to get dirty, or maybe the dirt just magically fell off.

"What do you say, feller? You want to go on an adventure?"

The unicorn seemed to take the question seriously, so Rhett held out a sugar cube from the Captain's personal stash. BB ate the offering and whuffed as if to suggest he'd think about it, and Rhett slipped the halter over his head and led him to the gate. BB followed willingly with Ragdoll trying to nudge ahead, and soon both horses were tied up side by side with Blue the mule, noses touching as they got to know each other. Ragdoll didn't dislike him, which was fine enough for Rhett.

Sam haltered his blue roan and picked out his usual flashy sort, a curly-haired black that one of the newer Rangers had brought. Winifred chose a sturdy little paint, almost a pony, and Rhett reckoned swinging up onto a sixteen-hand beast was soon going to be beyond the girl's abilities, once her belly started growing. Then again, if he knew anything about Buck and Kachina by now, he'd have bet good money that the mare would go back to kneeling whenever Winifred went to mount, just as she had when the girl's foot had been a bleeding stump.

Rhett went back into the herd to check the largest horse they had, a draft even bigger than Samson who should have no trouble pulling Cora's wagon, even now that it was loaded up with everything they could carry from the outpost. They'd taken every bullet, every arrow, every knife, and most of the books that were readable. They'd plundered bunks for clean shirts and pants and socks. The blue and purple wagon that had once housed a witch was now a rolling armory and library, the narrow bed inside crowded by bags and crates and stacks of heavy leather-bound books.

It still didn't feel like enough to Rhett. He'd been a fool to think the Rangers would ride out with him against Trevisan. It hadn't happened last time, when the Captain was still in charge, and it wasn't going to happen this time, now that everybody was dead. Rhett couldn't figure out if he was the best thing to happen to the Las Moras Outpost or the worst. It didn't really matter. The Shadow had no time for bellyaching or wishy-washying, so neither did Rhett. Sure enough, the wobble in his belly pulled east, toward San Anton and maybe the sea. Tomorrow morning, they'd head out. Or maybe...

"Let's leave now. Put some miles on these new ponies."

Dan looked up from saddling his mare and grinned. "I thought you might say that."

"Why don't we wait overnight?" Sam asked, massaging the patched-up wound on his shoulder.

The feeling that made Rhett's head duck down between his shoulders had to be guilt.

"Because I don't want to smell those assholes burning," he muttered.

CHAPTER 12

The more air Rhett put between his back and the smoking ranch house, the lighter he felt—at least as far as the Shadow was concerned. Part of him longed to shuck his clothes and his life and his feelings and his heart's desolation and take to the sky. But the rest of him felt weighed down with the Captain's star in his pouch and the responsibility dogging his every step. Being a bird meant he could forget the Captain and Earl. Being human meant he had to deal with how he'd failed them both. Being a bird also meant he could forget about his promise to his brother. If Revenge learned English and came here seeking Rhett, all he'd find were ashes. Rhett might never see his brother and mother again, and that was a hell of a blow on top of the rest of life's recent gut punches. Burning bridges, it seemed, sometimes meant you could never cross the goddamn river again.

He started out on BB, his rump rattling around in the Captain's bigger and far nicer saddle, which even had a side holster for the Henry rifle. Is this what the Captain had felt like, riding out with his posse? Unsure, guilty, worried that he wouldn't be up to the next task? The Captain had looked decades older in just a few weeks, and Rhett figured that the next time he looked in a mirror, he'd see time's toll in the curve of his shoulders and the worry wrinkles worming across his forehead.

The saddle would've made him sore no matter what, thanks to the healing wound from the silver bullet some bastard had shot in his rump. It had been humiliating, lying on his face with his buttocks bare in the air, letting his former lover dig around in his meat with a tweezer. But it was out now, and his other wounds were healing, if hurting. His body had just poked all those other bullets back out to fall one by one with a little plop in the sand. Sam was all patched up, and Rhett would gladly take a sting in the ass if it meant they could get on the road. The piss pan and bible he'd taken from the Captain's room stayed with him, though, tucked into a saddlebag. For a feller who could pretty much only die if he got shot straight in the heart, a little armor during a fight was not a bad thing.

They made good time in the crisp weather, all the horses trotting out with their heads up and hooves dancing high. First came Rhett, then Sam, then Winifred beside Cora's wagon with the ponies and Blue the mule tied alongside. Behind that... well, they'd brought the entire herd. Leaving a herd of horses penned up near a fire meant somebody was going to get hurt, and Rhett reckoned that some of the horses had never been wild and might've lost their instincts. That was a little how he'd felt, sitting at the fire with his mother and brother. He'd lost his chance to roam free and would chafe and fret at any bonds that kept him from his destiny. The herd was running loose now, which meant that any horses who felt the call could gallop right off and seek their own goddamn horse fortune, and welcome to it. Otherwise, they'd mostly stay bunched together, following the lead mare and the wagon containing their grain. Dan rode behind the herd, doing and thinking whatever the strange feller did and thought. Which Rhett didn't mind, as it meant he had Sam all to himself.

They didn't talk much. Rhett figured Sam was feeling the loss of the Captain and his fellow Ranger brothers pretty deep. Although Jiddy and the Scarsdales and their cronies had never approved of Rhett, they'd been just fine with Sam—at least in public. Everybody had. And Sam had killed some of 'em, all while they were firing on him.

"You doing okay, Sam?" Rhett asked.

Sam looked up, his kind blue eyes showing raw pain. "Hell no, I'm not. I never had my own people shooting at me. Never had to shoot folks when I wasn't sure if they needed killing at all. It got crazy in there. The feller who shot my shoulder, we trained up together. His name was Gene. He said he was sorry, kinda like he was surprised he'd hit me, and then I killed him." A sob broke, and Sam dashed at his eyes. "I killed him, Rhett. And I don't even think I did the wrong thing. We got to be better than that, than Jiddy and the Scarsdales. We got to be like the Captain, always."

"That's right."

"We got to get Trevisan. Captain should've done more about it. Should've known Haskell had gone bad. It's like he couldn't see that not all Rangers are good like him."

"Well, Sam, I reckon most folks think they're the good guys, even when they're dead wrong."

Sam's eyes met Rhett's. "We're the good guys now, Rhett. We got to be."

Rhett nodded. "It ain't fun and it ain't easy, but that's the way it is."

They rode on until evening, and Rhett fell into trail thoughts, his brain sort of floating away. The terrain was fine enough, rolling hills and scrub brush and rocks, familiar as the back of Rhett's hand. Dan shot a couple of rabbits with his bow, and they dangled from the back of the wagon, waiting to become supper and a winter hat, maybe. The posse had to go a little farther than Rhett would've liked to find decent grass and water, but the herd settled down to the trail peaceably enough. It felt good, going in the right direction at last. Still, the Shadow dogged him, making his heels dig into BB's sides, urging him to get east, and fast.

The hard part came when the posse went about their nightly chores and Rhett realized that no one was gathering the kindling for the fire. It might've been the job of the lowliest feller, but now their low feller was gone. Rhett left Sam to the horses and stumbled around in the dark, angrily yanking twigs and sticks and bunches of dried grass to put in the pile.

He hated it. He hated every goddamn moment of it. He hated the rasp of cold bark on rein-bruised palms, despised the wincing rip of a fingernail tearing. It wasn't until he'd dropped off his second armful of kindling that he realized he was crying. He dashed at his eye with his knuckles and went back out for more. Usually he was wary of snakes and scorpions and all the dangerous wild things that lurked in the desert, but just now, he would've welcomed a fight, or pain, or anything that didn't feel like Earl had chosen to die rather than keep on going with Rhett.

"Rhett."

Dan's hand landed on Rhett's shoulder, and Rhett dropped his load of sticks and swung wild. Dan stepped back, his hands up in peace. Rhett's failed punch took him into moron territory as he flailed around and regained his balance, ending up with his hands on his knees, feeling like he wanted to vomit.

"There's enough, Rhett. You brought enough kindling for three fires. You need to sit. Rest. Drink." In the low light,

Rhett could feel Dan looking him over. "You don't look well," he finally said.

"How the hell would I be well when I killed a bunch of my own folks this morning? Goddammit, Dan. How could anybody be well after that?"

Dan nodded and squatted to start the fire. With his back to Rhett, Rhett found it easier to recompose himself and stand, although he was full of nervous energy and paced around, kicking stones with his dusty boots.

"Anyone who feels good after what happened this morning is a true monster. But we have to find a way to go on," Dan observed.

"I reckon I see now why fellers drink so much. If we had a saloon handy, I'd be out of quarters by midnight and yarking in an alley by dawn."

"Perhaps I can help with that."

The man who'd spoken wasn't part of the posse. Rhett had his pistols out in a hot second, pointed at the figure that had emerged from the darkness. Dan's fire caught, but Rhett didn't need the growing flame to see who'd showed up at their camp uninvited and unexpected. And, for the most part, impossible. His flopping belly and sense of disquiet told him fine enough who he now faced. He shoved his pistols back in his holsters, considering they probably couldn't do a lick of damage, anyway.

"Howdy there, Mr. Buck. Welcome to our camp."

Buck tipped his black hat and grinned, teeth flashing white in the scant light. He was a god, of sorts, and looked it. "Thank you, Mr. Walker. I've brought gifts, if that'll soften your welcome for me."

Every hair on Rhett's body was standing on end, his senses casting out to find all his people as they went about their chores in the darkness. "It's not the gifts that cause alarm, but the fact that you found us in the first place. A bit far from your grove, ain't you?"

Buck laughed and tossed something on the scant flames, which roared up into a bonfire.

"Not that far, no."

The man—or god, really—looked just as he had in Rhett's dream last year and then again in his saloon, the Buck's Head. Sturdy, muscled, as manly as a rutting stallion, dressed all in black like a gambler who never lost. As always seemed to happen around Buck, things got a little wiggly, and then there were comfortable logs placed around the fire and food set out on silver platters that had no goddamn reason to be in the middle of the Durango desert.

"Y'all come on over," Rhett hollered. "Buck brought magic food."

Buck snuck his arm around Rhett and pulled him away from the fire in a grip that felt somehow charming and utterly dominating at the same time. Rhett allowed it, seeing as how he'd been warned against raising the god's wrath.

"I'd like a private word, first." Buck's whisper sent an unpleasant squirm through Rhett, as if the Shadow was both pulled toward and away from such a peculiar sort of monster, one both mortally dangerous and possibly unkillable.

"I reckon I can't stop you," Rhett said, going along with it.

Buck steered him over near the horses. As Sam walked toward the fire, he cast a careful glance. "All right there, Rhett?"

"Just fine, Sam," Rhett answered. "Don't start drinking without me, though, okay?" Because he knew well enough what happened when folks ate Buck's food, and he'd be goddamned if he'd let anybody else sit near Sam in such a state.

"So you remember the grove," Buck said as if only mildly

interested but clearly goddamned perturbed. "You weren't supposed to."

"Reckon I'm special."

Buck grinned, and even here, the fire danced against the wet white of his teeth. "Reckon you are. You seemed to enjoy my hospitality more than most."

Rhett looked down, fought the flush creeping up. "Well, that cheese was mighty fine."

Buck's laugh was a low rumble, like thunder still far-off but threatening. "Let's say that, sure. Tell me, Mr. Walker. How goes the lady's travails?"

Rhett didn't rightly know what the hell Buck was talking about until Buck turned slightly to where Winifred watched from the fire and tipped his hat to her. She nodded warily but respectfully and nibbled on grapes.

"If by *lady* you mean Winifred and *travails* you mean your get in her belly, I reckon she's doing fine. Had a bit of the sickness at first, but Cora said that was a good thing, meant the babe was sticking and healthy."

Buck smiled and nodded. "Good. Good. Now listen close. I expect you to take care of her. More than just what you're doing already. Think of her as a stagecoach carrying very valuable cargo. She crosses a river, you're by her side, holding her pony. There's a fight, you save her skin first. You get me?"

Rhett snorted, his head snaking back. "Oh, I hear you. Just like I heard her brother when he said the same thing. You think you can scare me into taking care of my friend? That's a shitty thing to ask, Mr. Buck. I already take care of her, and what's more, she takes care of herself. You don't own that girl." He spat on the ground. "Hell, nobody owns that girl. Nobody ever could. She'd have none of it."

Buck tsked and shook his head. "I don't own her. Nothing wild can be owned. But I own maybe half of what she carries, and I like to protect my investments."

"And what are you gonna do to me if something happens to her?"

With a long sigh, Buck crossed his thick arms and looked Rhett up and down. Rhett knew he didn't look like much, but he also knew a feller like Buck could see beyond what was on the surface. "That'll depend on the circumstances. I'm no monster." His grin could've swallowed up the moon. "But I'm asking you as a friend, and I make a bad enemy. Take care of her."

"Her brother might be a better person to carry that burden than me."

Buck watched the scene around the fire for a moment and chuckled. "Yeah, and we both know that if I asked him for any such boon, he'd set his mind to killing me. He might know, deep down, where that baby came from, but he won't want to hear the words aloud, I promise you."

Rhett kicked a stone and looked off into the distance. "You know she's under a curse, right? Cat shaman, so I hear. She's gonna die nine times, and the last one's final. So she's got a few deaths left in her. That should ease you some."

"Even the impossible to kill can be killed, as you well know. And that curse doesn't cover what she carries."

Buck took a step toward the fire, and Rhett stopped him with a hand. When Buck looked down at Rhett's hand, it jumped right back to Rhett's side with no interest in ever returning.

"So the baby—it ain't really Earl's?"

"What do you think?"

Turning to face him, Buck seemed to step sideways out of space, and he wasn't the cushy black gambler anymore. He was eight feet tall with a spreading rack of antlers, naked but for a deerskin breechclout, his muscles glistening with sweat and blood in the firelight and his eyes full of stars.

"Take that as a no," Rhett muttered.

Rhett blinked, and Buck was a gambler again. "Any more questions?"

"Uh, that food. And wine. Is it the same stuff we had in your saloon?"

Buck's smile was amused, a parent looking down on a naughty child. "Do you want it to be?"

"I..."

Rhett remembered back to what had happened in the high roller room at the Buck's Head Tavern, surrounded by velvet and gilt and filled up with sweetmeats and liquor. The feeling of Sam's fingers unafraid on his skin, the sweet slurp of peach juice, the look in Sam's eyes as Rhett took to his hands and knees. Did he want that again? Hell, yes, with every fiber of his goddamn being.

Would he settle for it on Buck's terms when he was this close to maybe getting it all on his own?"

"Don't reckon I do," he decided.

Buck nodded, considering him.

"You surprise me, Shadow," the god said.

Rhett nodded. "Yeah, well, sometimes I surprise myself." He headed for the fire, where the scent of Dan's roasting rabbits merged with the syrupy headiness of Buck's wine. "Reckon you're welcome to join us," he added, knowing Buck didn't need an invitation but would probably be waiting for one.

"Saved you a seat," Sam said, patting the long log he sat on, and Rhett gladly took it, wondering if Buck had placed it there for just such an occasion. Sam had a loaf of bread in hand, and he tore off a chunk and handed it to Rhett, their fingers brushing with the transfer.

Buck took a place beside Winifred, but not so close as to make the girl uncomfortable. Cora was on Winifred's other side, regarding him with outright suspicion.

"Cora, this here's Buck. Buck, this is Cora," Rhett said.

Buck tipped his hat and gave her a charming smile. "Well met, darlin'."

Cora slitted her eyes. "What are you?" she asked.

"A friend," Rhett said, figuring it was better to interrupt a god than let him take unkindly to Cora. "A peculiar friend, but a friend. A friend who don't like being insulted." When she opened her mouth, he added, "Even by a magnificent and dangerous dragon, if you catch my meaning."

Cora's mouth snapped shut, and she gave Buck a nod. "Greetings," she said coldly, but not so coldly as to offend.

"Please, friends. Eat," Buck said, arms spread to encompass the platters of fruit and cheese. "Drink." He uncorked a green bottle with his teeth and poured out into tin camp cups that he'd apparently conjured out of nowhere. It was unsettling and all too familiar, Rhett figured, but right handy. Knowing he didn't have much choice, and that the god would drug or poison his food as he wished, Rhett took the cup, clinked it against Sam's, and drank.

It tasted the same as it had last time and went to his head immediately. He took another sip and was focusing so hard on feeling for magic, trying to decide whether or not Buck had drugged him, that he forgot Sam was beside him. Right up until Sam's hand landed on his knee. At that, Rhett went stock-still like a mouse in a hawk's shadow.

"Uh, what?"

"I asked if you wanted some meat," Sam said, holding out a skewer of rabbit parts.

It wasn't the most romantic thing Rhett had ever heard, but it was a damn good start.

"Thanks kindly, Sam." Rhett plucked off a leg and set to gnawing on it before he realized Sam was still watching him. He closed his mouth, chewed, swallowed, and ran his cuff over the grease on his face.

"You look right thoughtful," he murmured, sipping at the wine to cover the awkwardness.

"I'm having that thing where it feels like you've done something before, or maybe dreamed it," Sam said.

"Déjà vu," Buck offered.

"Bless you," Rhett said. Then, hoping to learn if Sam actually did recall any of their time there, and if it was a happy recollection, "What seems familiar, Sam?"

Sam looked around, innocent and scruffy and perfect, as always, by firelight. "I remember sitting next to you, and Buck was there, and we were drinking this wine and eating something…"

"Peaches," Rhett supplied.

"That's it, and then things got right fuzzy."

"My wine is stronger than most folks are accustomed to," Buck said.

"So that's why you're feeling that way." Rhett cast Buck a disapproving glance. "Because it's pretty similar to what we did at Buck's tavern. Had a hell of a hangover the next day, though, so maybe we ought to slow down on the wine?"

Sam gave him a mischievous grin and chugged what was left in his cup. He silently held it out to Buck, who refilled it. "I think you might be wrong there, Rhett. We had a rough day today. We could use a little bit of carousing."

Rhett stared down into his wine and saw a glimmering and dark reflection of himself there, his one eye looking slightly terrified. He gulped it down before he could start thinking about how ugly he was, and how Sam could never want him without the benefit of the god's drink or a dark wagon and a near-death experience. Those thoughts weren't much good. He glanced around the fire to see what everybody else was doing. Winifred and Cora were turned toward each other, foreheads touching as they giggled. So that was fine, then; those two couldn't get into too much trouble together, and from what Rhett assumed, they'd already done just about anything the god could encourage them to do, and on their own.

Dan, as usual, sat aloof. Back straight, arms crossed, he frowned into the fire as if he didn't like what he saw there.

"Not gonna eat, Dan?" Rhett asked.

Dan looked at him, looked down at Sam's hand, forgotten on Rhett's knee, and stood. "I don't believe red wine agrees with me," he said. Everyone stopped to watch as he shrugged out of his clothes and stood there, naked and unafraid, wearing nothing but a bland smile, his parts as limp as a slug. "Please forgive me for my bad manners." He nodded to Buck, transformed into a coyote, and loped off into the night.

"You ain't offended?" Rhett asked when Buck didn't strike Dan down with lightning but merely shrugged and went back to filling the women's cups with wine.

"A man's predilections aren't my business," Buck said. "I serve the thirsty, and you can't make a man drink if he isn't thirsty. There are always plenty of folks who like what I'm serving." He winked and leaned over to refill Rhett's cup.

"I'll drink to that," Sam said with a whoop, tossing back the wine like it was a watered-down shot at the Leapin' Lizard back in Gloomy Bluebird.

Rhett put his hand on Sam's wrist. "You're drinking mighty fast."

Sam's pulse leaped under Rhett's fingertips as Sam clinked his cup against Rhett's. "I'm a big boy, Rhett. I can take it."

Having clinked cups, Rhett was duty bound to drain his glass. As he wiped the red from his lips, he looked at Buck, who was on the ground now, leaning back against a log and plucking grapes from a bunch held in one hand.

"You eat your own food?" Rhett asked.

Buck's grin said a lot of things. "I take what I want, whether it's mine or no."

Rhett wanted to leap in front of Sam and pull out his pistols, but he knew well enough what he was dealing with, or at least he knew enough to recognize that Buck could end him faster than a regular human or monster. Plus, if he stood up, Sam might move his hand from Rhett's leg where it had crept up from his knee to his thigh, sending all sorts of tingles through Rhett's middle. His head felt all spinny, and when he looked at Sam, it was like stars lived in the boy's eyes, and Rhett couldn't decide if that was the drink or the god or just how he felt most of the time, anyway.

"Do you feel funny, Sam?"

"You're asking a lot of questions, Rhett. You do that when you're nervous."

Rhett swallowed hard. "Do I? Am I?"

Sam's grin was a sweet, curling thing. "Yep. And I don't feel funny at all. I feel...free, maybe. Some of the Rangers weren't so kind to me, you know. I told you Scarsdale caught me and beat me down, but I guess I didn't mention he told some other fellers, and they...treated me bad. I didn't say nothing, but there was a scuffle, and the Captain put a stop to it for good. But I always felt like there were maybe some Rangers just waiting to take a shot at me, and today they did, and I'm still standing. It's a hell of a relief." He held out his cup to Buck. "If you'll be so kind, sir."

Buck nodded and refilled the cup, and Sam drank and looked all thoughtful. "It's like my secret died with 'em. Or at least..."

"The shame?"

Sam looked up, and his eyes went from raw and open to... something very different. Rebellion and anger. Rhett found it as intoxicating as the wine.

"Not shame. Maybe just the fear of being judged by idjits. I can do what I want now."

His hand left Rhett's thigh, and Rhett mourned its loss until it landed on his jaw, Sam's fingers warm and calloused as a cowboy's ought to be. Caught as he was, Rhett's eye darted around. Winifred and Cora were a hazy blur, disappearing into the wagon, laughing as they leaned on one another. Dan was long gone. Buck was just an antlered shadow across the fire, and Rhett reckoned that anything that might happen here was something the god had seen a million times or more. His due, he'd called it, back at the grove.

"Rhett. Look at me." Sam's voice was husky, his fingers pulling Rhett's face closer.

Rhett focused on him, wishing to hell he had two good eyes. One eye didn't seem enough to behold the man before him, a man Rhett had longed for when he was still a girl in pigtails, sitting on a white board fence.

"I'm looking," he said, his voice just as low.

So slowly, like he was sneaking up on a kicky colt, Sam's face moved closer and closer, his fingers never loosening. Rhett felt like he was being pulled down into a swirling river and wished for the surety Buck's wine had given him last time he'd been this open with Sam. Then, he'd felt compelled, pushed, caught in a tornado and unable to stop. Now, he was only himself, and whatever happened, he had only his heart and body to blame. Or to thank.

Sam's lips landed on his, softly, a question. Rhett answered back the only way he knew how: honestly, and with enthusiasm. Every touch was a revelation. Warm lips, warmer tongue, rasp of beard on raw cheek, flutter of eyelashes, a thumb pad stroking his temple. He was there in every moment, as awake as he'd ever been, sober as hell and so brimming with joy that he thought his heart would explode. The one time his eye opened and wandered to Buck, he found the log empty. The god was gone.

So they were alone under the stars, him and his Sam.

The kiss went on and on, and Rhett wanted it to go on forever. Sam's hands roamed over Rhett's shoulders and down his sides, carefully skipping over his wrapped front. Emboldened, Rhett slid his fingers up Sam's firm arms before pulling away in shock.

"Sam! Your shoulder. I'm sorry. I forgot."

Sam shook his head in surprise, his mouth deliciously open. "It...It doesn't hurt. It's like I was never shot." By firelight, he unbuttoned his shirt and slid it down to show smooth skin with a tight pink scar on either side of his shoulder. "Hellfire, Rhett. What was in that feller's wine?"

Rhett reached back to his buttock, where Cora had removed the silver bullet. It didn't hurt anymore, nor did any of his bruises or contusions. Even his broken nose felt less squashed. It usually took him at least overnight to recover from a fight, if not longer, but he felt fit as a fiddle now.

"I'm all fixed up, too. Pretty good magic."

Rhett's eye strayed to Sam's shoulder, and he licked his lips and reached out, all tentative, to touch the skin there. Sam's eyes blinked shut, long lashes sweeping down, and Rhett ran his fingertips up the taut side of Sam's neck, down his throat to where curly golden hairs disappeared down Sam's shirt. Sam didn't say anything, didn't move, didn't blush or run away screaming. Rhett briefly wondered if it was a dream, because his life thus far hadn't included such freedom to do as he wished.

"Something about you is so familiar," Sam murmured. "Like I've known you forever."

Don't remember me as I was, Rhett thought. *Not the ranch, not the grove. Don't remember the past at all.*

But what he said was, "We been traveling together awhile. Reckon you can't be too scared of me now."

Sam's grin made Rhett's middle buzz. "Oh, it ain't fear. Just...like a memory."

Decision made, Rhett took a deep breath and ran his fingers up Sam's face to cup his bearded cheek. "I'd rather make memories than think about the past," he said.

And there by the fire, wine forgotten, all alone, they made some goddamn memories.

CHAPTER 13

Rhett woke up in a tizzy.

Something was touching him.

And it was Sam Hennessy.

Hellfire.

Sam's arm was under Rhett's head, Sam's front pressed to Rhett's back. They were fully dressed at least, and this time Rhett remembered everything that had happened in stunning detail. Glancing around the camp, he saw nothing unusual. The fire had burned itself out, Dan was still missing, and the wagon was closed up tight and silent. Sam was snoring, just a little, and Rhett gave him a small, secret smile.

Quietly, gently, he extricated himself from the sleeping cowpoke and went out a far piece to take care of his personal business before poking around the fire for breakfast. Buck's silver platters were still there, as was the food—not even wilted or dusty or browned. Rhett realized he was starving. His mouth was fuzzy from wine and other things, and he fell on the food with more gusto than he'd ever let Buck see. Grapes, cheese, and bread went down mighty fine with cold, clear water from his canteen. It was a damn shame Earl was gone; he would've loved to enjoy Buck's hospitality again.

The wagon door opened, and Winifred hopped down lightly, rubbing sleep from her eyes. She was always one of the first ones up, and whatever changes her body was going through usually meant she had to hit the bushes more frequently than anybody else. When she had done so and came to the fire, Rhett held out a chunk of bread, which Winifred took and set to chewing.

"Peculiar night," she observed.

"Most peculiar," Rhett agreed, glad that they could start off on the same side, for once.

He watched her subtly while she ate. She had a glow about her, like there was a fire just under her skin, and her hair was somehow more lustrous than he'd ever seen it. She'd traded her worn trail clothes for clean duds at the outpost, but the man's shirt hung off her a bit and the leggings were soft doeskin. If Rhett wasn't wrong, her bosoms had grown in a bit, too.

"What's it like?" he asked without really thinking.

"What's what like?" She bristled, and he hurried to smooth things over.

"None of my business. Sorry."

"No, it's fine. My temper's a thin thing these days. You sounded curious, not teasing."

Rhett's eye slashed at her and away toward the grapes. He plucked one and rolled it around between two fingers. "Being...in...your current state." Goddamn, there was no good way to say it. "In a family way?"

Winifred gave an indulgent chuckle. "It's just different, I suppose. The ladies in town wear corsets as long as they can and hide themselves away as soon as they swell, but the way I grew up, it's just part of life. I'm glad to not feel sick anymore, and I'm sick of making water every five minutes, but it's a hell of a lot better than missing a foot."

"You still got a limp, though."

"And I'd still vastly prefer my current state over what I suffered before. Having a child isn't a defect, Rhett. It's a natural enough thing for a woman to do."

"Even if you don't know the father?"

Winifred picked up a grape and tossed it at Rhett, striking him right on the nose.

"I know well enough. It's a blessing. And I got a mighty fine horse out of it, too."

"You reckon he'll be born with antlers?"

He watched her carefully to see if she'd take offense, but she just laughed in that light, infuriating, teasing way she had.

"Of course not. The antlers will grow in later."

The girl had a calmness about her, a patience she'd sincerely lacked before. It was right peculiar for Rhett to see the subtle changes in a body he knew well and to recall that his own body was supposedly capable of doing the same thing. Thanks to Earl's instruction and his own iron will, he thought of himself as one hundred percent man, most of the time. Carrying a child was a prospect so impossible and strange as to boggle the mind.

Still, it seemed to suit Winifred, body and soul, and he was glad.

Cora wandered up next, looking beautifully rumpled, her top tied slightly askew. For just a second, Rhett remembered what it was to want her, but then her hand brushed Winifred's shoulder, and the girls shared a secret smile, and Rhett was glad for them. Anything he could've ever had with Cora had fallen down dead the day he'd headed west instead of after Cora's sister. And even if she'd admitted he was right to do so, he still knew the truth of it. Hell, if it was him wanting to go after Sam Hennessy and somebody else had told him no, he'd have burned down the world on his way to Sam's side, giant scorpions or no.

Cora picked up some grapes and nibbled before sighing softly and saying, "I miss tea."

"And coffee," Rhett added.

She nodded and smiled in an easier way than they'd had in a while. "But at least there is plenty to eat. Rhett, what was that man?"

Rhett shrugged. "A god, close as I reckon. You'll have to ask Dan if you want to know more. All I know is that peculiar things happen when he's around, and I don't want to make him mad."

"It's early in the morning to be telling tales about me." Dan sat down on Cora's other side, fully dressed, and began plucking feathers off a fat prairie bird speared on one of his arrows.

"We were talking about Buck, you peacock," Rhett muttered.

Dan, too, smiled. They were a regular bunch of Happy Howards today. When Sam finally woke, sat up, rubbed a hand through his golden hair, and smiled right at him, Rhett joined them in being stupidly, unreasonably, irresponsibly jolly.

The day went pretty smooth, considering. Rhett was a bit sore after last night by the fire, but it was less a pain and more of a fond reminder. And this time, he was able to keep all of his memories without the hangover or the blurry aftereffects of Buck's influence. Wherever the feller had gone, he'd left no sign besides the food. The posse took his silver platters along in the wagon, figuring they'd trade pretty well somewhere along the way, should they get in a bind.

Nobody mentioned anything about the evening's entertainment. Dan didn't say where he'd been. But Sam kept giving Rhett a sweet smile whenever they looked up at the same time, and they rode side by side at the head of the bunch. Everyone stayed in a good mood, and Rhett was glad to be settled on Ragdoll's back. The Captain's unicorn was a fine, handsome mount, but the scraggly appy just felt like home. She even pranced a little, like she wanted to show him she was just as good as BB.

The days passed as they did on the trail, and the air stayed nice and cool without veering into cold. When it rained too hard, they all huddled in the wagon, crowded as it was, and those who could read took up the Ranger books by lantern light, hunting for any sign of alchemists and liches and how to defeat them. With nothing to contribute and feeling like he was missing out on a big ol' secret, Rhett just curled up on the bed and went to sleep, noting the peculiar scent of Winifred and Cora mixed on the pillow. He woke every morning facing southeast, tasting the air, anxious to be back on the road.

They lost a horse to lameness and killed a fine deer and came across what looked like more buffalo tracks, thousands upon thousands of *U* shapes carved into mud. The sun wore a short, easy path across the sky each day, and the moon reigned long and cold. Rhett's buffalo coat became his favorite possession, and Sam inched his bedroll closer and closer until he was under it, too. Nobody said a goddamn thing about it. Rhett's heart just about exploded from happiness. Dan didn't seem to mind and didn't chide Rhett or try to teach him the bow anymore. The entire group was content to follow the Shadow's path to the alchemist they all wanted to see dead and in the ground. The farther they went, the more anxious and wrung-out Cora looked. The tension dogged them all.

And then one day Rhett woke up at dawn as taut as a bowstring. He bolted upright, and Dan joined him.

"What is it?" Dan asked.

Rhett's belly wobbled so hard he had to close his eye. "Monsters. Coming in fast from the north."

"How many? Who?"

Rhett glared. "How the hell should I know, Dan? I'm a god-damn dowsing rod, not a banker."

"What do we do?"

Rhett stood up, stuck his feet in his boots, buckled on his gun belt, ran a finger over his Ranger Scout badge, and considered his camp, his heart yammering all the while. Whatever was coming wasn't far off, and it felt pretty goddamn malevolent. And fast. There wasn't much time for a meeting or a discussion. "We got to head 'em off. Get the women in the wagon and post Sam to guard 'em. I wish like hell we had more people, but you and me have got to handle it ourselves."

Dan, bless him, nodded once and sprinted for the horses, where Rhett knew he would saddle Ragdoll and be on his own chestnut in a blink. Rhett squatted by Sam and gently nudged his shoulder under the buffalo skin.

"Sam?"

Sam's sleepy smile made Rhett want to crawl right back under the warm furs. "Hey there, handsome."

"Sam, you got to get up. Trouble's coming, and I need you to protect the womenfolk."

Sam's smile disappeared, replaced by the sturdy look of a Ranger ready for a fight. He hopped up, put on his boots, adjusted himself, and put a hand on Rhett's shoulder. "You can count on me."

Rhett grabbed his shoulder back and gave it a squeeze. "I know it."

Sam pulled him in for a quick pound on the back, almost a hug, and then he was buckling on his holsters and checking his guns and bullet pouch. With the women taken care of, and knowing Sam would be the one to tell them so, anyway, Rhett took up his Henry and ran off for the small herd milling nervously around the wagon while the larger herd had stopped their grazing and looked to the north. Dan was a quick hand, and Ragdoll was already licking at the bit of her bridle. The little mare knew well enough that something serious was up, and she was alert and dancing, ready for it. Rhett slid the Henry into the Captain's saddle and hopped up. Dan was ready, too, reining his chestnut over and looking to Rhett for orders.

"Over that hill. Let's just run like hell and get ready to shoot."

Dan nodded, bow in hand, and Rhett wheeled his mare and kicked her harder than she liked. They galloped through camp, in a plume of dust, and Rhett didn't even bother looking back at the wagon. That was Sam's problem now, and Rhett's problem was stopping whatever was coming from harming his people. As they passed a little tree, a murder of crows exploded, cawing into the dawn sky. He'd never noticed crows before, but now they seemed to him like the dour fellers in town who went to every funeral, standing there, frowning, all holier-than-thou, like the same future didn't one day await them.

The wobble grew stronger, and Rhett stood up in the saddle and gathered the reins in his left hand so he could pull his pistol with his right. They topped the rise side by side, and Rhett saw a danged peculiar sight: seven Injun fellers on horseback, riding right for them.

Rhett started shooting on the assumption that fellers who wanted to have a nice talk rode up to your campfire a fair bit more slowly. One of the men fell off the back of his paint horse, and several others started shooting their own guns. One pulled out a bow and arrow, and Rhett felt a hot punch and saw the arrow sprouting out of his shoulder.

"Goddammit, Dan!" he shouted as the Injuns rode right past them.

Ignoring the arrow, he yanked on his reins, and Ragdoll stopped so fast she almost sat. He wheeled her, and she reared and squealed to let him know she wasn't a goddamn bit pleased before leaping right into a gallop headed back the other way. Dan followed, and side by side, they rode like hell for the six fellers who were now headed for their camp. Dan started shouting something in his language, but one of the Injuns shouted back something that sounded right rude, and the rest just kicked their ponies harder and shot their pistols backward over their shoulders, not hitting a damn thing but making one hell of a ruckus.

They topped the ridge he and Dan had already crossed once, and Rhett realized what was happening.

These Injuns wanted their horses.

Funny thing was, Rhett didn't even mind. He'd gladly give over most of the herd if the fellers were in need. Hell, they'd mostly just kept the Ranger herd so the critters wouldn't get hurt around the burning buildings.

"Dan, tell 'em they can have most of the horses! No fight! They can have 'em!"

Dan hollered a few different things, and the men slowed just a little and shouted back. Now they were almost neck and neck, and if there hadn't been so many guns and arrows in the mix, it would've been pleasant enough, just galloping along with some fine riders on fast horses. As they rode into camp, Sam stood in front of the wagon, legs spread, and put Virgil Scarsdale's Henry to his shoulder to pop two more Injuns off their ponies. One man hollered, and the fellers stopped then, stuck between Rhett and Dan's pistols and Sam's Henry. It was four to three now, so far as the Injuns knew. Those weren't good odds, especially considering who had superior firepower and that Rhett was the sort of man to yank an arrow out of his shoulder, snap it in half, and toss it to the ground like it was a pesky fly. Which he did now as they watched him, wary.

"Dan! Tell him he can have half the herd and keep all his men if he'll just stop being stupid," Rhett hollered.

Dan said it, or something like it, and the leader wheeled to stare at Rhett. He was a lean man in a threadbare shirt and dirty breeches, but his horse was well-kept and well-mannered, which made Rhett like him.

"Why would you give us half your horses?" the man said in perfectly good English.

Rhett shrugged. "We don't need 'em, and we don't like killing."

The man pointed at Rhett's badge. "But you're Rangers."

"We ain't that kind of Rangers."

The man threw his head back and laughed. "There is only one kind of Ranger, which is why we're so hungry."

"There's clearly at least two kinds, because we're happy to share a meal with you and let you-all have the horses we don't need," Rhett shot back. "And if your fellers are alive and need doctoring, we got someone who can help."

The man said something to his men, and they talked among themselves in their own language.

"He says you're crazy, but he likes you," Dan muttered.

"Well, that's better than the opposite, I reckon."

A short while later, Rhett was walking through the herd with Little Eagle, talking about the merits of certain horses as mounts or breeders and other unfortunate critters as food. Little Eagle's band had suffered bad luck recently and needed meat as much as they needed transportation. The bad luck came in the form of Rangers and Lobos, unrelated but close set, which Rhett considered pretty goddamn unfair for quiet people just trying to get along. As far as Rhett was concerned, it was a fine way to lessen his own worries, especially regarding horses that had a mean look about them or hooves that tended to twist. They cut a little more than half the herd, with Rhett's posse keeping mostly the already-trained-up mounts and a larger draft cross to pull the wagon should Samson or his second suffer.

Fortunately, all the fellers they'd shot were shifters, and none of them had taken their bullet in the heart, nor did they hold the scuffle against Rhett's people. Cora didn't even have time to prepare her kit before the bullets had popped right out of the fellers, who were more interested in chunks of Dan's breakfast bird and the bunches of grapes left behind by Buck, which seemed, strangely, to never be absent of fruit. The fellers had never had grapes before and found them to be hilarious and wonderful. Little Eagle and his second-in-command, Slippery Snake, were the only ones who had any English, but they all got along well enough. Sam made them nervous, so he mostly stayed quiet. When Rhett discovered they were Javelina, he asked after the band he'd met while tracking the Cannibal Owl, but there was no way to know if they were related.

"We lost three babies then," Little Eagle said with a shrug. "Not good. But could've been worse. The Rangers killed four children."

Hearing such atrocities, Rhett wanted to shove his badge into his pocket. When the Captain had been alive, he'd been able to take pride in being a Ranger, but now that he'd seen the true colors of most of his outpost and felt their hatred in the form of a silver bullet dug out of his own buttock with tweezers, his opinion was changing.

The groups exchanged information: Rhett and Dan told the Injuns about what they'd seen to the west, and Little Eagle told them what to expect as they headed east. The band's shaman had said it would be a dry winter, which surprised no one. Rhett asked if they knew anything about alchemists or trains, and they just shrugged. Their concerns were much smaller things, mostly Ranger territories, white settlements, and the chupacabra vaqueros that seemed to raid farther and farther east every year. They didn't know Rhett's mother and brother. They'd never heard of his father. But they were awful grateful for the horses and laughed a lot, and that made them better than most of the folks Rhett had met in his life.

As they prepared to return to their band, Rhett helped them separate their new herd from the bunch and offered some rope for them to make into halters. They laughed easily as they hopped onto their own ponies bareback and trotted back up the trail. Rhett watched them go, not missing the horses so much as he missed a life he might've had, if the Cannibal Owl hadn't taken him from his home as a child. A small life, but a good one. No destiny, no troubles, growing up with love and respect instead of hate and derision, being part of an easygoing group of hunters held together by trust and hard work. Part of him would've liked to ride off with Little Eagle and Slippery Snake and the other fellers, to return to a band with what looked about like a miracle and see the faces of friends and family as they watched the horses top the rise. Instead, he had to keep on his current path, headed toward an enemy who'd already bested him once and who still owned a chunk of his very bones.

"Dan, what happens when I kill Trevisan?" he asked as they kept back the remaining herd, several of whom were whinnying at their friends as they trotted away.

"You know what will happen. Something else will call the Shadow, and you will answer with violence."

"What if I wanted to just... live?"

Dan looked at him, his face a mix of pity and amusement. "We're all prisoners of our birth and circumstances, Rhett. Most folks wish they lived bigger lives, but they aren't strong enough. They would crumble if they got what they wanted. You're different."

Rhett snorted and patted the neck of the horse currently pulling at his halter to rejoin the parting herd. "Same as always."

"As if you could be content doing nothing."

"Still, I'd like to give being ordinary a try."

Sam came up and put a hand on Rhett's shoulder. "I don't think you would."

When Sam looked at him like that, Rhett wouldn't trade his life for anything.

He didn't feel quite the same, that night.

CHAPTER
14

Everything was relatively calm as they settled in that evening. Losing half the herd lightened the load on Rhett's shoulders, and he also got to experience something completely new: helping somebody without killing anything. His heart felt all swole up, but in a good way. Dan had shot a nice little antelope for dinner, and Rhett's belly was pleasantly full. Sam was already asleep, just inches away under the buffalo robe and radiating heat like sunshine. The horses had calmed back down, and the women were in their wagon, and all was pretty much well with the world. Rhett closed his eyes and smiled, settling his head back into the worn seat of the Captain's saddle.

He was just drifting off when he felt something skitter over his bare foot, and before he could brush it away, he felt its bite. A hard, hot pinch, and the skittering disappeared. Rhett bolted upright and threw back the buffalo skin to find possibly the worst thing he'd ever seen: spiders. Huge ones. Hairy ones. Dozens of them. As he watched, horrified, one reared its front legs back and sunk its fangs into Sam's ankle.

"Spiders!" Rhett roared, slapping them away from Sam with his bare hands. "Wake up, goddammit!"

Sam was up and brushing the spiders away, dancing toward

the fire and shouting curses. Across the fire, Dan leaped to his feet, slapping spiders off his bare chest and into the flames. The ground seemed to move and shift, the hairy brown spiders crawling everywhere. Rhett stuck his feet in his boots, hard, feeling spider bodies squash and gush, and ran to the wagon, hating every second. He threw open the door and shouted, "Wake up, y'all. Spiders. Bad ones!"

"Spiders don't hurt anybody," Winifred said sleepily.

Then one of them must've got to her, because she screamed and hopped out of bed, dragging a mostly naked and spider-covered Cora with her. They were soon outside, shaking spiders from their clothes and blankets and hair.

Shots rang out, and Rhett looked up to see Sam shooting at the ground and then, to his horror, at Dan.

"I'll kill the big one," Sam shouted. "If it'll just hold still."

Rhett ran up behind Sam and yanked his arms down right as the Henry jerked back with a bang, putting a hole in Dan's leg instead of his chest. Dan fell over hollering, gushing blood and covered with spiders. But Rhett wouldn't let go of Sam, and Sam wouldn't stop trying to wrestle the gun away, claiming he had to kill the big spider. After getting his nose slammed and his feet stomped on, Rhett finally got the big rifle out of Sam's hands and threw it down, wrapping Sam in a bear hug. The cowpoke was stronger than he should've been, violent and thrashing and mad.

"She got my Henry!" Sam shouted, as if he didn't even know Rhett was there. "A giant spider stole my goddamn gun!"

"Shh, Sam. It's me. I'm right here," Rhett said, doing his level best to sound soothing.

Pain was radiating out of his foot where the spider had bitten him and Sam had stomped him, pulsing and swollen against his boot, but it was almost as if he could feel the magic in his body overtaking the venom, pushing it back out. Judging by the fact that Winifred, Cora, and Dan weren't trying to shoot one another, he had to assume that the crazy part of the venom only affected humans. And that meant that Sam was poisoned, didn't it?

"Goddammit, spider. You let me go. I got to help Rhett," Sam growled.

"I am Rhett, fool!"

"You're a goddamn lying spider is what you are, and I'm gonna kill you!"

Sam managed to elbow Rhett in the gut, grab one of his pistols, and put a hole in Rhett's thigh before Dan got close enough to snatch the gun away. Together, they relieved him of both his remaining guns and his Bowie knife, but Sam continued to fight them with the strength of three men, cussing them and insulting them and assuming they were giant spiders hellbent on stealing bullets from good men. No matter what Rhett said, no matter how sweetly or gently he whispered to Sam, he couldn't get past whatever madness gripped his best friend, and it just about broke his heart to see Sam's face twisted in hate as he tried to beat and stomp on whatever came into contact with him, all while striking out at anyone who tried to hold him back.

"I hate spiders, you asshole!" Sam hollered.

"A little rope would help!" Rhett yelled at the women, who were still dancing around as spiders kept trying to run up their legs.

Dan managed to get Sam's lariat off his saddle, and together, they trussed up Samuel Hennessy like he was a furious bull calf about to lose his nuts. Poor Sam struggled on his side, tied at ankles, waist, and wrists, angry enough to spit. The spiders seemed to be running in from every corner of the prairie, and it was all Rhett and Dan could do to stomp on every hairy body that tried to bite poor Sam. The girls finally got their wits back and picked up rocks to smash their own share of eight-legged monsters. Rhett kept waiting for the spiders to join together and form into a giant spider, but the insidious little bastards did just fine on their own, skittering into crevices and lunging out from every shadow. For every ten he killed, ten more rushed up, stupid but determined. He got bit more times than he could count, but he'd just swoon a little and recover. And get back to crushing.

"Goddamn Bernard Trevisan," Rhett muttered as he stepped on another spider.

"You're sure it's him?" Dan asked.

Rhett took a moment to glare at the man. "You know anybody else who commands hundreds of God's worst creatures, full-up with poison and hell-bent on my vexation?"

Slam. Dan squished a spider with a rock. "Are you sure you don't have any more of his possessions?"

Smack. Rhett stomped on one with his gut-splashed boot. "Yes, I'm goddamn sure."

Slam. "Then how is he tracking you?"

Squish. "If I knew, I would put a stop to it."

Dan stuck a stick in the fire and held it to an encroaching spider, setting it aflame. The spider made a screaming noise and bumped into another spider, setting it on fire. Rhett and Dan stared at one another and realized that the entire desert could burn up if they let these spiders get loose while on fire. *Slam. Squish.* The spider fires went out under their boots.

Rhett stomped on another eight-legged fire, grimaced at the white, creamy guts oozing out from under his boot toe, and smacked his own forehead.

"Goddammit, Dan. I already told you how. He has a piece

of my bone. He took one of my toes. Probably one of my teeth. So maybe it's not me. Maybe it's him."

Dan stared at him like he was an idiot. "Then I guess we're out of luck."

"Would you two spiders shut up and find my friend Rhett?" Sam howled.

Rhett and Dan watched him struggle against the rope, inching across the prairie on his side, his pupils so wide that they swallowed up his pretty blue eyes in black.

"This is a goddamn inconvenience," Rhett offered.

For once, Dan just nodded in agreement.

"You think he'll recover?"

The look Dan gave him was one of pity. "I don't know, Rhett. Poison is poison, and humans are easily poisoned."

Rhett looked at Sam, struck to the marrow. The man was still on his side and trussed, unmoving. Rhett couldn't even tell if Sam was breathing. He was so accustomed to his own ability to bounce back from every wound that he'd never considered that something as piddly as a spider might be able to take Sam from him.

"Then we got to get rid of the poison. We got to fix Sam."

The look Dan gave him was brim-full of pity. "We don't know how."

They went back to stomping on spiders.

Dawn was a long time coming. It took another hour to kill all the remaining spiders, which wanted nothing so much as to sink fangs into anything moving. Sam didn't sleep a wink, just kept hollering and going totally still at intervals all night. The horses were jittery and single-mindedly stomping whatever spiders came their way, but it was hard to settle down when an entire herd of horses couldn't settle down. The women slept by the fire, claiming that there were now spiders hiding in the wagon, which was chock-full of dark crevices. Rhett didn't enjoy lying next to Sam when Sam was bugnuts crazy and shouting at him, and his brain was wide-awake and jumpy, in any case. He kept telling himself that Sam would pull through, but Sam wasn't doing so well. His color was bad, his eyes sunken, and his lips dried out and covered in froth and spittle. His visible wounds were an angry red, hot and hard.

Rhett tried to pop one of the bites, but nothing happened. He tried to suck out the poison, but none came, and Sam just got more addlepated, screaming that a spider was clamped on him and after his blood. Dan poked through the wagon for a book on magic potions, but in between the dark and the spiders, he couldn't find anything. Rhett took to helping Sam sip a leftover bottle of Buck's wine, hoping that whatever had healed their wounds last night would help again tonight. He chewed Buck's grapes, just a little, pulled off their skins, and slipped them between Sam's lips, helping him swallow. It was almost as bad as his night with the Captain, but even that had held a certain peace. Now, watching Sam's shallow breathing, peace and sleep were things much longed for.

Sometime near dawn, Rhett saw the thing he'd both dreaded and expected: a spider, larger than most, scurrying right for him. It had a body the size of a stack of dinner plates and legs as long as Rhett's arms, and it could skitter like a bastard. Rhett stood, feeling his back creak all the way up to his neck, and tried to stomp the thing, but it was wily and sidestepped him every time. Instead, he took up his gun and shot it. Chunks flew off it, but it kept lunging for him until he'd shot off most of the legs. Even then, like the giant scorpion, it didn't stop trying to end him, even when it had only one fang left, and that one dangling by a gooey thread. Finally, Rhett put a boot on top of what was left and poked his fingers through its hairy back, hunting for the ball of wax he knew he'd find. It was slimed in white, but it crumbled easily enough. The spider shivered apart into brown sand shot through with long, whiskery hairs.

Exhausted beyond belief, Rhett picked through the mess in his hands and found bits of a regular spider crushed among the wax, along with the usual chips of bone and gold. Holding up the bone, he couldn't tell what it was from, but he had his suspicions now.

All the little spiders were suddenly dead, curled on their backs and still. Sam shut the hell up and slept, and Rhett fell to uneasy dreams wriggling with spiders and scorpions and centipedes. Then he was the bird, soaring overhead, watching a tiny girl drive a settlers' wagon pulled by two brown mares. It was Meimei, her bright red jacket traded for a light blue coat like the mayor's children had worn in Gloomy Bluebird. As the bird hovered overhead, Meimei set down her reins and crawled into the wagon bed, where an array of horrible notions were laid out. Bottles, jars, a crow's leg with the toes curled in death. Meimei—or Trevisan, really—unwrapped something from a scarf and pulled out a chunk of bone. Using a peculiar knife, she sliced off a little chip of the bone and picked it up from where it had fallen on the scarf and smiled a smile that no small child should know how to make, empty of sweetness and full of madness and horror. She took up a bit of wax from a melted black candle and began shaping it with her tiny fingers. The bird that was Rhett couldn't quite see what she was doing, but he understood the message well enough. Trevisan was riding toward his goal and using Rhett's toe bone to send monsters against him, just as Dan had suspected.

Rhett woke with a shuddering start, and it was full light out.

The first thing he saw was Sam sleeping. The man's cheeks were pink and feverish, his brow wrinkled as he moaned and fought against a nightmare. Rhett put a hand on Sam's shoulder.

"Shh, Sam. It's okay," he murmured.

Sam relaxed and smiled, and Rhett rubbed his shoulder. For a strong man, Sam was so fragile. The spider's venom that couldn't touch anyone else in their group had driven him to shoot at his own friends. Cora had inspected the first wound, the big one, while he was tied up last night and found it red, hot, and hard. When she'd gently poked it with a knife, vile white fluid had leaked out, what she considered to be a worrisome amount. Rhett almost wished he'd left Sam somewhere safe, some lily-white town or maybe with his own mother, rather than bring him along on a journey with this many dangers. He'd rather live without Sam for a time than see him hurting. So this must be how Dan felt about Winifred, then— not wanting to be bossy so much as to save himself the torture of watching someone he loved suffer.

Rhett helped Sam sip more of Buck's wine, which seemed to calm him some. He slipped more skinless grapes and bits of cheese between his lips. Sam wasn't calling him a giant spider anymore, but the boy was weak as a kitten, and they were far away from any sort of sawbones. Cora couldn't help him any more than she already had, and the wendigo doc probably wouldn't have offered up his services, anyway, now that the Captain and all the Rangers were gone under damning circumstances. If Buck's wine couldn't fix Sam, chances were nothing could.

"C'mon, Buck. I know you're watching. What's the point of a god if you can't make miracles happen?" Rhett whispered to himself.

When Sam quit drinking and fell into an uneasy sleep, Rhett closed his eye for what felt like a heartbeat. Almost immediately, he startled awake and sat up and stretched, feeling the noon sun on his face. When he opened his eye, he held stock-still. All around the camp, crows and ravens were feasting on the dead spiders, which hadn't turned to dust. Hundreds and hundreds of birds, pecking and swallowing like they'd found a blood-soaked battlefield. The sight was repulsive and fascinating, but Rhett had nothing left in his heart for black birds, other than hatred.

"Get on!" he shouted, throwing a stone into the throng. "Get the hell out!"

The birds rose in an angry cacophony, spiraling up into the sky with furious shouts. Rhett didn't know if they were Trevisan's things or just wild birds who'd found a feast, but he was having none of it.

"Stop the shouting," Dan said, hands over his ears. "Everything I've got hurts, and I just want to keep sleeping."

"We got to leave," Rhett said, standing and looking about in disgust. "This place is nasty, and the faster we find Trevisan, the faster he'll stop sending bullshit animals to do his work. Sam ain't looking good, and pretty soon something's gonna get him permanently. I got to find a creek and wash off the spider guts." He looked at his boots, dreading what he was going to find inside once he pulled them off his feet.

"Sam'll pull through," Dan said, but Rhett could tell when he was being lied to.

The birds settled in the scrub trees overhanging the creek. While Rhett washed himself and his boots and cried to himself, they laughed and talked among themselves. He counted one new bullet hole, sealed over with fresh pink scars, and twenty-two spider bites, red and pulsing, but nothing as bad as Sam's.

For the first time, Rhett began to realize the truth of it: Sam might not make it.

Rhett felt a little better once they were back on the trail—but not much. Sam's color was improved and his many spider bites weren't as angry, but he wouldn't wake up, either. His chest barely moved with each shallow breath, and his heartbeat was so slow that even Cora found it worrisome. She gave him what few curatives she'd managed to keep with her on the trail, but nothing seemed to help. They could only settle him into the bed in the wagon and hope for the best. Rhett bolstered him with pillows and tucked the buffalo blanket around him and whispered sweet things about how they'd ride together again one day soon, with nothing more vexful than a frachetty bull to deal with.

The trail to Trevisan brought little comfort but some relief at being on the way to revenge. Rhett's anger was always a simmering thing, but now it was goddamn personal. The morning was cool and sunny, the wind high and blowing crispy leaves across the prairie. BB felt solid and warm underneath him, the beast's fine spirit and gentle gait making Rhett's firm frown twitch the tiniest bit. The best part was being far away from thousands of stiffly curled spider corpses, but he always felt better in transit. Winifred rode Kachina while Cora drove the wagon with Sam inside. Dan rode in back, partly to keep the smaller herd together but mostly, Rhett figured, to give him some space. For all his vexfulness, Dan cared about Sam, too, and he hadn't gotten preachy or sassy since Sam had fallen ill.

Cora, poor girl, was all et up with guilt in addition to her ongoing dread for Meimei. As a healer with a wide range of practical knowledge, she had never seen a spider that could inflict such damage, even though Dan swore the spiders were just Durango brown tarantulas and should've been completely lacking in venom that could harm a man. Nobody contested that Sam had been hit hard, and it was clear to see that the alchemist's control of critters wasn't natural. The sense of comfort Rhett had experienced was gone. He wouldn't let himself fall into it again. That first scorpion had just been an appetizer for the challenges Trevisan would let loose on the world, all to stop Rhett.

And no mistake—Rhett wanted to stop. To give up. To turn around. To take Sam back to Tanasi and safety.

But he never would. No matter what the lich threw at him, Rhett would keep going with his last breath.

For himself, for Earl, for Cora, for everyone who'd died at the train camp. And now for Sam.

His face, so scarred and damaged, was fresh out of smiles. Every step was a promise. The Shadow was no longer messing around. Like his oft-broken nose, there was no going back to the straight and narrow simplicity of life before he'd been broken.

The days blurred together. They were in the saddle from dawn to dusk, and even if the days were shorter and the nights colder, Rhett fell asleep almost the second his head hit the stack of books he used as a pillow, curled up in the wagon by Sam's sleeping body. If Sam sensed his presence there, felt his gentle touches and heard his sweet words, he didn't show any sort of response. Cora took care of the doctoring, keeping Sam clean and doing what she could to calm him. The Captain's laudanum came in handy every time Sam roused and jerked to sitting, screaming about spiders with his eyes wide-open and seeing nothing. But Rhett held hope. That's why he stayed away when Cora turned and bathed Sam's still body—he prayed that one day he'd see that body whole again and yearning for him. Cora seemed to understand, and her kindness was a gift. For all her own worry, she never begrudged Rhett for adding Sam's nursing to her own tally of concerns.

Sam wasn't the only one struggling. Winifred grew tired easily and almost tumbled out of the saddle one afternoon after falling asleep, her chin on her chest. If not for Sam's resting place and thrashing spells, she could've napped in the wagon, but she didn't even bring it up. Watching her grunt as she stood or sat about made Dan right tetchy, and Rhett made sure to stop the group early in the evenings when he could, finding various little reasons that no one could argue. This creek was just right, the horses were getting spooky. Winifred looked at him, lips pursed, but said nothing, and she was always the first one asleep. Rhett didn't begrudge her such rest; she was making another person from scratch, after all. Rhett took first watch, most nights, and it was like a long, waking dream, him staring into the fire and losing track of time, hoping to give his posse just a little more relief before falling into the wagon beside Sam, his dreams dogged with foolish hope.

One night, Dan was staring at their Ranger map by the light of the fire, chewing on his chunk of jackrabbit and looking generally vexed, which wasn't a new look for him, but it was aimed at the map instead of at Rhett, which was peculiar.

"What's got your breechclout in a wad, Dan?" Rhett asked.

Dan looked up and gave Rhett the sort of look Rhett expected. "You're leading us where the Shadow calls you, yes?"

Rhett nodded. "Yep. I don't mosey through the desert for fun."

"So when I look at the map and at the direction we're headed, it seems we should be headed slightly south, toward the sea. If Trevisan is on the move, and you're taking us to Trevisan, why does our path remain firmly east?"

"Maybe Trevisan's holding still," Rhett said. "Maybe he's doing something dirty in San Anton. Fetching more bones or making friends with spiders or doing whatever asshole alchemists do when they're running around in the bodies of little girls. That ain't my business. I just go where I'm..." Well, *told* wasn't the right word. "Pulled."

"Then either he's settled in San Anton for now or the Shadow is leading us somewhere else."

At that, Rhett snorted and snatched a piece of rabbit from Dan's stick, just to be ornery. "Why the Sam Hill would the Shadow send us anywhere other than after Trevisan? Not like there's something worse than him roaming around the damn prairie while we're being chased by skittery monsters."

Dan nodded like he actually agreed with Rhett, for once. "That's what bothers me."

As Rhett liked to be the only thing needling Dan, it rankled him as well. If they weren't heading for Trevisan, what the hell else was calling him in San Anton?

And would Sam be alive to see it?

One day, they woke up to frost gilding the prairie, and Rhett had never seen a prettier sight. He wasn't so fond of the cold outside of his buffalo robe and the wagon where he'd slept beside Sam, but for a moment there, the world looked like it was made of glass, and the sunrise sparked it red like magical fire. They rode until dusk and came upon a building. It wasn't a white man's sort of thing, and it wasn't a cattleman's sort of thing, neither. It was an old mission, humpbacked and beat down, made of soft clay cooked hard by the Durango sun. It hunkered down amid the scrub like an old toad, the cross at the roof crooked and the front door flanked by two statues. There were no fences, no horses, no herds of cows, no barking dogs to let the posse know they were unwelcome. Just an empty hitch out front and candles burning, warm and welcoming, behind oiled skin windows.

Rhett's belly was doing somersaults, a sure sign that this was exactly what the Shadow had wanted him to see. He stopped his horse, looked at Dan, nodded in a manly sort of way, and pulled out one of his pistols.

"Do you suspect trouble in the church?" Dan asked.

"I reckon if I expect trouble, I got a better chance of living through it."

Winifred cantered up on Rhett's other side. Her pistol, taken from the Rangers' stash, was likewise at the ready. "Or causing it," she added.

Dan barked a rare laugh. "She called it."

Rhett rolled his eye. "For a feller who keeps talking about my destiny, you sure seem certain I can change it just by handing out flowers instead of bullets."

Dan shook his head. "Be careful, but don't assume the worst. Perhaps the Shadow brought us here for a different reason. Didn't you say the Captain once spoke of a nun? In an old mission near San Anton? He told you she might have the answers we need to defeat Trevisan. And perhaps she'll have a curative for Sam, so tread lightly."

Rhett rolled that around in his head for a minute. "I don't think the Shadow has a great affection for books."

It was Dan's turn to snort. "Rhett Walker doesn't have a great affection for books, but the Shadow is often smarter than Rhett Walker." Dan kicked his horse toward the mission, and Rhett was pretty sure he heard him mutter, "Thank goodness."

Rhett spun and trotted back to the wagon. "I don't know what's going on, but this is where the Shadow's been leading me. You'd best hang back." He looked sternly from Cora's place on the wagon to Winifred on Kachina. "Both of you."

Cora nodded, but Winifred kicked her mare to a canter and went up ahead with Dan.

"Goddammit, Winifred," he muttered, whickering at BB to catch up.

They cantered up together, three abreast, the tug on Rhett's center growing stronger with every hoofbeat. He still had his gun drawn, as did Dan, but Winifred just defiantly leaned over her mare's neck and urged her on. The horses skidded to a dancing stop in front of the hitching post, and Rhett hurried to tie BB up before Winifred went on and beat him to doing something stupid.

"At least let me go in first," he said, struggling with his reins.

"It's just a mission," she shot back. "And considering I lived in one as a nun for a few years, I've got more experience than you."

"But the Shadow—" he started.

"Isn't the only one who gets to make choices," she finished, giving him a dark glare before throwing open the door.

"Wha—?"

The word was cut off, and Winifred went totally still.

Stiller than still.

She had turned to stone.

CHAPTER
15

Goddammit, Coyote Girl," Rhett muttered under his breath. He rustled around in his saddlebag and brought out the Captain's piss pan and bible, stuffed them down his binder over his heart, and swung off the horse. Samson's second had picked up the canter, despite Cora yanking on the reins, and now the wagon shuddered to a stop in the dirt before the mission, the excited herd milling around it.

"Cora, I'm begging you, let me go first. Hang back and protect Sam. I can't lose... anybody else."

"What happened?" she asked, but then she found the still form in the doorway, her features cracking down from alarm to worry. She nodded and stood on the wagon box, feet spread. "I will protect him."

Anybody else might've thought she had a weapon hid somewhere on her slight person, but Rhett knew the real weapon was the dragon she could become.

"You're not going to tell me to hang back?" Dan said, lips pulled back over his teeth like he was already half coyote and feral to boot.

"I don't waste my breath on shit that won't happen. She's your sister, Dan. We can go in side by side if you like. I'll even give you a first shot at whatever's on the other side of that door."

In the silence, Rhett could hear his own breathing and Dan's, as well as the slow slide of something on hard-packed dirt. Whatever was in the mission was headed for them, and not in a stupid animal sort of way. In a measured, thoughtful, cautious way. Which made Rhett suspect it had some wits, which is not what a feller wants to realize while he's staring at a stone statue of his friend and holding a gun.

"You know anything that can turn a body to stone?" he whispered.

"Cockatrice. But it doesn't sound like a cockatrice. They sound more like chickens. And that's no chicken."

From within: *Step, slide. Step, slide. Step, slide.*

"Maybe whoever's in there keeps a cockatrice in a cage by the door. Pretty good guard dog, I reckon, if you have a fondness for statues of curious strangers." Rhett glanced at the door, and another thought just about slapped him in the face. "Cockatrices—it's their eyes that's dangerous, right?"

"Right."

"Then maybe I should go in with something over my eye."

"Only you, Rhett, would consider facing a foe blind. But you could try something reflective, perhaps. The Captain once killed one by watching it with a lady's pocket mirror and shooting backwards over his shoulder."

Rhett had to shove his pistol into his holster to pull the Captain's pan out of his binder. It wasn't the shiniest metal he'd ever beheld, but it would do. "Close your eyes, Dan, and go in with me. I'll tell you if you need to shoot."

"Your plans never fail to surprise me, Shadow."

"Shut up and come on."

"Oh, I will. I look forward to shooting whatever's inside."

Rhett turned his back to the door, pulled his pistol with his right hand, and held the pan in his left, out in front of him so he could sort of see what was behind him reflected in the metal. Right now, he mostly saw darkness and stone, but as they passed a window, the light glimmered there, warm and flashy.

"Here we go," he whispered as they approached the frozen gray figure of Winifred and the double doors she'd thrown open. Stepping into the space with Dan's shoulder against his, he glared into the pan and saw...a nun.

She looked calm enough, not the usual gibbering monster Rhett faced. Clad in a long black dress, her hair and face were covered in a veil. Her hands were clasped together under her sleeves, but as she saw Rhett, they whipped out and pulled the veil back to show glowing green eyes and a stern frown and—Sweet hellfire, her hair was...moving?

"Shoot her, Dan! But don't look at her! Her eyes are..."

"Monster eyes?

"Crazy murder eyes!"

Dan's pistol barked five times, the gunpowder tickling Rhett's nose. As he watched in the plate, the nun absorbed each shot but didn't stop her stately walk toward them. His ears were ringing now, and his heart was thumping like crazy.

"Your other gun! Keep shooting. Hit the heart."

"I would if I could see her," Dan growled.

"Then aim up. Her hair is moving or something. Snakes? Hell!"

Dan fired a shot over the nun's head.

"She's shorter, and she's getting close, fast."

Dan's next shot landed right in the nun's swarming hair, and at that she cried out in pain, one hand disappearing into the knot of writhing whatever-the-hell she called hair.

"You got her, but she ain't stopping, Dan." Dan's last shots went wild, and Rhett growled, "Goddammit." And then he dropped the plate, ran backward, and rammed the nun, landing on top of her with his full weight, his back to her front. She crumpled beneath him, thrashing uselessly. She was a tiny little thing, after all.

"Cover her eyes, Dan!" Rhett shouted, pretty certain that the nun would manage to wiggle out from beneath him sooner or later, as he wasn't a large man himself. "But don't get bit. Her hair is all snakes, and angry."

As he fought her, spreading his weight and trying to make himself heavier, he stared up to where old wood beams crisscrossed the ceiling. When the first snake nipped at his face, he slammed his head back into hers, hard. Whatever this nun was doing, he wasn't about to get snakebit by her fool head while Dan did his work. The back of his skull cracked hard enough to make him see stars bursting against the dark ceiling, but the blow did its work, as the woman cried out and went limp beneath him.

"I'm here," Dan said.

Rhett didn't trust the woman not to budge, so he stayed in place until Dan had fixed the bandanna and held out a hand to help Rhett up.

When Rhett stood, he felt dizzy and hot for a moment before getting his bearings. The chapel was full of wood pews and dripping candles, a contrast in light and dark. When he stared down at the swept dirt floor, he could see just what he'd been grappling with. The nun was indeed quite small, short and slender, her dark habit covering every bit of her, right up to her neck. Her chin was pointed, her lips full, her skin the rich brown of the Aztecans who had once lived in this part of Durango and still fought to steal the cattle the white men grazed in their ancestral lands. Dan's bandanna covered her eyes and the top of her head, and a whole tangle of skinny little black snakes shoved and bit at it, hissing and striking. They weren't vipers, as far as Rhett could tell, but they didn't seem particularly friendly, and they sure as hell didn't like the cloth.

"You know what the hell she is?" Rhett asked.

"Gorgon. I read about them in your grimoire. I knew something about turning creatures to stone was familiar. We've got to keep her eyes covered."

"Did the book say anything about turning the statues back into people?"

Hands on his hips, Rhett dusted off his rump and spun around, real slow-like. The edges of the mission were lined with stone figures, mostly men. Rhett walked to one that seemed centrally placed, behind the altar and holding a cross overhead. As he got closer, he noted that the statue didn't have the kind, holy, my-shit-don't-stink expression of the usual sort of church saints. This one looked angry, and the two-handed grip on the cross would've better suited a knife. Putting two and two together, Rhett backed away from the statue, wondering if the people inside were still alive and able to see folks glaring back at them, or if they'd been reduced to stone forever.

"The book said nothing of this." Dan stood by Winifred, one hand up as if he wanted to touch her but was terrified to do so.

Whether he was frightened that being made of stone was catching or maybe he was worried about breaking her, Rhett couldn't have ventured a guess. He hurried to Dan's side and looked Winifred up and down, noting the determined but playful expression on her face. He reckoned that if she had to be stuck one way forever, that was a proper enough representation of the girl within.

"Maybe we should go get Cora and look through the books," Rhett ventured.

"Maybe you should tie up the nun and go do that work yourself," Dan hissed, teeth clenched together.

"Fair enough."

Rhett untied the rope belt around the unconscious nun's waist and used it to bind her hands together tightly. There was still some length left, so he dragged her across the room by her feet, careful to avoid the snakes. But when he got to the fancy chair by the altar, he couldn't figure out how to get her in it without getting snakebit. Dan seemed preoccupied with walking around his sister and glaring, so Rhett tugged another rope down from an old curtain and tied the woman's feet together, too.

"I'm leaving her here, Dan," he called. "Going outside now, like you told me to."

Dan didn't answer, and Rhett figured that if he got turned into a statue after so many warnings, it was his own goddamn fault.

Back outside, he found Cora parked in front of the wagon, Sam's Henry ready, if awkwardly held.

"What happened?" she asked, and Rhett exhaled a breath that at least Sam was mostly safe, for now.

"It was a gorgon that turned Winifred into a statue. Dan sent me out for information on how to turn her back. Naturally he'd send the feller who can't read to fetch a book. Cora, you know anything about gorgons?"

Cora schooled her terror and worry into a calm mask and nodded silently, as she tended to do when thinking hard. She put the Henry down on the driver's seat and disappeared back into the wagon. A few moments later, she jumped down from the back door carrying a stack of heavy books, several of which she offloaded into Rhett's arms.

"I have heard of gorgons, but they are not native to my

homeland. With cockatrices, there is no way to turn someone back once they are stone, but perhaps the gorgon herself will tell us."

Rhett followed her as she walked purposefully toward the mission. "Yeah, well, she's out cold right now. But I tied her up first."

Cora huffed. "Well, that should certainly make her willing to talk."

"She attacked us!"

"I begin to see why."

She stomped past Winifred and into the mission, and Rhett muttered under his breath, "I will never in my life for a single moment understand how the female mind works."

Cora didn't even stop to inspect Winifred. She marched up to the brightest spot in the mission, dropped the books, and began flipping through them. When Rhett didn't follow fast enough, she pierced him with a look and pointed to the stack of books with a claw. A small curl of white smoke hissed from her nose. He hurried to deposit his books and get the hell away before she became more dragonish.

Back outside, the night air was one hell of a relief. Dan still stood by his sister, one hand on her shoulder like he was offering her support.

"Does Cora have the right book? Can we fix her?" he asked.

Rhett shrugged. "Damned if I know. Considering there's statues all over the mission. I reckon that if the nun could do anything about it, there wouldn't be so many." Another thought struck him. "Unless she likes it that way. Maybe she ain't a friendly kind of nun."

"Are you sure she's a nun?"

"Hellfire, Dan. She's wearing a nun's black duds and a veil, so I don't know what else she'd be. A waiter in a tuxedo? But

I reckon now she's a nun with a broken nose. Serves her right if it heals cattywampus." Ever since Rhett's nose had healed crooked after tasting Jiddy's silver knuckledusters, he'd pretty much begrudged everybody whose nose was straight and slender still. "In any case, seems like you'd do more good reading than you would standing here, being tetchy."

Dan released Winifred's stone shoulder. She rocked a little, and he winced. "Perhaps, for once, you're right."

Cora was still reading and had already discarded a couple of books, which were tossed away, their spines cracked open like they'd dared to insult her. Dan sat down beside her and took a book into his lap. His finger ran down page after page, and every so often, he'd glance up at the statue of his sister, his brow furrowed and his eyes gone soft and sorrowful.

Across the room, the nun was sitting up, conscious now and writhing against her bonds. Her shoulders rubbed at the cloth over her eyes, the snakes straining to bite the air before her face.

"Listen, nun. We got to talk," Rhett said as he walked up.

The nun gritted her teeth, hissed, and let out a stream of sounds that made no sense to Rhett but seemed to promise death and dismemberment.

"She only speaks Aztecan," Dan said, all surly. "And she said you will be punished for your sins."

Sadness gripped Rhett's heart, thinking about Earl's last confession. "I reckon I don't believe in sin, and she's not much in the position to punish just now, anyway. Ask her how to make Winifred a person again."

Dan stumbled over his words a bit, but whatever he said made the nun laugh, and a dark and evil sound it was, especially coming out of someone who looked so saintly on the outside. When she spoke again, Dan said, "She says nothing can make my sister a person again, that she will join the sinners who watch the door. Such is her curse: to punish and to keep the books."

"Wait. Keep the books? So this is the place the Captain told us about?"

Dan translated, and the woman's voice when she next spoke was less evil and more curious. Rhett caught the words *el Capitán*, which sounded pretty familiar.

"She wants to know which Captain told you? And who you are."

Rhett dug in his pouch and pulled out the Captain's badge. Careful to hold back the sharp pin, he ran the woman's fingers over the metal. "Las Moras. And I'm the Captain now," he said gently. "He even gave me his name. I'm Rhett Walker, and this is my posse."

Even with her hands bound, the woman went still as she touched the metal, her fingertips light over the carved letters. She spoke, and Dan spoke back, although he had to stop and think a bit.

"I don't know the word for sand wyrms," he explained. "But she seems familiar with them from my descriptions."

Dan and the woman conferred, and soon he stood with a tired sigh. "She liked our Captain. Won't deal with Haskell, since he called her some unkind names."

"Goddamn Haskell. I should've killed him myself," Rhett fumed.

"She says they had a signal so the Captain could approach without losing any men. She's willing to help us because we didn't kill her, but you should know...she would rather be dead."

"So why don't she kill herself?" Rhett asked, but his voice broke on the last word.

"Suicide is a sin," the woman said, her English perfectly

understandable. "This is my punishment and my task: to stay here and cause suffering and in turn, to suffer."

"Well, why the hell didn't you just start talking right off?" Rhett hollered, exasperated.

The nun gave a small, sad chuckle. "You learn more about a man when he thinks you can't understand him."

"Goddamn, lady. If you'd just dealt straight with us from the beginning, we'd all be in a hell of a better mood. Now can you help Winifred or not?"

The woman's head turned toward the door, where the night wind whistled in past Winifred cast perfectly in stone, gray and mottled and hard, hands outstretched.

"I cannot."

Dan growled and swore.

"Can anybody?" Rhett asked, feeling like he was asking a bunch of stupid questions but that somebody by God had to.

The nun shook her head, and as the cloth fell away from her eyes, Rhett lunged for Dan and tackled him to the ground while shouting, "Close your eyes, Cora!"

They landed hard, and Dan grunted but didn't complain, and Rhett climbed up so that he was blocking Dan's face completely from anything the nun might do. But she didn't move, and nothing happened.

"My eyes are closed," she said softly. "And if I could use my hands, I would put my veil down. You will be safe."

All of a sudden, Rhett realized he was plastered all over Dan, and it was damned awkward. He clambered off carefully, whispering, "I want to trust her, but I don't yet. Keep your eyes closed, you hear?"

Dan nodded, and Rhett braced his hands on the dirt floor and stood, circling around to walk toward the nun from behind.

"This your veil, falling down your back?" he asked.

"*Sí.*"

"Reckon that means yes. I'm gonna try to flip it over the snakes now."

The nun chuckled. "Perhaps they will allow it."

Holding his breath and ready to whip his hands back, Rhett gingerly plucked the white fabric from the nun's back and tried to sweep it over the nest of snakes that writhed and hissed where her hair should've been. It took several tries, but he finally succeeded. It was a rumpled job, but when he checked from the side, the nun's face was completely covered. She lifted her tied hands and arranged it as well as she could until she looked like nothing more than a simple nun.

"The serpents have no venom, you know," she said.

"I'll keep my distance, just the same."

"You said you came here as a Captain, for information?"

Rhett knew that tone. It was the sort of tone a person used when they wanted something and knew they had something valuable to trade in return.

"I did. And let me guess. You'll help with that information if I untie you."

Her laugh was a lively thing, for a snake-haired nun. "Exactly so."

"But nothing anyone can do will fix our friend?"

At that, her head hung low. "I am sorry, but no. It is permanent. Ask me anything else I can grant you or tell you, and it is yours."

"Once you're untied."

"Once I'm untied."

"And you're not lying about our friend?"

"Look around you. These statues are my constant companions. If I could save anyone, it would lighten the load my soul bears. This is not a destiny I wished."

Rhett looked to Dan, who walked to the mission wall and punched the stone with his fist, hard enough to draw blood. He stalked back to Winifred.

"My sister will not sit here, in a church, watching sins punished for eternity. She hated the church. I forced her to go there once, to seek solace and contemplation and safety within a cloister's walls, and she rebelled. I will not force her again." With both hands, he shoved the statue, hard, in the chest. The statue rocked backward, wobbled for a long second, and fell back, smashing against the floor.

CHAPTER 16

No!" Rhett yelled, running toward the toppling statue.

He was too late, of course, and he skidded to a halt as the statue crashed against the dirt. The gray rock exploded and skittered across the floor. Rhett was completely flummoxed to see Winifred's skin revealed underneath it, as if the stone had been merely a crust. She landed on her back, eyes wide open, totally still. And then she drew a deep, sucking breath and pushed it back out.

Dan was across the room in a heartbeat, whooping fiercely in joy and kneeling by his sister's side.

"How can this be?" Cora muttered, her face bathed in wonder as she came to kneel at Winifred's other side.

"I keep forgetting she's cursed," Rhett muttered back.

Dan put an arm around his sister's shoulders and took her hand, helping her to stand. Her face showed complete shock, her hand going immediately to her belly.

"Gorgon," she whispered.

"We know," Dan said, grinning.

"What happened?" the nun called. "You broke the statue, and...she's alive? She was within?"

"Exactly so," Rhett said, giddy with joy and mimicking her earlier clever tone.

"It can't be." The nun struggled, trying to stand on her tied feet. "It can't be so easy."

"You never tried to break one before?" Rhett asked.

"Of course not! I can't help turning them to stone, but smashing them would be cruel, blasphemous."

"Except she's alive," Cora said wonderingly.

"Please. Help me stand. I have to try. I have to see."

Rhett looked at Dan. "Your call."

Behind Dan's joy was his usual canny wisdom. "Free her feet and retie her hands behind her. And then we'll see."

The task that had seemed impossible while the nun was unconscious was far easier with her eager help. As soon as her feet were free and her hands were behind her back, she ran to the statue Rhett had inspected, the one with arms upraised and brandishing a cross. The nun threw her body at the statue, again and again, trying to make it topple over. Finally, Rhett took pity on her, walked over, and pulled it down with one hand. It smashed against the floor, and everyone stopped, waiting for the same magic that had revealed Winifred's copper skin under the hard stone coating.

All they saw was smashed gray stone.

"No!" the nun cried. "No! Not Eduardo. My love. Gone now. Truly gone. Why did I believe you? Why was I so foolish to hope?" She fell to her knees and dragged her veiled face through the rubble.

"Hey, now," Rhett called. "Keep that veil on."

"Or what? What could you possibly do to punish me more than this life?"

Winifred broke away from Dan and went to the nun, careful to keep her face turned away to avoid any accidental eye contact. Kneeling, she caught the nun by the shoulders and helped her to sit up, smoothing down her veil and patting her like a baby.

"It's never foolish to hope," Winifred said. "It's what keeps us going."

"But you're alive, and he isn't," the nun wailed.

"I'm under a curse. I die nine times, and the ninth time, I stay dead."

The nun swallowed hard and hung her head. "Ah, so you tangled with a cat shaman."

They shared a small chuckle, and Rhett looked at Dan and shrugged.

"Come. Stand up. We have to move forward. It doesn't do to sit in the dust of the departed, my mother used to tell me," Winifred said, sounding kinder than she'd ever been to Rhett.

"My hope is dead," the nun said. She took a deep breath and sighed. "But we are not. Close and bar the doors, and I will show you what I know."

An hour later, they sat in a warm kitchen around a long table on benches much like the ones in the Ranger cabin, roughly hand-made but long worn by years of buttocks. In blessed peace, they ate chicken soup and beans as Winifred and Inés, for that was the nun's name, discussed stew recipes. The room was homey, lit by candles and with a cleanly swept flagstone floor. Rhett would've been angry and bored if the food wasn't so good and if the womenfolk hadn't all been too pleasant to harp on him for his bad manners. As it was, he at least had a full belly and didn't have to bother with building up a fire. He'd checked on Sam before coming inside, but nothing had changed. Nothing had changed in days. Sam wasn't getting any better, but at least he wasn't getting any worse.

"How did you come to be here?" Winifred asked. Rhett was surprised to find that the girl who'd been turned to stone had a softness for the woman who'd nearly killed her.

Inés sat down with her own soup bowl, carefully spooning the rich broth under her veil with a delicacy that suggested long practice. "Your Captain found me when I was in a dark place, soon after I took over this abandoned mission. I arrived with only my husband, Eduardo—but he was stone, by then. I dragged him behind the wagon because I could not lift him. He was always bigger than me. He was the first statue, and it was your Captain who helped move him to where he stood, until this day."

She dropped her soup spoon and went to a cabinet, returning with an old, sack-wrapped bottle and a wax-dappled candle cup. After pouring a sloppy shot, she held the cup under her veil and drank it in one gulp.

Seeing Rhett's confused stare, she murmured, "Tequila can be curative."

"A drunk nun. Who'd have thought?"

"Sometimes a dash of strength is needed before telling one's sad story, boy. Now listen. I was left at the doorstep of a mission in Santa Lucia when I was just a little girl. I don't remember my parents, but I do remember that I was always kept blindfolded. A mortal sensitivity to sun, they said. The sisters were pure of heart and couldn't see the evil I hid under my habit." Rhett raised an eyebrow, and she could apparently see well enough through the veil to laugh at him. "The snakes are biddable when I will them so. I knew well enough that if the nuns were displeased, I'd be alone in the world, so I was a good little girl. I grew up almost like an ordinary novice, but before I took my orders, I wanted to experience the world. It's not uncommon, and I soon fell in love with a boy named Eduardo in the nearby town. We married, and had a daughter, and she was born like me. My sweet Maria. Eduardo could not see what she was, couldn't see the tiny snakes. I kept her eyes covered, like mine, telling him she had the same light sensitivity, and he was understanding. Oh, Eduardo."

Winifred put a hand on Inés's back as the woman's head fell. "But one day, she was angry, as babies can be, and her snakes attacked him while he took her for a walk outside. He couldn't see what was happening, and before I could stop him, he flung her away. It was such bad luck, so impossible. She landed on an old branch, and something pierced her heart. So tiny, so fragile she was. She turned to sand, and when I cried out, Eduardo looked to me and saw what I am. We fought, and he ripped the blindfold from my eyes, and then... he was stone."

"Looked like he was holding a knife to kill you at the time," Rhett observed.

"He was. What would a normal man do, finding a monster in the body of his wife? How could he understand what he was seeing for the first time? I do not blame him. For her, or for this. Losing them both, I knew I had to withdraw from life. To live alone, and to find some kind of work that would make up for my sins. This mission had a fine library, and your Captain brought me many books over the years. It would appear that the monks knew of monsters, and the way I found their bones suggests they were killed by the creatures they studied. Ripped apart violently. Partially eaten." Her veil tilted as she looked around the room, filled with sturdy but simple furniture and hanging herbs. "Oh, yes. This place is very haunted. It is what I deserve."

The hairs on the back of Rhett's neck went up, and he, too, looked around. He could see, now that he was looking hard, the dark splashes on the limed white walls where rusty red couldn't quite be scrubbed away. He imagined what it might have looked like, this table full of quiet men in brown robes eating their supper, and then the door flew open to reveal... hell, anything. Sand wyrms, Lobos, chupas, some critter no one had lived to tell about yet.

"Why didn't the Captain mention you earlier?" Dan asked, ever the logical one.

Inés shrugged. "Because we agreed it was best kept a secret. People who come here don't leave. This is not a boardinghouse or a saloon. I protect information that would change the very fabric of the world. Such things must be kept secret at all costs."

Rhett finished his soup and stood. "So where's this library? Because we got a lich to kill and a sick friend who needs medicine for what the lich's poison has done to him."

Even through the fabric, he could feel the nun's glare. "Where are your manners?"

"I like her," murmured Dan.

Rhett sat back down as everyone else finished their soup. Not like he could do much with a library on his own, anyway. Despite Sam's repeated attempts at teaching, he could barely understand the letters that made up his own name, much less parse out an entire book about killing alchemists. Ever since Winifred had turned back to flesh and blood, he'd felt the Shadow's tug renew, pulling him east toward San Anton proper. It made him feel restless, almost itchy, as if sitting anywhere but in a saddle on a moving horse was a godforsaken waste of his time. He glanced at Cora, who sat back with her arms crossed and her mouth pursed. He reckoned she felt about the same way as him: ready to go kill a lich.

Still, as a man who hated rudeness, he figured he'd get more help out of Inés if he let her finish her goddamn soup, even if it was a dainty sort of business that took for-goddamn-ever. It took everything he had to sit still, not fidget and be vexful, but he by God did it. And there was no sweeter sound than the nun's spoon scraping on pewter.

"Now, if you're ready," the nun said, prim but amused. She took a lantern off the table and walked into a long, shadowy hall.

Rhett stood, cracked his back, and followed. Inés kneeled and pried up a large, flat stone, revealing a dark hole and the top of a wooden ladder.

"It's a priest hole. It was open when I arrived here. I carted the bones up in sacks."

She descended halfway into the hole to a pitch-black hell, took the lantern back, and kept going down, down, down. When her feet hit the ground, it echoed.

"Come on down. Only one on the ladder at a time. It's very old. I'll light the way."

Rhett stared down into the hole as Inés lit a candle far below. It occurred to him that he was more scared of going down that ladder than he was of a shoot-out with twenty fellers who wanted him dead. But he wasn't going to let anybody see that, especially not Dan, who would never let him live it down.

"I'll go first," he said, backing carefully onto the ladder and taking the rungs slowly, feeling the wood accept his weight with a slight bounce on every step down. It was cold belowground, and the scent reminded him all too well of the Cannibal Owl's lair, of cold stone and blood and evil left alone to fester too long. The shadows seemed to shift around the candles, making wraiths and eyes and claws twitch on the walls. The sound of Inés's footsteps echoed down a short hall, each sound ending like a dying sigh.

"Haunted was goddamn right," Rhett whispered to himself.

The dirt was the same orangey-brown as it was aboveground, but there were stains everywhere that showed where blood had soaked in to stay. The ground was hard and pebbly, and square niches cut into the dirt walls held more dripping candles that Inés lit as they passed.

Rhett followed the light to a larger chamber, hewn from the dirt and rock and filled with flickering shadows. Rough wooden shelves were built into the walls like carven dentures in an old man's uneven gums. Rows and rows of books lined the shelves in all shapes and colors, faintly emanating menace like a growling cat. Inés prowled among them, taking down books and inspecting them more closely. A table, shiny with use, held years' worth of melted candles, and the stool beside it was dimpled from being sat on. Rhett tried to imagine the life Inés had led, alone here with only the souls of damned monks and endless silence. Here, she could take off her habit and veil, knowing that she couldn't do any harm. It was goddamn sad, and coming from Rhett, that said quite a bit.

Rhett attempted to lean against the table, but it groaned dangerously, so he settled for putting a shoulder against the cold wall. He saw a flash, almost like being punched in the nose, of the bookshelf on its side as giant black-and-yellow lizards tunneled in and tore brown-robed men to shreds using knife-like teeth and stubby black claws. Shivering, he pulled away from the wall and went to the bookcase he'd seen in the vision, pressing against the wood gently to test it.

"It's fixed," Inés said sharply. "The Captain sealed it himself after he and his men determined the giant Gila monsters might come back. Now, tell me of your alchemist."

"He ain't mine," Rhett barked. After clearing his throat, he went on. "His name is Bernard Trevisan. He's a railroad tycoon. Said he's a few hundred years old, originally from somewhere in Europa. He's not just an alchemist, though. The Captain called him a lich."

"A necromancer," Winifred added, having appeared from the dark hall. She hugged her arms around her middle and shivered. "And he's in the body of a little Chine girl, about six years old."

"My sister, Meimei," Cora added, sliding her arms around Winifred from behind.

Inés nodded. "Tell me more. Tell me everything."

Rhett recounted his time in the railroad camp while they waited for Dan to join them. He skimmed through his own experiences and failures and tried to focus on describing every moment he'd spent with Trevisan. From their first meeting in the evaluation tent when Rhett had lost a toe, to their final showdown in Trevisan's locked train car, he recollected hard enough to give himself a headache. Inés and Dan broke in, here and there, to ask a question, and Cora chimed in when she had information from her own interactions with the railroad boss.

When they were done, Rhett felt like he'd been interrogated in Trevisan's damn doctor chair all over again, and the unnaturally encroaching shadows in the cellar crypt didn't help, either. All along, Inés had been tracing her fingertips over the books, plucking one here and there and either shoving it back home or placing it in a stack on the rickety table. By the end, Rhett had very little faith that the table could stay upright a moment longer. He felt the same way about himself.

"And what of your sick friend?" Inés pressed.

"The lich sent spiders," Rhett said. "They didn't trouble any of us much, but Sam took dozens of bites. Went mad, started seeing things. Tried to shoot us. We tied him down and gave him some...magical cures. But now he's just sleeping. Only wakes up to scream. I fear..."

He trailed off, but Cora finished for him. "He's only human, and it's killing him from the inside."

Inés nodded and went straight to a big book with gold lettering on it. Of all the books, something about this one struck Rhett as good, like the book had its own thoughts and held miracles for anyone willing to just give it a friendly look-through.

"Poisons I understand more," Inés said. "Ah! Here. See?" She tapped the book. "Bewitched spider bites. I think I have all the ingredients."

"Then you can save him?" Rhett asked, his voice high with feeling and hope.

"I can try," Inés confirmed.

"Then I'd best get back to Sam." His heart stuttered in his chest. "Hellfire, he's all alone right now!"

"We have work to do here, Rhett. You can't do anything to help Sam up there," Dan said solemnly.

"Well I can't read, so there's nothing I can do for him down here, either. Don't you get all preachy with me, Dan," Rhett said, shuffling toward the door as if waiting for someone to shoo him on, which is exactly what he was hoping for. "You're in a mission. You ain't the most preachy thing here."

Inés considered him through the veil, which was right disconcerting. Rhett couldn't read her facial expressions, see how her mouth was turned, but he could sense the sharpness of her gaze. "Your friend is safe. Almost no one comes here, maybe one lost soul every few years. That's why I stayed in the first place. Help us move the books up the ladder, and then go to your friend."

Rhett smiled to finally be getting his way. "Let's get those books up, then."

Inés's head turned to the wall. "Perhaps it's for the best. The shadows seem to follow him."

Rhett's spine went over cold at that, and he tried not to look at the stains or the shadows or anything snapping at the candle flames in a space where there was no wind.

"Faster's better than slower," he muttered, picking up a stack of books and hightailing for the hall.

It was a bulky operation, carrying the heavy, dusty tomes down the hallway and handing them up the ladder carefully so the rickety rungs wouldn't break. They made like a bucket brigade, one or two books at a time moving from person to person. Rhett stood at the top, being both smallish and hard to hurt.

And because he was the only one with his head above ground level, he was the first one to hear Sam scream.

CHAPTER 17

Sam had woken up screaming at least a couple of times a day since the spider attack. But this time, it was much louder, and Rhett knew there was something sincerely wrong. In a heartbeat, he was up and running, guns drawn.

Down the hall and out the chapel he ran, his boots skidding on the gravel left behind by Winifred's burst statue skin. Throwing the door open with both hands, the first thing he saw was a giant lizard eating one of the spare ponies and making a goddamn mess out of it. The next thing he saw was the tail of one of the creatures poking out the back of the wagon as it tried to squeeze inside. They looked a lot like Gila monsters, with pebbled black skin and yellow stripes and tiny beady eyes. But the ones he could see had a hell of a lot of teeth and were bigger than Samson.

Rhett emptied his gun into the lizard in the wagon as he ran to yank the halters off the tethered ponies, all of whom were pulling and rearing away from the wagon, desperate to join the rest of the herd in scattering into the desert night. He couldn't have them pulling the wagon over with Sam inside it.

A horse screamed, and Rhett looked around to find Samson fighting one of the lizards, his massive haunches pressed back against the wagon box as he reared and kicked.

"Goddammit, lizards," Rhett muttered, running around to the front of the wagon and aiming for the Gila's heart. Three shots in, and it burst into acrid black sand that billowed into Rhett's mouth like ashes and coated poor Samson until he looked black instead of bay.

"What's happening?" Dan called.

Rhett patted Samson's sweaty neck before hollering back peevishly, "We're fighting giant Gila monsters, you idjit. What's it look like?" He cut Samson's traces and ran for the lizard in the wagon just as Sam screamed again.

Ducking into the wagon, he saw Sam trying to drag himself back as the lizard fought its way inside. Bellowing his rage, Rhett emptied his other pistol into the creature at point-blank range, finally hitting its heart and filling the wagon with sand.

"It's okay, Sam," he murmured, trying to dust the sand off Sam's pale face and ease him back down onto the bed.

"The spiders are back," Sam whimpered. "Oh, lord, they're gonna go for Rhett!"

"Rhett can take care of himself. You just stay here, okay?" He almost pulled one of the Ranger pistols out of the trunk but didn't know if Sam was seeing straight these days. "Just hide under this blanket."

Tugging the sandy buffalo robe over a shivering Sam, he slammed and locked the wagon door from the inside and hurried out into the driver's seat, where he pulled the canvas taut and tied it shut. That would at least make it a little harder for the lizards to get Sam while Rhett did his best to end all the bastards.

Dan was just outside the mission and had managed to kill the Gila he'd been working on. Rhett was about to ask him if he needed more bullets when another lizard slammed out of the night and knocked him over, which set Rhett's blood boiling.

He hopped up and flung himself on top of the Gila, wrenching an arm under its neck to hold on while he tried to stab it in the heart with his Bowie knife. The lizard, for its part, didn't particularly want to get stabbed, and it was the bronco ride of Rhett's life trying to get the monster to focus on him instead of Dan, who was frantically reloading. More and more lizards were appearing like vultures to a carcass, too many for Rhett to handle on his own, especially considering he was holding on to one for dear life.

"Anytime you wanted to help, I'd be much obliged," he hollered.

But when he looked around for Dan, he couldn't find him.

Rhett fell with a sudden jolt in the middle of a cloud of black sand, dropping his knife and landing hard enough to knock out his breath. Winifred's hand appeared to help him up, and Rhett took it and resheathed his knife.

"It's always interesting with you, Rhett," she said.

"Well, I'd hate for you to get bored," Rhett said as soon as he could speak again, looking down at her belly to make sure it was still whole. Which was a bad move, as a Gila monster bit down on his shoulder and shook him like a dog.

"Where's Dan?" he yelled, punching the lizard in the throat before he realized his Bowie knife would make a much better argument. As soon as the blade sunk in past the hard skin, the monster dropped him and looked at him in utter surprise as its skin started to knit again. That's when he stuck the knife right in its chest, jagging the blade around until the lizard disappeared in its own puff of sand.

"Getting real sick of sand," he offered.

"Uh, Rhett?"

Winifred's back was to him, and Rhett soon realized why. A circle of the fat lizards had surrounded them. Rhett spun around, putting his back to hers and trading his knife for his pistols, which he swiftly and fumblingly reloaded from the bullet pouch on his belt. There were at least a dozen of the monster lizards, and they'd apparently given up on the swift horses to focus on the only critters dumb enough to stick around. With no sign of Dan, Cora, or Inés, it looked like he and Winifred were in for a hell of a fight. At least the lizards were going for lively prey and no longer poking around in the wagon for Sam.

Cora and Inés being scarce he understood, but Dan should've been here, and maybe a fire-breathing dragon would have more of an impact on the smaller, less fire-breathing monsters. No time to resent his absent friends, though. He had to fight.

"Let's do this, girl," he said. And then he started shooting. So did Winifred.

The lizards didn't much know what to do with a fight, and they weren't too fond of guns. It was right peculiar, watching them act like the usual shy lizards and then getting brave enough to screech and show their teeth. Rhett killed one, and Winifred killed one, and then Rhett reloaded while Winifred kept at it with his Henry, which she must've snatched off BB's saddle. Damn, but Rhett wished he had Sam's Henry, which was locked up in a trunk, in case Sam should again confuse his friends for tarantulas.

"Rhett, Winifred. Close your eyes!"

Rhett's head spun toward the mission doors, where he found Dan standing behind Inés. The nun was a peculiar thing to see outside, in the middle of the prairie. Her long black habit swayed in the wind, her white veil shining like a beacon in the night.

Rhett didn't generally like doing what Dan said, but as Inés started to lift her veil, he screwed his eye shut and put a hand on Winifred's arm.

"Don't look, you hear?"

"Once was enough for me, fool."

Even if he couldn't see what was happening, Rhett could hear the results of Inés's dastardly power. The lizards made a sucking puff as they turned to stone. Now and then, one would fall over, and then sand sprinkled down onto the prairie and got whipped around on the night wind. He could feel it dancing over the skin of his cheeks and the backs of his hands.

A long pause made him a little nervous, as he could still hear lizards moving but couldn't tell how many or what prey they were currently after. But Inés's boots swished closer as she yelled something in Aztecan, so he assumed she had the lizards in hand, or was at least getting a bit more proactive about getting their attention.

"Rhett! In front of you!"

As Dan's words reached him, Rhett heard it, a lizard scurrying toward him on giant claws. He took the chance of opening his eye, just a tiny bit, and emptied his pistol into the attacking Gila monster, which soon popped into sand and blew away.

The night got real quiet after that, and he ventured to ask, "Is that all of 'em?"

It took a few long moments for Dan to answer, as of course the feller would want to be extra sure. "I think so."

"My veil is down," Inés said.

Rhett scrubbed the sand from his face before opening his eye. He and Winifred stood in a small circle of orange dirt, and around that was a much bigger ring of sparkling black stone lizards.

"Goddamn," Rhett murmured. He looked at Inés, again fully swathed in fabric, the nun's small hands clasped in front of her. "You're pretty good in a fight."

Inés inclined her head. "Only when the cause is righteous. I did not think the Gila monsters would return here. After the monks' slaughter, the Rangers sealed the hole. They attacked from underground last time, swarming, and I understood them to generally be lone, stupid creatures who stay in their caves and tunnels and come out only to feed. This has never happened before."

Dan looked at Rhett, his arms crossed. "Yes, well, strange things seem to happen around Rhett. Almost like he calls trouble to his side."

Rhett bristled at that, crossing his own arms and approaching Dan nearly close enough to touch boot toes. "I take offense at that, Dan. I get rid of trouble, not bring it."

"I'm not saying you mean to bring trouble. You are too unpredictable to make plans on that scope, as I've learned through repeated suffering. I'm saying that we know the Shadow is called to trouble, but perhaps, in turn, trouble is called to the Shadow."

"You know," Winifred said thoughtfully, "I've actually seen more monsters in the last year than I have in my entire life combined. Even in Nueva Orleans, we were carefully hidden and controlled."

Rhett looked from one to the other, but neither of them seemed to be pulling his tail. "So life ain't normally this..."

"Chaotic?" Winifred offered.

"Dangerous?" Dan countered.

"...peculiar," Cora said, stepping out from behind Inés.

Rhett took a step back, casting about for an answer that didn't make him seem like a walking bear trap for anyone foolish enough to throw their lot in with him. "Maybe it's just Trevisan's curse," he said. "Maybe whatever calls his creatures calls other things as well. We don't understand his magic. Right?"

"Perhaps," Inés said, sounding amused. "Either way, the

books are inside, waiting. I've learned to trust books more than people."

Rhett looked around the mission yard, hands on his hips. "Well, considering I can't read for shit, I'll just rustle up the horses." Pulling all the halters off the wagon and draping them over his arm, he walked off without looking back. "Horses I understand," he muttered, mostly to himself. "But people'll turn on you in a heartbeat."

"We're not turning on you," Dan said, jogging to catch up with him and taking a handful of halters for himself. "We're just trying to figure out how things are supposed to work. When you showed up, the rules changed. People need a while to adjust to something new. Like horses. A transition, the Captain called it. You have been going through your own transitions, and the rest of us are struggling to catch up while trying to stay alive."

Not sure what to say to that, Rhett whistled for Ragdoll and waited to hear hoofbeats, hoping the mare had regained her wits and not ventured too far into a night that could contain worse things than a passel of oversized lizards. Sure enough, the scraggly appaloosa appeared shortly at full gallop, several of the other horses in her wake. She'd become the lead mare of their regular herd, and Samson, Kachina, Blue the mule, Blue the horse, two chestnuts, and Sam's new curly were with her. BB thundered after them, and with him, most of the small herd following behind like baby ducks. Rhett rubbed Ragdoll's forehead the way she liked, scratched her withers, and tried to stay standing when Blue nudged into him with his long, hard mule nose, begging for the same affection.

Yep, Rhett understood horses. And he was starting to understand people pretty good, too. For all Dan's preaching and occasional bellyaching, he was a stand-up sort of feller, and he was trying to help Rhett find the right path. It wasn't easy. And Rhett owed him something in return.

"I guess I've had to get used to change, too," he said slowly. "I do tend to shoot first and ask questions later, but I think that's because I often know what I want from the start, and I'm willing to do anything to get it. Even wait. Even if it means I have to throw a little hissy fit first. A long time ago, somebody smart told me you had to let horses get used to you before you tried to ride 'em. I reckon it was good advice. Smart horses don't take to dumb people. Smart horses, they test you first. Make sure you can be trusted."

"Wise critters, horses," Dan said as they slipped halters over noses and scratched favorite spots and brought the herd back to the wagon.

"Well. You're pretty wise yourself," Rhett said. "For a coyote."

Dan gave his old, tricksy grin. "Let's go back and see if the killer nun can save Sam. I think you and him have a lot to talk about."

CHAPTER
18

When Rhett and Dan had tied up all the horses, they found Cora waiting, leaning against the door to the mission.

"We think we found something," she said. "For Sam. We moved him inside."

That's what her mouth said, at least. Her eyes danced in a mischievous sort of way that raised Rhett's hopes.

"Guess we should go on in, then," he answered.

They followed Cora into the mission, which felt right homey now that nobody and nothing inside it was trying to kill them. It was getting late, and Rhett couldn't stifle his yawn as he stumbled into the kitchen. The long table was cleared from supper and covered in dry old books and tall, leaning candles, which looked downright precarious to Rhett but wasn't his problem. Right down the middle was Sam. Rhett startled and hurried over, but Sam was still breathing, for all that he looked to be laid out like a corpse.

"What'd you find?" he asked, thumbs tucked into his gun belt.

Inés walked over carrying a mortar and pestle, grinding something in the old stone that smelled of spices and grave dirt, the most putrid sort of medicine. "This is a counter to magical poisoning," she said. "Most such things, like venom and contagion, reach the heart and kill the victim. But Cora tells me you had some magic of your own—"

"A god's wine," Rhett supplied.

Inés bowed her head. "Yes. So perhaps it was enough to keep him from dying, and yet his fragile mortal body can't get rid of the poison within. It's trapped inside like liquor behind a cork. And this will...let's say, get rid of the cork."

"Sounds messy," Rhett said, but he bounced on his toes. He didn't care if it was messy. He just wanted Sam.

Inés stopped by Sam's head and put the pestle on the table. "Before I give him this potion, you must consent for him. I don't know what it will do. It could cure him. Or it could kill him. Do you think he would wish to take this chance?"

"Yes," Rhett said. "Hell yeah, he would. Do it."

Dan shifted and made a little noise that suggested his quick answer was more about what Rhett wanted than what Sam wanted, and Rhett turned to him, one hand unintentionally on his pistol.

"You got something to say, Dan, you'd best go on and say it."

"I can't tell if you call the shots or if the Shadow does, but I've always known Sam to be a fighter. So I agree with you, but I still think your reaction is rooted in selfishness."

"Most people wouldn't choose to keep dying if they could maybe live."

Dan nodded to concede the point.

"Well, then." Inés scooped the thick, black mixture up with a spoon and stirred it into a waiting cup of water. "Help him sit up."

Rhett and Dan moved, one on either side of Sam's still body, and helped him to sit up. He felt floppy and too thin in Rhett's arms, light as a feather. No wonder the womenfolk had been able to wrestle him out of the wagon and onto the table. Rhett was forced to recognize how much the boy had wasted away in the past days. Sam's cheeks were gaunt, his temples sunken in. All his sunshine was gone.

"Hurry," Rhett urged.

Inés tipped Sam's head back and dribbled the liquid into his mouth. Sam sputtered and coughed some up, but Inés shook her head and kept pouring it down. It foamed black around Sam's lips, and his eyes flew open as he choked and spat.

"Hold his nose," Inés said. "He will fight it, but he must drink it, or it's all for nothing."

"Sorry, Sam," Rhett said. He pinched Sam's nose and forced his head back.

Dan held Sam's chin so he couldn't close his mouth, and Inés kept pouring the foul brew down, no matter how much of it came back up. Sam's blue eyes rolled to Rhett, pleaded as he weakly struggled.

"You got to drink it down, Sam. You're dying. You're dying, and I can't lose you."

Sam gave the tiniest nod and tried to swallow, but the stuff was fighting its way back out. Finally, the cup was empty, and Inés set it down and gestured for Rhett and Dan to close Sam's mouth.

"Keep it closed," she said. "Let the magic work."

Sam shook and flailed between them, eyes wide and panicky and bloodshot, trying to escape them or the medicine. Cora stepped close to watch with the detached sort of look she got when she was doctoring. Winifred hovered a way back, a few ragged towels in her arms. The waiting seemed to go on forever, and then Sam jerked and fell back, unconscious again. Rhett shrugged at Dan, and they helped ease Sam's body back down flat on the table.

"What now?" Rhett asked.

"We wait. We wait, and we watch." Inés stepped back, arms crossed.

For the longest time, nothing happened. And then Sam moaned, his head falling to the left and then the right. His shoulders hunched up around his ears, and his belly gave an evil gurgle. His body convulsed, and Rhett recognized what was happening.

"Sit him up quick," he shouted. "He's gonna—"

Before he could finish his sentence, Sam's moan turned into a goddamn geyser of vomit. Blacker and thicker than the medicine, it splattered all down's Sam shirt, burning through the fabric and turning his skin red. Rhett brushed it away, feeling the sting of ichor, and flopped Sam over on his belly with the boy's face over the floor as he kept on retching and retching and retching.

"Goodness," Inés murmured.

Because the sum total of everything that was coming out of Sam was more than his whole body could've held, much more than a stomach's worth and much more than he'd eaten in weeks. The floor was covered in black, syrupy tar, the white walls splattered with it as flecks ate through the years of white-washing. Winifred tried to clean some away with her towel, but it just ate through the fabric. Rhett kept his hand on Sam's back, hoping the black stuff wasn't burning up the poor man's innards as it came out.

"Is that supposed to happen?" he asked Inés.

She shook her head. "I've never seen anything like it."

As time wore on, Sam came up dry heaving, and Rhett took another towel from Winifred and dabbed the black stains away from Sam's lips.

"A salve," he muttered. "Get me some kind of salve. It's burning him. It's burning him, goddammit!"

Inés hurried away and came back with a little pot of grease,

which Rhett smeared over Sam's lips and chin and chest, anywhere the black poison had burned him and left angry red
stains behind.

"Rhett?"

Rhett looked up, every part of his being focused on the man
who had finally spoken again.

"I'm here, Sam."

"There were spiders."

"I know."

"They were trying to get you, Rhett. I tried to stop 'em, but I
wasn't . . . wasn't strong enough."

"It's okay, Sam." Rhett helped Sam sit back up and their eyes
locked. "We can fight the spiders together."

And then Sam smiled, and it was like the first time seeing
the sun in weeks.

Rhett smiled back.

⟍⟍━

They moved Sam to one of the old cots in the monks' sleeping
chambers. Rhett collected what moldering cushions he could
to make his friend more comfortable, but it wasn't an easy task.
For his part, Sam seemed happy to be alive for all that he was
weak as a kitten and could barely lift his arms.

"What's wrong with me? Why am I so thin?"

"You got bit by one of Trevisan's spiders, and you took it
badly. Tried to shoot everybody, fought us, screamed about it.
Then we couldn't get you to wake up."

"Tried to shoot you?" Sam said, eyebrows going up like he
was already feeling guilty.

Rhett poked a finger through the hole in his pants. "Not
your fault. No harm done. Barely tickled a little."

"Oh, lord, Rhett. I couldn't be more sorry."

"It's okay, Sam. You got Dan, too. It was fun, watching him holler."

He didn't want Sam to feel bad about what he'd done under the influence of poison, but he wasn't going to start lying now, not when things had been going so well for them.

For the rest of the night, Sam wandered in and out of sleep, but it wasn't the sleep of the venom. He didn't lie like a dead man and then rise up, screaming at things that weren't there. He just slept like a normal feller who was recovering from an awful illness, something that had come within a hairsbreadth of ending him. Whatever the rest of the posse did, Rhett didn't care. He settled in on the next cot over, content with his own thoughts. It was enough, for Rhett, that Sam was alive.

Some time later, whether hours or days, Rhett couldn't say, he woke up right as Dan showed up in the door with the old sparkle in his eyes.

"How's Sam?" he asked.

Rhett nodded to show he appreciated the politeness. "Better. Sleeping easy. Says he's going to be fine."

"When do you think he'll be able to travel?"

Rhett stood, stretching, considering. "As soon as we can carry him out to the wagon, I reckon, although he won't like not being in the saddle."

"Good. Because we found something."

"Well, what the Sam Hill is it?"

Dan grinned. "A book on necromancy. It's written in Italian—"

"Which is very similar to Aztecan," Inés finished, coming up behind him. "I can't translate entirely, and I'm sure some sensitivity is lost, but there are spells here. You said this Trevisan has a familiar?"

"A what?"

"An animal he keeps with him."

Rhett looked up into the rafters, just to make sure there weren't any black-feathered birds staring down at him, hungry for secrets to take back to their master. "Ravens," he said. "Or crows. Ravens *and* crows. Hell, I don't know. If it's black and beady-eyed and full of malice and feathers, I reckon he's fond of it. He kept one in his train car beside Meimei."

"In identical cages." When Cora said it, smoke curled from her nose. She was so silent that Rhett didn't know when she'd arrived, but she was in the doorway just the same.

"And when he jumped bodies, what happened to this bird?" Inés asked. She curled a finger at Rhett and headed back to the kitchen, everybody falling in behind them.

Rhett frowned as he walked and tried to remember. "It died. Went all dry-like, its feet curled up. But he can also make 'em out of wax and gold and bone." Even through her veil, he could feel Inés staring, waiting, so he added, "I can't tell which ones are real and which ones are made up anymore."

"Ha!" Inés spat a vicious little laugh and pointed at a huge black book on the table where Sam had been. Someone had cleaned up all the black spatters. "The book agrees. The life force of the familiar is used up, drained by the transfer. Jumping to a new vessel takes more life than one body can hold. Without the familiar, without an animal of some sort nearby to use as kindling, the alchemist will fail."

That perked Rhett up. "By fail, do you mean die? Really die?"

Inés nodded. "But the necromancer need not be picky. A rat, a pigeon, a squirrel. Just enough for a spark. He will have to be isolated."

"What about lizards? Bugs?"

Inés shook her head. "Bigger than that, I think. If the spark is too small, the fire sputters and dies."

"So that's how to keep him from jumping to somebody else, but how do we get him out of Meimei in the first place?"

Inés hummed and held up the book. The thing had to be as thick as Rhett's forearm, and he knew personally just how heavy it was because he'd huffed and puffed helping deliver it up from the basement.

"It will take me time to unravel that," she answered.

Rhett shook his head. "But we got to go! We got no time to sit around reading. Trevisan is holding still right now, but he could go anywhere."

Cora nodded. "And he could jump again. My sister's body is not ideal for his purposes."

"We can bring the book," Dan said. "I can read a little Aztecan—"

"It ain't good enough to read that and you know it," Rhett said, cocking his head at the book. "We need an expert. So what do you say, Inés? You want to take this show on the road with us?"

The nun looked around the kitchen. With her veil down, and not knowing her particularly well, anyway, Rhett couldn't begin to guess what she was thinking. Would she go? Would she stay?

"You don't want to stay here," he said, not quite pleading. Yet. "With us, you can go out in the world. You can help us right this wrong. Do some good." He looked right at her veil, right at where her eyes had to be. "Save another little girl's life."

They waited, each person staring at Inés, willing her to join them.

"We got a wagon," Rhett said. "If you don't like to ride. You can bring all your books. Well, some of your books. We got some books, too. You can tell us which ones might be useful, and you can have whatever of 'em you want for your own library. They're from the Las Moras Ranger Outpost. I reckon the Captain would've wanted you to have them. He told me to find you, you know. He wanted you to help me. And once we kill Trevisan, we'll bring you right back here or take you to the nearest city, as you like."

There was a low chuckle from under the veil. "Stop trying to convince me, Rhett. I have already made my choice."

She paused for a maddening goddamn amount of time, and Rhett had to bite his tongue to keep from begging harder. Good thing his tongue started to heal the moment he withdrew his teeth.

Finally, Inés said, "I will go. Perhaps I have hidden from the world for too long."

Rhett exhaled a huge sigh of relief and felt a hand fall on his shoulder. When he turned around, he was amazed to find Sam standing there, one hand on the wall for support. The feller was shaking from exertion and as white as milk but still staring at Rhett like he'd hung the moon. He grinned back.

"But I don't know what we'll do with my cow and donkey," Inés said.

Rhett grinned. At least that question he could answer. "Easy. Eat one, bring the other."

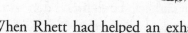

When Rhett had helped an exhausted Sam back to his bed and stayed nearby to doze while the cowpoke slept, Inés settled down at the table, poring through her necromancy book. When he woke up and lumbered back into the kitchen, she didn't look like she'd moved an inch. She'd merely asked Rhett to milk the cow before killing it so they'd have fresh milk, and he enjoyed the hell out of it, not having tasted milk in years. Together, he and Dan slaughtered the scrawny critter in the mission's dusty yard.

For all that Dan was a fine hand around a ranch, Rhett

missed the hell out of Sam. Even butchering a cow was fun with Sam. Up to their elbows in gore, each silent and steady in his work, Rhett kept looking up, expecting to see blond hair and blue eyes and finding serious, frowning Dan instead. He briefly remembered when he'd butchered a cow with a boy named Chuck who'd later become a chupacabra and tried to kill Rhett's mentor, Monty, but Rhett pushed that right back out of his mind. What was past was past, and the present had its own trials and tribulations. For one, Inés had promised to make a great feast before they left the mission and her clay oven, and Rhett would be glad for softer beef tonight and freedom from hunting and carving until the cow's meat and parts ran out on the trail. San Anton wasn't so far now, just a day's ride, Inés said. And even that was how long it took her on her donkey, a shaggy thing that screeched at them indignantly the entire time they wrestled with what was left of the cow, like they'd murdered his best friend right in front of him. Which, Rhett realized with a chill, they basically had.

"You might want to shut your pie hole. We already lost one donkey," Rhett told it, knowing full well he sounded unnecessarily peevish. "And we don't got room for another. So unless you're gonna become a rude Irishman and help build fires, I don't need another donkey's thoughts and I don't want to hear it."

The donkey eventually shut up, and it didn't become a person, so Rhett figured it wouldn't be half as much trouble as Earl had been.

"Do you miss him?" Dan asked after a few long moments of sawing and chucking bits of meat into pots.

Rhett looked up and sighed. "I miss him being alive." It was an honest answer, but it wasn't enough. "But, no, I guess I didn't like his personality in particular. He helped me once, and you can't put a price on that. I reckon some folks are just around long enough to teach us something, but that doesn't necessarily make 'em a pleasant companion."

Dan looked at him sharply, and Rhett's gut went cold. "It's strange, that the Rangers managed to shoot him in the heart during such a heated battle."

Goddammit, Rhett hated lying, especially when the other feller knew he was lying. But he owed it to Earl—to let Dan and everybody else believe their companion had died nobly. "I can't believe it, either, but there it is. His sadness was killing him, anyway. Maybe he's happier wherever he is now." Sick of the way Dan was looking at him, he stood up by Inés's cauldron. "I'll take this in. You go on and help with the books so we can get on the road." Instead of arguing, Dan just nodded thoughtfully.

"You might consider having a wash," he said, and it sounded more a kindness than a ribbing. "You know how fussy Sam can be about baths."

Rhett at first took offense, then looked down. He was a mess of blood, sand, dirt, black ichor, and weeks' worth of trail dust. Once Sam was back to himself, he might be a bit put off. "That's a right fine idea, Dan. I do feel a bit mussed."

"Best get to it, then."

The look Dan gave him—well, if Dan didn't know everything in Rhett's head, Rhett would've been surprised. The coyote boy was too clever by half, and Rhett was right glad to get out of the room with him before Dan laid all his secrets out on the dirt like the cut-up cow.

As he brought the dinner beef into the kitchen, Rhett found Inés, Winifred, and Cora laughing as they sorted through books on the long table, deciding what could stay here in the mission's secret library and what was needed with them on the road. Dan came and went, taking the books they'd indicated down to the cellar or out to the wagon, looking stern and businesslike but more than happy to do as they asked.

"What're you-all laughing at?" Rhett asked when they all giggled like hens.

"Girl business," Winifred shot back.

"And none of yours," Cora finished.

For once, Rhett didn't like being left out, but he wasn't about to say a thing. If they all thought of him as a man and nothing else, then he wasn't about to change their minds just for the sake of knowing what the joke was.

"Well, Bessy wants to join in," he said, putting the old iron kettle at their feet. He didn't stop to see their reaction to the pile of raw meat, just turned around and walked right back out to do his washing at the trough by the well.

What he saw there just about made his jaw fall off. The sun broke through the clouds, and there was Samuel Hennessy, his shirt stripped down to his waist, pouring water down his neck and shoulders, letting it run in rivulets down into his britches, flowing over all those interesting muscles and into crevices and through little patches of honey-gold hair. He was thinner than he'd been, but it only served to make the lines of his body more raw, more real. Rhett swallowed hard, transfixed.

"Well, howdy, Sam," Rhett murmured. "Didn't know you were up to bathing yet."

Sam's eyes popped open, and he looked up and started to pull on his shirt. "Oh, hell, Rhett. I didn't know you were there. Inés fed me a good breakfast, said she put some kind of potion in it, and once I had a full belly, I got all jittery. Full of energy. I just had to wash. I felt all gritty from the trail, and now there's blood and black junk mixed in it, and who knows when we'll find the next creek. Didn't know if we'd get the chance to bathe before we hit San Anton. Those city folks, they look down on a feller who hasn't changed out of his duds since last winter. I didn't want to look disreputable. As a Ranger, you know."

Rhett looked down at himself. He was rumpled, covered in cow blood and lizard sand, too. His hair had kept on growing out and was starting to get in the way of his hat. He let the battered thing fall down his back and ran a hand over his head.

"I reckon you're right. We look like no-good rustlers, don't we?"

"Right disreputable."

Rhett's eye trailed down from Sam's bluer-than-blue eyes, down his throat to the water droplets caught in the golden fuzz on the man's chest. For all that Sam had looked about dead yesterday, he seemed full of goddamn life at the moment. Fuller than full.

"Then I reckon we'd better bathe. It's the right thing to do."

Sam swallowed hard and started buttoning his shirt... with one button off.

"It's our duty," he said. "Let's see if they got better facilities."

Rhett grinned, went to grab his saddlebags, and headed back to the kitchen with Sam in his wake. "Inés, you got a bathtub in here? Or a convenient creek?"

Inés inclined her head to the hall. "There's a cistern and a copper tub out back. The water will be cold."

Rhett's eyes met Sam's. "Oh, I think we'll do okay."

"I bet you will," Winifred murmured, and she and Cora giggled.

"Buncha damn fool hens," Rhett muttered, stomping out back.

But Sam was following him, so who cared what the damn fool hens thought?

His Sam was back.

They had a hell of bath, although Rhett kept his binder on until Sam gently tugged it off. It was a new thing, being in his altogether in the middle of the day with another person, but Rhett was so glad Sam was alive that he didn't care if maybe his body wasn't how he felt it should be. Sam wasn't complaining. He would've expected Sam to be weak and easily tired, but the man was goddamn ravenous, as if trying to make up for time lost while he'd been asleep.

When Rhett asked him, "Sam, are you sure...?" Sam just grabbed him by the hips and put him where he wanted, and Rhett didn't complain. It was like a dream, and after they'd messed around, they had to go on and bathe again. Nobody from inside the mission ventured outside, and Dan kept to his book-hauling around front, and Rhett figured baths weren't so goddamn horrible after all. They changed into their clean duds and went to the trouble of washing their trail clothes and hanging them to dry on Inés's lines. When they were done, the trough was a dirty, oily mess that they emptied out and refilled from the deep, cool well. When they reentered the kitchen, every good smell rode the air, and the books spread over the table had been replaced with platters. Inés was grinding masa on a stone board while Cora chopped green things and Winifred stirred something in a kettle.

"You're looking much improved," Inés noted, watching Sam closely.

He grinned, his color high. "Whatever you put in that breakfast did its work, Señora Inés."

Rhett couldn't see it, but he imagined she smiled fondly at Sam. Because everyone did.

"How'd you like to take some clippers to me?" Rhett asked, poking Winifred in the back, and she laughed and limped over to knock off his hat and said, "It is always fun to have scissors so near your throat, fool."

Soon he was shorn down to where he liked it, and Sam was

shaving with his knife using a tin plate for a mirror. The effect was rough and lovely and made Rhett's throat ache. As Sam pinned his badge back on his clean shirt, Rhett's heart sunk back down. They'd almost had a normal day, hadn't they? Good work, laughter, the smell of dinner that wasn't Dan's rabbits over what should have been Earl's fire. Damn that donkey for up and killing himself right when he'd figured out exactly how to build and bank a fine fire. Everywhere he went, it was like Rhett carried ghosts with him. Monty, Chicken, Regina, Grandpa Z, the Captain, all those bitty babies the Cannibal Owl took while Rhett was stumbling around, trying to find his way as the Shadow. Even Chuck, who was a chupacabra now—unless somebody'd killed him—that was on Rhett's conscience, too, heavy as a stone around his neck.

He stood from the table, where the women were about to serve dinner and the men were joshing as men do, and shook the fuzz from his shoulders. After giving Winifred a nod of thanks, he walked alone back toward the chapel. As Sam finished his ablutions, Rhett suddenly felt like the kitchen was a very full place, and he needed a quiet moment alone.

With every step down the hallway, with every lit candle he passed, his pace slowed. A wind whispered from somewhere, cool as water in the desert. The chapel looked about like it always did, flickering with candlelight and rounded and warm. Welcoming, even. He'd never been in the town church back in Gloomy Bluebird, never much approved of the stern preacher and his pucker-faced, hateful wife, which meant Rhett didn't know what a church was supposed to be, really, or what was supposed to happen there. He'd never heard a real prayer, outside of that hogwash Earl had spouted right before he'd done the goddamn unthinkable.

Rhett walked first to a rough statue of a skinny white feller in a breechclout, nailed up to some sticks and looking pretty mournful about it. As a figure, this one held no appeal for Rhett. Instead, he wandered toward a painting of a sleepy-looking lady in a fancy blue nun suit holding a fat white baby. She looked pretty kind but also harmless, which likewise offered no connection. Moving around the room, he passed banks of candles and small portraits of various serious-looking fellers, and even one skinny boy stuck full of arrows, but the first thing to appeal to him was a skeleton lady in a fancy dress with black holes for eyes. Around her feet were a few coins, a piece of brown stuff, and several hand-rolled cigarettes.

"Santa Muerte," Inés said, somewhere behind him. He hadn't even heard her approach, nor recognized the slight wobble he felt every time he was near a monster.

"Bless you," he muttered back.

He could hear the smile in her voice. "I did not sneeze. The statue there is of Santa Muerte, Lady Death."

"Don't sound much like a church lady," Rhett observed.

"Yes, well, there's more than one church and more than one god. She calls to you, does she?"

"She's more interesting than all these other sad-looking white folks."

Inés stepped closer but didn't touch Rhett, and he didn't turn around.

"Winifred says you have no love of women."

He snorted. "Oh, I got a use for 'em, from time to time. Even like a few of them, more or less. It's useless folks I can't abide. In a life like mine, if you can't kill what's coming at you, you don't deserve to walk away from the fight. You just stand there, screaming and tossing your skirt over your head, I figure you deserve to get bit by whatever's running at you. But this lady..." He stretched out a finger and traced the carved wood of her hem. "She looks like she gets it. Like she'd drink with you, then laugh during a bar fight."

"She might at that, if she was in the mood. This was once a strict mission of monks, but now I invite any gods or saints who need a place to rest. There is a place for each of them. Santa Muerte only understands death, but she is honest about it. You two might get along. Every person, after all, needs to believe in something."

Rhett looked skeptically into the statue's dark eyes. "Long as she don't expect me to pray."

"Just keep killing things," Inés said, her voice moving back down the hall. "She likes that."

Rhett tipped his hat. "At your service, I reckon." He turned away, but before he left the room, something pulled him back. Hunting around in his pocket, he found an old nickel and tossed it at Santa Muerte's feet. He wasn't sure it was the proper way to do things, but he figured that when a feller found something bigger than him that he couldn't kill, he ought to give it a gift and a wide goddamn berth.

"Thanks for not taking Sam," he said.

They slept in the monks' cots, taking watches just in case the Gila monsters—or something worse—arrived, drawn to Rhett like flies to honey, or possibly vinegar. Nothing arrived. Rhett spent his few hours at watch sitting outside near the sleeping horses on a rock with a good view, trying hard as hell to draw the old comfort from their warm simplicity. But life had grown too complex. He could feel Trevisan, not far away but still out of reach. Everyone's expectations weighed heavy on him: Cora, Dan, Sam, even the Captain's ghost, entirely imagined though it was. Problem was, he knew deep down that his usual method wasn't enough. He'd killed Trevisan once already in his own way, and the killing hadn't stuck. If his friends couldn't find what they needed in all those goddamn books, it didn't matter how ready Rhett was, how dangerous or lucky or well trained or well armed or dastardly.

If he killed Meimei, Trevisan would just jump into somebody else, and then Cora would probably stab Rhett in the goddamn heart for failing her. They had to find a way to stop that crucial jump. So it was down to what they could find in the books. Which Rhett couldn't read. He pulled out one of his pistols and pointed it at his old adversary, the moon. But he didn't pull the trigger. If he did, he knew damn well the others would run out in their bare feet, weapons in hand, thinking there were more Gila monsters or scorpions or whatever monster got called up next.

"Bang," he said, mimicking the gun's kickback.

But he did throw a few rocks, just to have something physical to do.

When he found himself sitting upright on the rock, wobbling, eyes drooping closed, he went in to wake Dan and send him out for his own turn at watch. Considering the long line of cold cots, he came to a decision. Kneeling by Sam, he placed a soft kiss right behind the feller's ear.

"Howdy," Sam said, all breathy and welcoming.

"I know it's a small bed, but you got room for one more?"

Sam rolled over to make room, and Rhett shucked his boots and settled in with another kiss on Sam's cheek. Relaxing into the space, body to body, he felt himself tenderly held in the lingering scent and warmth of the person he liked best, all his questions silenced by a rare sort of comfort. Sam was already snoring, and it made Rhett smile fondly. He fell into a deep, sweet sleep and woke to the cawing of crows.

Chapter 19

The bastard black birds were everywhere, but the biggest ruckus came from the chapel. It was barely dawn, but they cawed in every niche, on every pew, sitting on the skinny feller's outstretched arms and Santa Muerte's head and lined up along the rough wooden rafters like they were waiting for a show. All the candles had blown out, and the church was cold and smelled like a cave, like a one-way trip to the bowels of cold, dark hell itself. Even the saints somehow seemed to be looking the other way. Rhett pulled out a pistol, but Inés appeared behind him and pushed down the barrel, pointing it at the ground.

"Don't waste your bullets on devils," Inés said.

Rhett did not argue.

When Inés walked back toward the kitchen, he followed her. Soon the rest of the crew, accustomed to early waking, sat around the table looking downright tense, their bags puddled at their feet. Cora's foot tapped, her mouth pinched down. This close to hitting the road and finding Meimei, she just about couldn't handle herself. But Rhett's thoughts, as usual, moved to Sam. He watched his friend from under cover of his hat, noting that Sam's usual sunniness seemed...dampened. The feller's blue eyes were fixed ahead, his movements preoccupied. He was being right quiet. Something was bothering Sam.

Rhett scooted closer on the worn old bench until their knees touched under the table.

"You okay, Sam?" he asked, real low.

Sam looked at him, kinda panicky, and tried to muster up a grin. He partially failed.

"Well, it's bothering me, I guess. Seems like I feel the bullet hole more when it's rainy. Makes me think about that shoot-out back at Las Moras. I got a hole in me right now, and I reckon I'll feel it for the rest of my days, even if Buck helped move along the healing and Inés finally got the poison out. And then, I think about what would've happened if I'd been the first one to open the doors here. I'd be dead. Or stone. I don't know which is worse. I guess that I'm starting to feel pretty fragile, for the first time. Up till now, I thought I was gonna live forever."

Down the table, Inés chuckled. "Feeling foolishly immortal is a symptom of youth, and of a life that hasn't fully tested your mettle. The only cure is middle age or death."

Sam shook his head. "I liked it better then, though. Now it feels like shadows are always pressing in, like something's always waiting to get me. I never had any trouble falling asleep before, but last night it took me a right long time, and my heart just about skittered out my mouth, and I couldn't stop think-ing of all the times in my life I coulda died." He set down his spoon. "I envy you-all being hard to kill, I guess."

"No." Rhett turned to Sam, feeling tight all over. "Don't say that. You're the best of us, Sam. You're good to the core, and we're..."

"Say 'monsters,' and I'll turn into a coyote and bite your leg," Winifred muttered.

"We're not natural," Rhett finished.

Dan pointed his spoon at Rhett. "Bullshit. Again. We're as natural as he is. That's like saying a wolf is less natural than a mouse. Stop thinking of us as good and bad and just realize that we're all animals. We all have our purpose. I'm tired of you placing value where value doesn't matter. I'm sick and tired of you hating yourself. For being born a girl and a monster."

"I don't hate myself," Rhett said.

"You think women are useless and monsters are unnatural," Winifred said, her color high.

"It's not that," Rhett said, but he felt his own cheeks flash red in return. "It's just that..."

"You're too hard on yourself," Sam murmured. "They're kinda right. But it's a compliment. We think more of you than you think of yourself. You got to start seeing yourself as somebody."

Rhett's head hung down, his eggs forgotten. What they were saying was true, but it was awful hard to swallow. He didn't know what to say.

"Being a white man is not the greatest thing on this planet," Winifred added. "So stop thinking it."

"We can't help sinning," Inés said sadly. "They can, but they do it anyway."

"Again with sin." Dan dropped his spoon. "Why would any god create creatures that started off already failing him?"

"And why would God be a man?" Winifred said tartly. "Only one of us here is making life out of nothing."

Rhett stood, his head full to swollen with thoughts he wasn't ready for, and especially not at breakfast. "I ain't here to argue philosophy. What is, is, and that's all I got. I'm here to fight, and I want answers on how to kill that goddamn lich. I may not value this sin business, but I know without a doubt that he's a bad man, and I'd like to end him sooner rather than later, so finish your breakfast and get ready to go. Now where's the damn water bucket?" Inés pointed to a basin by the back door, and Rhett went to clean his breakfast plate and scour it with sand. If there was one thing he recalled from his life with Pap and Mam, taking out your anger on dishes was better than taking it out on people.

As his posse finished their breakfast, Rhett took their plates and cleaned them, one by one, taking a peculiar comfort in the work. Inés dried the dishes silently and put them back in their places, banked the stove coals, and blew out all the candles.

"I think we are ready now," she said quietly, for all of them.

In contrast to yesterday's cheery blue sky, it was a dull gray day, the wind brisk and cold and threatening as a bad boss. The horses felt it, too—something wicked in the air. They stomped their hooves and pinned back their ears and nipped irritably as their girths were tightened. Right before he mounted up, Rhett felt the pinch of pain and hot rush of blood that he'd been dreading but expecting and hurried off to tie on his rags, cussing every step of the way.

The mission was dark without the nun's presence. Every candle was blown out, every cupboard closed up tight. Rhett didn't bother with the outhouse out back for his rags, just went into the bunk room for some privacy. On his way out, he was drawn back to the chapel. The crows and ravens and blackbirds, whatever they were, were still there, acting like they owned the place. As he stepped from the hallway into the larger room, a ripple went through the flock as they seemed to laugh at him. He pulled his pistols, considered, and chose not to waste his bullets, knowing full well what waited for him in San Anton. But he wasn't going to let those birds just sit around and have a good guffaw at him, neither. Picking up the discarded, cold candles, he threw them as hard as he could into the biggest concentration of black-feathered bodies.

The birds rose up, shrieking indignantly with each candle he threw. The air filled with their cacophony, and they fluttered up and settled back down every time. It wasn't enough for him. He needed violence. His lips curled into a snarl as he unbuckled his holster, unbuttoned his shirt, and shucked his boots and pants and hated rags. And then he was the bird, big and clumsy on the ground but a flawless machine in the air. The birds screamed for real now, not just fluttering up and down but flapping hard, trying to escape a very physical threat. However they'd gotten in, there weren't many windows offering escape, and feathered bodies hit the walls hard, knocking down the paintings and sending the remaining tall candles toppling over. As for Rhett's part, he gave over to the bird completely.

Some birds he ate, some he snapped in half, some he merely batted aside with his great, broad wings or snatched and shook with his talons. It was an orgy of blood and feathers, and he delighted in it and didn't stop until all the birds were gone or fallen. The mission wasn't a large place, and he couldn't really stretch his wings, so when his belly was full and his rage was slaked, he flapped down to the dirt floor and turned back into Rhett Walker.

It was a hard transition from beast to man. Limp, dead bodies crunched under his bare feet as feathers twirled down from the ceiling. He dressed quickly, the sensations of being human unwelcome and small and painful. The bird's fierce glee became the human's petty shame. The birds had merely been dumb animals, after all, something more than wax and magic but something far less than the evil he imagined.

The room was destroyed, no longer holy. He had to get the

hell out before Inés discovered what he'd done. Adjusting his badge, he forced himself to spin around and see the disaster he'd wrought. The feller nailed up to the wall had fallen, as had all the portraits of ladies and saints. The candles were tossed everywhere and, in the cold light, looked all too much like bones. Only Santa Muerte still stood, her arms outstretched. Rhett seemed to think she was smiling, as if she'd enjoyed the morning's entertainment.

He got the hell out of there, and fast.

The road to San Anton was gloomy and quiet. Inés sat on the wagon bench with Cora, her veil pinned down on the sides so an errant wind couldn't get anybody accidentally turned to stone. A book lay open in her lap. Rhett, as usual, rode out ahead with Sam, and he was damn glad to have his best friend back where he belonged instead of always feeling like his heart was back in the wagon. Dan came last with the rest of the herd, plus one noisy donkey that trailed behind them on his own, honking at intervals as if complaining about his undignified treatment. Blue bellowed irritably back at him in mule as if agreeing that they were all sorely aggrieved, and for good reason, but he might as well shut his donkey trap.

Rhett was a creature of pure misery, in between the dull ache of his middle, radiating down his thighs and back, and the headache pressing down behind his skull like a goddamn vise. His stomach roiled, as it often did if he didn't give his bird stomach time to absorb whatever he'd eaten before turning back into a puny human. The world seemed hell-bent on crushing him between the heavy gray clouds and the hard, dusty ground like an ant under a boot.

Sam nudged his horse a little closer, their boots brushing in a right friendly way every few steps. "You okay, Rhett?" he asked, eyebrows tilted up like a worried puppy. "You scared?"

Rhett looked up ahead and nodded, trying to sort out his feelings and then figure out which bits of that to share with Sam without scaring the feller. No matter how sprightly he seemed, Sam had stood on death's door yesterday, and Rhett didn't want to give him a fright. He settled for complete honesty, which made him feel downright fidgety, as he wasn't accustomed at all to talking about twisty things like feelings and fear and how he wasn't nearly as calm and collected as he made it a point to act in front of the others.

"I reckon I'm not so much scared of Trevisan as I'm worried about being in a big city. Lamartine's as close as I've ever been to a town bigger than G—Gosh, I don't know." Thank goodness he'd caught himself before he said Gloomy Bluebird. Far as Sam knew, Rhett Walker was no relation to Nettie Lonesome of Gloomy Bluebird, and that was how Rhett wanted to keep it. "Hell, the railroad camp had more folks than most towns I've seen. Made me feel downright itchy."

Sam broke out in a smile that gleamed as bright as the sun that refused to shine. "Is that all? Well, hellfire, Rhett. The city's not such a problem. When there's that many folks, they don't pay much mind at all to cowpokes who ride on through. It's like a herd of cows. You notice one when it's off alone in the middle of the prairie, but when you got a whole herd, they all just blend together. Hiding in plain sight, like."

Rhett's head sunk down without his consent. "Maybe for you, but I figure I stick out like a buffalo among cows, Sam. You don't know what it's like. You always fit in."

Sam snorted, a rare and weary enough sound that it caught Rhett's attention. "I always fit in? Damn, son, that just ain't true. Folks look at me. Call me handsome. They always got...

expectations. Go into a town with the cowpokes or the Rangers, and the prettiest whore always picks me first." He leaned in close. "What am I gonna do with a whore, Rhett? I got no choice but to play along, go upstairs with her, and then fake like I'm sick. That's why I drink so hard, when I'm in a saloon. It's the only excuse I got for why my... Why I can't... Why I don't wanna..." He closed his eyes and shook his head in frustration. "Honestly, it's easier when they're vamps and I can just pretend I don't know what they're up to."

Rhett let this sink in. He'd always wondered about such things but couldn't have figured out a way to ask in a million years. For all his own personal problems, he'd never considered that a bad thing had happened to Sam in his life—well, before the spiders. There was this whole other layer to Samuel Hennessy, a layer of clouds under the perpetual sunshine. Out in public, in cities and even among his brother Rangers, he had to hide what he was as much as Rhett did. Probably hurt him as much as it hurt Rhett, too.

"I had no idea," Rhett said softly.

"I know you didn't. Wouldn't expect you to. Ain't so bad."

But Rhett could tell it was, and he wished to hell there was someplace they could go, just the two of them, where nobody would ever narrow their eyes or ask pointed questions or take offense at something neither one of them could control.

"Hellfire," he muttered. "Other people are shit."

As if Sam's mind had followed down the same path, he asked, "Rhett, what do you think you'll do after you take care of Trevisan? We ain't got the Rangers anymore, and...I mean, would you want to maybe find a ranch up north, get on as cowhands? We can change our names, pretend we were never Rangers. It'd be just like this, like the good days on the trail. Broncs, chores, falling asleep by the fire. Right cozy."

Rhett's heart just about sunk into his feet. He wouldn't lie to Sam about this, but he hated to be the rain on Sam's parade. "I'd like that, Sam. I would. But I reckon the Shadow will have other plans."

Sam's sullen silence after that was like a slap to the face. He edged his horse away from Rhett's, his shoulders slumped.

"Yeah, I reckon so," he said, all hangdog.

"If I had my way, Sam, you know I'd do that. I'd do whatever you wanted. If it were up to me, I'd give you your own goddamn cattle company. I'd shoot anybody who looked at you wrong. But you can't run away from destiny. I can only hope that wherever I go, you'll stick with me. Not because I'm your Captain, because I sure as hell don't think of myself that way. But because you want to." He nudged his own horse closer to Sam's so he could look the boy in the eyes. "Because I want you to."

Sam's mouth twitched. That he was even considering such a thing meant the world to Rhett. "I don't know how long a feller can run around like this, Rhett. The Rangers, they got a week or two off in between assignments, usually. Or the fellers take turns sitting at the ranch house, if they get overworked. Do a day or two of chores. But...well, damn, Rhett. You never stop. Like a frog hopping from one pot of boiling water to another. My bones would like a rest now and then."

Rhett's head dropped. "Yeah, I'd like a rest, too."

Sam exhaled forcefully, like he was trying to blow his nose, almost. Rhett's eye flicked to him from under his hat, watching and waiting.

"Let's make a promise, Rhett. I promise I'll stay with you as long as I can, and you promise that you'll try to relax every now and again. Take a day off. Let somebody else chase the bad guy. I understand that with the Cannibal Owl and Trevisan, you got to stop 'em so they'll stop killing. But you can't save everybody."

"I...I got to try."

Sam punched Rhett's shoulder gently. "I know you do, fool. Big damn heart of yours."

"It's not my heart, it's—"

"Your destiny." A real chuckle now. "Yeah, sure it is. Keep telling yourself that, Rhett Walker. But don't expect me to believe it." And then he turned the full force of his smile on Rhett, and Rhett realized Sam was just about his only weakness. For Sam, he'd try.

Anything.

The ride was a lot easier, after that.

With the wagon so heavily laden, the ride to San Anton took longer than anticipated. Considering it didn't seem like Trevisan was on the run, Rhett decided they could stand to enjoy one more night of quiet outside the city before subjecting themselves to the eternal bullshit of society. If Rhett squinted up ahead, he could see a glow of too many damn people squashed up together, or maybe his aching head was just overwhelmed with showing him waking nightmares about what would happen once he entered that teeming mass of squalor.

Considering how miserable he felt, it wasn't a lick of trouble to fetch the kindling and start the fire, because at least it didn't take him any closer to San Anton. It was honest work, making a fire, and Rhett loved honest work done by his own choice. Walking around the scrubby brush eased some of the ache in his thighs and lower back while also giving him plenty of privacy to switch out his rags and wash the old ones in a convenient but freezing-cold stream. He'd drape them over a rock tonight to dry and collect them in the morning before Sam was awake, if possible. It was one of the many reasons he was grateful that Sam always slept in, just a little, given the chance.

His fire soon roared up in a satisfying sort of way, beating back the cold, heavy air. The posse crowded close to the flames, nursing second bowls of Inés's stew, reheated in the kettle and licked off fingers and carved wood spoons. Inés finished hers quickly and dove right back into her book, holding her veil up just a sliver to read by the fire's light. Dan took off as a coyote for a bit and returned, unsettled and twitchy, to take up a book of his own. Cora was quiet but on edge, startling at every strange noise and turning her head toward San Anton like she could hear music no one else could, calling her forward. Sam seemed happy enough to sit next to Rhett and have a third helping of stew. Apparently, Rhett's decision to stop tonight seemed close enough to relaxing to make him feel settled and like maybe Rhett was capable of listening.

Winifred appeared to be having more trouble with her foot than usual, and when Rhett tried to take her bowl from her hands and scour it clean for her, she snatched it back and said, "I don't need your help."

"It's okay if you do. Your foot—"

"Is fine. The cold makes it stiff. It's none of your concern."

"I have a liniment," Cora said quietly, and Winifred nodded at her. They retired to the inside of the wagon, and Rhett was glad to have Cora stowed away somewhere that he didn't have to watch her worry and feel like he was failing her.

It was a right peculiar feeling—anxious but calm. Rhett enjoyed his part of the chores more than usual, combing the prickers out of Ragdoll's tail and brushing down BB's face like the unicorn preferred. Old Blue followed Rhett every step of the way, butting him and snuffling at the ticklish place in his neck. Time became a peculiar, strung-out thing, almost like a blanket unraveling. Rhett could feel, for the first time, that there was an end to that string. That somewhere, sometime, there'd be nothing left. The good parts and the rough parts were all just little knots on the same rope, and pretty soon that rope might become a noose. There was something about facing a feller after you'd already killed him once that didn't sit well.

Such thoughts made him jumpy as hell, and he hurried back to the warmth of the fire, where Sam had laid out his saddle and blanket, which he inspected closely to make sure it wasn't planning to unravel anytime soon.

"Something wrong with your blanket?" Sam asked, his face open and smiling.

"Just smoothing it out."

Rhett flapped it a bit, refolded it, and put it just so. Before he lay down, he checked for each of his people. Inés and Dan sat across the fire, the books piled between them. Inés had brought coffee, strangely enough, and the scent of it warmed Rhett to his toes as it bubbled and perked in the fire. The girls were in the wagon, safe and still. Satisfied that all was as well as it could be, considering, he curled up on his side and pulled his buffalo coat over him, hoping Sam would edge under the corner, which he did.

"Good night, Rhett."

"Good night, Sam."

Rhett settled in, watching as Sam frowned and twitched for a bit before relaxing into his usual smiling sleep.

Everything should've felt right fine.

Considering.

But it didn't.

Rhett turned one way, then he turned the other, then he flopped over on his back and longed for the stars he couldn't see. The clouds hung low, thick and hateful. The air tasted cold, sharp and metallic. The ground was like ice, the rocks seeming to settle in all his most tender spots. Just when he thought he might figure out how to drift off, he felt a grueling ache followed by a hot gush of blood. He pretty much couldn't have been any more uncomfortable if he'd tried, which he wasn't about to do. And he didn't want to get up alone and wander away into the darkness, because it felt like the sort of moment when something terrible would happen.

So he just curled in tighter, gritted his teeth against the pain, and waited for morning to come.

A hand clutched his shoulder, shaking him out of a sleep as deep and sucking as a swamp. Rhett jerked awake and whipped out the Bowie knife under his saddle in one swift and violent motion.

"Don't," a sharp voice said.

His brain caught up with his instincts right before he jabbed Inés with the blade. Or worse, cut her veil.

The nun knelt beside him, her black habit merging with the edges of darkest night and the white of her veil bright as a dove. He slid the knife back under his saddle, although his suspicion didn't lessen.

"Why?" he simply said.

"I found something." Inés stood gracefully and inclined her head to the other side of the fire, where she had several of her stubby candles lit on a rock surrounded by open books. Even Dan was asleep now, on his back like a corpse, his chest bare.

Rhett checked Sam and found the cowpoke half-covered with the buffalo robe, his face soft in sleep. Rising, he walked in his sock feet to where Inés sat beside her rock. When she patted the ground nearby, he sunk down, rubbing sleep from his eye and wishing he was cruel enough to drag his buffalo coat off Sam, because it was cold as hell outside the warm cocoon they'd made together.

"See here?" Inés said.

"None of it means shit to me," he grouched. "Told you. I got no letters."

"The picture, Rhett. Even children understand pictures."

Rhett looked, his eye sliding uneasily over the scrawled letters to the ink-drawn pictures Inés wanted him to see. The book had to be very old, as the fellers in the pictures seemed to be wearing long dresses and had right peculiar hairstyles that made them look like idjits. One in particular was a nasty sort, in all black with black eyes and a large owl sitting on his shoulder. As Inés pointed from one image to another, Rhett tried to follow along.

"To switch bodies, a necromancer needs these: a great confidence and conviction. The bones of a man and the bones of the earth." When he shook his head in confusion, she clarified. "Bone and gold. Which you've already seen. The necromancer also requires a familiar, an animal with enough life force to power the change."

"We already knew all that," he said, preparing to go back to sleep.

Inés caught his sleeve. "Wait. I'm not done. Don't test my patience. Yes, we already knew all that. But we didn't know this. To remove him from a body, we must remove the bone and gold he's hidden within it."

Rhett perked up at that. "Wait. How's he get bone and gold in a body?"

"I have a theory." He could almost see Inés smiling under the veil, smug as a cat with a face full of feathers. "You said you saw a jar full of teeth?"

"Well, sure."

"That means he removed teeth from his victims."

"I know that, too."

"And we know that gold can be used to replace a tooth. What if he mixes gold with a tooth and implants it in a man's jaw? Or perhaps, in the case of a growing child like Meimei, he pierced her ears and made earrings merging bone and gold."

Rhett thought back to his brief time with the child.

"Yeah, she had ear baubles, sure enough," he said. "So if I take out her earrings, Trevisan will pop on out?"

At that, Inés actually laughed. "Would that it were so easy. You must remove both earrings and any other such gold and bone mixtures she might be holding. And you must say this spell." She pointed to a string of letters just as jumbled and scrawly as any others.

"Then I reckon we're shit out of luck, because I don't know what that says," he muttered, rubbing the back of his head and feeling just as prickly.

"Then this is our task tomorrow. I will read it and you will repeat it to me until you can say it flawlessly, from memory. And then, if we are very lucky, you can save Meimei and defeat Trevisan." She closed the book with a satisfyingly heavy thump, leaving a long blade of grass to mark her page.

"You say that'll get him out. But where will Trevisan go? What if he tries to go into somebody else?"

Inés nodded thoughtfully, and Rhett wished he could see her face, her eyes, the set of her mouth, any clues as to what the woman actually thought. Did they have a chance in hell? Or was this another cruel, useless errand guaranteed to disappoint and leave scars, as the Cannibal Owl had?

"This is why Trevisan must be brought outside the city, to a place of our devising. In the city, there will be too much interference, curious onlookers and distractions. Anyone wearing gold could become his next victim. We need to get out here." She raised her hands to indicate the quiet prairie around them. "We must keep him quiet, prevent Meimei's mouth from speaking. We must remove all gold and bone from the child's person and be sure that no one else in the area is holding such objects. Rather than destroy his familiar, we must keep it nearby to power our own magic. And then you must speak this spell."

"That sounds downright complicated," Rhett said.

"Magic always is."

"Pretty convenient how you found that, the night before we arrive."

Inés chuckled. "Funny how the muse finally shows up when you get down to business and demand her attention."

Chapter
20

Rhett's dreams were always twisty things, but it seemed to him like Santa Muerte watched him now, always on the periphery, a dark and skeletal spectre with a knowing smile. It wasn't like the dreams where the Injun woman or Buck had spoken to him, when he'd mostly had control of his own mouth and thoughts. It was more like the skeleton lady was standing over him, listening and scheming. He could sense her but not holler at her or shoot at her. It was downright frustrating, but he knew better than to ask Inés about it. He didn't need anyone doubting his sanity or destroying his confidence. Of course, he didn't need death goddesses spying on him in his own mind, neither, but he could face that problem after Trevisan was taken care of. Life had been so much easier when he'd figured there was maybe just one god, and that one pretty boring.

He woke up feeling like maybe he'd et a spider in his sleep. But when he rinsed his mouth with the water in his canteen, he immediately spat it out. Because it wasn't water. It was ... warm and thick and sweet?

Rhett stared at the brown splatter on the tan dirt, then sniffed his canteen. It was maybe a tiny bit like coffee but nothing Rhett had tasted before.

"What's that?" Sam asked.

Rhett handed him the canteen. "I don't rightly, but it sure as hell ain't the water I put in it last night."

Sam sniffed it and sipped cautiously. "Why, Rhett," he said, looking surprised. "That's hot chocolate."

"Hot what now?"

Sam took a deeper sip and handed the canteen back. "Hot chocolate. Had it a few times as a boy, back in Tanasi. You never had it?"

Rhett considered his own childhood. Hell no, he hadn't tasted chocolate. It was about the only thing as rare as gold. He'd only ever had one piece of candy, and he'd spent two weeks licking it down to nothing. But Sam didn't know any of that.

"Nope."

"Well, taste it."

Rhett did, and this time he found it good. The first time, when he'd spit it out, he'd been too surprised and confused. There was something in the slurry texture and warmth that spoke too much of spilt blood. But now, knowing what it was, it warmed his middle, bitter and sweet all at once.

"How'd you get chocolate?" Sam asked as Rhett finished it off.

"I have no idea."

But he did. He thought back to Santa Muerte on the edges of his dream last night, then even further back to the statue in the mission, the pieces of something brown sitting at the hem of her robe. Chocolate. Which made sense. If the boring saints liked waxy white candles and bits of bread, of course the goddess of death would like something as rare and bitter and sweet and strange as chocolate.

Sam got up and left, and Rhett closed his canteen, murmuring,

"If that's how you want to play it, lady, you go on and show up in my dreams anytime you want. But don't go thinking I owe you."

Yesterday, the clouds had pressed down, and the cold earth had reached up as if to claim him. Today, the sky snapped blue and bright, the wind cutting and pulling at every exposed inch of skin, tugging at the corners of Rhett's eye and drying out his lips. His hands cracked where they clutched the reins, and his feet rattled around in his boots. His nose ran like a leaky roof. He rode Ragdoll today, even though it made two days in a row, because he knew well enough that this was a fight he might not be able to come back from, and he wanted her to know she was his favorite, even if she was an ugly little thing. BB didn't seem to mind. Sometimes Rhett figured the unicorn reckoned him a poor substitute for the Captain, and Rhett himself had to agree.

They hit the road all too soon for Rhett's taste, navigating around slower wagons and holding back the horses as cowpokes and stagecoaches dashed rudely by. They'd packed up the books since they had their answers now, and Inés sat beside Cora on the wagon bench, her fingers curled over the seat. Cora was...hell, Rhett tried not to look, most of the time. She looked anxious and angry and worried, and he couldn't blame her for it, not a bit. She'd waited a long time to see her sister again, and she'd had to wait even longer at a chance to truly have her Meimei back. And they still might not save the child. Hell, Rhett might have to kill the poor thing.

Turned in the saddle to watch Cora, Rhett recognized that he'd been acting like a chickenshit coward all this time. The truth of it was he felt shame over losing Meimei to Trevisan, and it was flat-out easier to avoid Cora than deal with how he'd failed her.

Muttering "Goddammit," he turned Ragdoll and trotted her over to the wagon.

Cora looked at him like someone with a fever, half dull and half on fire. She'd once looked at him with nothing but a different kind of fire, and he'd vastly preferred it.

Figuring it was best to just say what needed to be said, he blurted out, "Woman, I owe you an apology."

Cora's lips twisted up in a grim sort of way. "Why, in particular?"

He exhaled, shut his eye to think, and just said it. "For everything. I wasn't good to you. You were upset with me, and I just let you go. Pushed you away. I did the best I could in Trevisan's car, and I reckon you know that, but you're still unhappy with the outcome, as am I. And I'm making it right in the best way I can, which I figure you don't like, either. But…I should've been better to you. More understanding, I guess. What you been through ain't easy. And I'm a man of action, not words. Feelings just slow me down, make my job harder. But for what it's worth, I'm sorry. And I'm going to fix things in the only way I know how."

He sucked in a big gasp of air, after all that. Cora watched him, bemused and angry and thinking. It was funny, how he'd come to know her from afar as they traveled. Theirs was not a relationship of secrets and trust and whispers. It was like two birds flying free, sometimes bumping into each other and caroming away. But he'd always liked her, even when she hadn't thought much of him.

"Red-Eye Ned, know this. If you have to kill her to kill Trevisan, I will forgive you. I will have to go far away, but I will be grateful. Better I lose my sister than she continue to be a pawn for such evil."

Knowing that she meant it and that it was hard as hell to say, he nodded. "I understand. And I will do my best for you. And for her."

She nodded back, her face hard. "Good."

"Then that's all, I reckon. I'm just sorry. For everything."

He tipped his hat, nodded, and spun his horse, cantering back up with Sam before she could...say something. Which was still a bit chickenshit, but at least he'd tried.

"What was that all about?" Sam asked, brow wrinkled down adorably. Rhett was stunned to realize that Sam was maybe a bit jealous. And that he, Rhett, liked it.

"Just apologizing."

"What for?"

"Everything."

Sam chuckled. "Did it help?"

Rhett shrugged. "Hell if I know. She hasn't turned into a dragon and eaten me yet, at least."

"Women seem like a fair bit of trouble."

"Truer words were never spoken, Sam."

That afternoon, the first huts and shop stalls showed up along the road, reaching out from the city like a hungry child's skinny arms. The smell slunk up Rhett's nose, making him flinch. It was all bodies and sewage and beasts and smoke and the great piles of trash left to rot because folks weren't made to live all cheek to jowl. The wobble in his belly was happy, though. It went from being a tugging sort of ache to a satisfied expectation. Reminded Rhett a bit of the way a man's feelings could turn from starving to appeased the moment he knew food was on the way. A monster like Trevisan...well, it was food for the Shadow, wasn't it? And, finally, the Shadow was close to sinking claws into deserving prey.

Dan galloped up front and reined in beside Rhett.

"We should sell some horses," he said tightly.

Rhett looked back at the herd, about thirty horses now, and

noted the folks along the street staring at them in a hungry, calculating sort of way.

"Fair enough. Everything but the mounts and mule. You know well enough who can go."

Dan's jaw twitched, his eyes hard. "The local folks won't want to do business with me."

Fury burned up Rhett's spine. "Then let's just take the herd back out five miles and let 'em loose."

A snort from Dan, and then a smile. "While I appreciate your indignation, I'd rather just have the money. Sam and I can go sell them off while you and the women secure a room."

Rhett looked at Dan like he'd grown two heads. "How the hell do I secure a room?"

"Ask Winifred. Better yet, let her do all the talking. Come on, Sam."

Dan turned back toward the herd and tugged on the rope halter of the stubborn black mustang mare who was second fiddle to Ragdoll. Where she went, the rest would follow, all except the horses tied to the wagon.

Sam gave Rhett an encouraging grin. "It'll be fine, Rhett. We'll meet in the city tonight, maybe go out for a drink. You can usually find somebody selling good tamales on the street, almost as fine as Conchita's. Me and Dan, we can sell the horses, no problem."

He tipped his hat, and Rhett tipped his hat back, and they both knew now that it meant more than that. Then Sam rode off with Dan, taking the herd of horses along. They turned off the road just past the first of the rickety stalls and headed for a prosperous-looking cattle company up on the hill with a fancy sign and boards that had been recently painted white. Rhett hated to watch the horses go. As far as he was concerned, a feller who had enough horses could do anything he pleased, and for the rougher end of a small herd, there was still some fine horseflesh hiding among the hopeless beasts. But he had Ragdoll and BB and Blue, so he had everything he needed. As the Captain had once told him, things tended to weigh a man down.

What was currently weighing him down the most was wanting to kill a goddamn lich.

Winifred rode up beside him on Kachina. Rhett hadn't paid her much mind that morning, but she was back in her city duds, a blue-sprigged dress that hid road dust pretty well over her soft doeskin leggings and an Aztecan shawl tied over her shoulders. Her hair was in a long braid down her back, and she wore an old hat that shouldn't have suited her but did.

"It's going to be hard to find someone who'll let a room to us. Bunch of folks, only one of us white and him not with us at the time. If we didn't have so much gold, we'd have to rough it out here on the outskirts. But I think we'll be able to find something—maybe upstairs in a saloon. And we'll need to find a hostler for the beasts and the wagon."

"That's bullshit," Rhett growled. "We don't need any such thing. Pay a man to brush our horses?" He spit in the already filthy street. "Hell, I could hunt down Trevisan right now, gag him, and drag him out into the country. I don't need to get all homey in a place that smells like an outhouse. I'm not trusting some no-good fool with my mounts or getting shoved out the back door by some pinch-faced old shrew."

"This is the city, Rhett." Winifred acted like she wanted to pat his arm but knew he'd bite her fingers off. Her voice went soft, as if she were speaking to a wild animal. "We must act like we belong here if we're to have any hope of accomplishing our goals."

Rhett looked down the road into San Anton. It was a teetering mess of buildings leaning this way and that, cut into blocks and rows by dirty streets knee-deep in mud and shit. It reminded him all too much of the railroad town, except that instead of having the good sense to up and move to fresher country every couple of days, San Anton just kept on festering like a mesquite thorn stuck deep in feverish, putrefying skin, building up a world of muck around its mud-black heart. He would've vastly preferred to make camp out in the wilds.

Cities were places for fools.

As they passed a big, stout wooden pen with a sturdy barn attached, Rhett asked Winifred, "That there. Is that a hostler?"

"Yes, but—"

Rhett kicked his mare and rode up to a smallish boy standing by the gate. "Hey, boy," he called. When the boy looked up, he held up a penny and added, "You understand me?"

The boy looked at him like he was a damned fool. "Yes, sir."

"Feller who owns this barn. He a nice man? Good to his horses?"

The boy looked back toward the barn and crept closer. "No. He shorts you on grain."

"If you had a horse, where'd you take it?"

The boy's mouth twitched as he looked around. "Two streets up, go right. Mr. Marko."

Rhett flicked the penny up in the air, and the boy caught it easily. Rhett almost wished he had a horse to give the boy, as the child looked at Ragdoll not as if she were a scrubby little appaloosa mustang, but like she was a fine thing worth having. A penny would do, though. It was more than Rhett had ever had as a child.

"Thanks kindly." He tipped his hat and led his posse up two streets and then right.

He liked the look of Marko's place right away, and even though the feller's speech was right peculiar and had the same guttural accent as the dwarves Rhett had met in Burlesville, they struck a decent enough deal for the keeping of the horses and wagon.

Pointing up at the hay loft overhead, Rhett asked Mr. Marko if he was willing to let folks sleep up there, but Marko wouldn't have it. Turned out his mother-in-law ran a boardinghouse across the street. That's where they ended up, eating peculiar German grub at a long table with a whole crew of laughing Germans. Rhett had no idea what most of 'em were saying, but they seemed friendly enough and nobody frowned at him, so he liked them fine and ate the rich food until he was close to bursting a button. He'd grown accustomed to white folks taking to Sam, and it felt strange to be among strangers without Sam there as a buffer.

"Wait," he said, overcome with panic. "How will Dan and Sam find us?"

Winifred pointed at her belly, or just above it, and then at her nose. "Same way Dan always finds us."

That's when it struck him. As Rhett looked around, amazed that nobody was hating him by sight or being rude to him by mouth, he realized something right peculiar: He couldn't sense a single monster. Besides his own friends, there wasn't any kind of wobble in the area, and he'd gotten sensitive enough to notice such things from a far piece. He hadn't felt another monster since the giant Gila lizards, and nothing in the city had raised his nerves a jot. Although he could feel the slight tug of Trevisan almost like a little fish testing the bait, the Shadow—or destiny, or whatever the hell—seemed pleased that Rhett was near his quarry and that the quarry was staying put. So between his sensitivity to monsters and his coyote nose, even in the stinky city, Dan would find them.

And so Rhett ate the strange German foods set before him and drank the dark German beer until he was full and punchy, and by the time Sam and Dan showed up, he was singing a German song with his arm around Mr. Marko, hefting his beer stein and grinning.

The newcomers were easily absorbed and fed, and Rhett enjoyed Sam's hip pressed close to his on the bench and the warm giddiness inspired by the drink. He'd only ever had the rotgut liquor served in saloons and stolen from Lobos who had probably stolen it from saloons, plus Buck's heady wine full of who-knows-what, but the German beer was a right friendly sort of drink, and it made him love everybody. Sitting at that long table with his friends, surrounded by folks who seemed happy just to be alive, he kept on drinking and eating until he just about couldn't move and crawled upstairs to the room he was set to share with Sam and Dan, as Frau Schafer wouldn't dream of letting genders mix in nightclothes. Good thing that little old lady couldn't see into the hearts of the degenerates she was renting to. Meaningless gender lines didn't slow their dirty thoughts down a bit.

The room had only two beds, so Dan chose to sleep on the floor. Before he settled in, he gave Rhett a grim frown, and Rhett knew he was in for some of Dan's signature preachin'.

"You look happy for a man about to chase down his destiny," Dan observed.

"Beer agrees with me, even if you don't," Rhett answered. "Did you get a good price for the herd?"

"Good enough," Dan allowed. "Sam did well. Once Trevisan is destroyed, we should have enough to keep our people fed for a good, long time."

"I'm gonna miss the Rangers, though," Sam said, all hangdog.

"Me, too, Sam. But we can't go back. Only way is forward, holding a gun."

The way Dan was looking at him just now, Rhett felt like a little baby caught soiling itself again. "I have asked you this question many times, Rhett, and your answer has never satisfied me, but I will ask again: What is your plan for tomorrow?"

Rhett shucked off his boots and lay back on his bed, marveling at the softness of the freshly fluffed mattress. "Well, Dan, I been thinking about it a long time, and I got me a good plan this time. See, I'm gonna get all my weapons loaded, and I'm gonna eat my breakfast, and I'm gonna get on my ugly horse, and I'm gonna follow the Shadow to wherever the hell Trevisan is hiding, and I'm gonna gag him and drag him out of town. Then I'm gonna say some fancy words Inés taught me to kick him out of Meimei's body, and then he'll be dead. Or at least gone."

Dan ran a hand over his grimace. "There are so many loose ends in that plan that it's got to be doomed to fail."

"Except I'm the Shadow."

"Except you're the Shadow," Dan agreed. "But you'll still have a better chance of succeeding if you take us with you. We don't know how Trevisan is living, whether he's alone and hiding or if he's got associates. Don't tell Cora I said so, but it's very possible he's already abandoned Meimei's body for a better vehicle. He might run, he might throw spells. The local sheriff might see you dragging a child away and interfere, and a diversion would come in handy. We're going with you."

"Except Sam," Rhett said sharply.

"And except Winifred," Dan added with a nod.

"Why not me?"

The hurt in Sam's voice just about made Rhett's eye tear

up. He sat up and turned sideways on the bed to face Sam, their knees nearly touching in the confines of the small room. "Because like I already told you a hundred times, you're the only one of us that can get killed easy, and I can't fight my best if I'm worried about you."

"I don't need to be protected," Sam snapped. "I rode with the Rangers for years before I ever met you. I'm trained, I'm deadly. Captain said I was a man he could count on in a fight."

Rhett leaned close. "Yeah, and the Captain didn't feel about you the way I do. You were just one of his men, but you're more than that to me, okay? So just stay back and protect Winifred so me and Dan can take care of business." When Sam just glared hurt at him, Rhett did the unthinkable and added, "Please."

Dan stared from one to the other, stood, and walked out the door without saying a word. Rhett liked him more in that moment than in all previous moments combined.

Sam leaned close, his head in his hands. "The thing you forget is that it works both ways. I care about you, too, and the thought of you going into a fight without me at your side is like…hell, like you going in without one of your best weapons. It would kill me if something managed to hit you in the heart and I wasn't there like a shield."

"Sam, if somebody hit you, they've already hit me in the heart."

Sam reached out and curled his fingers around the nape of Rhett's neck, pulling him in so their foreheads were touching. A shiver went down Rhett's spine, and it felt right intimate, for all that he couldn't see Sam's eyes, only the tops of their knees touching.

"Is it always gonna feel like this when the Shadow calls?" Sam asked. "I'm worried and angry and scared and ready to kill anything that looks at you wrong."

"I don't know, Sam. I never done this before. I just know it's got to be done so I can get to the other side of it. I don't know if I'll succeed. I don't give it a good chance of Meimei coming out of this alive, and Cora will most likely roast me where I stand if the child is gone, no matter what she says now. I just know that I'll fight better knowing I have you to come home to."

"And where is home, Rhett? We burned our home."

Rhett's fingers curled around Sam's neck, and they held each other there. "My home is where you are, and that's all that really matters."

"Then take me with you."

"Sam, don't you get it? You nearly died the last time we tangled with Trevisan's magic. Do you know how many nights I lay by your side, terrified you were gonna quit drawing breath? You shot me, and it didn't hurt half as much as watching you suffer. I can't have that happen again."

"But I pulled through it. I always do. You need me there, Rhett. At least let me be nearby, watching. Just in case. And I won't interfere unless it's down to your life."

Rhett bit his lip and rubbed his forehead hard against Sam's. The man spoke some truth. Thing was, Sam had to live with Rhett being the Shadow, but Rhett couldn't expect Sam to stay home and make soup. Sam was a man, just like he was, and his business was to do what he thought right. And clearly, this time, Sam wanted to be part of Rhett's destiny. Rhett couldn't deny him without making Sam seem less a man.

"All right, Sam. All right."

He lifted his head, and Sam did the same, and they looked at each other, searching and finding and being amazed with what was there, and Rhett slid his lips across Sam's, and then it was a goddamn good thing that Dan had left the room.

CHAPTER
21

So it was that Rhett set out the next morning with a small posse and a mouthful of magical mumbo jumbo to memorize. Sam just about had to grab Winifred around the middle to keep her at the boardinghouse with him, but considering every damn person was against her, she ended up slamming the door to her room with a shriek of rage and staying put. Cora would come get Sam if they needed him, but nobody was telling Winifred that. Inés and Cora were coming, and Rhett felt mighty fine with a dragon and a gorgon on his side. Inés carried a big bag full of magic shit, not to mention her book knowledge and the constant threat of her eyes. Cora just brought herself, but that was enough. Dan was his usual stolid self; for all that he could be vexful, he was damn handy in a fight.

As they walked the streets of San Anton, Inés murmured the spell to Rhett, over and over. As far as they were both concerned, he would've been a crappy necromancer at best. The words felt like old, lumpy gravy in his mouth, no matter how many times they went over it. It just didn't make a lick of goddamn sense.

"If I am able, I will say the spell when the time comes," Inés said, slamming the book shut. "You are hopeless."

"The Shadow's meant to kill things, not yap." He touched his guns and felt for the sack hanging off his gun belt that was packed full of bullets. The Henry was strung over one shoulder on its strap, his saddlebags over the other, and he had two pistols and a Bowie knife, and there were several handkerchiefs in various states of cleanliness planted about his person for gagging Trevisan so he couldn't speak a spell of his own.

But something felt off. He was nervous, whereas he usually felt like a bear wading into a rabbit fight. Part of it was that they weren't on horseback. But the rest of it was a mystery.

"I've got a bad feeling about this," he said.

"That's as it should be," Inés snapped. "There is nothing good about it."

The city was just waking up, roosters crowing and folks yelling at the roosters to shut up and old women in ratty shawls already selling breakfast made of yesterday's roosters from steaming kettles set along the road. Rhett walked in front, following the wobble in his belly, his three companions arrayed behind him. He keenly felt Sam's absence, and he wouldn't let himself think about the loss of Earl and how even if the donkey had mostly just caused trouble and complained, it was still nice to have another body on his side. He was glad to have Inés and Cora backing him up, though, and he knew he could count on Dan. They were solid folks, all of 'em.

"If something bad should happen today, I'm glad to know y'all," he muttered, almost too low for them to hear.

"Did you just say something nice?" Dan sounded more amazed than he should have.

"I didn't say nothing." Rhett spat on the ground and stormed on.

The Shadow led him deeper into the city, down streets lined with the tallest buildings Rhett had ever seen and over bridges and rivers and past missions and down filthy alleys where he felt much more at home. The farther they went, the more certain he was they were going to find Trevisan waiting around every corner. His belly was flipping like crazy, and being at the end of his courses didn't help a goddamn bit, just as it had not helped last night. He let his mind drift back to those stolen moments in the narrow room, all mouths and hands and Sam teaching him something new, since his betraying goddamn body was a mess at the time. One hand drifted up to the piss pan and bible under his binder, over his heart. It would be a goddamn shame if he died today, after he and Sam had finally said what they'd said the night before.

If things got bad, Cora was to run and fetch Sam. But Rhett knew he could end it before Sam had to get involved. No matter what had passed between them, he still wanted to keep Sam safe. For all his fights and wounds, he'd never given much thought to his own dying before. Now he did. Because now he had something to lose.

Rhett had to stop thinking about Sam, get out of the clouds, and be ready to head-butt anybody who gave him trouble. He said the words Inés had taught him under his breath, practicing, but he quit when she corrected him sharply from behind. How could she even hear him with her ears under that goddamn veil all the time? The wobble intensified as they crossed a street, and Rhett edged his pistols out of his holsters, jumpy as a cat on a stove, waiting for an ambush. He walked two more blocks and stopped, every part of him screaming for a fight.

When he looked up, he stood before a fancy two-story building with wrought iron and sparkling white paint. He longed to rush in through the door for the shoot-out he knew was coming, but he could tell it wasn't that sort of place, so he just stood there, vexed as hell.

"He's in there, somewhere," Rhett said.

Dan put his hands on his hips and whistled. "Well, that's a problem."

Rhett bristled like he usually did when Dan said such things. "Why the hell's that, Dan?"

"Because this is the nicest hotel in San Anton, and they're not going to let you walk in the lobby bristling with weapons and start knocking on doors and tossing children around."

"Because I'm brown?"

"Because you're not rich. Or a guest. Or safe-looking."

"Didn't you just sell thirty fine horses? Don't we have a shit ton of money? I reckon I'm rich enough to get a room and be a goddamn guest if I please." He held out his hand, and Dan counted out a stack of worn cash, more than Rhett had ever seen, not that he was going to let on about that. Ten whole dollars, and there was more in the roll Dan returned to his pocket. "How much does a room cost, anyway?"

Dan pointed at a sign. "Two dollars a day, room and board. But I'd bet you two dollars that for you, the cost would be three, if they even have a room available, which they might say they don't. I guarantee that if the four of us mosey in, there will be no vacancies."

"Which of us is the most respectable, in their eyes? Besides Sam, because he ain't here."

Dan inspected them, and Rhett forced himself to try to look upright and harmless, standing up straight and taking his hand off his gun.

"Inés, I think. Especially with the habit and veil. Perhaps you can be her guard, escorting her to her convent. You'll need two rooms, side by side."

"But that's a waste of—"

"Real nuns don't share rooms with men," Inés reminded

him. "Come, let's see if you can keep your mouth shut." She held out her hand and wiggled her fingers, and Rhett pulled out six dollars and gave it to her.

"Should be enough for two rooms, even if they charge us extra. I'm keeping the other four. Just in case."

He'd never held cash before, and it felt damn good in his pocket. It felt like an extra weapon, one he didn't need yet but was glad to have on hand, just in case. Neither Dan nor Inés made any comment on it, and it felt, for a moment, like a well-earned reward.

"Let's go, then." Inés hid her hands in her sleeves, and Rhett could tell she was being very careful about her accent, and that she could almost sound white, if she wanted to.

"But how will they get in?" Rhett hooked a thumb at Dan and Cora.

"I can fly to the roof," Cora said, and Rhett realized it was the first time he'd heard her voice in a while. She'd never responded to his apology, and he didn't know if that meant she accepted or rejected it, but at least she hadn't slapped him. "There is usually a door there. I can sneak inside."

"And I can become a coyote." Dan grinned his coyote smile. "Dart inside, and they'll see some rich man's yappy dog."

"But won't you both be nekkid after that?"

Dan flapped a hand at him. "We've got bigger problems than nudity. We'll figure it out. Go in and get a room, and we'll work from there."

Inés started walking, and Rhett hurried past her to go first until he remembered he was supposed to be her guard. Slowing, he tried to relax his face and hands, make himself seem smaller and less murderous. It was a new kind of fear that he felt, holding the grand door open for Inés. The lobby was tall and imposing, and the ceiling seemed like it was made of glass rainbows, casting glittering colors all over the floor. Fine chairs waited everywhere like they were begging to be sat in, and there were paintings on the wall that looked so real Rhett mistook one for a window. A life-sized deer—an eight-point buck—was stuffed and posed by the hearth, where a merry fire crackled and two white men in bowler hats sat arguing in striped waistcoats.

"Close your mouth before a fly wanders in," Inés murmured, and he did.

She walked to a desk, her tapping steps echoing. Rhett all but scurried behind her, feeling rough and raw and small in such a place. The white man behind the counter inspected the nun through his pince-nez, his head cocked to the side.

"I'd like two rooms, please," Inés said, her accent barely detectable as she placed four dollars on the table, keeping her hand hidden by long sleeves. "My chaperone will need to be next door for my safety. Only one night's room and board, each."

"We don't want any trouble," the man said, all fussy, looking at Rhett like he figured being dangerous might be catching.

"Neither do I," Inés said. "I'm carrying valuable relics." She held up her bag, then slid a coin across the table. "For your trouble."

The man had already slid the dollars into a little drawer, but the coin he slid into his pocket. His sneer suggested he'd noticed the color of Inés's hands when she held up her bag. Right before he was about to say something, Inés drew a cross in the air and murmured, "And may our Lord guide and keep you, my son."

The man frowned and fetched two keys from the wall behind him, where many such identical gold keys hung in orderly rows according to numbers.

"If you'll sign in," he said, indicating a book, pen, and ink-well. His face suggested he hoped Inés would fail at this test, but she simply smiled and nodded and wrote something very elegant and pretty.

"Supper's at six and breakfast starts at dawn. Have a pleasant evening, ma'am."

Inés nodded to him, nodded to Rhett, and palmed the keys. Rhett followed her through the lobby and up a carpeted set of stairs, and Rhett marveled at the strange, soft feeling under his boots and the lack of hobnails tapping. On the next floor, they went down several halls, passing a maid carrying a pan of ashes. She turned to the wall as they walked by, as if her look-ing away meant they couldn't see her. Rhett felt right sorry for the girl, stuck cleaning up after a bunch of rich assholes on her hands and knees while wearing a starched uniform.

Finally, Inés stopped in front of a door like every other door, save for a number carved into a small brass plaque. "These are our rooms. Mine is one-oh-nine, and yours is one-ten. You can match the numbers, see? Line, line, circle."

"I know my numbers," Rhett said irritably, although he didn't. But she was right—the combination of lines and circles was easy enough to remember. "So I go in here and...what?"

Inés...well, he didn't know if she was staring at him. All he could see was her veil. But he got the distinct impression she was silently laughing at him.

"You go in and rest, or sleep, or watch people through the window." She did laugh, then, a surprisingly light and girlish chuckle. "You are like a wild dog forced inside, aren't you? Just keep yourself occupied until supper. Then we'll go down to the during room and see if we find your lich...wait. Can you feel him? Where he is?"

Rhett faced one direction down the hall, then the other. "I think he's downstairs."

"But you haven't felt him move since we arrived?"

Rhett wanted to spit, but he didn't dare, not on the thick, fine carpet. "I don't think so, but I'm not a goddamn bloodhound. I never done this before, really. Cannibal Owl scooped me up at the last, had me carried right to its door. Trevisan had me trussed up in his trailer. I'm pretty good once a monster's got me cornered, I guess. Can I just mosey on downstairs and grab him?"

Inés shook her head. "No. You're in a civilized place now, or so we tell ourselves. Every move you make, someone is watching. See there?"

She pointed down the hall, and Rhett's eye flicked that way just in time to see a little white girl gasp and duck her sleek blonde head back inside her room.

"So I sit in my room and sip tea with my pinky up and wait until it's time to eat with the queen? Hell, Inés, I could just storm on down there now and end this."

When Inés put her hand on his arm, he went totally still. It was like being touched by a snake, like if maybe he didn't move, he wouldn't get bit. "It's about self-control. You must learn if you wish to survive. Your natural face isn't the only one you can show the world. Practice patience. Do this right. If you are not patient, innocents will die, and neither of us need more blood on our hands. *Sí?*"

He exhaled, let his head hang. *"Sí."* He took out his key and held it while he stared at the door. It should've been easy, but he'd never actually used one of the damned things before.

Taking pity on him, Inés stuck her key in her own door, turned it, and pushed the door open. She waited while he did the same, then pulled out her key and waited. After he'd managed to open his door, she softly called his name.

"Rhett?"

"Yeah?"

"Do not leave your room until supper."

Her door clicked shut, and he realized that he was being treated like a naughty child. Which maybe he was. Good thing Inés hadn't seen what he'd done to her chapel before they left. That had been one hell of a temper tantrum. He could do just as much damage to the hotel, if he lost his temper. He could picture it: the pretty white hallway filled with bullet holes, the paintings and mirrors and gas lights just shot to hell, broken glass fallen on the soft carpets. Women and children ducking into rooms, screaming as their soft, citified men barreled out, silver guns drawn.

Inés was right, much as he hated to say it. The chances of him getting into a locked room and dragging a six-year-old child out against (supposedly) her will was very small, especially once somebody raised a call to the local authorities. Seeing a feller like Rhett, badge or no badge, they'd shoot to kill. He'd just have to do his least favorite thing: wait.

The room inside was fancier than just about any place he'd ever seen, with clean swept wood floors and a nice rag rug and a bed with turned-back blankets and two fluffy pillows. He closed the door gently and hopped onto the bed, admiring the cushy mattress that felt like he was lying on a cloud. It would be mighty nice, being in here with Sam—

The door pushed open, and he had his gun out and pointed. Inés peeked around the dark wood, the small brass key dangling from her fingers.

"You must take the key, or else anyone can open your door," she explained, placing it on a chest of drawers.

"Well, sure," he said, as if he already knew. He didn't know if he had to lock the door from the inside now, or what, but he wasn't about to reveal his ignorance again, so he just said, "Many thanks."

Her veil hovered outside his door for just a moment, making him nearly squirm. "Do not," she said stiffly, "leave this room. I will fetch you when it's time to go."

"You already said that."

"I'm saying it again."

If her eyes could've burned a hole through the fabric, he reckoned she would've enjoyed that. And Rhett refused to kowtow to anyone, not even a gorgon nun, so he just inclined his head the tiniest bit to let her know he'd consider it. His response must've been sufficient, as she closed his door and left him in peace.

The peace lasted about five minutes. Then he started to get itchy. Although the room was about the size of Mam and Pap's entire shack, Rhett had since grown accustomed to living under the stars or having the freedom to come and go at the ranch or the Ranger outpost. Not since being locked up in the train camp had he been so goddamn penned in like a cow in a chute, blocked in every direction. The neck of his shirt started to feel tight, and he tugged on it and took off his hat and set his Henry on the floor and got to pacing, but that only made him feel more desperate. Pacing wasn't much fun when a feller's boots didn't even clomp. Going over to the window, he tugged it up and sucked in the gust of cold air that rushed inside, glad to smell the stink of the street and the pleasant whiff of horses, at least. Once he could breathe again, he closed the window most of the way and sat in a tall chair in the corner, daring to put his boots up on a little tufted stool.

Before he knew it, Rhett Walker was asleep.

A knock woke him up. The room was dark and cold, and he was huddled down in his chair. The knock came again, more urgent, and he jumped up and slammed the window down, muttering, "I'm awake, goddammit."

"Supper, Rhett," Inés called softly through the door.

He used the chamber pot and was glad to find his courses finally over, which meant he'd be a hell of a lot more comfortable without his rags, although he had no idea what to do with them now. He ended up just stuffing them under the chest of drawers in the corner, although he felt bad for the maid who would have to deal with it eventually. That taken care of, he went to the mirror and arranged himself into as respectable a figure as he could. Tied a clean kerchief over his eye, got his hat on straight, rebuttoned his shirt. He'd kept the piss pan and bible in his binder and had grown accustomed to its weight, and he reckoned he might as well keep it there, over his heart, just in case Trevisan had men with guns nearby. And even though he'd heard hotel rooms were generally safe, it wouldn't do to have the Captain's bible stolen while he was out chasing Trevisan. Just before he left, he remembered to take the key Inés had left on the dresser and lock the door, which would keep his Henry safe and help him not feel like an idjit.

Inés waited outside, watching silently as he locked and tested the door.

"You were good," she said.

"I was asleep."

"So I assumed."

"Well, what the hell did you do, then?" he said, annoyed.

"I did what needed to be done. I read the books, looking for more answers."

"But you already found the answers."

A chuckle. "That's the thing about books: There are always more answers. It's never over, really."

She led him down the hall and back downstairs, where a loud din was echoing throughout the lobby. They followed the noise to a big dining room filled with long tables and folks helping themselves to what smelled like a mighty fine supper.

"This ain't so bad," Rhett observed.

But then he realized it wasn't just his hunger talking. His belly was flip-flopping all over the place, and it wasn't long before he found his prey.

Trevisan.

In the body of Meimei still, thank goodness. She was no longer in her little red jacket and Chine silk outfit, but was now dolled up in a long, white dress like any fancy white child in town, her hair in neat pigtails. And she was staring daggers at Rhett from her place at the long table. The eyes may have been Meimei's, but the cold look was all Trevisan.

"That's him," he said to Inés, giving a big, toothy grin. "But why the hell is he just sitting there?"

Her head swiveled to follow his gaze. "I couldn't say. There are open seats. Let's go see how the cards fall."

"Didn't take you as one to gamble, nun lady."

"I'm not. But I wasn't always what I am now."

Inés headed for the table where Trevisan sat and found two seats. Inés sat first, and Rhett squeezed in beside her, barely noticing the press of bodies in his hunger for his prey. He wanted nothing so much as to leap across the table and throttle Trevisan to death, for all that he looked like a sweet if grumpy little girl. Trevisan was staring back through Meimei's dark eyes, furious and disgusted and full of hate. Rhett drank it in, loving that his enemy was finally so close, and yet unable to do anything. Because sitting next to Trevisan were two of the most dangerous creatures Rhett could imagine.

Rich white folks.

A lady and a man, just a little too old to have babies of their own, probably, and full up with righteousness and evidence of too much cash. The lady was big and busty like the lead heifer, all dripping with diamonds and lace, and she had a long ribbon tied around her wrist and attached to Trevisan's belt, almost like he was a dog on a leash. The man looked like an over-stuffed chair and had a bristly mustache and a very tight hat, and Rhett felt at any moment the feller's buttons might start popping off and pinging across the room. He was very busily eating, but the lady was fussing over Trevisan.

"Here come the delicious greens! Open up like a bunny!"

Trevisan's dead, angry eyes stared at Rhett. He did not open up like a bunny.

Rhett helped himself to fried chicken and smothered a laugh.

"What a lovely child," Inés said, and the woman just ate that up like syrup.

"Oh, how polite of you to notice. An orphan, the poor dear thing. We're adopting her. But she just won't eat her delicious greens, will you, Mildred?"

Rhett took a big bite of his biscuit and leaned over. "C'mon, now, Milly. Be a good little girl and take a bite." His grin just about split his face in half.

"Your boy's a bit familiar," the lady said to Inés, and Inés put a hand on Rhett's arm.

"Let the child eat, Rhett," she said.

He nodded and leaned back. "Yes, ma'am. Wouldn't want to get between a child and vittles, that's for sure."

"Is the child giving you trouble?" Inés said, one hand

indicating the ribbon. And, Rhett noticed, the second ribbon attaching Trevisan to a bored-looking feller sitting on the child's other side, a teddy bear stuffed under his arm and huge pistols poking up at his hips.

The woman tsked. "Oh, you know how these abandoned foreign children are. Feral as wild coyotes. Poor Mildred keeps trying to run off. She doesn't know what's good for her. So we've had to take precautions, with good Mr. Franck to help keep her safe. I don't know what she thinks she's running off to that's better than us, but we'll get through to her. I'm sure of it. Love always finds a way."

Inés nodded. "I will pray for you, *Señora* . . ." She trailed off, questioning.

"Josephina Mallard. And this is my husband, Herbert."

Herbert took a moment out of stuffing his face to tip his hat and mumble something.

"And are you just passing through, or have you plans in the area?"

Josephina put a hand over her heart like she was about to tell her favorite story. "Sister, you'll appreciate this. The hand of God brought little Mildred into our lives. We were scouting a ridge for our ranch when we saw a figure on a dying mare struggling across the prairie. And I told Herbert he had to go see what it was, because it was either someone who needed our help or someone trespassing, and he sent one of his boys down, and they brought back this poor heathen child, just kicking and screaming. She was skinny and dirty and carrying saddlebags filled with all sorts of filth, bones and jars of smelly plants and great, ugly books, and if you'll believe it, a box of gold. Even a crow in a little cage. The horse was wearing old wagon traces attached to her bridle. I imagine her whole caravan of people got ambushed, and she's the only one who survived, and God sent her right to us, right onto our land. She tried to escape, but we had our boys bring her up on the wagon box with us, and now we've decided to build the ranch on the very spot where we found her. We'll call it Provenance Ranch, and the sign will have a little horse in traces. Isn't that perfect?"

"Just perfect," Rhett said. Then, quickly, "What'd you-all do with the crow and the bones?"

Josephina's mouth puckered up like a cat's angry butthole. "They seemed downright unchristian, so we had the trail boys start up a fire and just throw everything in. You should've seen it! I swear those flames turned green. Thank the Lord!"

Trevisan's hate was like a fog rolling across the table, and Rhett just wallowed in it. To think: All this time he'd been chasing the man, and now Trevisan was stuck here. Whenever Josephina had burned his things must've been when the animal attacks stopped, and Trevisan had been trapped ever since under the watchful eye of this well-meaning lunatic and her paid muscle. As for Josephina, Rhett wondered what kind of fool would set themselves up as guardian to an unholy terror and keep at it even when it was clearly not working. The woman had to be raving mad. Or richer than God and bored to death. Probably both.

Mr. Franck, he noticed, didn't take his eyes off the child. He was clearly being paid well to prevent Trevisan from escaping again. Even as he took out a fine, antler-handled knife and picked his teeth, he didn't look away. Silent but deadly, that one, Rhett reckoned.

"So you're staying here at the hotel while your ranch is built," Inés said. "How lovely."

Josephina nodded. "It's a bit rustic, but the doctor said Herbert needed a dry heat for his gout and eczema. He looks healthier already. And soon sweet little Mildred will have her own suite of rooms to explore. And she'll be the luckiest little girl on earth, won't you?"

She reached over to pinch Trevisan's chubby cheek, and he grunted and turned away. His arms were already crossed, and the sight nearly made Rhett pee his pants in amusement. The three-hundred-year-old necromancer, stuck in the body of a child and trapped by these great fools, shackled to a hired gunman. It was a fitting punishment. But it was nowhere near enough. Meimei might still be in there, and Trevisan still had to pay for his sins.

Rhett refilled his plate and kept eating as he scanned the dining room. There were windows everywhere, opening out onto the front street and into a brick-walled alley on the other side. The folks eating at the table were all human and mostly white, but the men were in general all armed, and several of them looked like they might actually be familiar with the trigger. Women and children were in full force, as well as old folks and a couple of small dogs. It was not a good place for a gunfight, nor would it be possible to steal Trevisan and hurry out the door without someone calling an alarm—or Mr. Franck throwing that shiny knife. Wherever the sheriff's office was, it was bound to be close. You didn't build a hotel like this one unless you had the law nearby and on your side.

So his posse had been right, then. This job would take more than his usual frontal attack. He had to get Trevisan away from the assholes who'd adopted him and drag him into the desert, alone.

"Until Sunday, then," Inés said, and Rhett realized Trevisan's folks were getting up from their meal. Herbert had gravy stains all down his front, and Josephina and Mr. Franck had their hands full with trying to hold Trevisan's arms. The child very clearly did not like being carried around like a sack of grain and was fighting like a mad badger.

"Good night, Mildred," Rhett called.

When Trevisan glared at him from under Mr. Franck's arm, Rhett blew him a kiss.

He was pretty sure Trevisan would've killed him for that alone, had he been able.

"You shouldn't taunt him," Inés murmured, lifting her veil just enough to slip a spoonful of soup underneath.

"I can't help it," Rhett whispered back. "He's my enemy. He cut off one of my toes. If I can make him squirm, I'm gonna."

"Did you hear the last of the conversation?"

Rhett pulled over a pie and helped himself to a generous slice. "Nope. I was busy figuring out how to kidnap the little shit without killing everybody."

"You don't have to. We're going out with them Sunday morning, to see the new homestead."

Rhett dropped his fork with a clatter. "Well, damn, nun. You done good."

Inés slid his pie across the table and used her own fork to finish it. "I have my uses. I told that fool woman I would consecrate her ground in the name of God. If she knew anything about religion other than how to show up on Easter Sunday in her finest dress, she would know that I don't have that power, but lucky for us, she has no idea. So be ready. Sunday morning is our chance."

Rhett nodded. "Grab Trevisan, spook their horses, and start the spell. Day after tomorrow."

"Day after tomorrow. As long as nothing goes wrong."

"But something always does."

"Amen to that, Sister."

CHAPTER 22

Rhett knew how to work his ass off until midnight and then fall asleep, but he was utterly unfamiliar with finishing supper and going to his room to be alone all night. Nobody to talk to, nothing that needed mending, no horses to pat and brush until a feller felt tuckered out. He kept waiting for Dan and Cora to show up, maybe figure out a way to sneak Sam and Winifred into the hotel, too. He sat in his room, then paced it again, then looked out the window at the folks scuttling down the street in the dark. He knew exactly where they were going. The saloon was lit up like Christmas and featured the only monsters in town, if the harmless little wobble in Rhett's stomach was any indication.

Vampire whores. Lots of 'em. And plenty of other trouble, too, if you considered the human men gambling and drinking within. Rhett could use some trouble. He had all of tonight, then tomorrow, then another fool night to get through before he could make his move on Trevisan, and there wasn't a goddamn thing he could do until then.

Well, supposedly.

But considering Trevisan was locked down in his room with the Mallards and Mr. Franck and whatever other hired muscle got set on babysitting, the necromancer was stuck here, just like Rhett. Just like he had been for weeks. So odds were he wasn't gonna be able to do anything naughty tonight.

But Rhett could.

Well, hell, maybe not naughty. Not without Sam around. But entertaining. Inés had ordered him to stay put, but she wasn't his mama. He could mosey on down to the saloon, have a drink, play a hand of cards. It almost felt like he'd be stepping out on Sam, but he told himself a sort of story about what it could be like if Sam had the same idea. Rhett would walk in the front door and stop, and he'd feel a tug across the room, and there would be Sam Hennessy, sitting alone at the bar. No—a little table. In the corner, shadowy and private. Rhett would flip a coin to the bartender for two shots of whiskey, head over to where Sam was sitting, and slide one across the table, cool as you please. Maybe he'd turn his chair around, spin it so he was sitting on it backward, resting his arms across the top. And the noise of the saloon would be friendly and the air would be warm and he'd lean over to Sam, secretive-like, and whisper something like, "What's a tall drink of water like you doing in a shithole like this?"

And Sam would blush like he did sometimes and maybe look down, but he'd be smiling, and he'd say something like, "Waiting for somebody like you, I reckon."

And Rhett would lean in, and—

Was that someone scratching at the door?

Was it Sam?

Feeling a bit flushed and flustered, Rhett loosened the kerchief around his neck and settled the gun belt on his hips and walked to the door.

"That you, Sam?"

One long, suggestive scratch was all it took, and Rhett thanked his lucky stars and opened the door.

Or tried to. He turned the knob, and the door flew open, knocking him onto his back. A huge shape bounded into the room, taking up most of the space. With the light of just the fire and a few candles, and with his brains rattled around from the fall, Rhett couldn't quite tell what it was. More than anything, it looked like a giant deer with strangely shiny antlers. The creature's great head swiveled around, its eyes finding Rhett.

"That you, Buck?" he asked, hopeful that it might be someone he at least partially considered a friend while still pretty sure it wasn't.

But when it lowered its head at him, he saw that the beast's eyes were black and dead and its antlers were tipped with knives.

That's when he knew it wasn't Buck, or anything like him. It had to be one of Trevisan's creatures.

Which meant bullets wouldn't kill it, although they would draw other guests and staff to the room, likely getting them killed. As the monster deer stabbed at him with its antlers, Rhett rolled sideways and drew his own knife. Like the big black cat, he was going to have to get uncomfortably close with this thing if he wanted to live long enough to kill its maker.

With a snort, the monster swung its head, sending a lamp flying and nearly slicing Rhett's arm. As Rhett crawled away, breathing hard, he realized that the stag was having trouble navigating the small room filled with dainties. It knocked over a little table and got its hooves tangled in the rug as it stalked him. Being small and limber and possibly clever was the only way for Rhett to survive.

Still, it was a monster covered with knives, and at every stage of the fight, it tossed its head, the blades slashing the air and leaving the wallpaper in strips. When Rhett was too slow scrambling away, he took a hot slice to the shoulder, and he could've sworn he heard the monster's lips part in a fiendish and un-deerlike grin.

"You're Trevisan's thing," he said.

The monster gave no answer, choosing instead to pause in chasing him around the small room and paw at the rug, rumpling it. Well, hell. If the room was going to be destroyed anyway, Rhett might as well stop pussyfooting around and get down to business.

Picking up a vase of flowers, he threw it in the stag's face, hard, and used its surprised snort to crawl across the floor and wedge himself up under the bed. It was a narrow thing, barely big enough for two even if they were skinny, and it wasn't nearly the kind of cover he liked to have in a fight. The door hung open, and no one had yet come to investigate the sound of hooves and slashes and a scared boy rolling around on gangly knees and elbows as sixteen knives rent the air where he'd just been.

Good. He didn't need anybody else to worry about just now. That's why Sam and Winifred were staying somewhere else.

The stag stepped close to the bed, worrying it with his antlers, and Rhett pulled out his Bowie knife and slashed hard at the slender tendons of the thing's fetlock. Whatever it was made of, the flesh there was softer than the bones and bits of a real deer, and its hoof soon dangled from a thin black string. The beast bellowed its rage and flipped the bed off him with its rack, and Rhett did the usual sort of thing he did, the thing that would've seemed downright stupid to anybody watching: He crawled toward the stag, past its bad leg, and around back to slice at another leg.

Black ichor spilled out, just like it had with the other creatures, burning up Rhett's forearm like fire. No time to worry about that—the beast was falling, and Rhett barely had enough time to roll away before it landed and started thrashing around like a goddamn fool.

Rhett stood and backed away, considering. Problem was, he needed to get to the stag's heart, but it was on the same side as the blade-tipped antlers. Whether he went in from the back or the front, the thing would twist its monstrous head and fillet him like a nice steak. But at least it couldn't stand up anymore, seeing as how he'd cut both its left feet.

Knife still in hand and dripping black ichor, Rhett stood and dashed back over to the bed, stripping off the puddled coverlet and tossing it over the stag's rack like a tablecloth. It didn't cover all the bladed tips, but it covered most of 'em and the monster's eyes as well.

Saying a brief prayer to whoever was listening, he slid to the floor on his back and managed to waggle in right up against the stag's chest. It tried to bite him, but its mouth couldn't reach him, and it was still fighting the blanket, and he shoved hard with both hands until his Bowie knife juddered into the thing's chest, all the way to the hilt.

As he sawed the knife around, hunting for the heart, the stag flailed against him, landing hard blows with its front legs and remaining hooves. But Rhett was Rhett, and he wasn't going to budge until the goddamn job was done, no matter how much punishment the creature rained down on him, which was turning out to be quite a lot.

The stag didn't take the cut like a sensible beast. No, the flesh of its chest had the consistency of a log, hard and unyielding, and Rhett wasn't finding the heart no matter how hard he jabbed or how he dug around with the point of his blade. The monster landed a punch in the gut with its good front hoof, and Rhett muttered, "Fuck you, deer." Yanking out his knife, he stuck his hand into the mangled hole he'd created, ignoring the burning pain as his fingers reached for something that wasn't a heart exactly. There. A ball of wax. His fist closed around it, and he yanked it out through the jagged hole and crushed it.

The stag gave a bleating sigh and just...collapsed, melting around him in a puddle of black glop and fur and a tinkling storm of blades that hit the ground with all the power of a mirror's useless, broken shards. Rhett rolled away from the growing puddle, certain that Inés was going to kill him if the snotty little hotel man didn't beat her to it. The monster was no longer a monster, just a soggy black mess with bits of metal stuck here and there, as if it had melted on a hot day. Rhett hoped the already-ruined rug would help protect the floor and wondered what he would sleep under now that the coverlet was in tatters.

Dragging himself away to sit with his back against the chest of drawers he took a moment to catch his breath and let his heart find its rhythm. It took time, forcing his clinched fist to open. There was the crushed ball of wax he expected to see, although it wasn't the shiny black wax within all the other creatures. It was whitish-gold candle wax, just like the candles still burning around his own room. And stuck in the middle of it were three things, both exactly what Rhett expected to find and utterly different: Mr. Franck's antler-handled pocketknife, folded closed; a gold shard of ceramic from a doll baby; and a child's tiny tooth.

He plucked out the tooth and held it up to the nearest candle's light. It still had a dab of blood on the inside. He had a few such teeth in his little pouch, as he'd saved them when he'd lost them as a child. Pap and Mam took everything he found, back then, and he'd just assumed they'd have some nefarious purpose for his teeth, were they to discover he'd been foolish enough to let them fall out. He'd been surprised as hell when new teeth grew in in their places, and then furious that no one had told him that such was the way of things.

So this must be one of Meimei's teeth, and whether it had fallen out on its own or Trevisan had found an easy handhold and yanked was anybody's guess. Rhett had known that Trevisan's spells required bone and gold to run, but now he better understood that they also required some small shard of the animal they were based on. The birds had been powered by feathers. The seed of this stag was an antler-handled blade, which explained its goddamn bladed antlers. For the cat and the scorpions, Trevisan must've used what he found on the trail. Maybe all it took was a housecat's single whisker and Trevisan's words to send the panther out hunting.

Pulling out the knife, Rhett had to wonder if Mr. Franck was still alive. Had Trevisan killed him or merely stolen the man's fine knife? The worst thing Rhett could do right now would be to run downstairs and bang on the Mallards' door, demanding answers. He'd just have to show up at breakfast tomorrow like nothing had happened, eat his vittles, and play nice so they wouldn't get uninvited to Sunday's picnic.

Rhett stood, cracking his back and flexing his fingers. He went to the ewer to wash off the black gunk, but it clung like hot mud and burned. When he wiped it off on a bit of the rug that hadn't been destroyed, it pulled long strips of skin off with it. By the time he'd gotten it all off, his fingers were mottled pink and brown.

"This job's making me ugly," he observed to no one in particular.

He tried to kick the stag, or what was left of it, but it had dissolved down into nothing but a stain. Hell, maybe it had dripped down between the floorboards and onto Trevisan's damn head. With a grunt of annoyance, Rhett smashed what was left of the ball of wax in his hands, glad to see the stag's remains turn to proper sand, black and sparkling. That, at least, could be swept up. If only getting the stains off his hands were so easy.

He righted the bed, collected and fluffed the pillows, and went to close and lock the door. The wood had scratch marks on it from the stag dragging his bladed antlers down the front. When he turned back around, the room looked like...well, like an annoyed feller had gotten into a hell of a fight with a bucket of sand.

Rhett sighed deeply. He was just fine with fighting monsters, but he wasn't a big fan of doing the same kind of useless cleaning he'd been forced to do at Pap and Mam's. Still, he couldn't get tossed out of the hotel before their picnic with Trevisan, so he snuck out into the hall in his sock feet, went to the closet where the maids kept their cleaning supplies, and spent most of the night sweeping the floor and sewing his blanket back together with the kit he kept in his saddlebags. He mixed some ash from the fire with water and rubbed it into the scratches on the door, glad that it was dark wood and not painted, and that the scratches mostly disappeared unless you were really looking hard.

When he was done, he returned the broom and dustpan to the closet, the dustpan brimming with sand. Not his problem anymore. At least this time nobody could beat him, even if he did a middling to poor job cleaning up. He went to sleep aching in every crevice from the stag's hooves and didn't wake up until Inés started beating on his door the next morning.

"Go away," he murmured from under his stitched-up coverlet. "I been killing monsters all night."

"Wake up!" Inés shouted again. "You must guard me at breakfast."

Rhett grunted and rolled out of bed. He'd used up all his

ewer water last night, and his face looked ten years older and bore new scars from flecks of dead stag. He dragged a hand over his hair and shoved his hat on low. Feet into boots, gun belt over hips, mouth into something like a smile. He pulled the door open to find Inés standing there looking like somebody'd ironed her clothes while she wore 'em, starched and upright as the nun she had once been.

"You look like hell," she observed.

Rhett pointed to the barely visible scratches on his door. "He sent one of his friends to say hello last night. The conversation was not pleasant."

"But you won."

"Lady, I always win."

He knew she was inspecting the damage because her veil twitched, this way and then that. "And you tried to clean up." Kneeling, she brushed fingertips over the floor and stood, dusting away sand. "You should probably stay in your room all day so no servants enter. They won't like this."

He shook his head. "Small spaces make me itchy. I got to get to breakfast and see Trevisan for myself. And then I got business in town."

Inés hummed to herself. "That will be tricky. Remain silent when I speak to the hotel staff."

"As if I was really looking forward to that conversation," he groused.

It took him a moment to relock his door, as he still wasn't accustomed to the key system, and he followed Inés downstairs. She went directly to the big desk, and Rhett stood behind her, staring down at the sparkling white floors with their fancy black designs. He could imagine all too well how many hours with a scrub brush it took to keep such an extravagance clean in a place as dirty as Durango.

"Can I help you, ma'am? Er, sister?"

It was a different stuffy white feller this time, but they were all about the same to Rhett. This one was too big for his waist-coat, bulging out like an overdone sausage.

"I wish our rooms to remain undisturbed," Inés said, sounding stern. Keeping her hands hidden, she slid a coin across the desk, and it disappeared down the man's cuff. "I must pray and do my readings. See that no servants enter rooms 109 and 110, and there will be another coin before we leave." She snapped her fingers at Rhett. "The money, boy." He tried not to look too annoyed as he handed her the four dollars, and she slid that across the desk, too. "We will be staying one more night as well."

"You don't wish to have your, ahem, water changed?"

Inés drew herself up as tall as she'd go. "I do not."

The man dipped his head. "I'll see it done."

Inés inclined her head like a queen and swept off toward the clamor of the breakfast table. Exhausted and drooping, Rhett followed, finally perking up when he smelled bacon sizzling. As they entered the room, Josephina flapped a napkin at them.

"Sister Inés! Sister? There's room down here."

The sight that greeted them was so ridiculous that Rhett had to stifle a laugh. Trevisan was wearing...some sort of pajamas with arms that wrapped around his front, crossing, and then tied around his back. His hands were all tucked up in there, and he clearly couldn't figure out how to escape. He was radiating fury from Meimei's eyes, and as Rhett slid his long legs over the bench opposite him, Trevisan bared his teeth, showing a fresh gap where a tooth was missing.

"Oh, I'm so glad you're here. Herbert had to do business, and Mr. Franck was...well, he had an accident last night, and I've had to care for poor Mildred alone. It just won't do. I haven't been able to take a bite of my breakfast, and I swear I'm going to faint."

Josephina did look flustered, her hair slightly askew and her food nearly untouched.

"I'm not sure how we can help, but you should take care of your needs," Inés said, her voice tender and caring. No one had ever spoken to Rhett like that in his entire goddamn life.

Josephina sighed and sat down, shoveling breakfast into her mouth in a way that suggested she wasn't as gently bred as she would've liked folks to think. As soon as her hands were off his shoulders, Trevisan began to thrash about, trying to escape from the confines of his shirt.

"Rhett, why don't you hold sweet Mildred down," Inés suggested. "Gently. As gently as if she were one of your new foals." Leaning in to Josephina, she added, "He's a great hand with young things, Rhett is."

Rhett toned down his grin and nodded enthusiastically. "Yes, ma'am. I can soothe that little one while you have a bite."

About the only thing better than eating a breakfast he didn't have to cook was the chance to torture Trevisan, so Rhett abandoned the plate he'd been filling and moved around to the other bench, putting a hand on each of Trevisan's shoulders and gently but firmly shoving Meimei's little body back onto the bench. Trevisan's tension and fury all but vibrated up Rhett's arms.

Rhett leaned in close and whispered, in a singsong voice, "Rockabye, asshole, in the treetop. When the wind blows, your stag turned to glop."

Trevisan growled and flailed in his arms, and Rhett smoothed his hair. "She's feeling feisty today, seems like. She ever get any exercise? Little things like to run free."

Josephina swallowed and glugged her coffee before dabbing

her lips with her napkin and answering primly, "It's not safe. She might do herself damage. Why, she bit off one of her own toes, once! And she can be, well, violent toward others. Poor Mr. Franck didn't believe me, and look where he is now."

"Where is that?"

She rolled her eyes heavenward. "The infirmary."

"So why do you keep her, if she's so . . . troubled?"

Her eyes flashed defiance as she glared at him. "Fate delivered this precious child to us after many years of fruitless heartache. I just know that with enough love, she'll find her way."

Inés sketched a cross in the air. "Amen. The Lord provides."

That got Josephina smiling again. "He does. Perhaps you'll come have tea with me this afternoon, sister, after I've hired on another nursemaid. I could use some company in this wild, rough place." She looked down her nose at Rhett and added, "Your boy won't be necessary. We have plenty of muscle in our suite." Then, more pointedly, "You're squeezing her rather hard, Mr. Rhett. Please release her and give us some privacy."

It was true enough that Rhett's fingers were dug into Trevisan's shoulders as he pinned his foe to the bench and considered how easy it would be to kill him right here. But it was also true that Cora wouldn't let Rhett see another sunrise should he take that route, and also that his face would be up on Wanted posters from here to New Amsterdam. So he pasted on a shit-eating grin and held up his hands.

"Just trying to follow directions, ma'am. That little biscuit sure can squirm."

"The jacket will keep her from self-harm. Good day, Mr. Rhett."

"And a fine day to you."

Before Inés could give him any orders, Rhett scooped up a biscuit, tipped his hat, and hightailed it for the door. The day was fine, clear, and warm if a bit windy. As soon as his boots hit the muck of the street, he could feel all his muscles uncoil, his blood pumping and his lungs sucking in all that sweet, free air. When they'd first come to the city, the stench had nearly made him ill. But compared to the stale air indoors, he'd gladly gulp down the collective stink of every beast in Durango. A city was a trap, but once you went inside a building, the trap had sprung, and you'd already started dying.

Rhett chewed his biscuit and whistled as he practically skipped down the street. It was like there was a string attached to Sam, and Rhett danced on the end of it like a fish being reeled right in. He found Mr. Marko's hostelry, and he went on in to check on his horses first, half hoping he'd find Sam there. As luck would have it, he did.

It was like a daydream: Sam Hennessy still mussed from sleep, caught in a sunbeam as he curried his blue roan. Bits of hay danced in the light, and everything seemed touched with gilt. Rhett's heart just about exploded.

Blue's welcoming yodel pulled him out of the reverie, and Sam looked up in surprise and smiled in that particular way that made Rhett's heart do somersaults. Rhett gave his old mule a scratch, but his eyes never left Sam.

"Well, there you are. I been missing you, Rhett."

"Likewise, Sam. How's the horseflesh?"

"Right as rain. That Mr. Marko keeps a good barn. What's the news?"

It went like that, back and forth, easy as sugar. Rhett told Sam about Trevisan, the Mallards, the upcoming picnic, and the monster he'd killed the night before. He didn't mention that he only let the critter in because he was hoping against hope that it was Sam. As for Sam, he made the appropriate scared and impressed noises throughout Rhett's story and even looked worried about the blade-antlered stag.

"Hellfire, Rhett. You need somebody there with you. I told you it ain't safe alone."

"Oh, I took care of it, Sam. All in a day's work." He said it with some swagger, thumbs in his gun belt, and Sam gasped and stared at his hands.

"It burned you, Rhett!"

Rhett blushed and pulled his hands away, stuffing them in his pockets. "Aw, hell. It didn't hurt so bad. I reckon I'll just be nothing but a mess of scars, one day."

Sam dropped the curry comb and stepped close, closer than two smart cowpokes would be in a public place. Even though he didn't want to, Rhett stepped back. Anybody could walk into Marko's barn at any time, and as much as he didn't mind getting in fights with monsters, he sure as hell didn't want to feel the brunt of a human who saw the way he and Sam looked at each other and decided it wasn't acceptable.

As soon as Rhett stepped back, Sam looked about as hangdog as a feller could look.

"What's wrong, Rhett?"

"Hellfire, Sam. You know a place where we can talk? And just...be? Somewhere private-like?"

Sam nodded and pointed at the hayloft and started climbing. Rhett skittered up the wooden ladder behind him, indulging in a glance at the cowboy's fine rump. Up top, the loft was tidy just like below, full of neatly stacked hay and a table with four chairs and an old ceramic jug on top of it, just waiting to welcome hardworking fellers for a poker game away from the crowd. Sam looked like he was going to sit there, but the whole setup seemed cold to Rhett, and he couldn't imagine saying anything real to Sam with that stained table separating them. Instead, he inclined his head toward the sunny side of the loft and took a seat on a bale of hay. When Sam sat down beside him, their legs almost grazing, Rhett's heart just about floated away.

Rhett looked down and saw his hands on his knees, all mottled brown and puckered pink. He slipped them under his thighs, even though the hay itched like hell.

"You don't have to hide your hands. Your scars are part of you," Sam said, looking down at his own calloused pink palms. "You can trust me. I don't get scared off easy."

Rhett's throat closed up, and he forgot about his embarrassment and grabbed for Sam's hand without thinking about it too much, covering it with his own. "I know, Sam. I know you're tough. It's just...I never had anybody look at me like this before, like whatever I am and whatever I become is perfectly fine. It makes me jumpy. Like maybe one day you'll look too deep and see what I really am."

Sam turned his hand and squeezed Rhett's fingers hard enough to make the little bones rub together. "I see you fine. And I know everybody's got secrets, and they ain't all pretty. But you got to let me in. Let me see the things you hide from other people. That's what a partnership is: showing somebody what you keep from everybody else and trusting them not to hightail it."

"Maybe I'm scared of what you'll see. I don't ever want to hurt you." Rhett gulped and looked down. "I'm broken, Sam. In ways I haven't even figured out yet. And that means I'm still breakable. Maybe not so much on the outside, when I'm fighting monsters. But on the inside."

Sam held up their hands, tangled together, brown and pink and white and rough. "Nobody and nothing is perfect. Scars inside, scars outside. I got 'em, too. You haven't heard all my stories yet, but we can trade, by and by. Maybe I don't have as many scars as you, but I still got more than most. I rode with the Rangers for years before you showed up. I'm a survivor. A fighter. Just like you are." His grin was a come-hithery thing. "You tend to forget. I'm bigger than you."

Rhett turned a little and looked up. "Oh, I don't forget that."

Sam's eyes darted around the hayloft before he cupped Rhett's jaw and pulled his face into the proper angle for kissing. Rhett went all melty inside and forgot, for a moment, everything that dogged him. The Shadow drove him with whips and shouts but Sam beckoned him forward inexorably. Sam was the least magical person in his life but somehow made Rhett truly feel the magic in the world. He was the opposite of monsters, the counterpoint to the darkness, the personal sun around which Rhett orbited. This, Rhett thought, was the whole reason he fought so hard. So that maybe, every now and then, he could feel this way. Truly alive in every part but whole and happy, even with everything he was missing. The Shadow emptied him out, but Sam filled him back up.

Breaking from the kiss for a breath, Sam ran his knuckles over Rhett's cheek. "No stubble burn. Never thought I'd find the perfect feller, but here we are."

Rhett was lit up inside like kindling and couldn't find words for all the things he wanted to say. All he could do was cup Sam's hand with his own and try to put his feelings into his one good eye. It had been hard enough with two eyes, but now he felt like he was never enough, especially not to hold all the goodness of Sam Hennessy's heart.

"Know how you feel," he managed to whisper.

The ladder creaked down below, and they broke apart. Not quite guiltily, because Rhett was damned if he'd feel guilty for such stolen moments. More for the reason deer flash their tails and bolt when they hear a twig snap. They knew how rare a thing they possessed and didn't want to lose it. For deer, it was their own lives. For Rhett, well, he reckoned Sam was the most important thing in his life, and he'd bolt to keep him, every time.

As the ladder groaned under someone's weight, Rhett leaned back against a hay bale and stuck a slip of hay in between his lips to seem nonchalant. Sam inspected his fingernails.

"Marko said he saw you two head up here," Winifred said, head and shoulders peeking up through the hole in the loft floor.

"You climb right back down," Sam shouted. "Dan'll string me up if he knows you been climbing haylofts in your condition."

Winifred rolled her eyes and clambered up onto the honey-gold boards to stand, hands on hips. "You're not my nursemaid, Sam Hennessy, nor my jailer. So don't go telling me what to do. Greater men have tried. And failed."

She looked like some sort of a goddess, just then—natural and unkempt and fearsome. Her hair was loosely braided, long and shiny, and her skin seemed to glow from within. Even in her rough clothes, she was like a queen, and Rhett didn't doubt what she said. He wouldn't want to tangle with her just now, that was for damn sure. There had been a certain secretive, stolen safety in their time together, in the darkness of the wagon in the deep of night. But out in the daytime, in the sun, Winifred was more than a little terrifying.

"Tell us what you want, then, and go on back to being dangerous," he muttered, noting to himself that there was nothing in the world quite so uncomfortable as a former lover sneaking up while a feller was with his current lover.

She walked over with purpose and sat on Rhett's other side, and it felt about like being bracketed by two dogs that weren't exactly friendly. Sam scooted a little closer, which made

Winifred scoot a little closer, which made Rhett feel like a draft horse squeezed between the traces of a goat cart. He bolted up to pace the loft nervously, his fingers drumming on his pants legs.

"Well, go on," he urged. "With whatever you got to say."

Winifred gave him that private little smirk that reminded him how much she enjoyed needling him. "I just wanted to know what you found out. Is Trevisan still in Meimei's body?"

"He is. Got taken in by some white folks, richer than they are smart. They keep him under lock and key, guarded by well-armed fellers around the clock. Say it's for the child's own good. Last night, he must've gotten loose. Sent a monster after me, big ol' stag with blades for antlers. Made a mess of my hotel room, I'm not afraid to tell you. But Inés sweet-talked the fool lady who wants to be that necromancer's mama. We're going on a picnic with 'em tomorrow, out to the land where they're building their homestead. That's when I'm gonna do it. I haven't seen Dan and Cora, though. Have you?"

Winifred laughed at that. "They couldn't get in last night. Apparently someone in the hotel has a yappy little dog that kept having a hissy fit any time Dan tried to mosey in as a coyote. He about wanted to wring its neck. Since he couldn't get in, he couldn't unlock the attic door for Cora to come in from the roof. Dan will try to get in today, while folks are likely out and about."

"Could've used their help last night."

Her head whipped back like a snake. "Oh, you could've used some help? Sorry to disappoint you. Perhaps you forget that none of us are here because we must be. Or because we're paid well. My brother's sense of obligation to you is his own business, but I find it ridiculous. He is worth more than acting as your shield against the world."

That irked more than Rhett would ever admit. "Then why

the hell are you-all along? Stay here in San Anton, or go travel with my mama. There's plenty of places that would be glad to have you and your wee-un, I'm sure. But I got enough to worry about. I don't plan to start accepting complaints from aggrieved parties."

Winifred took a deep breath and sat on her hands as if trying to keep from clawing at his face like a harpy. Rhett figured it was a good skill for her to learn before the god's baby was born. "My brother is here because he feels it is his duty. I came here because...well, I just knew he needed me. Don't ask me how. It tugged me right out of Nueva Orleans. And now I'm staying here because Cora needs me."

"And what happens when she gets back what she really needs?"

Winifred looked like she'd been slapped, which Rhett found satisfying. If the coyote girl wanted to get honest, he could give as well as he got.

But Winifred's eyes just went cold as the November sky. "You don't know what she needs. You never bothered to ask. You didn't stick around to find out."

She spun and headed back for the ladder. Sam nudged Rhett's shoulder and whispered, "Rhett."

That's all it took, and Rhett was ashamed, for both of them. "Winifred, wait." When she turned around, he gave a sorry-type smile and asked, "How are you feeling? You need me to smuggle some biscuits out from the fancy hotel? They got pats of butter shaped like flowers."

She chuckled like he was a naughty child. Which, in many ways, he reckoned he was. "No, thank you. Mrs. Schafer is a fine cook, and the German ladies cluck over me and make sure I'm more than full. I'm feeling better. Not as sick. But I miss the open air. When you're used to the wide sky, being in such a big city is..."

"Right stifling," Rhett filled in.

Winifred nodded. "I don't know much about what the future holds, but I know this baby wants to be born on the prairie, not looking up at a pressed tin ceiling and a white woman's fine, soft hands."

Hearing her say that, Rhett remembered what he liked about her. She was a wild thing, like he was, and containment chafed at them both.

"Then I reckon I'll do my best to end that goddamn alchemist and get you back on the trail so you can squat in the mud," he said with his old teasing tone.

"What a gentleman," she answered in kind.

"Are you worried at all, Winifred?" Sam asked. "It seems right scary, birthing a baby. I know my ma squalled her head off. And it didn't seem to do well for Ms. Regina."

Winifred shrugged. "In my band, women simply stop on the trail, put down a piece of leather, and do what comes naturally. Not in the dirt." She gave Rhett a look that told him he was a fool. "But near enough. It's hard to do something more natural than that. Sometimes, women die. Sometimes, the child is lost. Sometimes both, but that wouldn't be a problem I would have to deal with personally, would it? As far as I see it, if Buck wanted this child made, that means he wants it born and growing and healthy. And he probably wants me to raise it, as I suspect he doesn't have time for that sort of thing, so I most likely won't fall during delivery. I'm fortunate, compared to some. Charmed, perhaps."

"But won't you feel trapped? With a little thing needing you all the time?" Rhett asked.

She flapped a hand at him. "Babies aren't boulders. You just carry them with you. I suppose I shouldn't get into as many fights as I currently do, thanks to you. But a few years off won't

316

dull my aim. How like a man, to assume that new life carries an impossible burden. It's a blessing, Rhett."

His breath hitched, and he had to look away. "Perhaps I come from a place where I was only ever a burden. I've never seen a child that folks seemed glad to have around."

"Well you're going to, so prepare yourself. Keep my brother safe until then, you hear?"

With a nod, she sauntered over to the ladder and gracefully swung around to climb down. Rhett watched her go, feeling the usual swirl of mixed feelings around a girl both too complicated and vastly fascinating, inviting and ferociously hostile.

"I don't reckon I will ever understand her," he said to Sam.

Sam sat beside him, hip to hip, and smiled. "You don't have to," he said.

And then they kissed for a good while more.

CHAPTER 23

Rhett spent the rest of the day with Sam in the hayloft trying his hardest to forget about everything that could go wrong the next morning. Private time with Sam was quickly becoming his favorite activity, second even to galloping on horseback. As dusk fell, they were forced to part, and he wandered back over to the hotel, his lips puffy with kissing and his belly woozy and sated in a different sort of way. Trevisan and his folks weren't at dinner, and neither was Inés, so he scooped up what he could right quick, before somebody noticed that he was the darkest person at the table and tried to kick him out. Upstairs, he found Inés in his room with a book in her lap, and he could feel her glare through the fabric of her veil.

"You stayed away," she observed, letting the book fall shut with a loud clap. "All day."

"I had business."

Her head nudged up and down like she was inspecting him for mismatched buttons. "You appear to have many kinds of business, some more pressing than others."

Rhett grinned. "Everybody does. There's still supper downstairs, if you're hungry."

The nun's belly growled as if on cue, and she left in a cloud of annoyance. One hand on the door, she turned to look back at him. "If something attacks you tonight, knock on my wall. You don't have to fight alone."

He didn't agree, but he didn't argue. Just stared at her and shrugged.

That night, not really meaning to, Rhett slept like a damn baby. At least, right up until he heard a key turn in his lock. His eye flew open on the sort of darkness that a man never finds on the prairie. Something about walls and ceilings seemed to create impenetrable shadows that just couldn't survive outside under the honest stars. Real quiet-like, he rolled off the bed, which he'd been lying on top of in all his clothes, just in case something untoward happened, which it seemed to be doing just now.

His gun belt was on the floor under his fingertips, and he slipped out a pistol with his left hand and his Bowie knife with his right. Barefoot and silent, he had just enough time to get behind the chest of drawers before the door creaked open. The next noise was the sharp click of his revolver cocking, just giving his intruder a warning. He had his gun aimed right where he figured Trevisan's head would be, but the loud, bemused snort from slightly higher up suggested it wasn't an ancient necromancer in a little girl's body, coming to throttle him in his sleep.

"It's just us, fool," Dan said in that tone of his that said Rhett was a damn idjit.

Rhett felt what he should've felt a full minute earlier: the wobble of his belly letting him know that monsters were right close. Was the Shadow getting some finesse at telling when monsters meant harm and when they didn't? The wobble of Little Eagle riding hell-bent for leather to steal his horses had woken him up, but this time he'd nearly slept right through

Dan's invasion. It was worth considering some other time, when he was fully awake and not annoyed. It was also right fascinating, he realized, that even though Trevisan wasn't a born monster, the Shadow was still called after the necromancer. Maybe it was all the monster bones he'd possessed over the years, but Rhett felt Trevisan's presence now, throbbing like a sore tooth that needed pulling.

"Goddammit, Dan," he muttered, uncocking his gun as he waited for his heart to stop pounding. "I was sleeping pretty good, too."

"Go back to sleep, then."

Rhett's heart sank as he realized the second person in the room wasn't Sam, as he'd hoped, but Cora. Which he should've known, considering their plan depended on Sam and Winifred staying the hell out of trouble—at least until it was time to take down Trevisan. Instead, it was the person who made him feel awkward and twitchy and ashamed, right here in the room where he'd been sleeping.

"Well, make yourselves comfortable, I reckon. I wasn't using the blanket, considering it got all torn up by a blade-antlered stag monster. And there's a chair over there and a couple of little pillows."

His eye had adjusted to the low light filtering in through the window, and he did a double take.

"What the hell are you-all wearing?"

Dan held up his arms to show a lady's nightgown, finely embroidered and with a ribbon at the neck. "First thing I found. I just needed something until I got into your room. And Cora can't fit through the halls as a dragon, so I grabbed one for her, too. You should've seen me stealing a key in this get-up. Like a thieving granny."

Cora laughed softly behind her hand. She was beautiful in

the scant moonlight, her hair loose and windswept and her body almost visible under the thin white fabric. Rhett caught himself ogling her and looked away quickly, settling back into bed and shoving his gun and knife under his pillow. Dan was right—he was like the town tomcat that just couldn't stop his roaming damn eye. He would've felt shame, but he'd known plenty of men in Gloomy Bluebird like that and plenty among the ranchers and Rangers, so why should he feel any different? Still, he didn't look at her again, out of loyalty to Sam.

"Well I'm glad you're settled, Granny. Can we sleep, then?"

"Tell us the plan, first."

So Rhett told them, and Dan reckoned it was better than most of Rhett's plans.

"Inés is a good influence on you, Rhett."

"Anybody who can turn me into stone has me at a disadvantage. Cora, you want the blanket? Or the pillow?"

Being in the small room with her was making him right twitchy. Dan was already on his back on the floor, but Cora stood by the window, looking down into the street, frowning.

"She's here," she said softly. "In room twenty-one. I checked the register. I could walk to her room and knock on the door, and perhaps catch a glimpse of my sister."

Rhett sat up, already shaking his head. "You can't. You shouldn't. We got a good plan going. We'll get her back tomorrow. But not tonight. Trevisan sees you, there's no telling what he'll do. And he's got plenty of armed guards who won't cotton to looky-loos at midnight."

For once, Dan agreed. "Tomorrow is soon enough."

Cora didn't look any happier, so Rhett added, "I can feel him, too. Here, in the hotel. Not moving. Not even pacing around." And then it occurred to him. "Hell, I bet those crazy people have to drug him at night, otherwise he'd escape. That's got to be it. Laudanum. Maybe we should go steal him while he's unconscious..."

"No." Dan's growl was harsh from the floor, closer to a coyote's bark than a man's chiding. "Don't be fools, either of you. The both of you. Egging each other on. Tomorrow is soon enough, and if either of you go for that door, I'll make sure you're bleeding before you hit the stairs."

"I am not a child," Cora said, colder than Rhett had ever heard her.

"Then don't act like one. Have patience."

Cora threw herself into the chair, arms crossed, looking very much like a child.

"I could fly out that window and set this entire city on fire."

"That would make you a murderer, and Rhett would probably be obliged to hunt you down next," Dan snapped. "Now go to sleep."

Cora looked out the window and exhaled smoke. "No."

Rhett grinned. It was nice to see someone else giving Dan shit.

Nothing attacked that night, and the party began at breakfast, where Mildred—or Trevisan, so far as Rhett was currently concerned—was dolled up in a little blue party dress with layers of ribbons and petticoats. The fighting man on her other side, not Mr. Franck, kept one hand on the back of her gown, his thick fingers twisted in the fabric. The red around the child's blurry eyes suggested she had indeed been drugged and was still feeling the effects. When Josephina rolled up Mildred's sleeve to clean off one of the child's hands, Rhett saw the marks where she had been tied down. These good-hearted souls were going out of their way in their kindness to an orphan child, and they weren't going to take no for an answer, it appeared.

Trevisan deserved it, and it surely helped Rhett that Trevisan hadn't escaped, but he felt bad for the child hidden within, whose skin should never have felt restraints. It was a good thing Cora wasn't in the room, or she couldn't have kept the fire from steaming out her nose and setting the tablecloth aflame.

"We haven't been out to see the home site in a few weeks," Josephina burbled. "What a lovely picnic! Isn't it, Mildred? A lovely picnic?"

Trevisan gave her a stare like something seen on a dead fish, and for just a moment, the woman's mask of kindness and sweetness wavered, showing rage and impotence, as if she wanted nothing more than to slap the child for her constant ungratefulness. But the smile snapped right back up like a white picket fence, and she held out a cup of milk.

"Better eat up, darling. It's about an hour's ride, what with the wagon's slowness." Still smiling grimly, she forced the milk cup against the child's lips until Trevisan either had to drink it or have it spilled up his nose. He drank. And he looked so miserable Rhett almost felt sorry for him.

After breakfast, Rhett and Inés walked to Mr. Marko's place to saddle up their horses, joined by Dan and Cora, who had changed back into their regular duds once they were out of the hotel. Dan let Inés ride his smaller chestnut, and Rhett took Ragdoll, not wanting Herbert to take a liking to BB, as regular folks so often were attracted to unicorns for some reason they could never quite explain. Dan turned into a coyote, and Cora headed for the edge of town, where she'd transform into a dragon and fly overhead. Inés had a decent enough seat for riding, and Rhett finally felt at home as Ragdoll trotted out of town just ahead of the Mallards' fine wagon. Herbert drove, and Josephina held her Mildred tightly in the open back, one arm wrapped around the child and the other clinging to the wagon seat for dear life. Facing them sat the new guard, and the man didn't even blink, so carefully did he watch his charge. Rhett didn't know a thing about the man, but he hoped he'd stay out of the way when things got twitchy.

It was peculiar to Rhett, seeing Trevisan like this. Helpless. Without his bones and gold and potions, physically trapped by these fools, Trevisan was as powerless as the little girl he so resembled. But that didn't mean Rhett could relax. He was all too aware of the crows that always seemed to be around, sitting on the buildings and fences of San Anton and then, later, on rocks and pecking at dead things as the party traveled past on the prairie. Whether they were Trevisan's creatures or simply drawn to him, they were everywhere, and Rhett badly wanted to shoot every damn one of them.

He caught sight of Dan every now and then as he glanced back toward the receding town. It felt good to leave San Anton. The room, the hotel, the very streets seemed to press down on Rhett, pinning him in place in a right uncomfortable way. He felt free outside, and it was an unusually fine day. Being this close to his prey put him in a downright jolly mood. And if the plan was working correctly, Sam would be even farther behind them on his dancing pony, far enough away to avoid trouble, hopefully, but close enough that he felt vital to the operation.

"You locals call this an Injun Summer, don't you?" Josephina asked him, letting go of the bench to hold on to her hat. "Why, I swear it's as fine as a summer day."

"We just call it November, ma'am," he responded, insulted on behalf of most of his friends and half of himself.

A shadow passed overhead, and he looked up to find Cora.

So long as he lived, he would always be filled with wonder to see a dragon, even more so to consider one a friend. It was downright amazing, how far his life had come since he'd been nothing but a slave at Pap and Mam's not even a year ago. The world was so much bigger than he'd ever guessed.

Herbert looked up at Cora and grunted. "Damn buzzards," he grumbled.

Rhett blinked away from Cora and back to Trevisan. Even with three of his posse by his side and one as backup, he had to keep an eye on the necromancer. Perhaps in the city there were too many fail-safes to allow him to escape his captivity, but out here, on the prairie? With only Josephina and Herbert and the new Mr. Franck as witnesses? Trevisan would gladly slice all their necks if he could get his tiny hands on a straight razor. And if Rhett wanted to stay on the right side of the law, he'd continue his Ranger pledge to keep these humans safe, even if they were godforsaken idiots with no clue what kind of trouble they carried in their laps. He had to give them some credit, though. With money and pure stubbornness, they'd managed to capture, corral, and hold one of the most dangerous creatures in the Republic, even if they had no idea.

With every clop of Ragdoll's hooves, Rhett's heart seemed to speed up. The moment was coming. The skeletal frame of a ranch house was just visible on the horizon. He said Inés's spell in his head, over and over until it was as natural as the roll of his hips in his saddle. He touched his guns, his knife, his bullet pouch, his Henry where it rested in his favorite place for it, the specially made sheath on the Captain's old saddle. To think, that mighty man's rump had been just here as he'd fought and galloped and hunted and saved folks all over his corner of Durango. Even if the Captain had refused to help with Trevisan, Rhett knew the Captain would want to see this job done, that wherever he was, he was watching Rhett. And Rhett wanted to make him proud. Sam, too.

If he could just end Trevisan and free Meimei, he'd finally get some small rest with Sam. Plenty of money, no Rangers to fuss at him, and all of Durango waiting. It was a pretty enough daydream, and Rhett even allowed himself to savor it for a short while.

Right up until Josephina called out, "It's just right over this ridge. Herbert said so!"

The ridge wasn't much of a ridge, as far as Durango went, but Rhett wasn't going to argue the matter. Beyond, the land went flatter, and a fine homestead was rising up from the prairie, finer than anything Rhett had ever seen. It was a big ranch house, two stories tall with an attic, and the board skeleton was shiny and yellow and spread out big enough to house a hundred people right comfortably. Wagons nearby held more wood, plus shingles and supplies and pretty much everything builders needed aside from the builders themselves. Crows and ravens sat here and there, on scrub trees and piles of wood and the bones of the house, staring silently.

A little thrum of worry went up Rhett's spine.

"Where's the builders?" he called.

"Sunday," Herbert barked. "They won't work, the bastards. Overseer will be around, somewhere, to protect the goods."

Which was, of course, part of the plan. They needed as few witnesses as possible. Not only so no one could report them as gunslingers harrying fine rich folk, but also so there were fewer bodies into which the lich might leap. After several rounds of shouting, even Herbert had to furiously assume the overseer had likewise taken the day off—or was drunk. He sent the hired gun out to find the rascal. Even better.

Because that meant the entire building site was empty. Rhett found Cora circling overhead, sought out the shape of the coyote skulking along behind them, and touched his own guns again. Far behind, up on a little ridge, he saw a flash that was probably the sun hitting Sam's Ranger star. Everybody was in place.

When the wagon stopped, he looked to Trevisan and found him...smiling.

Josephina seemed like a woman who wouldn't abide an inconvenience, and when she realized she couldn't set out a picnic and watch her charge at the same time, she naturally turned that labor over to somebody else.

"We haven't found a proper maid or governess yet, so I'll have to do the work myself. This little bumpus should be no trouble to a Ranger," she said, fluttering her eyelashes as she walked toward Rhett, towing Trevisan along firmly by the hand. "I don't know why you didn't just wear your star in the hotel. We would've gotten off on a much better foot."

Rhett bit his tongue and tried not to curse and get himself taken off of child-wrangling duty. "Well, ma'am, when a feller walks into town wearing his Ranger star, folks start bringing us problems. And my first charge, as given by my Captain, is to help Señora Inés. But I am glad that you appreciate my pedigree."

But before Trevisan could be turned over to Rhett, Inés stepped in.

"All God's children are precious," she said, arms open.

Rhett was right vexed until he realized that Trevisan's hands weren't bound and Rhett was just bristling with weapons.

Josephina gave Inés a beaming smile, transferred Trevisan's wrist to the nun's keeping, and returned to the wagon to set out a picnic. Rhett was pretty curious to see why the woman needed three boxes and two big blankets, but he wasn't about to take his eyes off Trevisan.

Inés had both of his hands now, tight, and Rhett kneeled a few feet away to squint at the child.

"How you doing in there, you piece of shit?" he whispered.

"I'm going to kill you slowly," Trevisan said in his peculiar accent but with a little girl's high-voiced lisp. "I'm going to slit your throat and pull out your tongue through the hole. I'm going to cut off pieces of you and shove them into other pieces of you. I will—"

"Unless you got a chunk of bone and a chunk of gold handy, I don't think you will. But look! What's this behind your ear? A penny! Aw, but that's made of copper, not gold, ain't it?"

Rhett pretended to pull a penny from the air generally over Trevisan's ear but didn't dare touch him. Not only because his protective mother was a lunatic, but also because he could feel Cora circling overhead, feel her shadow pass over him. If he dared to gently slap Trevisan's cheek, Cora would probably swoop down on her leathery wings and set him on fire like a goddamn pile of brush. But the twitch of Trevisan's head did reveal to him that the child wore gold earrings. And if Inés had been right about the necromancer's spell, that meant they might contain bits of bone. He'd have to snatch them out, and soon.

With a growl, Trevisan tried to launch for him, but Rhett just stood and stepped back, easy as pie, and Inés held the child-sized body easily. It didn't matter how much magic you had if you were just a little thing, Rhett reckoned.

"It's a good time to get rid of them," Inés said, jerking her chin toward the wagon, where Josephina was standing in the wagon bed as Herbert mopped sweat off his brow from the driver's box, neither of them watching the scene. "I can hold the child."

"Fair enough," Rhett said. "Hey, Mr. Herbert, sir!"

He ran toward the horses, flapping his hands, but the beasts were steady enough and merely twitched their ears at the wild scarecrow rushing at them. Figuring it was now or never, Rhett gave a loud yip, pulled his gun, and shot in the air. Still, the horses merely danced around irritably like any well-trained prairie beasts. Josephina screamed at the gunshot, and Herbert dropped the reins to stare at her, and then Rhett was close enough to swat one of the horses on the rump with his hat and send them both farting and running.

Josephina fell flat down on her back in the wagon bed, but Herbert tumbled over the side and landed in the dirt. Since Rhett had been running in that general direction, he just kept on running until he stood over the man, feeling slightly guilty.

"You all right?" he asked.

"No, I'm not all right, you simpleton," Herbert howled. "Why the hell did you spook my horses?"

But Herbert did not get up, just turned redder and redder as he lay on his back, and Rhett began to suspect he couldn't sit up. Whether his back was broken or he was just too fat remained to be seen, but Rhett didn't offer his hand.

"Just seemed like the right thing to do. Are you armed?"

"How dare you!" Herbert blustered, arms in the air like a bug, so Rhett snuck his fingers inside the feller's jacket and felt around until he'd discovered a tiny pearl-handled revolver.

"I reckon you *think* you're armed," Rhett said, dangling the little popgun in the air.

Herbert kept on blustering, and Rhett stood and put the pistol in his own pocket. "You'd better stay where you are," he warned. "Things are about to get peculiar. That little girl you-all found...she ain't a little girl."

"She's a monster," Herbert said.

"More than you know."

Just then, Inés shouted, "He got loose! Rhett!"

Rhett drew his gun as he looked up, but Trevisan wasn't

running toward him, hell-bent on blood like Rhett had expected. The little fool was running toward the half-built house, fast as his short little baby legs would carry him.

"Goddammit," Rhett muttered, running over that way, too.

Trevisan was closer to the house and fast enough, and he quickly squeezed in among the timbers like a swift darting into a barn. Rhett couldn't get a clear shot, and he hopped up onto the unfinished wood floor to get a better view.

"Where is he?"

"Nice of you to show up, Dan," Rhett said dryly. He glanced down briefly and smirked at Dan's usual way after changing over from his coyote skin. "And in your altogether. Always prepared for a gunfight."

"I was prepared to lay out that hired gunman wandering toward the still full of whiskey. One rock to the head, and he's not a problem. Any other complaints, Shadow?"

Rhett snorted a laugh. "You could use some pants."

"Where is Meimei?"

Rhett didn't even bother trying to look at Cora once he heard her voice. He had to keep all his concentration on the monster that looked like her sister.

"Somewhere in here, I reckon," he said, jerking his chin at the house. "I feel him near, but not exactly where."

Inés had arrived, too, a small knife in her fist. She didn't bother apologizing for letting Trevisan get loose, and Rhett liked her all the more for it. He handed Dan one of his guns and held out Herbert's little peashooter to Cora, his eyes carefully averted from her nakedness. "Don't forget, y'all—he's human. I know Cora wants him whole, but I'd rather have Meimei with a shot leg than Trevisan escaping in fine fettle." He did meet Cora's eyes this time, now that he'd had a troubling thought. "Wait. Is Meimei human? Or is she...?"

"A dragon? No. Like my father, she is human. Otherwise, we would not be in this mess."

"Then everyone do your best not to shoot. But if it comes down to it—"

"Still don't shoot," Cora snapped. "She is a child."

"And Trevisan can hear us," Dan observed. "Most likely."

Rhett grabbed Cora by the shoulders, feeling desperate down to his bones. "Cora, you got to listen. This might be our only chance. Do you want Meimei to go on like this, or would you rather have an end to her suffering? I say shoot if you can. We don't take chances."

Cora looked down, tears in her eyes. "You are right. Shoot if you must. I would rather she be free, either way."

The half-built house was big and full of pits and walls and staircases and fireplaces and unruly stacks of lumber and piles of bricks. Rhett would never have guessed a place could be so full of pitfalls and hidey-holes. With his posse nearby and Trevisan in the general area, he was having a hard time honing in on the feller's wobble.

"Everybody...stop being monsters!" he shouted. "Or at least shut up!"

They hadn't been talking, but they didn't start up. And they couldn't control that monster sense that plagued each of them to some degree, pulling this way and that. Outside of birdsong and crow caws and footsteps, the morning was quiet. Right up until Rhett heard something he usually loved more than any other sound but that made him sick to death, just now.

"Rhett, he's running for the feller on the ground! What do you want me to do?"

It was Samuel Hennessy. And he wasn't supposed to be here until Rhett was in mortal peril.

But he was here anyway, goddammit.

CHAPTER 24

Stay away from him, Sam!" Rhett shouted, and his voice sounded just like a scared girl, and for once, he didn't give a shit.

He was up and running like a mad thing, jumping over wood and squeezing through corners and leaping off the house to land in a puff of dust and take off running again. He registered Sam running in the same direction, toward the fallen Herbert. Josephina was on her knees in the sand beside him, fussing with smelling salts and handkerchiefs and whatever city fools did when faced with tragedy.

"Sam, stop! Josephina, watch out!" Rhett called as Trevisan zoomed across the yard, something held in Meimei's little fist.

But neither person did as he'd commanded, damn them.

Josephina looked up at him sharply, frowning. Then, seeing the child heading toward her, she smiled like she was seeing heaven and held out her arms, calling, "Mildred! Come to Mama!"

Trevisan ran right into her arms, and Josephina hugged the child tightly, crying like she'd gotten her fondest wish.

"Get away from it!" Rhett shouted again.

Trevisan pulled away from Josephina, and the woman put

a hand to the child's soft cheek. Trevisan turned his head into her palm, nuzzled close, and then...

Josephina started screaming and held up a hand spurting blood.

The child—Trevisan—had bitten off part of the woman's finger.

Putting two and two together, Rhett put on a fresh burst of speed and got close enough to shove Trevisan to the ground. The child's body was so light that it flopped back into the dirt, and Rhett stood over it, a boot planted on its frail chest— because it wasn't Meimei, and it wasn't Trevisan, it was an *it*— and cocked his gun.

"Drop the finger, Trevisan," he said.

Behind him, he heard Sam tending to Josephina. Dan and Cora finally arrived, drawing a circle around Trevisan.

"Meimei?" Cora said, voice wobbly.

"Sister?" the little lispy voice said, and Cora sobbed and kneeled.

"Cora, don't fall for it," Rhett barked. "Don't let him near you."

"I can see her in there. In the eyes. Trapped in a cage again."

"Then you stay the hell back, Cora, and let me get her out. Don't go complicating things."

Rhett felt like he was trying to fend off twenty rabid dogs, but everything was happening too fast. He was trying to call Cora off, wishing Josephina would stop blubbering, wishing Herbert was moving a little more, wishing Dan and Sam could just flat-out read his mind.

But when he heard Trevisan lisping a spell in Meimei's voice, he knew he had to act.

Trevisan was still on the ground, something clutched in each of his fists, and Rhett dropped down beside him, pinned each tiny hand under a knee, and tried his damnedest to stuff his bandanna into the child's mouth. Trevisan fought him like a cat, twisting and bucking and pinning Meimei's lips, but Rhett grabbed his little snub nose and pinched it closed until Meimei's mouth opened. In went the handkerchief, and Rhett snatched the earbobs out of the child's ears, leaving little drops of blood as thanks for his rough quickness. Cora made a sound of fury, and he turned around to see why nobody was helping him.

Josephina was acting like a damn fool, on her back and screaming, and good ol' Sam was tending to her wound, or trying to. Cora was watching Rhett with terror in her eyes, alternating with softness when she looked at the body of her sister pinned cruelly beneath his knees. Dan just stood there, naked, waiting.

"Help pry open his hands, Dan," Rhett said, and Dan chose not to be irksome. He kneeled down, parts flopping everywhere, and set to getting Trevisan's fingers open, which was harder than it seemed. For Rhett, it was hard as hell to do anything that might hurt the child's body. Everything in his heart and soul rebelled against damaging the tiny bones and soft little fingers, especially after he saw the scrapes on Meimei's knuckles from his own knees driving them into the stony ground.

Rhett worked the other hand, pulling away each tiny finger, terrified that he would break a bone. He was lucky—his hand held only a gold ring and a dead lizard, squeezed to death by the struggle. He finally got both objects out and tossed them over his shoulder. Dan's hand revealed a worse prize: Josephina's finger, raggedly bitten and leaking slurry blood.

"So that's bone, gold, spark, and spell, stopped," Rhett said in the peculiar silence.

Josephina had finally settled into soft sobs, and Trevisan

could only squeak through the bandanna. Rhett exhaled, his heart settling back down. Finally, after all this time, they had Trevisan right where they wanted him.

"Inés, you want to do the spell, or you want me to?" Rhett hollered.

"It might be best if I say it." She was so quiet he hadn't noticed her behind him, but he was glad as hell that she was willing. He knew he was gonna mess up that spell, no matter what.

"Dan, you and Cora take Meimei's hands. I'm gonna grab us a familiar."

When they each had one of the struggling child's hands, Rhett stood and aimed his gun for the crows lining up over Herbert's half-built castle. He took aim at the biggest bastard and pulled the trigger. The raven fell over backward as its inky friends took to the sky, screeching. They swirled up in peculiar patterns, whirled around like a tornado, and took aim...right at Rhett and his posse.

"Everybody take cover!" he shouted, diving to protect Sam with his body.

The birds beat down like rain made of fists and knives, and Rhett buried his face in the nape of Sam's neck. How he longed to turn into the bird and cut a swath of destruction through the flock, but somehow, these birds were different. The last ones that attacked him had been alchemy, feathers and wax and gold and bone. But these birds were solid, angry, and sharp. Beaks pecked at the curve of his neck, claws pricked through his shirt. Somewhere nearby, he heard heavy thunks and realized Inés had to be turning birds into stone. The enraged yipping and growling—that was Dan in coyote form, using his best weapons of teeth and claws. And then he felt the hot licks of flame overhead, searing the hair under his hat. Cora's fire, demolishing the pesky birds.

As the breath of flame ended, Rhett dared to look up. Most of the birds were dead, dying, or flying away with all their might. Only problem was, Trevisan was gone.

"Goddammit!" Rhett hollered. "Find Trevisan!"

Sam shifted under him, and Rhett briefly buried his face in Sam's neck. "Not you, Sam. You got to stay safe. He's a wily little bastard, and he's still got his magic."

"I know that. You think I don't? But you need me now, Rhett."

Rhett brushed a swift kiss along his earlobe. "Just stay safe. Keep away from him."

And then he was up and spinning, hunting for that wobble he felt when the Shadow's quarry was near. There. Trevisan was on the other side of Herbert, fumbling with the big man's limp hand. Ring or bone or both, he damned well wasn't going to get it.

Cora was just transforming back into a woman as Rhett landed a vicious kick that sent Trevisan skittering away from Herbert.

"Rhett, no!" Cora shouted, and even Rhett felt guilty for the violence of his boot striking that tiny body.

Trevisan looked up at Cora, letting Meimei's lip tremble. Cora couldn't see that he was in the process of slipping Herbert's gold ring off the man's bloated finger, that he had recovered Josephina's bloody finger, that he had the body of a half-dead bird beside him, the last ingredient for his spell.

If Trevisan had been in any other body, Rhett would've busted in his teeth, yanked out his tongue, made damn sure he couldn't say his shifty goddamn spell. But this was Cora's Meimei, and she'd kill Rhett herself if he damaged that little body more than he had to. And yet he had to stop the necromancer, or he'd hop bodies, and then they'd be in real trouble.

The disturbing thought occurred to him that he'd never asked what would happen if Trevisan jumped into a monster's body. Surely the man could, or he wouldn't have tried with Rhett in the train car. So was that his plan, now—to take over one of Rhett's posse? Or would he settle for a weak thing like Josephina? Or Herbert? What good would it do Trevisan to be in a corpulent body with a broken back? Although that form would be best for his financial schemes, it wasn't gonna do him any good when it came to hiking back into town.

"What's your play?" Rhett murmured under his breath as he circled around Trevisan, trying to pick the right angle of attack. Finally he just gave up and threw himself at the child, knocking Trevisan backward and landing hard on top of him.

That's when he felt the hot punch of a knife, just to the side of his heart. The next breath he drew was a wispy, incomplete thing.

Lung, he thought. *That ain't good.*

But it wasn't a killing shot, either, so long as Trevisan wasn't strong enough to drag that knife sideways. Rhett popped up and backward, taking the knife with him. Grabbing it by the hilt, he tossed it down. Just a little pocketknife. Trevisan had probably grabbed it off Herbert, thought he could end the Shadow with a good stick to the heart.

Dumbass.

Rhett was back on Trevisan in a moment, but now his hands were slippery with blood, and Rhett still couldn't draw a full breath as his lung twitched and pulled closed, and Trevisan managed to slip out of his grasp. When Rhett went to grab him, he got a kick in the face from a tiny boot.

"You little turd," he wheezed.

Trevisan was a mess of skirts and blood and black feathers and kicking boots, and Rhett needed his lung to heal back up completely so he could get a full breath. "Somebody grab him!" he squeaked, and Dan circled around obligingly.

Trevisan picked up the knife, threw it hard with terrible aim, and tried to dart away, but Dan caught him, driving him to the ground on top of the bird corpses. Cora was frozen in place, but Rhett was done being gentle. He'd nearly taken a knife to the heart for his troubles, and Meimei could just get a little banged up and heal later. Rhett smacked Trevisan's fist, making him drop the finger. Then he pried out the gold ring. Swiping them both from the ground, he threw them in opposite directions out into the prairie, as far as he could. If luck was on his side, one of the fanged jackrabbits would make quick work of the finger and take the meat down into its burrow, where Trevisan couldn't get to it.

While Dan held the struggling necromancer, Rhett stuffed another handkerchief into Meimei's mouth.

"Inés, say the thing!" he shouted.

Somewhere behind him, she shouted back, "I can't. You do it."

"But Inés!"

"No, Rhett! You! I'm needed here!"

"Goddammit," he growled. He cleared his throat and said, "Cora, bring me a living bird." Once she'd handed him an angry crow with a broken wing, he clutched it by the legs, feeling all guilty and squirmy with fellow feeling as it squawked and flapped, hating being trapped.

Rhett stared Trevisan in the eyes, in Meimei's eyes, and began to say the spell Inés had taught him. Every word, every peculiar syllable, no matter how they fought to twist his tongue. He didn't stop, he didn't pause, and he could tell it was working. The bird in his fist screamed in earnest, in agony, and Meimei's brown eyes went over-wide and terrified. Trevisan struggled frantically in Dan's arms, but Dan, at least, would not let go. Cora whimpered but kept her distance.

So close. Just the tricky part left, and then the ending.

Every word. Every sound. Every subtle slithery accent.

He nailed it.

The final line, three repetitions. When the last one left his lips, the bird in his hand gave one final flapping scream and went completely limp and cold, its toes curling up. Likewise, Trevisan collapsed in Dan's arms, Meimei's little body losing all tension and looking far too dead for Rhett's taste.

They waited an endless moment for Meimei to breathe again.

"Inés, it ain't working!" Rhett shouted. "What happened to Meimei?"

But Inés didn't answer, and when Rhett glanced back angrily, he found her and Sam dealing with Josephine and a thrashing Herbert, just a knot of bodies.

"Don't bother with the goddamn Mallards, Inés. We got to bring Meimei back! Now!"

Inés growled and shouted, "Wake her up then, fool."

Dan still held the child's wrists, and he gently laid her limp body on the ground. For the first time that day, Rhett noticed that despite the unseasonal warmth, the ground was as cold and hard as the middle of winter, unforgiving and cruel. He tossed the bird aside and kneeled over Meimei, all too aware that the child wasn't breathing.

"Dan, do that thing you did with Winifred. When she drowned."

Dan glanced up at Cora, who nodded eagerly. "Do it. Whatever it is, do it."

Taking a deep breath, Dan fitted his mouth over Meimei's mouth and breathed out. The little girl's chest rose high.

Pulling back, Dan watched her chest go back down as the air left her. It didn't rise again on its own. He looked to Rhett, and Rhett wanted to scream.

It had to work, goddammit. It had to.

But it didn't.

"Do it again!"

Putting his face right up next to Meimei's, Dan shouted, "Wake up, Meimei!"

Still nothing. Tears pricked at Rhett's eyes. All this, for nothing?

"Cora, you try," he said.

Naked and beautiful, she curled over her sister. Rhett scooted to make room and wished he had the guts to touch her. A hand on the shoulder or back, some kind of human connection to help her get over what he knew was going to happen next. Instead, he just hovered, waiting for the inevitable. He knew what it was to be broken, after all.

Cora's voice went deep like it did when she was a dragon, and smoke curled out her nose and mouth as she put her lips to her sister's and said something incomprehensible. Her hands, now covered with glittering orange scales and sharp, glass-like claws, gently caressed the tiny face, the sweet curve of a cheek, the pink blossom of a mouth.

Nothing happened.

At first.

Then Cora dragged her hand down over Meimei's heart, and the little critter's chest rose as she coughed and began crying. Laughing and sobbing at the same time, Cora helped her sit up and murmured to her in their language, and the little girl answered her the same way, voice hitching and high and lisping with no trace of Trevisan.

"Is it her?" Rhett asked.

Cora looked at him and gave him a smile he'd only seen once before, in her tent at the train camp when he'd first brought the little girl from Trevisan's car.

"It is her. I'm sure. You have succeeded."

One time, perhaps, they would've hugged. But now Rhett just smiled back and said, "I'm glad, Cora. I'm real glad." And then, softly, over her shoulder, "Hey there, Meimei."

"Rhett," Dan said, real sharp-like.

"Now ain't the time to holler at me, Dan. I succeeded, remember?"

He meant it as a joke, but Dan wasn't smiling. He was looking over at Inés, and in all their time together, with all Dan's preaching and shouting and threatening, Rhett had never seen him look this stony, this somber.

"Rhett," Dan said again.

"Well, what's wrong now? Can't you let a feller take a moment to relax?" But Rhett could hear the pleading in his own voice because he knew something was desperately wrong, so wrong that Dan couldn't tell him what it was.

He swallowed hard and stood up, turning and shading his eye to see what Dan was looking at. It wasn't Josephina on the ground, nor Herbert, that had captured Inés's focus.

It was Sam.

Chapter

25

Rhett ran to Sam, uncaring of anything else. Trevisan was gone, or good enough. Cora was happy, and if she wasn't, he didn't give a shit. What had happened to Sam?

Sam, who was supposed to stay back with his Henry.

Sam, who Rhett had told again and again to stay out of the line of fire.

Sam, who was covered in blood, his normally sunny smile a grimace of pain.

Sam, whose bright blue eyes were wet and scared and latched onto Rhett like a starving baby.

"What happened?" Rhett asked, sinking to Sam's side.

"He . . . He got me, Rhett. I'm sorry. You were right. I shoulda stayed out of sight. Covered you with my gun. Like we talked about."

"No, Sam. No. You did just fine. I always knew you'd have my back."

Sam's hands were over his belly, but he pulled them away to show the hilt of Trevisan's pocketknife, the one he'd thrown at Dan . . . and missed. Or had he?

Blood burbled out, and Sam groaned and put his hands back over it. Rhett briefly put his hands over it as well, wishing that his magic could help instead of hurt. He'd trade everything he had to fix it for Sam, to take the pain away. Hell, he'd take the knife, right now. In the gut, in his other eye, anywhere. He'd carry it with him forever if he could change places with Sam. It didn't escape him that this was the same knife Trevisan had stuck into his own chest. But unlike Sam, Rhett had simply plucked it out and kept fighting.

"We can fix this, right? Inés? We can pull out the knife?"

The nun sat back on her heels, hands on her lap. He couldn't see her face, and it was a good thing, because her silence said more than he wanted to know.

Her head shook, just the tiniest twitch. "It's in his guts."

"So pull it out and…"

"It's not the same for him. His body won't seal off and heal as quickly as yours did. If the knife comes out, the contents of his intestines flood his body. It's septic, Rhett."

"I seen it before," Sam said, voice quavering. "A man can't survive it. A man can't…"

He trailed off, his eyes finding the sky.

Rhett looked to Inés. "Then what? What can we do?"

He wanted to hold Sam's hands, wanted to draw the man close and hug him, but Sam seemed as fragile as a dying butterfly, his body rigid and his hands firmly pressing down and his face as white and tight as a hotel bedsheet.

"We can do nothing," Inés said. "Humans are fragile. That's their curse."

"Nothing?"

Her head shook. Rhett looked to Dan, whose face was grimmer than grim.

"This is not a wound that humans can survive, Rhett."

Rhett had to touch Sam, so he put a hand on the boy's shoulder as he looked around the home site. He found no one and nothing that could help. Cora and Meimei, Josephina and Herbert, two monsters, four horses. No medicine, no sawbones, no magic. He'd beat Trevisan. He'd won. But he would trade it all to have Sam standing and whole. No victory was worth this.

"Necromancy?" he asked.

"No!" Inés snapped. "That way lies darkness. Sam would not kill another so that he could live."

Sam's eyes fluttered open. "I wouldn't, Rhett. Not that way."

"But there has to be a way, Sam."

Sam coughed, his voice wheezing. Little bubbles of blood popped at the corners of his mouth, dribbled down into the golden fuzz of his beard. "It's okay, Rhett. Not your fault. I'm a Ranger. Was. Always figured...I'd go this way. S'not so bad. Looking up at a fine blue sky and my best friend."

"I'm with you to the end, Sam."

Sam looked up at Rhett, his eyes unfocused and as blue as a sunny day and his smile as sweet as sugar.

"I reckon we're there already, Rhett."

extras

meet the author

Photo Credit: Von Tuck

LILA BOWEN is a pseudonym for Delilah S. Dawson, the writer of *Star Wars: Phasma*, *The Perfect Weapon*, and *Scorched*; the Blud series, the Hit series, *Servants of the Storm*, and the Ladycastle comic. She won the RT Fantasy of the Year Award for *Wake of Vultures*. Delilah lives in Florida with her family.

if you enjoyed
MALICE OF CROWS

look out for

THE TETHERED MAGE

Swords and Fire: Book One

by

Melissa Caruso

In the Raverran Empire, magic is scarce and those born with power are strictly controlled—taken as children and conscripted into the Falcon army.

Zaira has lived her life on the streets to avoid this fate, hiding her mage mark and thieving to survive. But hers is a rare and dangerous magic, one that threatens the entire Empire.

Lady Amalia Cornaro was never meant to be a Falconer. Heiress and scholar, she was born into a treacherous world of political machinations.

But fate has bound the heir and the mage. And as war looms on the horizon, a single spark could turn their city into a pyre.

Chapter One

Here, my lady? Are you sure?"

As the narrow prow of my boat nudged the stone steps at the canal's edge, I wished I'd walked, or at least hired a craft rather than using my own. The oarsman was bound to report to La Contessa that her daughter had disembarked at a grimy little quay in a dubious corner of the Tallows, the poorest district of the city of Raverra.

By the time my mother heard anything, however, I'd already have the book.

"Yes, thank you. Right here."

The oarsman made no comment as he steadied his craft, but his eyebrows conveyed deep skepticism.

I'd worn a country gentleman's coat and breeches, to avoid standing out from my seedy surroundings. I was glad not to risk skirts trailing in the murky water as I clambered out of the boat. Trash bobbed in the canal, and the tang in the air was not exclusively salt.

"Shall I wait for you here, my lady?"

"No, that's all right." The less my mother knew of my errand, the better.

She had not precisely forbidden me to visit the pawnbroker who claimed to have a copy of Muscati's *Principles of Artifice*, but she'd made her opinion of such excursions clear. And no one casually disobeyed La Contessa Lissandra Cornaro. Her word resonated with power in every walled garden and forgotten plaza in Raverra.

Still, there was nothing casual about a Muscati. Only twelve known copies of his books existed. If this was real, it would be the thirteenth.

As I strolled alongside the canal, my mother's warnings seemed ridiculous. Sun-warmed facades flanked the green water, and workers unloaded produce from the mainland off boats moored at the canal's edge. A bright, peaceful afternoon like this surely could hold no dangers.

But when my route veered away from the canal, plunging into a shadowy tunnel that burrowed straight through a building, I hesitated. It was far easier to imagine assassins or kidnappers lurking beyond that dim archway. It wouldn't be the first time I'd faced either in my eighteen years as my mother's heir.

The book, I reminded myself. Think of the book.

I passed through the throat of the tunnel, emerging into a street too narrow to ever see direct sunlight. Broken shutters and scarred brickwork closed around me. The few people I passed gave me startled, assessing glances.

I found the pawnbroker's shop with relief, and hurried into a dim wilderness of dusty treasures. Jewelry and blown glass glittered on the shelves; furniture cluttered the floor, and paintings leaned against the walls. The proprietor bent over a conch shell wrapped with copper wire, a frown further creasing his already lined face. A few wisps of white over his ears were the last legacy of his hair.

I approached, glancing at the shell. "It's broken."

He scowled. "Is it? I should have known. He asked too little for a working one."

"Half the beads are missing." I pointed to a few orbs of colored glass still threaded on the wire. "You'd need an artificer to fix it if you wanted it to play music again."

The pawnbroker looked up at me, and his eyes widened. "Lady Amalia Cornaro." He bowed as best he could in the cramped shop.

I glanced around, but we were alone. "Please, no need for formality."

"Forgive me. I didn't recognize you in, ah, such attire." He peered dubiously at my breeches. "Though I suppose that's the fashion for young ladies these days."

Breeches weren't remotely in fashion for young ladies, but I didn't bother correcting him. I was just grateful they were acceptable enough in my generation that I didn't have to worry about causing a scandal or being mistaken for a courtesan.

"Do you have the book?" I reminded him. "Muscati's *Principles of Artifice*, your note said."

"Of course. I'd heard you were looking for it." A certain gleam entered his eye with which I was all too familiar: Cornaro gold reflected back at me. "Wait a moment, and I'll get it."

He shuffled through a doorway to the rear of the shop.

I examined the shell. I knew enough from my studies of artifice to trace the patterns of wire and understand the spell that had captured the sound of a musical performance inside the shell's rune-carved whorls. I could have fixed a broken wire, perhaps, but without the inborn talent of an artificer to infuse new beads with magical energy, the shell would stay silent.

extras

The pawnbroker returned with a large leather-bound book. He laid it on the table beside the conch shell. "There you are, my lady."

I flipped through the pages until I came to a diagram. Muscati's combination of finicky precision in the wirework schematics and thick, blunt strokes for the runes was unmistakable. I let out a trembling breath. This was the real thing.

The pawnbroker's long, delicate fingers covered the page. "Is all in order, then?"

"Yes, quite. Thank you." I laid a gold ducat on the table. It vanished so quickly I almost doubted I'd put it there.

"Always a pleasure," he murmured.

I tucked the book into my satchel and hurried out of the musty shop, almost skipping with excitement. I couldn't wait to get home, retreat to my bedroom with a glass of wine, and dive into Muscati's timeworn pages. My friend Domenic from the University of Ardence said that to read Muscati was to open a window on a new view of the universe as a mathematical equation to be solved.

Of course, he'd only read excerpts. The university library didn't have an actual Muscati. I'd have to get Domenic here to visit so I could show him. Maybe I'd give the book to the university when I was done with it.

It was hard to make myself focus on picking turns in the mazelike streets rather than dreaming about runic alphabets, geometric diagrams, and coiling wirework. At least I was headed in the right general direction. One more bridge to cross, and then I'd be in polite, patrician territory, safe and sound; and no lecture of my mother's could change the fact that I'd completed my errand without incident.

But a tense group of figures stood in the tiny plaza before the bridge, frozen in a standoff, every line of their bodies promising each other violence.

Like so many things in Raverra, this had become complicated.

Three broad-shouldered men formed a menacing arc around a scrawny young woman with sprawling dark curls. The girl stood rigidly defiant, like a stick thrust in the mud. I slowed to a halt, clutching my satchel tight against my side, Muscati's edge digging into my ribs.

"One last chance." A burly man in shirtsleeves advanced on the girl, fists like cannonballs ready at his sides. "Come nice and quiet to your master, or we'll break your legs and drag you to him in a sack."

"I'm my own master," the girl retorted, her voice blunt as a boat hook. "And you can tell Orthys to take his indenture contract and stuff it up his bunghole."

They hadn't noticed me yet. I could work my way around to the next bridge, and get my book safely home. I took a step back, glancing around for someone to put a stop to this: an officer of the watch, a soldier, anyone but me.

There was no one. The street lay deserted. Everyone else in the Tallows knew enough to make themselves scarce.

"Have it your way," the man growled. The ruffians closed in on their prey.

This was exactly the sort of situation in which a young lady of the august and noble house of Cornaro should not involve herself, and in which a person of any moral fortitude must.

Maybe I could startle them, like stray dogs. "You there! Stop!"

They turned to face me, their stares cold and flat. The air went dry in my throat.

"This is none of your business," one in a scuffed leather doublet warned. A scar pulled at the corner of his mouth. I doubted it came from a cooking accident.

I had no protection besides the dagger in my belt. The name Cornaro might hold weight with these scoundrels, but they'd never believe I bore it. Not dressed like this.

My name meant nothing. The idea sent a wild thrill into my lungs, as if the air were alive.

The girl didn't wait to see what I would do. She tried to bolt between two of the men. A tree branch of an arm caught her at the waist, scooping her up as if she were a child. Her feet swung in the air.

My satchel pulled at my shoulder, but I couldn't run off and leave her now, Muscati or no Muscati. Drawing my dagger seemed a poor idea. The men were all armed, one with a flint-lock pistol.

"Help!" I called.

The brutes seemed unimpressed. They kept their attention on the struggling girl as they wrenched her arms behind her.

"That's it!" Rage swelled her voice. "This is your last warning!"

Last warning? What an odd thing to say. Unless...

Ice slid into my bone marrow.

The men laughed, but she glowered furiously at them. She wasn't afraid. I could think of only one reason she wouldn't be.

I flattened myself against a wall just before everything caught fire.

Her eyes kindled first, a hungry blue spark flaring in her pupils. Then flames ran down her arms in delicate lines, leaping into the pale, lovely petals of a deadly flower.

The men lurched back from her, swearing, but it was too late. Smoke already rose from their clothing. Before they finished sucking in their first terrified breaths, blue flames sprang up in sudden, bold glory over every inch of them, burying every scar and blemish in light. For one moment, they were beautiful.

Then they let out the screams they had gathered. I cringed, covering my own mouth. The pain in them was inhuman. The terrible, oily reek of burning human meat hit me, and I gagged.

The men staggered for the canal, writhing in the embrace of the flames. I threw up my arm to ward my face from the heat, blocking the sight. Heavy splashes swallowed their screams.

In the sudden silence, I lowered my arm.

Fire leaped up past the girl's shoulders now. A pure, cold anger graced her features. It wasn't the look of a woman who was done.

Oh, Hells.

She raised her arms exultantly, and flames sprang up from the canal itself, bitter and wicked. They spread across the water as if on a layer of oil, licking at the belly of the bridge. On the far side of the canal, bystanders drawn by the commotion cried out in alarm.

"Enough!" My voice tore out of my throat higher than usual. "You've won! For mercy's sake, put it out!"

But the girl's eyes were fire, and flames ran down her hair. If she understood me, she made no sign of it. The blue fire gnawed at the stones around her feet. Hunger unsatisfied, it expanded as if the flagstones were grass.

I recognized it at last: balefire. I'd read of it in Orsenne's *Fall of Celantis*.

Grace of Mercy preserve us all. That stuff would burn anything—water, metal, stone. It could light up the city like a dry corncrib. I hugged my book to my chest.

"You have to stop this!" I pleaded.

"She can't," a strained voice said. "She's lost control."

I turned to find a tall, lean young man at my shoulder, staring at the burning girl with understandable apprehension. His wavy black hair brushed the collar of the uniform I wanted to

356

see most in the world at the moment: the scarlet-and-gold doublet of the Falconers. The very company that existed to control magic so things like this wouldn't happen.

"Thank the Graces you're here! Can you stop her?"

"No." He drew in a deep, unsteady breath. "But you can, if you have the courage."

"What?" It was more madness, piled on top of the horror of the balefire. "But I'm not a Falconer!"

"That's why you can do it." Something delicate gleamed in his offering hand. "Do you think you can slip this onto her wrist?"

It was a complex weave of gold wire and scarlet beads, designed to tighten with a tug. I recognized the pattern from a woodcut in one of my books: a Falconer's jess. Named after the tethers used in falconry, it could place a seal on magic.

"She's *on fire*," I objected.

"I know. I won't deny it's dangerous." His intent green eyes clouded. "I can't do it myself; I'm already linked to another. I wouldn't ask if it weren't an emergency. The more lives the balefire consumes, the more it spreads. It could swallow all of Raverra."

I hesitated. The jess sagged in his hand. "Never mind. I shouldn't have—"

"I'll do it." I snatched the bracelet from him before I could think twice.

"Thank you." He flashed me an oddly wistful smile. "I'll distract her while you get close. Wits and courage. You can do it."

The Falconer sprinted toward the spreading flames, leaving the jess dangling from my hand like an unanswered question.

He circled to the canal's edge, calling to get the girl's attention. "You! Warlock!"

She turned toward him. Flame trailed behind her like a

queen's mantua. The spreading edges crawled up the brick walls of the nearest house in blazing tendrils.

The Falconer's voice rang out above the clamor of the growing crowd across the canal. "In the name of His Serenity the Doge, I claim you for the Falcons of Raverra!"

That certainly got her attention. The flames bent in his direction as if in a strong wind.

"I don't belong to *you*, either!" Her voice was wild as a hissing bonfire. "You can't claim me. I'll see you burn first!"

Now she was going to kill him, too. Unless I stopped her.

My heart fluttering like an anxious dowager's handkerchief, I struggled to calm down and think. Maybe she wouldn't attack if I didn't rush at her. I tucked my precious satchel under my coat and hustled toward the bridge as if I hoped to scurry past her and escape. It wasn't hard to pretend. Some in the crowd on the far side beckoned me to safety.

My legs trembled with the urge to heed them and dash across. I couldn't bear the thought of Muscati's pages withering to ashes.

I tightened my grip on the jess.

The Falconer extended his hand toward the girl to keep her attention. "By law, you belonged to Raverra the moment you were born with the mage mark. I don't know how you managed to hide for so long, but it's over now. Come with me."

The balefire roared at him in a blue-white wave.

"Plague take you!" The girl raised her fist in defiance. "If Raverra wants my fire, she can have it. Let the city burn!"

I lunged across the remaining distance between us, leaping over snaking lines of flame. Eyes squeezed half shut against the heat, I flung out an arm and looped the jess over her upraised fist.

The effect was immediate. The flames flickered out as if a cold blast of wind had snuffed them. The Falconer still recoiled, his arms upraised to protect his face, his fine uniform doublet smoking.

The girl swayed, the fire flickering out in her eyes. The golden jess settled around her bone-thin wrist.

She collapsed to the flagstones.

Pain seared my hand. I hissed through my teeth as I snatched it to my chest. That brief moment of contact had burned my skin and scorched my boots and coat. My satchel, thank the Graces, seemed fine.

Across the bridge, the gathering of onlookers cheered, then began to break up. The show was over, and nobody wanted to go near a fire warlock, even an unconscious one.

I couldn't blame them. No sign remained of ruffians in the canal, though the burned smell lingered horribly in the air. Charred black scars streaked the sides of the buildings flanking me.

The Falconer approached, grinning with relief. "Well done! I'm impressed. Are you all right?"

It hit me in a giddy rush that it was over. I had saved—if not all of Raverra, at least a block or two of it—by myself, with my own hands. Not with my mother's name, or with my mother's wealth, but on my own.

Too dangerous to go to a pawnbroker's shop? Ha! I'd taken out a fire warlock. I smiled at him, tucking my burned hand into my sleeve. "I'm fine. I'm glad I could help."

"Lieutenant Marcello Verdi, at your service." He bowed. "What is your name, brave young lady?"

"Amalia Cornaro."

"Well, welcome to the doge's Falconers, Miss..." He

stopped. The smile fell off his face, and the color drained from his bronze skin. "Cornaro." He swallowed. "Not...you aren't related to La Contessa Lissandra Cornaro, surely?"

My elation curdled in my stomach. "She's my mother."

"Hells," the lieutenant whispered. "What have I done?"

if you enjoyed
MALICE OF CROWS
look out for

ONE OF US

by

Craig DiLouie

They call him Dog.

Enoch is a teenage boy growing up in a rundown orphanage in Georgia during the 1980s. Abandoned from the moment they were born, Enoch and his friends are different. People in the nearby town whisper that the children from the orphanage are monsters.

The orphanage is not a happy home. Brutal teachers, farm labor, and communal living in a crumbling plantation house are Enoch's standard day to day. But he dreams of growing up to live among the normals as a respected man. He believes in a world less cruel, one where he can be loved.

One night, Enoch and his friends share a campfire with a group of normal kids. As mutual fears subside, friendships form, and living together doesn't seem so out of reach.

But then a body is found, and it may be the spark that ignites revolution.

One

On the principal's desk, a copy of *Time*. A fourteen-year-old girl smiling on the cover. Pigtails tied in blue ribbon. Freckles and big white teeth. Rubbery, barbed appendages extended from her eye sockets.

Under that, a single word: WHY?

Why did this happen?

Or, maybe, why did the world allow a child like this to live?

What Dog wanted to know was why she smiled.

Maybe it was just reflex, seeing somebody pointing a camera at her. Maybe she liked the attention, even if it wasn't the nice kind.

Maybe, even if just for a few seconds, she felt special.

The Georgia sun glared through filmy barred windows. A steel fan whirred in the corner, barely moving the warm, thick air. Out the window, Dog spied the old rusted pickup sunk in a riot of wildflowers. Somebody loved it once then parked it here and left it to die. If Dog owned it, he would have kept driving and never stopped.

The door opened. The government man came in wearing a

362

black suit, white shirt, and a blue-and-yellow tie. Hair slicked back with gel. His shiny shoes clicked across the grimy floor. He sat in Principal Willard's creaking chair and lit a cigarette. Dropped a file folder on the desk and studied Dog through a blue haze.

"They call you Dog," he said.

"Yes, sir, they do. The other kids, I mean."

Dog growled when he talked but took care to form each word right. The teachers made sure he spoke good and proper. Brain once told him these signs of humanity were the only thing keeping the children alive.

"Your Christian name is Enoch. Enoch Davis Bryant."

"Yes, sir."

Enoch was the name the teachers at the Home used. Brain said it was his slave name. Dog liked hearing it, though. He felt lucky to have one. His mama had loved him enough to at least do that for him. Many parents had named their kids XYZ before abandoning them to the Homes.

"I'm Agent Shackleton," the government man said through another cloud of smoke. "Bureau of Teratological Affairs. You know the drill, don't you, by now?"

Every year, the government sent somebody to ask the kids questions. Trying to find out if they were still human. Did they want to hurt people, ever have carnal thoughts about normal girls and boys, that sort of thing.

"I know the drill," Dog said.

"Not this year," the man told him. "This year is different. I'm here to find out if you're special."

"I don't quite follow, sir."

Agent Shackleton planted his elbows on the desk. "You're a ward of the state. More than a million of you. Living high on the hog for the past fourteen years in the Homes. Some of you are beginning to show certain capabilities."

"Like what kind?"

"I saw a kid once who had gills and could breathe underwater. Another who could hear somebody talking a mile away."

"No kidding," Dog said.

"That's right."

"You mean like a superhero."

"Yeah. Like Spider-Man, if Spider-Man half looked like a real spider."

"I never heard of such a thing," Dog said.

"If you, Enoch, have capabilities, you could prove you're worth the food you eat. This is your opportunity to pay it back. Do you follow me?"

"Sure, I guess."

Satisfied, Shackleton sat back in the chair and planted his feet on the desk. He set the file folder on his thighs, licked his finger, and flipped it open. He produced a black pen and clicked it a few times while he read.

"Pretty good grades," the man said. "You got your math and spelling. You stay out of trouble. All right. Tell me what you can do. Better yet, show me something."

"What I can do, sir?"

"You do for me, I can do plenty for you. Take you to a special place."

Dog glanced at the red door on the side of the room before returning his gaze to Shackleton. Even looking at it was bad luck. The red door led downstairs to a basement room called Discipline, where the problem kids went.

He'd never been inside it, but he knew the stories. All the kids knew them. Principal Willard wanted them to know. It was part of their education.

He said, "What kind of place would that be?"

"A place with lots of food and TV. A place nobody can ever bother you."

Brain always said to play along with the normals so you didn't get caught up in their system. They wrote the rules in such a way to trick you into Discipline. More than that, though, Dog wanted to prove himself. He wanted to be special.

"Well, I'm a real fast runner. Ask anybody."

"That's your special talent. You can run fast."

"Real fast. Does that count?"

The agent smiled. "Running fast isn't special. It isn't special at all."

"Ask anybody how fast I run. Ask the—"

"You're not special. You'll never be special, Dog."

"I don't know what you want from me, sir."

Shackleton's smile disappeared along with Dog's file. "I want you to get the hell out of my sight. Send the next monster in on your way out."

Two

Pollution. Infections. Drugs. Radiation. All these things, Mr. Benson said from the chalkboard, can produce mutations in embryos.

A bacterium caused the plague generation. The other kids, the plague kids, who lived in the Homes.

Amy Green shifted in her desk chair. The top of her head was itching again. Mama said she'd worry it bald if she kept scratching at it. She settled on twirling her long, dark hair around her finger and tugging. Savored the needles of pain along her scalp.

"The plague is a sexually transmitted disease," Mr. Benson told the class.

She already knew part of the story from American History and from what Mama told her. The plague started in 1968, two years before she was born, back when love was still free. Then the disease named teratogenesis raced around the world, and the plague children came.

One out of ten thousand babies born in 1968 were monsters, and most died. One in six in 1969, and half of these died. One in three in 1970, the year scientists came up with a test to see if you had it. Most of them lived. After a neonatal nurse got arrested for killing thirty babies in Texas, the survival rate jumped.

More than a million monster babies screaming to be fed. By then, Congress had already funded the Home system.

Fourteen years later, and still no cure. If you caught the germ, the only surefire way to stop spreading it was abstinence, which they taught right here in health class. If you got pregnant with it, abortion was mandatory.

Amy flipped her textbook open and bent to sniff its cheesy new-book smell. Books, sharpened pencils, lined paper; she associated their bitter scents with school. The page showed a drawing of a woman's reproductive system. *The baby comes out there.* Sitting next to her, her boyfriend Jake glanced at the page and smiled, his face reddening. Like her, fascinated and embarrassed by it all.

In junior high, sex ed was mandatory, no ifs or buts. Amy and her friends were stumbling through puberty. Tampons, budding breasts, aching midnight thoughts, long conversations about what boys liked and what they wanted.

She already had a good idea what they wanted. Girls always complimented her about how pretty she was. Boys stared at her when she walked down the hall. Everybody so nice to her all the time. She didn't trust any of it. When she stood naked in the mirror, she only saw flaws. Amy spotted a zit last week and stared at it for an hour, hating her ugliness. It took her over an hour every morning to get ready for school. She didn't leave the house until she looked perfect.

She flipped the page again. A monster grinned up at her. She slammed the book shut.

Mr. Benson asked if anybody in the class had actually seen a plague child. Not on TV or in a magazine, but up close and personal.

A few kids raised their hands. Amy kept hers planted on her desk.

"I have two big goals for you kids this year," the teacher said. "The main thing is teach you how to avoid spreading the disease. We'll be talking a lot about safe sex and all the regulations about whether and how you do it. How to get tested and how to access a safe abortion. I also aim to help you become accustomed to the plague children already born and who are now the same age as you."

For Amy's entire life, the plague children had lived in group homes out in the country, away from people. One was located just eight miles from Huntsville, though it might as well have been on the moon. The monsters never came to town. Out of sight meant out of mind, though one could never entirely forget them.

"Let's start with the plague kids," Mr. Benson said. "What do all y'all think about them? Tell the truth."

Rob Rowland raised his hand. "They ain't human. They're just animals."

"Is that right? Would you shoot one and eat it? Mount its head on your wall?"

The kids laughed as they pictured Rob so hungry he would eat a monster. Rob was obese, smart, and sweated a lot, one of the unpopular kids.

Amy shuddered with sudden loathing. "I hate them something awful."

The laughter died. Which was good, because the plague wasn't funny.

The teacher crossed his arms. "Go ahead, Amy. No need to holler, though. Why do you hate them?"

"They're monsters. I hate them because they're monsters."

Mr. Benson turned and hacked at the blackboard with a piece of chalk: MONSTRUM, a VIOLATION OF NATURE. From MONEO, which means TO WARN. In this case, a warning God is angry. Punishment for taboo.

"Teratogenesis is nature out of whack," he said. "It rewrote the body. Changed the rules. Monsters, maybe. But does a monster have to be evil? Is a human being what you look like, or what you do? What makes a man a man?"

Bonnie Fields raised her hand. "I saw one once. I couldn't even tell if it was a boy or girl. I didn't stick around to get to know it."

"But did you see it as evil?"

"I don't know about that, but looking the way some of them do, I can't imagine why the doctors let them all live. It would have been a mercy to let them die."

"Mercy on us," somebody behind Amy muttered.

The kids laughed again.

Sally Albod's hand shot up. "I'm surprised at all y'all being so scared. I see the kids all the time at my daddy's farm. They're weird, but there ain't nothing to them. They work hard and don't make trouble. They're fine."

"That's good, Sally," the teacher said. "I'd like to show all y'all something."

He opened a cabinet and pulled out a big glass jar. He set it on his desk. Inside, a baby floated in yellowish fluid. A tiny penis jutted between its legs. Its little arms grasped at nothing. It had a single slitted eye over a cleft where its nose should be.

The class sucked in its breath as one. Half the kids recoiled; the rest leaned forward for a better look. Fascination and revulsion. Amy alone didn't move. She sat frozen, shot through with the horror of it.

She hated the little thing. Even dead, she hated it.

"This is Tony," Mr. Benson said. "And guess what, he isn't one of the plague kids. Just some poor boy born with a birth defect. About three percent of newborns are born this way every year. It causes one out of five infant deaths."

Tony, some of the kids chuckled. They thought it weird it had a name.

"We used to believe embryos developed in isolation in the uterus," the teacher said. "Then back in the Sixties, a company sold thalidomide to pregnant women in Germany to help them with morning sickness. Ten thousand kids born with deformed limbs. Half died. What did scientists learn from that? Anybody?"

"A medicine a lady takes can hurt her baby even if it don't hurt her," Jake said.

"Bingo," Mr. Benson said. "Medicine, toxins, viruses, we call these things environmental factors. Most times, though, doctors have no idea why a baby like Tony is born. It just happens, like a dice roll. So is Tony a monster? What about a kid who's retarded, or born with legs that don't work? Is a kid in a wheelchair a monster too? A baby born deaf or blind?"

He got no takers. The class sat quiet and thoughtful. Satisfied, Mr. Benson carried the jar back to the cabinet. More gasps as baby Tony bobbed in the fluid, like he was trying to get out.

The teacher frowned as he returned the jar to its shelf. "I'm surprised just this upsets you. If this gets you so worked up, how will you live with the plague children? When they're adults, they'll have the same rights as you. They'll live among you."

Amy stiffened at her desk, neck clenched with tension at the idea. A question formed in her mind. "What if we don't want to live with them?"

Mr. Benson pointed at the jar. "This baby is you. And something not you. If Tony had survived, he would be different, yes. But he would be you."

"I think we have a responsibility to them," Jake said.

"Who's we?" Amy said.

His contradicting her had stung a little, but she knew how Jake had his own mind and liked to argue. He wore leather jackets, black T-shirts advertising obscure bands, ripped jeans. Troy and Michelle, his best friends, were Black. He was popular because being unpopular didn't scare him. Amy liked him for that, the way he flouted junior high's iron rules. The way he refused to suck up to her like the other boys all did.

"You know who I mean," he said. "The human race. We made them, and that gives us responsibility. It's that simple."

"I didn't make anything. The older generation did. Why are they my problem?"

"Because they have it bad. We all know they do. Imagine being one of them."

"I don't want things to be bad for them," Amy said. "I really don't. I just don't want them around me. Why does that make me a bad person?"

"I never said it makes you a bad person," Jake said.

Archie Gaines raised his hand. "Amy has a good point, Mr. Benson. They're a mess to stomach, looking at them. I mean, I can live with it, I guess. But all this love and understanding is a lot to ask."

"Fair enough," Mr. Benson said.

Archie turned to look back at Amy. She nodded her thanks. His face lit up with a leering smile. He believed he'd rescued her and now she owed him. She gave him a practiced frown to shut down his hopes. He turned away as if slapped.

"I'm just curious about them," Jake said. "More curious than scared. It's like you said, Mr. Benson. However they look, they're still our brothers. I wouldn't refuse help to a blind man, I guess I wouldn't to a plague kid neither."

The teacher nodded. "Okay. Good. That's enough discussion for today. We're getting somewhere, don't you think? Again, my goal for you kids this year is two things. One is to get used to the plague kids. Distinguishing between a book and its cover. The other is to learn how to avoid making more of them."

Jake turned to Amy and winked. Her cheeks burned, all her annoyance with him forgotten.

She hoped there was a lot more sex ed and a lot less monster talk in her future. While Mr. Benson droned on, she glanced through the first few pages of her book. A chapter headline caught her eye: KISSING.

She already knew the law regarding sex. Germ or no germ, the legal age of consent was still fourteen in the State of Georgia. But another law said if you wanted to have sex, you had to get tested for the germ first. If you were under eighteen, your parents had to give written consent for the testing.

Kissing, though, that you could do without any fuss. It said so right here in black and white. You could do it all you wanted. Her scalp tingled at the thought. She tugged at her hair and savored the stabbing needles.

She risked a hungering glance at Jake's handsome profile. Though she wanted to go further than that, a lot further, she could never do more than kissing. She could never know what it'd be like to scratch the real itch.

Nobody but her mama knew Amy was a plague child.